QUEENS' RANSOM

ALSO BY VICTOR DAVIS

The Ghostmaker

QUEENS' RANSOM

Victor Davis

VICTOR GOLLANCZ
LONDON

First published in Great Britain 1997
by Victor Gollancz
An imprint of the Cassell Group
Wellington House, 125 Strand, London WC2R 0BB

A catalogue record for this book is
available from the British Library.

ISBN 0 575 06532 X

Typeset by Rowland Phototypesetting Ltd,
Bury St Edmunds, Suffolk
Printed in Great Britain by
St Edmundsbury Press Ltd,
Bury St Edmunds, Suffolk

97 98 99   5 4 3 2 1

For my brother, Bernard Davis BEM, and his wife, Pat.

Prologue

In June 1980 a young Englishman, Terry Stevenson, scaled an ugly lava cliff overlooking Lake Baringo in East Africa and solved a mystery. Until then no one had known where an extravagantly feathered bird called Hemprich's hornbill nested.

Hanging perilously from a rock, Stevenson observed that, at the beginning of the ten-week incubation period, the red-billed male bird brought mud and sealed his mate into a hole in the lava. Only a slit remained through which he fed her.

During this time, in her secret place, the female undergoes what ornithologists call a catastrophic moult: she loses all her wing and body feathers. Consequently, if the male should meet with an accident or become victim to a more powerful predator, the female is marooned in her cell. If she should succeed in breaking out, her nude body plunges to the boulders more than a hundred feet below, her useless plumage drifting down after her.

Stay or jump, either way she is doomed.

Chapter One

From the moment the word came down from the Élysée Palace, the French took precisely ten hours to find Ringrose. The President of the Republic was involved. Everybody jumped to it.

The cops were instructed that Ringrose was on Corsica, touring with his wife Helen and their two daughters. *Bien.*

In anticipation of a result, a Dassault Mystère-Falcon jet of the *Groupe de Liaisons Aériennes Ministérielles* had been moved from Marseille to Ajaccio, ready to whisk Ringrose to London where *les rosbifs* were out of their skulls with worry. This was a sight the French would normally relish. But not now.

The gendarmes raced through all the usual checks – car-hire computers, hotel registrations – and got warmer by the hour. Finally they found Ringrose's hired Renault impeccably parked in the clifftop town of Bonifacio, alongside the quay where the ferry from Sardinia berths. It was unoccupied.

After all their efforts, *les flics* had been scooped by the French Foreign Legion.

Up on the cliff, above the ferry landing stage, squats a Legion barracks, the Citadelle Montlaur, in the final stages of closure, with the men being shipped out to Southern France. It is an unlovely pile, apart from the cream-walled area around the arched main gate where a sentry box is manned by a ramrod legionnaire in a white *képi*, and khaki uniform with extravagant, red-tasselled epaulettes. The setting is made for holiday snaps.

Ringrose, in ill-cut slacks held up by an old necktie knotted round his waist, was trying to get Helen and the girls positioned under the crossed tricolours for a photograph – and doing his best to ignore the knot of squaddies giving the eye to his pretty daughters in their skimpy frocks.

'Tom,' said Helen, sweetly unaware, 'we ought to have a

picture all together. Why don't you ask one of the soldiers?'

The squaddies watched him turn towards them, proffering his camera.

'Mais certainement – avec plaisir,' said a young hopeful, leaping forward. Grinning self-consciously, Ringrose joined his family line-up.

'Monsieur, le chapeau!' said the legionnaire.

'Daddy, he wants you to take your hat off. The brim's throwing a shadow on your face,' said Laura, the family linguist.

'Sorry,' said Ringrose, disengaging his arm from his wife's slim waist and removing the offending headgear to reveal a silver forelock that fell over the brow of a sleepy, tanned face.

The legionnaire raised the viewfinder to his left eye then slowly lowered it again. He gaped.

'C'est lui! Celui qu'on cherche!' he shouted to his comrades. They all looked intently at the English family. Then the legionnaire, still clutching the camera, broke into a run. He raced, shouting, through the gateway and into the guardroom on the right. Moments later a *sous-officier* returned with him.

The NCO took one look at the tall Englishman, brought his heels together and saluted. 'Commandant, voulez-vous venir par ici tout de suite, s'il vous plaît,' he said.

Commander Thomas Ringrose, head of Scotland Yard's Serious Crimes Branch, was baffled by the torrent of French and turned to his elder daughter. 'What's going on, Laura?'

She said slowly, 'As far as I can make out, they've been looking for you everywhere, Daddy. There's been a terrible crime. The Prime Minister asked the French to find you.'

'Bugger,' said Ringrose.

For the next half-hour pandemonium disrupted the austere routines of the Citadelle Montlaur but soon the bemused Ringrose family were watching a Super Puma helicopter set down on the parade ground, ready to carry Ringrose over the mountains to the waiting Mystère.

Ringrose swore under his breath. 'God knows why it has to be me,' he shouted into Helen's ear, above the racket, 'but I want you to stay and enjoy the rest of the holiday.'

Helen said firmly, 'You go, we go. I'm not having you coming home to an empty house.'

'Too right,' chorused his daughters. 'You need your home support team.'

At last the cops could join in. A car-load of blue uniforms tore off to collect the family's luggage from a nearby *pension*. In the guardroom, a Legion officer showed Ringrose a newspaper, *Corse-Matin*, which displayed the lurid headline: 'DISPARUES!' Laura translated: 'VANISHED!' Then she said, 'The story's about a large number of girls of different nationalities who have been kidnapped in London.'

Her father frowned. 'How many?'

'Forty-nine.'

'*Forty-nine?* Surely not!' Ringrose peered over her shoulder.

'Yes, Daddy, it definitely says forty-nine. The report says it should have been fifty but one girl got left behind.'

'Does it say whether or not the girls are still alive?'

Laura read to the end of the report and handed him the paper. 'They don't know.'

An hour later the Ringroses were London-bound.

The jet climbed fiercely, the G force momentarily making Ringrose's head swim. As his eyes settled back into focus he found he was still clutching the copy of *Corse-Matin*. He gazed out of the aircraft's window and pondered. What manner of man (a small voice added, 'Or woman,') could have concocted such a ridiculous criminal spectacular?

And hope to get away with it?

Chapter Two

Lucius Frankel circled Kew Green twice, watching his rear-view mirror for any sign that he was being tailed. Nothing. He had no reason to be so cautious – it was too early in the game – but he felt an almost obsessive need to make every moment into a drama, to savour to the full his commanding role in all that was to happen.

He parked and strolled across the grass, passed Gainsborough's tomb, and nipped across Kew Road. He turned his back on the Botanical Gardens and consulted his map before he plunged into the network of narrow streets that led down to the river.

The single-bedroom apartment was on the third floor of a small block. Its only notable feature was an unhindered view across the Thames to Strand-on-the-Green. Before he entered the building he pulled on plastic gloves.

As he let himself in, the person he had privately codenamed the Source stood up in a grubby black tracksuit. Over the chairback hung a cheap khaki jacket and on the table rested wire-rimmed glasses that gave the Source's face the cast of a revolutionary intellectual.

Lucius flopped into a worn tapestry chair and said shortly, 'I don't want to be here any longer than I have to. Give me a run-down.'

The Source said: 'I'm establishing a whole separate identity. I'm leaving the telephone in the previous tenant's name and paying all bills with cash.'

Lucius nodded. 'This crib's fine. It hits the right note of anonymity. There has to be a neutral clearing house for information and eventually for storage of the money.' He levered himself up and made a tour of inspection, tapping the walls.

'It's going to be essential to keep the telephone working and for you to be available here at pre-set times. You're going to get lonely. Your only contact will be my voice on the line. Once we've pulled it off, I shan't come near you. You'll get the jitters.'

The Source tried to object. 'Don't kid yourself,' said Lucius Frankel. 'You'd better listen to what I'm saying. This is going to be one scary game. You crack and we all go down.'

The Source was hardly listening. 'I just know this is going to be the most amazing event in my whole life.'

Lucius stared long and hard. He caught the starveling glitter in the Source's eyes and it made him uneasy. He struggled to conceal his irritation and pump sincerity into his voice. 'I know what you mean,' he said. 'Me, too.' Then he grunted. 'Let's start with the money.'

The Source fished in a veneered mahogany sideboard and dumped a brown-paper bundle on the table. 'It's twenty-five thousand exactly. My total stake. I'm not to be asked for any more, no matter what the final overall expenditure. In return, I collect one-fifth of the proceeds. Agreed?'

'Agreed,' said Lucius. 'Without you, the operation is imposs-ible. The remaining share-out is my worry. I say who gets what. Anyone doesn't like it, they get dealt with.'

The Source's neck hair prickled. Sometimes you could glimpse the cold, violent beast that crouched inside Lucius Frankel.

Lucius produced his notes. 'Our biggest preliminary outlay, by far, is going to be for the two coaches.'

'How's the recruiting going?'

Lucius hesitated. The Source asked too many questions but had to be kept happy. 'I've been researching the Great Train Robbery of the nineteen sixties,' he said. 'Those idiots doomed themselves with too many helpers with serious criminal records.'

'So?' The Source had poured some red wine.

Lucius sipped from a heavy-bottomed glass. The surgical gloves still covered his hands. He said, 'So some of their past crimes were big enough to earn them an automatic place on the list of suspects.'

He shook his head at the long-ago folly, the overhead bulb bouncing highlights off his sleek black hair. 'Our team will be much more compact – I see eight as the maximum. None of the principals will have a criminal record. It's the military I'm calling in.'

'Who . . . ?' began the Source.

Lucius rose from his chair. He smiled but shook his head. 'Not yet. Later,' he said.

Chapter Three

Why this damn fury all the time? Celia had once said to him: 'You know, Bruiser, it has to be some chemical imbalance. I think it's very sad for you, especially as you never appear to care a twopenny toss.'

He did care, of course.

Once, not so long before she took off for good, she had suggested, in a joke-that-wasn't-a-joke, a session with a Wimpole Street witch-doctor. 'I mean, it can't be right, can it, you constantly flying off the handle?'

Cee, whose loyalty had been exemplary for a long time, had been reacting to his latest asinine prank and the subsequent headlines.

In the tabloid press, Bruiser was appreciated as one of a disappearing breed of gentleman rampagers who roamed the upper reaches of London society. He knew he was being used by the media. He was fodder for the newspaper-reading mob, one of the cast of nobs, mountebanks, hairdressers and frock-makers who fill the daily gossip columns. The knowledge did nothing to moderate his irascibility.

Before Cee married him, friends had warned her, or so she told him later, that he was mad, bad and dangerous to know, but she had found him amusing.

Cee had once squeezed his arm, saying: 'You can be very endearing sometimes.' Bruiser did not understand that remark although, pondering later, he decided Cee had really meant quaint. Was she poking fun?

But there was no doubt about the laughter that had attached itself to his name after the incident at Buckingham's club. The evening, unsurprisingly, had been boisterous, because he had been in the company of Dickie Biggs-Salter and Rolly Ponsford.

They had reached Buckingham's famous treacle roll when Rolly had spotted the red-haired civvy, two tables distant, dining with – of all people – General Lingfield, retired, who had lately been recruited to the board of Edison Electronics. 'It's that oik Burt Spanner.' Rolly identified him accurately.

Despite his name, Spanner was a subtle, technically educated man with a BSc from London University, who had created the Association of Professional Computer Operatives. His members had demonstrated their ability to bring day-to-day government to a halt by shutting down the terminals into which for the previous fifteen years the bureaucracy had obligingly fed all its knowledge. Under his skilled command, the APCO had brought the government to heel in four weeks and the right-wing newspapers had found what they had long sought: a left-wing bogeyman to replace Arthur Scargill, the miners' leader.

Spanner's presence in the gentlemen's sanctuary of Buckingham's blighted the evening. Rolly fumed and Bruiser grumbled *sotto voce*: 'Damn fellow's got no right to be here. I've a good mind to say so to the General.'

Dickie pushed the port decanter towards him. Not unmindful of his own position as a serving officer, he drawled, 'Knock it off, Bruiser. You go anywhere near the old boy and he'll have you across the muzzle of a cannon. Spanner's a guest of the club and *noblesse* has to *oblige*.'

It was by the sheerest misfortune that the trio should leave the premises just as General Lingfield was bidding farewell to his guest and helping him on with his camel-hair coat while the hall porter sought a cab outside in St James's Street.

The General was mounting the staircase to the first-floor smoking room when Bruiser and Rolly confronted Spanner.

Slightly slurred, Bruiser said, 'C'mon. Let's debag him.'

The roly-poly trade-union leader's first reaction was one of terror: he was being mugged, he thought.

Then, as a massively built man of six foot three lifted him under the shoulders and another took him by the suede shoes, the terror turned to a bellow of indignation. His assailants cheered manically, but Dickie Biggs-Salter was appalled. 'For Chrissake, stop it!' he yelled. 'There'll be hell to pay!' He went unheeded.

Rolly dragged the trousers down Spanner's kicking legs just as General Lingfield, summoned back to the pavement by his guest's roars, advanced down the steps.

The next few minutes were a blur of struggle and shouting, but it might have been possible even then to salvage something from the sorry mess if the incident could have been contained within the circle of those involved. However, the photograph had appeared in next morning's *Daily Mirror*. It had been taken by a passing taxi driver, and it was a stunner.

It showed Spanner clean off the ground, his trousers around his ankles, Bruiser and Rolly, teeth bared in feral joy, the General, hand frozen in mid-air on its way to a vigorous connection with Rolly's cheek, and Dickie, arm crooked around Bruiser's neck, attempting to pull him off. The elderly club porter stood wringing his hands.

And, in public, that is what everyone else did. Bruiser and his party were nothing more than high-born hooligans. But through all the printed comments there ran an undertow of amusement: a large section of the public was gleefully ready to give its silent approval to Spanner's humiliation.

Buckingham's did not wait for General Lingfield's complaint: the committee sacked Bruiser and Rolly within the day because, the assault on Spanner notwithstanding, gentlemen should be able to hold their drink. Dickie, thanks to the evidence of the photograph, escaped with a reprimand. He was equally fortunate when the matter was brought to the attention of his colonel. But Bruiser and Rolly were required to resign their commissions. The regiment passed judgement with genuine regret: they had proved themselves resourceful, fearless officers in the Falklands, but none of it counted now in these politically sensitive days. Outside times of war, the British Army had no place for cowboys.

At this sorry time, the gossip columnists of the *Daily Mail* unearthed the origin of Bruiser's nickname. He wished they hadn't.

Chapter Four

In Bruiser's day, Eton College remained perversely proud in all twenty-five of its houses of the 'fagging' tradition, in which small boys waited on older ones. The system had flourished for three centuries until Headmaster Michael McCrum called a halt.

At twelve, Brewster Moxmanton was a dour boy, already well developed for his age, and for a whole term endured the boot polishing, the sausage cooking, the errands. That summer, at home, his mother had been absent as usual on the show-jumping circuit. His father visited intermittently, rarely taking time out from his business affairs in London or from the company of political cronies. In this family doldrum, Brewster had turned to a stimulating association with Colour Sergeant Wally Barnes.

The former NCO occupied a converted stable block on the edge of the Moxmanton estate, alongside the Maidstone road. He paid no rent: the accommodation was a reward from Brewster's father. In the war, during the commando raid on the Bruneval radar installation, the old man had taken a bullet in the thigh and Wally Barnes had hauled him to safety down the beach under enfilading fire.

Besides his Military Medal, Wally Barnes had another distinction: he was an expert in unarmed combat and when the Americans joined the war, before the main assault upon Hitler's Fortress Europe, had trained many of them in this form of mayhem.

'It's nothing fancy,' he told Brewster. 'It's not the stuff that looks like ballet. It's rough-house fighting that'll give you the edge on untrained people – just a means of kicking more shit out of your opponent than he'll ever kick out of you.'

The boy was thrilled. Wally Barnes was the first adult who had ever talked to him man-to-man.

Brewster first witnessed Wally's prowess at the village summer fête, held each July on Pilgrim's Green, a resting place in medieval times for the devout on their trek to Canterbury. Wally recruited half a dozen mates from the Royal British Legion and, on a canvas stretched over a bed of grass cuttings, gave a good-natured display of holds, throws and incapacitating blows. Naturally, he muted the strength of his attack but his volunteer victims were well rehearsed in blood-curdling reactions to his strikes and knuckle-thrusts into their flesh. It was a lively show, although Brewster discovered later that Wally excluded the section of his repertoire that encompassed instant death, eye gouging and testicle crushing.

However, in private, Brewster learned the lot. He marvelled as Wally Barnes, a chunky, cheerful man of only five foot seven – Brewster's own height at thirteen – disposed so adroitly of his adversaries. He knew then that, before cricket, before rugby, he had to master fighting.

Wally had been amused at the boy's pleadings, and subsequently surprised at the single-minded application he brought to the training sessions. Brewster practised relentlessly throughout the summer in the yard behind Wally's cottage. He had straw to break his falls, a punchbag and sandbox to turn his arms and hands into steel-tipped pistons. Even Wally became worried at the dedicated hours the boy put in.

His father came to hear of his son's new interest. Arriving to collect Brewster for three weeks at Cap Fleurie, he said briefly, 'Hear you're learning to look after yourself. Absolutely right. Be more use than cricket. And Sergeant Barnes is just the chap for you. Let me know if you need any equipment.'

By the beginning of the Michaelmas term, Brewster felt that Wally Barnes had given him the 'edge' of which he had spoken.

'And, remember,' said Wally, 'you'll not only have an edge if a bigger boy picks on you, you'll also have the crucial element of surprise. After all,' he added, with his open grin, 'who'd believe that a young lad like you could fight like a pro? Just remember to go easy. You're only out to hold your own and give a bully a fright.'

On the first day of the new half, Brewster had sought out Ellis, his house captain. He had stood squarely in front of him and said, 'Ellis, I want you to know that I've decided not to fag this term. If you want your shoes cleaned you should do them yourself.'

Ellis, a handsome, blond boy and cricket hero to the lower school, had risen up mottle-faced. 'You'll do as you're damn well told. You've fagged for one term and that means you've got at least three to go. Now get out.'

Brewster had stood even-eyed. He said, levelly, 'I mean it, Ellis. Be warned.'

Ellis threw a cushion at his departing, rigid back.

Within the hour, the cry of 'Boy up!' echoed down the staircase and Brewster, in his room, had listened to the fading sound of scampering feet.

Soon after the 'Library' of senior boys came for him. Ellis stood in the doorway. 'Moxmanton, I assume you heard the call. You are last boy. I need you to make tea.'

The others peered expectantly over Ellis's shoulders. Brewster sat unmoved. Finally, he said, 'I'm sorry, Ellis. I told you I wasn't fagging any more.'

He did not protest when ordered to change into his shorts for a beating. Silently he bent over a chair and Ellis administered six strokes. Brewster made no sound, neither would he run the errand. The 'Library' retreated. According to Eton rules, a boy could not be beaten twice on the same day.

The next morning Ellis was out in his running gear on Agar's Plough. He saw Brewster standing loosely on the cinder path ahead of him. 'Out of the way,' said Ellis, panting up. Brewster stood his ground.

'Out of the way, I said.'

'I did warn you, Ellis. I'm sorry you wouldn't listen.'

'You incredible little shit,' said Ellis.

Wait for him to touch you, thought Brewster.

Ellis was four inches taller than Brewster and now he reached out to take the junior boy by the shoulder and twirl him out of his path.

Brewster let the hand connect with his shirt then three of his knuckles thrust forward into Ellis's solar plexus. As his target's hands came down to protect himself, Brewster sliced inwards hard against Ellis's ribcage.

Ellis screamed with pain and grabbed at his attacker's hair. Brewster reached down, took Ellis firmly by the genitals, gave a sharp twist, then dropped to one knee, lifting his opponent by the crotch and propelling him clean over himself.

Ellis's humiliation was public and open-mouthed boys watched Brewster walk calmly away.

Of course, the seniors could not tolerate such insubordination and Brewster was beaten again. He still did not respond to the cry of 'Boy up!'

Brewster waited two days, which he deemed sufficient time for Ellis to recover from the first 'lesson'. Then, on the field in a gentle autumn mist, he confronted Ellis again.

'You're mad. Stark, blithering mad,' said Ellis, who, despite his rage, could feel the onset of a chill uncertainty.

'I'm truly sorry, Ellis,' said Brewster, as evenly as he had addressed him on the first occasion. 'All you have to do is take me off the fagging roster and I'll leave you alone.'

There was something frightening about Brewster's calm demeanour. In his steady gaze, there was nothing of boyhood or youthful bravado.

Ellis cursed, took up a boxer's stance and shuffled forward.

Brewster feinted with him for a few seconds, then screamed into Ellis's face. In the frozen moment after the shock wave of sound, he hooked Ellis's foremost leg with his own foot and threw him over onto the wet grass. Ellis, winded, scrambled to his feet and came forward again from a crouched position, roaring his anger. Brewster let him come, took a neat backward step, allowed Ellis's fading tackle to reach his knees, then spun round in a complete circle until he collided with Ellis's flank. He delivered two vicious blows in lightning succession to Ellis's lower thoracic vertebrae. The older boy dropped like lead, temporarily paralysed and howling into the turf.

Boys were already running towards the scene of combat but the fight was over. Ellis, feeling sensation return to his legs, ceased bellowing. He could see Moxmanton bending over him.

The voice was no more than a whisper. 'Ellis, next time I'll break your pretty face. You'll carry the marks for the rest of your life.'

Spittle bubbled at Ellis's mouth. 'You'll pay,' he swore. 'You'll pay.' But Brewster didn't.

The matter went to the headmaster, which everyone considered a bit off. After all, Moxmanton was only a kid. Ellis should have been big enough to fend for himself.

Brewster's fast-growing band of supporters and admirers, including Rolly Ponsford and Dickie Biggs-Salter, did not appreciate the skill that he had acquired from Wally Barnes, and Brewster took care not to brag about it. The best anyone at Eton knew was that he had faced up to a bigger boy and thrashed him.

'It's no bloody use you letting the other bloke know you can handle yourself,' Wally had lectured him. 'We're not concerned with fair play here, we're concerned with winning. And if you can hold on to that little bit of surprise until you've delivered a couple of telling blows, you're half-way home and dry.'

A few years later, Brewster received the same advice, rather more elegantly couched, from his instructor at Sandhurst. But right now the headmaster of Eton was in an irritable mood. He couldn't take seriously a senior boy's complaint that he was being harassed by a thirteen-year-old. Wasn't this a matter for the house master to sort out? 'And as for you, Moxmanton,' he said, '– or should I call you Bruiser in the light of your Christian name and your deplorable behaviour? – you appear to have got it into your head that fagging is a synonym for slavery. Well, let me disabuse you of this idea. A boy who can accept orders responsibly and legally given will be all the better fitted in years to come to give orders. And I don't suppose,' the headmaster failed to rid his voice entirely of a tinge of sarcasm, 'it has escaped your notice that boys from this school, once they go forth into the world, tend to give orders rather than take them?'

Brewster did not know the meaning of 'synonym' but his headmaster's drift was beyond misunderstanding. 'Yes, sir,' he said ambiguously.

'Well, that's that, then,' said the head, his mind already on higher things. 'Oh, yes,' he added vaguely. 'You'd better shake hands with Ellis.'

'Yes, sir,' said Brewster.

It was Ellis who gave the other members of the Library an account of what had taken place behind the headmaster's door: 'Moxmanton, or Bruiser as the boss called him, copped the sort of blistering he'll remember until his dying day.'

Within the day this account of the interview with the head filtered through the house and beyond. Brewster, who had neither comment to offer nor apology to make, was suddenly a boy of distinction. The headmaster of Eton had called him Bruiser. And so it would be for ever more. Ellis could have bitten his tongue for letting that out of the bag.

At the next cry of 'Boy up!' Bruiser sat alone in his room, bolt upright, waiting.

'Boy up!'

There were three seconds of drowsy afternoon murmur then came the sound of doors opening frantically. The din of a dozen pairs of stampeding feet echoed along the corridors and staircases of the redbrick, Victorian house. Bruiser remained coldly still.

Ten minutes later he knew his seniors were not coming for him. Expressionless, he changed into long trousers from the shorts in which he had been ready to take another beating, and got on with his prep.

He never answered the call again; neither was he punished. Bruiser did not crow about this: he had out-faced Ellis to pre-serve his own integrity, a regrettable incident, but Bruiser Mox-manton was never to be trifled with again. His self-containment was much admired by his contemporaries, especially by Rolly and Dickie. They became inseparable.

Bruiser failed to see the irony of his senior years at Eton when he enjoyed the convenience of the fagging system that he had so notably failed to reinforce. 'There are those who serve and those who exist to be served – and the world would be a happier place if everyone was clear in which camp he draws his rations,' he told Rolly and Dickie one day when they were on the river.

'We won't be drawing any rations at all unless we put some

slog into this,' said Dickie, raising his blade. From the towpath the abuse of the coach resounded across the water.

Bruiser stopped for a moment while he tried to get the future into focus. He then said something that gave his two friends a glimpse of another side to their friend. 'Let's promise ourselves to live the brave lives of conquistadors,' he said.

Rolly twisted in his seat and raised his eyebrows at Dickie. Bruiser could be an odd chap at times.

Chapter Five

The lives of conquistadors ... Unbidden, that long-ago day on the river came back to Bruiser as he sat in the airbus going to Nice. God! How he'd mucked things up. Bruiser glared truculently at the steward who was offering a plastic beaker of Beaujolais. He returned to his troubles. He knew he had been stupid – bloody stupid. The incident at Buckingham's was, in the grey light of a firing squad's dawn, inexcusable, alien to every measure of discipline he had ever imposed upon himself. And he should have done more to keep on the sunny side of his father. The dispositions made in the will had been a disaster.

The death of the old man after his second marriage had truly winded Bruiser. He was even more surprised when he found there wasn't as much in the family kitty as he had anticipated. He had the baronetcy but his widowed stepmother retained hefty rights in the estate. As old Jeavons read out the details in a quavering monotone, Bruiser knew he was deep in the hole.

His father had built up the estate around Moxmanton House to more than five thousand acres and, naturally, he had expected Bruiser, his only child, at some stage to take on the management.

Bruiser shifted restlessly in his seat as he recalled the quarrels. He had dragged himself reluctantly to the Cirencester agricultural college to learn estate management but after four months had got himself slung out. The old man had been livid but finally gave in to Bruiser's pleas that he might become a soldier. Bruiser hadn't wanted a total falling-out with his parent. After all, he controlled the Moxmanton money.

With his second marriage, the old man retreated to his place in the South of France. He was getting on and wanted, under-standably, to spend more time with his new bride, who was twenty-eight years younger. Moxmanton House stayed shut for most of the year and the land, including the extensive hop gardens, some of the finest in Kent, was let.

Soon after his father's death, Bruiser found himself at the centre of a financial whirlwind with which he was ill-equipped to cope. To provide an income for his wayward son, Moxman-ton had bought Bruiser membership of fifteen Lloyd's of London insurance syndicates, and while the fat cheques rolled in annually, he encouraged Rolly and Dickie to join him in what appeared to be a foolproof way for the upper classes effortlessly to maintain their lifestyles. When the insurance market nosedived after 1986 the three were trapped in a night-mare: they discovered that while a single one of their syndicates remained 'open' – subject to future claims – there was no getting out.

One syndicate's underwriters had rashly taken on the bulk of the insurance cover for a newly constructed hotel-casino in Atlantic City on the US eastern seaboard. A week after its official opening, it had been swept by fire. Arson by rival under-world interests had almost certainly been the cause but the devastation was so thorough that nothing could be proved. The syndicate was called upon to pay out.

Bruiser, then on an exercise in Oman on the Persian Gulf, was shocked to receive a demand for £540,000, his share of the losses. Gratefully, he allied himself with more than ninety other Names in challenging their unlimited liability in the suspicious circumstances. This was regarded as a most ungentlemanly act at Lloyd's, where a three-hundred-year reputation for financial rectitude was at stake. Emotionally, Bruiser stood with the gentlemen; financially he was obliged to wriggle with the cads.

Finally a High Court judge had decided that the Names should honour the claim. Bruiser now faced the demand for £540,000, plus his share of the court costs, plus a contribution to achieve Finality – the price of a permanent escape from Lloyd's. He was facing bankruptcy unless he could find a paint card in his dog-eared pack.

Bruiser was aggrieved. It had been his father who had bought him his Lloyd's membership and had left him now to face the creditors. The money to meet his obligations, Bruiser felt, should come out of the estate trust.

The airbus banked to port over St Tropez and began the descent into Nice airport.

Rawlings was waiting with the black Rolls that had been the Moxmantons' stately runabout in the Alpes Maritimes since 1960, when both Bruiser's parents had been alive. In those golden days, a French chauffeur in bottle-green livery went with the car.

Rawlings was capless but wore the discreet black jacket of the manservant.

'Oh, it's good to see you, Sir Brewster,' chattered the old man, as he stowed Bruiser's bag. 'Mrs Rawlings was saying only the other day how much she misses surprising you with a baked jam roll or treacle pudding.'

'Those were the days, eh, Rawlings?' grunted Bruiser.

'Indeed, sir.'

Rawlings and his wife were the last of the Moxmanton House retainers. During Bruiser's childhood there had been a staff of twelve, excluding the gardeners, a modest enough retinue but his father had preferred to entertain at the Arlington House flat in town and his mother was often away with her horses.

Bruiser's mother had ultimately gone the way she would have wished: out with the hunt, her mount had inexplicably refused a fence and Gertrude Moxmanton had sailed on, arse-over-tip, cursing volubly and landing badly. There had been an almost imperceptible crushing sound, as of a bamboo cane being twisted, and her ladyship had been launched into eternity, very irritated with God indeed.

Life at Moxmanton House had undergone a renaissance when her husband had remarried.

Bruiser was at first suspicious and resentful. He had never been close to his mother but he felt, somehow, that her memory was being slighted. And there was the matter of inheritance. He and Constanza were virtually contemporaries and, barring accidents, his expectations were diminished. Suspicions of gold-digging could not be dismissed.

The second Lady Moxmanton was the third daughter of an

English banker. Her first marriage had been to a Formula One racing driver, who never rose above sixth place in the world championship rankings and who had contrived to get himself cremated on the track at Sebring before a crowd of 25,000 people. When she met the older Moxmanton, she had grown tired of the noise, smell and eternal boyishness of the international racing circus. Moxmanton was an attractive baronetcy, and the only effort she'd had to make had been with the rather brooding son, and she understood perfectly why he did not welcome her with open arms. Constanza was no fool.

Bruiser came round grudgingly in the end. Constanza had opened up the house, redecorated, swept away the Victorian plumbing and the stabling and, until the English winters began to undermine her husband's health, invitations to her weekend house parties were widely sought. Bruiser's father shed years and paunch before his eyes, and Bruiser had to admit that Constanza seemed fond of the old man, who had demonstrably gone overboard about her.

Rawlings made a right turn round the old port at Nice. Despite the elderly limousine's adequate trafficators, he also gave a hand signal.

Bruiser returned to his reverie, shutting out the over-developed clamour of the passing scenery. Yes, Constanza had turned out all right. She was not noticeably greedy for jewels or expensive clothes but insisted that she shared his father's life. He was never again permitted to retreat into the masculine world of clubs and cronies.

The chill descended when Moxmanton, returning from a business trip to New York, had been gazing down at Greenland 38,000 feet below: he had given a polite cough and died.

The pathologist said it was a myocardial infarction. The cabin crew loosened his tie and thumped his chest but all that the regrettable incident succeeded in doing was to highlight the inadequacy of the medical equipment carried aboard the average scheduled airliner.

Bruiser stirred unhappily in the back seat of the Rolls, which was passing through Villefranche, a town he had once quite liked but – peering out at the dun-coloured apartment blocks – not any longer.

In the will, Constanza had been left the Villa Apollo at Cap Fleurie and income from the family trust. She shared with Bruiser a life-time interest in Moxmanton House. As Jeavons, the family lawyer, had put down his glasses, Bruiser realized there was no further provision for himself. His father, having bought him his place at Lloyd's in life, had seen no need to add to Bruiser's good fortune in death.

Of course, one day there would be a great deal for Bruiser's heir. But Bruiser and Cee had failed to provide one and only they knew why. After Bruiser had serviced Cee more than four hundred times, he had begun to wonder why he was seeing no results.

'Better have a doctor pull a piece of two-by-four through your tubes,' he had said, trying to make the matter sound light.

Cee had taken herself off to a gynaecologist and had returned, rather nervously, with the results. 'He says there's nothing wrong with me.'

Cee let the implication fall into the silence. 'So it's my fault?' Bruiser looked bellicose.

'No, of course not, Bruiser,' said Cee, hurriedly. 'I daresay there's nothing the matter with either of us and that we should just keep bashing away at it.'

And that is what they did for another six months. But one day Cee felt it her duty to say, 'Bruiser, perhaps it's some vitamin or hormone thing – you know, a deficiency. Mightn't it be a good idea to let the quack run the rule over you?'

Bruiser had tried to shrug the ghastly business aside, but the necessity to provide the Moxmanton dynasty with an heir was a primal urge. Finally he submitted to the tests, was told by the doctor: 'It's a question of a low sperm count. Nothing to worry about. It happens to many men.'

Subsequently he had swallowed pills and rogered Cee to a schedule dictated by her ovulation charts. She was still without child on the day she walked out on him.

No damn money. No damn heir. Christ! Bruiser gripped the Roller's leather upholstery to contain his frustrations.

Back in London, Lucius Frankel had begun to put some funny business to him that might meet his needs, and had roped in Rolly and Dickie at the same time.

'I'll not bullshit you,' he had said. 'What I have in mind is downright criminal, but it'll put all three of you back on your feet for life. Think about it.'

But Bruiser had not thought about it because he was playing his last card. He was going to see Constanza.

The Rolls was nosing along the lower Corniche into the main street of Cap d'Ail, which appeared dirtier than Bruiser remembered.

Rawlings drove past the church and cautiously edged the car into the maze of lanes criss-crossing the Cap Fleurie estates. Once through the high, surrounding wall, Bruiser could see that the villa had not changed much, although Constanza had had the shutters painted lemon and the flowering shrubs were better tended than they ever had been in his parents' day.

Constanza came flip-flopping in beach sandals down the curving staircase into the cool, bone-white marble hall. He was not a man whose aesthetic sense had been over-developed but one would have to be insensate indeed not to appreciate Constanza's looks. Her blonde, streaked hair hung about her shoulders, framing a face of pale fragility, which she was clever enough to keep from the sun.

Amidst the olive faces of the Latins Constanza stood out as a Nordic goddess of light. She was wearing a shantung blouse that hinted at unfettered breasts, and those French blue jeans, worn without undergarments, that delineate both the buttocks and the labia.

'Bruiser! A visitor from afar!' Constanza went *en pointe*, placed her slim hands on his wide shoulders and kissed him Continental-style on both cheeks. He'd always found her an open, friendly woman, if a trifle forced.

'Hello, Connie, sorry for the short notice, but something's come up. Hope I'm not upsetting the lotus life, barging in like this.'

She began to drag him by the elbow towards the terrace. 'Come on, there's some iced lotus juice waiting and Mrs Rawlings is in the kitchen having hysterics over tonight's meal. You'll have to go round in a minute and say hello or she'll burst into tears.'

Constanza had the impetuous, gazelle-neat movements of a girl.

However, her gaiety depressed Bruiser. He was here to beg – a role that ill became him – and he resented having to go cap-in-hand to anyone, let alone his youthful step-mother.

He ground his teeth. It had to be done. Fate had handed Constanza a great deal of power over his future.

Rawlings had unpacked his things, pressed his white jacket and hung it in the carved armoire in his room. Bruiser could detect no sign that anyone was here except Constanza and the servants. Surprising the gigolos weren't on to her, he thought.

The dinner was staged a little too graciously for Bruiser's blunt taste: candlelit table for two fanned by a gentle breeze from the open french windows. On the lawn a single Aleppo pine was theatrically spotlit. Constanza wore a simple mauve Kenzo dress with a firework display stitched up one side from her thigh to a point where rockets burst around one breast.

Bruiser waited until Rawlings had left them with coffee and liqueurs before launching into his woes. Constanza sipped and listened, occasionally making sympathetic noises.

'I've mulled my situation over, forwards, backwards and upside down,' said Bruiser. 'And every time I come back to one solution.' He leaned forward earnestly. 'I can get off the hook if you and I agree to make a joint approach to Jeavons and the other trustees, and get Moxmanton House and the estate sold off. We would split the proceeds. After all, you seem to have lost interest in the place and I'm only there for the occasional weekend.'

Constanza gazed thoughtfully into the candle flame and said nothing. Bruiser felt a need to fill the silence. 'I'm really up against it, Connie. I wouldn't come pestering you like this unless it weren't the last resort. Please believe me.' He could hear the wheedling tone in his voice and loathed himself.

His hostess stirred. 'Poor old Bruiser. I'd guessed you'd hit a bad patch but I never realized those City buggers had dropped you in so deep. Let me have a think overnight and we'll talk again tomorrow. Okay?'

Okay it had to be.

They'd sat chatting for a while, then Constanza had pecked his tense forehead with her pale pink lips, he'd captured a whiff of a musky scent, and she had drifted up the staircase to her bed.

Bruiser poured himself a balloon of Hine to help him sleep. He had the uneasy sensation that his life was being marched away from his own command.

Despite a fitful night, he was out of bed at seven. The English upper classes, lovers of the outdoors, share with the Army a taste for early rising, no matter what the exigencies of the night before. He showered and wet-shaved, and the sound of him moving about must have alerted the staff because when he arrived downstairs coffee, kedgeree and the other ingredients of a bulky English breakfast were waiting for him.

Afterwards, Bruiser strolled moodily down the sloping lawn to an ordinary wooden bench with a curved seat. It was an old friend – Bruiser had known it since childhood. The supports were raised on three layers of paving stones so that even a short person could gaze out over the boundary wall at the vista of the coastline winding along to the promontory of Monaco.

Constanza joined him at nine, tripping down the lawn in a turquoise shift and wide-brimmed straw hat. She parked herself on the grass at his feet, removed the hat and yanked the shift up and off. Bruiser blinked. Constanza was wearing a triangle and nothing else. Involuntarily he turned his head towards the house to see if any of the servants had witnessed this unrobing.

'That's better,' she said, ramming her hat back on and shading her face from a sun that was already beating down strongly.

She had kept her figure. Her ribcage was elegantly defined, neither too stark nor too padded with flesh, and above it sprang two small breasts, girlishly pink-tipped. Bruiser felt himself stir. God's teeth! Was it incest to be on heat for your own step-mother?

He said: 'My parents used to have me here during the holiday when I was a kid. Did you know that on the very spot where you've got your tits out to air Winston Churchill once sat and painted the view? His detective would bring him over from Max Beaverbrook's place. Or so they told me.'

Bruiser sighed at the greatness that had gone from life.

Constanza had turned onto her front. Her bikini bottom had all but disappeared into the crease of her buttocks. She was as unself-conscious as a little girl. She made no attempt to adjust it.

He wondered again if she had taken a lover – she was too handsome to be left alone for long but she had made no mention of one. Was she, perhaps, merely being discreet out of respect for his father's memory? It would not be good form to inquire.

Constanza was speaking. 'You know, Bruiser, there's something quite romantic about you. But you'll have to learn to live in the shitty world of today. It's a dilemma facing a whole generation of your kind of Englishman. Money gives the orders now. Breeding, background, tradition are all vaguely admired, at least by the shopkeeper class, but you have to do more than step forward and say, "I'm here to command and set the example."'

Bruiser was taken aback. 'I don't know what brought that on,' he said gruffly.

Constanza removed her hat again and tossed her hair impatiently. 'It's your daydreaming, Bruiser. You feel you have a right to income you haven't earned, a right to a country seat, a right to be treated as a special case. Yet you were too impatient at Cirencester to learn how to care for the land and you sacrificed soldiering on a drunken impulse. It's not a record to command respect. I'm not angry about it, as your father was, and had a right to be, but I'm saddened at the waste.'

She drew breath. 'Anyway, it brings me to the main point of this conversation. Selling Moxmanton House is not on. Jeavons would say no and a court action to break the trust would be long and costly. In any case, why should any of us throw a single penny at those ravening bastards in the City? Even if you go into bankruptcy, they can't sell the estate from under you because it isn't yours to sell. Your father was sentimental enough to foresee generations of Moxmantons safely tucked up in the ancestral home. One day you'll marry again and have children. Then you'll thank me.'

'I can't see anyone wishing to marry a beggar,' said Bruiser.

He felt rocked. He'd never had a conversation of such depth and candour with Constanza.

'Look here, Bruiser,' she went on. 'There's one way for you to get your hands on some readies – at least, enough to keep the wolves at bay while you look around. Surely, with your connections, someone will turn up to throw a lifeline?'

'*Downright criminal . . . put you on your feet for life . . .*' Lucius Frankel's words drifted lazily into his mind. What had the smooth bugger been on about? Ought he to have put Frankel in his place?

Constanza was saying: 'Your father's will is very specific on the point. The cellar is for our joint use and pleasure. Now he obviously envisaged us drinking it dry over several years and, indeed, replenishing the racks for future generations of Moxmantons as we went along. But there is nothing in the will to hold us to that, although I expect old Jeavons would start yelping if he knew what I'm about to propose.'

Bruiser was picturing the massive wine cellars that ran the length of Moxmanton House. His father had been proud of them.

'There was some judicious hanky-panky when the cellar was valued for death duties at fifteen thousand. In fact, the true value is nearer forty-five. Now if you're discreet, I'm willing to turn a blind eye while you sell the lot *and* I'll let you keep all the proceeds.'

'Jeavons'll twig.'

'Who's to tell him? Certainly not you or me. And not the servants. I think I've persuaded the Rawlingses that their future is with me and I'm staying here in France.'

Rawlings returned Bruiser to the airport to catch the afternoon flight home.

The last thing Constanza said was: 'Clear the cellar – fast. Find a private buyer and don't haggle him into the ground. And don't let your creditors get wind that there's money up for grabs. Try to use it in an intelligent investment.'

Within an hour of his return the telephone rang at Lowndes Square. 'How did you know I was back?' said Bruiser.

'I've been trying your number since yesterday,' said Lucius

Frankel. 'Have you given any thought to our little chat?'

'No, I haven't,' said Bruiser. 'I don't know what's buzzing around in your brain but it sounds a bit off and I'm not sure Dickie and Rolly would want to be dealt in. Despite what you may read in those bloody gossip columns, we are, deep down, all rather regimental fellows, you know.'

'That's why you're so right for what I have in mind. What can I do to persuade you?'

'Don't know about that,' said Bruiser, shortly, 'but there's one small service you can perform for me. Let's drive down to Moxmanton for the weekend.'

'Why?'

'Well, you buy wines in bulk for that club of yours, don't you?'

'Of course.'

'In that case, I'd welcome your advice and perhaps I'll have a business proposition to put to you.'

'Should I bring girls?'

'Best not.'

Lucius closed his eyes briefly and dropped the receiver back into the cradle. He was satisfied. He had not had to force the drift of the conversation.

Chapter Six

Lucius could not quite pinpoint the moment when he had begun to weave the Eton trio into the crime that was forming in his head. He supposed their appetite for decisive physical action was the first characteristic that had made him think of them in connection with the enterprise that was still only teasing his mind.

This had begun with a two-word question: What if . . . ? He had been sitting alone in his office, with its black leather walls and steel-and-glass furnishings, watching a desk-top television. He never went downstairs to the club before 11 p.m.

The sound was turned down and he was watching a parade of girls, flitting backwards and forwards in party frocks, swimsuits, on catwalks, climbing the steps of aeroplanes, posing for cameramen, waving and smiling. He reached forward and raised the volume. The programme was a documentary and the presenter had taken the result of that year's Queen of the Earth beauty contest, gone to some participating countries and recorded the reactions of winners and losers. Lucius watched as the presenter brought out the intensity of the partisanship that the annual event generated, the scarcely veiled hints of prejudice among the judges, girls laughing off or crying at the memory of their defeat.

The programme showed the fierce national loyalties whipped up by the event. The final ceremony had attracted an international television audience of more than three hundred and fifty million. The Queen of the Earth could expect to be £100,000 richer at her abdication, one year hence, when she lowered her crown onto the head of her successor.

The knock-out competitions sifting the contenders in each country that year had raised £2.5 million for local charities.

The semi-finals in New York and the crowning ceremony at the Wembley conference centre in London added a further £500,000. Bets totalling not less than £35 million had been placed on the fifty girls who had fought their way out of the human cattle markets to win a seat on the Boeing 747 airlifting the Queens of the Earth from Kennedy to Heathrow Airport.

The whole circus stirred Lucius to rare excitement. And that's when he had thought: What if . . . ?

The next morning Lucius bought a taped copy of the previous evening's programme and watched it. At several moments during the London sequences he froze the frame and studied the characters attending the Queens. In three instances he was able to identify the person he later codenamed the Source.

Lucius already knew the Source as someone who occasionally used his club. Months later, when he had turned this visitor into a close friend, when the shock of what he was proposing had been overcome, they'd played the What if . . . ? game with mounting enthusiasm. The Source was captivated by Lucius's hunger for liberating wealth.

In their games, Lucius would propose a money-making scheme involving the funds of the contest and the Source, using an extensive inside knowledge of the Queen of the Earth's global organization, would give a critique. Lucius would devise a plan as a military strategist might prepare an assault on enemy fixed positions. The Source would turn up the flaw that would lead to disaster.

Lucius asked the Source many questions and his schemes improved: the Source had to look harder and think longer before the weaknesses became apparent.

Finally, Lucius's scheme assumed a steely, refined quality. The Source said, 'It's not foolproof. With the right backing, it's sixty-forty in your favour, but there's still far too much that can go wrong.'

Lucius laid his final card on the table. 'The odds tilt heavily in our favour,' he said, flatly, 'if we're prepared to use guns. It is the principal reason why this scheme would not work in New York at the semi-finals – we produce a gun and a dozen cops and civilian passers-by produce theirs. Only England is still the land where the man with the gun is still master of his fate.'

There was a nervous silence.

Lucius plunged on. 'It's the only way. At the very least a gun ensures a reasonable prospect of backing off unscathed if things go wrong.'

The Source looked agitated.

'Make up your fucking mind,' said Lucius. 'We've played mental cops-and-robbers long enough. None of this can work without you on the inside, so if it's no we'll drink a bottle of champagne and no hard feelings. If you say yes, you'd better mean it because there'll be no backing away. I'm going to need to recruit some hard characters to make this thing work and they'll be a damn sight less charitable than me if you should suddenly blow out.'

'Yes,' said the Source, and added hopelessly, 'Christ! Why does it always have to be such a hard word to say?'

Chapter Seven

Bruiser used the Land Rover for the drive to the country. He picked up Lucius at the side door of the club and slung his bag into the back of the vehicle. 'Got your riding kit? I've telephoned one of the tenants to hold a couple of horses for us.' Lucius went back upstairs and fetched breeches and boots.

The drive through the drab suburbs of South London took two hours. Bruiser stopped briefly in the village at a modern brick dwelling that displayed the single word POLICE in blue and white glass over the porch. He spoke to the young woman in a pinafore who answered the front door, then climbed back into the Land Rover. Lucius noted what a light mover his host was, despite his bulk.

'What was that for?'

'Normal drill,' said Bruiser. 'Always let the village bobby know when I'm in residence. That was his wife.'

'Why does he need to know?'

'Matter of courtesy, really. It'll save him a wasted journey. This area isn't the Chicago of crime but our policeman, Bob Malley, likes to do random checks on the more isolated properties if they're unoccupied. Most evenings he'll do a run up to the house to check the doors and shutters. It's not visible from the road.'

'I know.'

Bruiser glanced sideways. 'You do?'

'Yes, I've been doing my homework. Do you mind?'

'Not at all, although I can't exactly brag about the glorious history attached to the place.'

'Oh, I think it has history enough,' said Lucius, not explaining further.

'All in the past,' said Bruiser regretfully. 'The original Tudor house burned down. What you'll see now was built in the early days of Victoria. Solid and reasonably comfortable but, as grand houses go, definitely second eleven.'

Bruiser drove along a leafy, curving lane until a high wall of crumbling, mellow brick came into view. The ornate twin gates, a fine example of the blacksmith's craft, were fully open. There was no gatehouse and Lucius noted with approval that metal sheets had been fixed over the wrought-iron tracery so that when the gates were closed it was not possible to see into the grounds.

'Not much point in keeping them locked,' Bruiser was saying. 'A paraplegic could scale that wall.'

Moxmanton House was, as Bruiser had described, handsome in a stalwart fashion, a grey-stone oblong, pilastered and balustraded, squatting on a gentle knoll that was mostly lawn and bloated rhododendrons. A small waterless fountain and pool formed a traffic island in front of the house around which vehicles could circle to arrive and depart along the gravelled drive. There were two main storeys and, glimpsed above the roof parapet, the semi-circular windows of the attic rooms under a slate roof. Cedar and stands of oak and beech shielded the house from view, although the rear terrace afforded a long view of distant farmhouses and conical oasts, white-caped vents swivelling at the whim of the wind. The set-up was ideal, thought Lucius.

Bruiser opened the back of the Land Rover to get at the bags. There were no servants to greet them, although Lucius discovered later that a telephone call from Bruiser had already summoned a woman from the village, a former full-time Moxmanton servant, to air a handful of rooms and prepare the weekend meals in one corner of the kitchen.

Lucius could see armorial bearings centred on the massive timber front doors. On close examination this turned out to be a coat-of-arms, displaying a proud lion incongruously set among three clusters of hops, a maladroit device got up by the College of Arms for the Moxmanton family. The motto read: *The brave cannot yield*. It had been overpainted numerous times and the fine edges of the carving were blunted. It seemed to

Lucius an apt commentary on the present-day condition of Bruiser and his friends.

Lucius was agreeably surprised to find his room tastefully decorated and the bathroom modernized. He had had previous experience of the threadbare décor and ramshackle plumbing that even the very rich often inflict upon themselves in the British Isles. The aristocracy were Spartan in their domestic arrangements.

The furnishings upstairs were sound, without any single piece being spectacular from a collector's point of view. The same could be said of the pictures and Lucius took it that much must have been lost in the fire that had consumed the house in the 1820s. The prize items, a Constable landscape and two Burne-Joneses, Bruiser explained, had gone for auction to ease the burden of death duties on the estate.

Lucius and Bruiser strolled half a mile to pick up the horses. They seemed adequate to Lucius, but, cantering along the edge of a field of corn stubble, Bruiser complained that they were more suited to a fairground roundabout. He was a disgruntled, unhappy man.

Drawing alongside, Lucius said, 'We really must have a talk – you, me, Rolly and Dickie. I honestly think I have an idea to give each of us a tremendous leg-up, something that will mean serious money.'

'It's my turn first,' said Bruiser. 'When we get back I want to show you the wine cellars. I have a proposition.'

Bruiser was showing his guest round the house, and was mystified when Lucius asked him to send away the woman in the kitchen for a couple of hours. 'I'd rather she didn't see me here,' he said. 'Don't take offence, it's just a precaution that will make sense to you later.' He gazed with approval around the kitchen, its wooden dressers, dangling copper pans and long work-surfaces. The ovens, capable of catering a banquet, had been converted to oil. The tank was concealed in an ice-house a few paces from the back door: the gauge indicated that it was nine-tenths full.

'This is the butler's pantry,' said Bruiser. The small room was lined with locked cupboards in which the household silverware had once been stored. He opened one floor-to-ceiling cupboard door to reveal a second door, set into the back wall, massively built and stoutly hinged. He sorted through his iron keys, selected one and unlocked the door. The switch was on the inside and, when he pressed it, low-wattage ceiling bulbs threw a weak light on to the stone steps. At the bottom the two men reached a curious structure: a barrier of iron bars that caged in the staircase. Lucius examined the points where the crude inch-thick metal rods had been inserted into the stonework and cemented fast. The workmen had done a slapdash job. The finish was rough, but the cement appeared solidly worked into the holes. A door of matching iron bars was incorporated into this grille and gave access to the main cellar.

Bruiser produced another key and, with effort, turned it in the heavy deadlock. He and Lucius stepped through. The dim lights, with the wiring housed in metal conduits, ran the length of the cellar, which was also the length of the house. The space was impressive, the atmosphere chilly but not damp. Most of the wine racks stood in arched alcoves, which had at some time been whitewashed, presumably to reflect and enhance the dim lighting. There was also evidence that the alcoves had once been walled-off rooms: Lucius noted the marks where the door frames had been removed.

Bruiser's father had laid down a formidable collection of wines. Lucius examined a few dusty labels.

'The fact is,' Bruiser was saying, 'all this lot has to go, quietly and soon. Is it your sort of thing?'

Lucius was examining the vaulted brick ceiling. 'There has to be an air supply,' he said.

Bruiser looked at him blankly. 'I'm talking about the wine,' he said, irritated.

'I know, but bear with me, Bruiser. Where does the air come in and the fug go out?'

'It's just a damn wine cellar. It doesn't need any ventilation,' said Bruiser, impatiently.

Lucius walked towards the far end of the cellar. He found what he was looking for set high in the stone wall: the mouths of two galvanized sheet-metal vents protected by cast-iron grilles. He reached up, palm flat, and felt a draught.

42

'Christ, it's perfect,' he whispered.

Bruiser came up behind him, baffled. 'Well, there's your bloody ventilation. I can't say I've ever given it much thought. But what about all these blasted bottles?'

'I'll take 'em,' said Lucius, absently.

'The whole caboodle?'

'The whole caboodle,' agreed Lucius. 'A fair amount of it is too good for the club, so I'll arrange a private sale on your behalf. Some of those clarets are stunning. But don't ask me about the money until I've taken more expert advice. Okay?'

'Okay!' said Bruiser, delighted. 'Let's take a couple of bottles upstairs to celebrate.'

'Fine,' said Lucius, 'but first would you tell me where those air vents lead?'

Bruiser was laughing now. 'What a nosy fellow you are, Lucius! As I remember, the damn things run up the east-facing end of the house to chimney level. You can't see them any more because my father had the gardeners train ivy across the wall.'

'The gardeners?' said Lucius.

'Only two now, employed part-time by the trustees. It's their responsibility to see that the grounds don't degenerate into a jungle.'

'So,' said Lucius carefully, 'you have domestic help in the house only when you summon it from the village and a police constable checks the outside regularly when you're not here?'

'That's about the size of it.'

'Do the gardeners come into the house?'

'Certainly not. There's a barn where tools, tractors and grass-cutters are kept. The men have no business coming to the house at all.'

Lucius clapped his hands excitedly. 'My God, Bruiser, you don't know how delighted I am at your set-up. I swear it could make you rich!'

'Sounds more like you're planning to burgle the place,' said Bruiser.

Lucius took Bruiser's arm, an unusual act of familiarity. 'Come on, let's broach the Mission Haut-Brion and I'll tell you why there just had to be vents in your father's cellar.' He selected the bottles and carried them gingerly up the steps.

The dust covers had been removed from the mahogany dining table and the tapestry-seated chairs. The mouldings and Victorian furnishings had been scrupulously preserved to the last fringe. On a sideboard, a selection of cold meat, game pie and salad had been set out.

Bruiser took his plate. 'All right, Lucius, what's all this about the cellar?'

Lucius tasted the wine and let it carry an intense pleasure down into his gut. 'I told you I'd been doing my homework. Did you know that while your father was away at the war, Moxmanton House was requisitioned by the Army?'

'Of course I know. When I was growing up the servants complained about nothing else. It was some sort of staging post for Jerry prisoners before they shipped them off to Canada or whatever.'

'Almost correct,' said Lucius, earning a sharp glance from Bruiser for the hint of patronage in his tone. 'From nineteen forty onwards this house was a classification centre for refugees from Europe suspected of not being what they claimed, and for captured Germans, first those taken in the battle that led up to Dunkirk and afterwards the crews of Luftwaffe planes shot down during the battle of Britain. The unit was run by the Intelligence Corps, who were looking for spies and senior German officers posing as other ranks. Those alcoves in your wine cellar were the holding cells. The inmates were subjected to heavy interrogation. If a prisoner looked a likely prospect, he was earmarked for treatment. The Military Police would collect him in a truck and he would be carted up to a mansion in London called the London Cage. The gentlemen who ran that establishment were skilled at getting answers to their questions.'

'Interesting,' said Bruiser. 'Though it wasn't anything my father ever talked about. But then, he was away doing his bit when these larks in the cellar were going on.'

'Yes,' said Lucius. He grinned and put his elbows on the much-polished surface of the table. 'However, whether you use it for bodies or bottles, your cellar makes a lovely prison.'

★   ★   ★

Lucius Frankel moved fast. He returned to Moxmanton House a week later with a wine dealer to make a detailed inventory of the cellar stock. Two weeks after that the racks and bins were emptied and the contents packed for transportation to London.

Six weeks on from their country weekend, the business was done and Lucius drove down again to go over the cellar with Bruiser and to give him his money. The wine had raised £55,000.

The two men could have returned to London in time for dinner. Instead they made the short journey to Maidstone, ate and celebrated further, then drove back to Moxmanton House for a night's sleep rather than risk the roadside breath-testing activities of the Kent and Metropolitan Police forces.

This proved an unlucky decision for Lenny Belcher, Teddy Triggs and his girlfriend, Jessie Moss, professionally known as Twirling Tess.

Chapter Eight

Teddy Triggs had been heard to tell friends that he was depraved on account he was deprived, a line that would have been familiar to his mother as borrowed from an American stage musical popular in her girlhood.

Teddy's father had been a London docker who clung grimly to his place on the dock register long after the container revolution, mismanagement, union greed and widespread pilfering had struck their fatal blows at the trade that for almost two thousand years had been borne on the river Thames into the heart of the capital. Ultimately, Teddy's father was faced with two choices: moving to a New Town and a new job, or taking a redundancy payment. He felt too old and too settled in his Southwark council flat to uproot so he took the pay-off. He was living on this when Teddy and his classmate Lenny Belcher left the Pickwick Street secondary modern aged sixteen. Overnight Teddy became the family breadwinner – but he and Lenny found themselves pitched into a commercial world in which there were only nine jobs for every eleven school leavers. The two boys faced this dilemma with their customary cheerfulness. They were both personable – Teddy, chubby and curly-haired, Lenny, slim, lank-haired and athletic – but were not particularly distressed when they discovered that the labour needs of the local brewery, clog-making factory and machine shops had been met by other youths more fleet of foot and earlier to rise. Like many of their peers they showed an increasing unwillingness to take on employment that would result in profits for others. 'Bleeding exploitation,' they agreed.

They were not alone in believing a little larceny their birthright. All his life, until the advent of the sealed containers had made it impossible, Teddy's father had extracted his tribute from the cargoes that passed through his calloused hands. No one thought anything of it, not even the police, unless a particularly flagrant case was thrust under their noses.

In this benign world, Teddy and Lenny grafted along. They did car repairs and stole one here and there. They helped themselves in multiple stores where goods were provocatively displayed. They broke into automatic vending machines and jemmied the cash boxes from parking meters. In the end, they graduated to housebreaking, an activity which, they were heartened to learn from Home Office statistics, gave them a four-to-one chance of never being caught.

Teddy's one consistent joy was that he had a way with women. While 'working' in Soho he met Jessie Moss, an indolent young lady, with gleaming golden hair. Jessie scurried between four strip clubs doing eight exotic dances a day. She was a tall, slim girl with shrewd green eyes and a spectacular bosom. She could make one breast spin clockwise and the other anti-clockwise at the same time. For an encore she could put each into reverse. Thus her billed name, Twirling Tess. This minor talent earned her an income a fraction more than that commanded by a competent secretary. It was not enough. Jessie had only the vaguest notion of where the future would take her but she knew that money would help.

After an apprenticeship of an hour, she became a masseuse in a sauna parlour, and had considered whoring but regretfully rejected that idea for three reasons. First, the ponces she encountered made her nervous, second, she might find herself alone one night with a psychopath, and, third, she had a mild distaste for male flesh. The men who frequented the sauna parlour generally possessed sad, doughy bodies. Rarely did a slim-hipped man with a lean, muscled abdomen come her way in either sense of the verb.

One reason she found herself attracted to Teddy Triggs was that he had a cuddly, unthreatening body and did not display that sexually aggressive streak that disturbed her. Her most enjoyable thrills came from a detached sexual electricity. She experienced a real moment of power as she stood over a man on the massage couch, gazing down at his moaning, shuddering nakedness as she manipulated his genitals with the tiniest movement of her fingertips. The same sensation of shivering pleasure came over her when she gazed out at those rows of slack-mouthed male faces as she performed her strip routine.

Her stage presence beyond challenge, Jessie turned ambitious thoughts towards making it as a pop singer. She and Lenny mastered a number of chords on the electric guitar and Teddy acquired a minimal proficiency on the drums, but the best public exposure they could get was at pub gigs, so Jessie continued to gyrate her breasts and Teddy and Lenny stuck to thieving as a more reliable support.

In their life of petty crime, the two men had made their mistakes and been punished accordingly. Both had served short terms in youth institutions and Lenny had done six months in an adult prison for being found in possession of stolen property, a silver teapot and sugar tongs, while Teddy had put in eighteen months for burglary.

Although he had worn gloves throughout, he was convicted on the evidence of his fingerprint on a windowpane of the house he had screwed. Teddy was baffled; how could this be?

It was not a question he could ask aloud without incriminating himself. However, the answer was simple: he had become a bloody nuisance to the local CID. Information from a snout led to Teddy and they'd had him in for questioning. They got no change from their indignant suspect and he was finally allowed to leave the station smiling.

On the wooden table that stood between him and the detective inspector who had conducted the interrogation, had stood a clean glass of water. Twice, when the questions had caused Teddy to squirm, he'd taken sips. Afterwards, the detective, humming happily to himself, had taken a strip of adhesive tape, pressed it lightly to the surface of the drinking glass and 'lifted' Teddy's thumbprint. This he had taken round to the plundered premises, still waiting in a line of similarly blighted homes for the arrival of a Scenes of Crime officer, and had transferred the dab to the windowpane. Which is where the conscientious fingerprint expert found it, corresponding beautifully in at least sixteen characteristics to Teddy's print in Criminal Records.

Justice was done in an unjust manner but Teddy bore no grudge, least of all towards the detective inspector who, to all appearances, had done his job in an affable, above-board way.

Teddy and Lenny were now in their late twenties, still undaunted by social disapproval but, nevertheless, beginning to wonder if they were not in a rut. They were having a drink in their local pub. 'It's our MO,' said Teddy flatly. He was fond of police television serials.

'What's that?'

'You know, that *modus* whatever-it-is. On your file at the Yard they always write down the details of what you've done and, after a while, it forms a sort of pattern. Like round here. Every time someone milks the parking meters, you and me are always on the list the filth turns over. They've got our cards marked and it stands to reason if we go on the way we are, we're a racing certainty to spend more time inside than out.'

Lenny pursed his lips. 'What'll we do if we turn it in? There's no bloody mileage in the pop stuff. What we made last year didn't keep the van in petrol.'

'I've been thinking,' said Teddy slowly. 'It's not so much a case of turning it in as turning to another line.' He warmed to his theme. 'Look, it's just a way of conning the Old Bill. If we do something different they won't clock us. And, anyway, knocking over drums around here ain't made us millionaires. We ought to be thinking bigger.'

'How much bigger?'

'Country houses,' said Teddy. 'Here, take a gander at this.' He produced a thick edition of *Country Life* and opened it at the illustrated property advertisements. 'Just look at the insides of these places,' said Teddy. 'Look at all that stuff – pictures, silver, knick-knacks, furniture. It's worth a bloody sight more than those TV sets and stereos we pick up. We find ourselves a better class of fence and we're in business.'

Lenny was dubious. 'Those kind of people rig the place with alarms and we don't know how to spike them. I hate that bloody system where the bell rings down the nick and you don't even know anything's wrong until the squad cars come screaming up to the door.'

'Yes,' agreed Teddy. 'This kind of operation wants a lot more preparation. You can't just have it off every time you find a drum where the lights are out and no one answers the doorbell.' Still Teddy waxed enthusiastic. 'Reconnoitring, that's what's wanted. Reconnoitring and observation. A proper plan. When I was in the Scrubs there was lots of faces along the landing who got nicked because they hadn't planned their getaway. They'd half-inch the stuff all right and shove it in the boot for the ride back to town. But what's the first thing Old Bill looks for in the middle of the night? A carload of likely looking villains. Right? And the second thing is he asks for a look inside the boot. End of story.'

Teddy paused for breath and Lenny went to the bar to get the drinks in.

Dumping down the refilled glasses, Lenny said, 'So can we box a bit cleverer than that?'

' 'Course we can,' said Teddy. 'We've got the perfect excuse for being on the road at night – the band. We're on the way home from an out-of-town gig, aren't we? We'll have the stuff in the van to prove it.' Almost as an afterthought, he added, 'We'll have to take Jessie along, of course.'

Lenny jumped. 'Now wait a minute. We ain't never done that before. She'll be scared out of her knickers.'

'No, you'd be surprised,' said Teddy. 'She's a great girl for a bit of excitement. Besides, she's cover – the upfront singer and her band out on the road. She can mind the van while we're inside and then help load. If we take the paintings out of the frames and keep the other stuff small, we can stick it behind a false wall at the driving-seat end. If we do it right, it'll work a treat.'

Teddy spoke no lies about their *modus* thingy, Lenny conceded. And they'd both had more than enough of the smell of excreta and boiling cabbage, the aroma peculiar to English penal institutions. 'All right, then,' he said. 'I'm in favour. But you can't kid me. You've already got a tickle in mind.'

Indeed, Teddy had. 'D'you remember, when I was a kid, my mum and dad used to go hopping?' Lenny remembered. His own family, along with millions of others, had discovered the existence of perpetual sunshine along the Mediterranean coast of Spain. They had privately sneered at Teddy's family for carrying on in the old-fashioned way.

Teddy was saying, 'I think we should start near where we

sometimes used to go. There's this big house in a park.' His eyes lost their sharpness and his thoughts wandered. Jesus, why couldn't life have always been like hopping? The bonfires outside every hut at night, the apples baking in the white ash, the scrumping, the grapefruit drinks and arrowroot biscuits passed out to the kids through the country pub doorways, the knees-ups and sing-songs and the daring ones touching up the girls when their mums weren't looking . . . He said, 'We'll take a run down in the van tomorrow and you'll see what I mean.'

Chapter Nine

Lights out came early at Moxmanton House. 'Early start tomorrow,' grunted Bruiser, speech thickened by the wine they'd drunk in Maidstone. 'But it's been a damn good day's work. I'm grateful to you, Lucius. You've done wonders. G'night.'

Lucius smiled privately. He closed his door on the darkened corridor, undressed and climbed naked into bed. Not expecting to stay, he had omitted to bring an overnight bag. He reached out, turned off the lamp and lay gazing up into the dark, his brain echoing with plans clamouring for resolution.

At dusk, Jessie Moss dropped off Lenny and Teddy in the deserted lane. She was told to drive on and return to the main gate of Moxmanton House in an hour. This she did and the two boys were waiting for her. They boldly directed the van into the driveway and reversed off the gravel into a clump of trees. Jessie switched off the sidelights.

'We've been watching the house,' whispered Teddy. 'Nobody's at home. If they come, it's at weekends. The ground-floor shutters are on the inside and they're all closed. We'd have to break a window to get to them and I don't think we should. If the place has alarms, that's where they'll be. So we're going back to see if we can find another way in. Jessie, you stay here and one of us'll come and get you and the van when we've got the stuff out.'

'Well, don't be all bloody night,' said Jessie, huddling into her quilted parka. 'These country places can get on your nerves.'

The two boys disappeared into the darkening landscape. Jessie fished out her cassette player, pushed back her blonde tresses and clamped the earphones into position. The fucking things she had to do for a living!

The two intruders moved up to the last shrubbery cover before the open space in front of the house. Teddy had not noticed Bruiser's Land Rover parked alongside the ice-house.

'This has got to be a knockover,' he said.

They surveyed the silent grey façade of the main building. 'I reckon,' said Teddy, 'that our best way is to get up to the roof and through one of those attic windows. They won't have wired them. Costs a fortune.'

They walked across to the corner where the ivy ended, the gravel crunching softly underfoot. The galvanized-iron air ducts under the vines ran up from the cellar, parallel to the house's brick chimney breasts, all the way to the roof. The gap between the brick and the iron was little more than two feet. Every four feet along the ducts a metal stay held the structure to the wall. 'See,' said Teddy, 'it's simple. We'll tie the rope round your waist so that when you reach the top you can hitch it to the parapet and I'll be up after you.'

Lenny could see that the thirty-foot climb was well within his competence. He chimneyed his way up the side of Moxmanton House in classic mountaineering style. He reached the top, grasped the parapet, then hauled himself over the edge into a wide gutter.

Lenny took the nylon rope from his waist, encircled the stone balustrade twice and double-knotted the end. Behind him was a double window, sealed against the weather and any jemmy. He peered into the uncurtained room, now faintly illumined by a quarter-moon. There was an empty cot in one corner, a blackboard on an easel and a miniature school desk.

Lenny took a small hammer from his belt. The head was taped to reduce noise and he gave a sharp, controlled tap to the pane nearest to the catch. The glass starred and splintered immediately; several slivers dropped onto the inside ledge without much sound and Lenny removed several more from the hard putty before putting in his hand and pushing up the catch.

The act of opening the window swept several pieces of the broken glass onto the wooden floor. They made a momentary clatter but Lenny was already turning back to the parapet and lowering the rope for Teddy. This job was a doddle.

In a second Bruiser Moxmanton's brain rushed from sleep into full awareness. His military life had trained him to the need for immediate alertness in the face of the unexpected. His brain was already scanning the possibilities. A sound had woken him. What sort of sound? Glass breaking? Yes. Or falling. He sat up abruptly. Definitely falling – and right above his bloody head! He remained absolutely still so that he could listen. He knew every nocturnal protest that the old house made and right now there was an alien noise as of weight bearing down on surfaces above the ceiling; a rustling that wasn't caused by a rodent; a creaking beyond that of a house settling for the night.

God's teeth! Bruiser flung back the bedclothes and swung his feet to the floor. The room was pitch dark because the curtains were drawn but he made his way unerringly to the wardrobe. The door squealed traitorously, but Bruiser got his hand to the back of a shelf and removed his old service Browning automatic in its polished leather holster. He groped again for a small box, and slapped a magazine into the butt. With the gun's safety catch off, he padded noiselessly on bare feet to the door.

The third-floor rooms in the roof were where Nanny and the servants had lived. They were normally sealed off from the rest of the house by a door, faced in green baize, through which Bruiser had been forbidden to go, except when he was very small, for lessons with his governess. It had always been understood that the servants' off-duty privacy must be respected, and that their living quarters were sacrosanct to them. But since the live-in staff had departed, the green-baize door had stood open to allow the circulation of air and the prevention of dry rot.

Bruiser, climbing the stairs cat-like and keeping to the sides of the treads to reduce the sound of his approach, could feel a draught on his face. It was stronger than it had any right to be. A window had been opened.

He slipped past the green-baize door, mentally picturing this floor in relation to his own bedroom. The sound had come from somewhere almost directly over his head, which meant the east end of the building.

The marble, polished elm and carpeting of the lower floors had now given way to linoleum underfoot and Bruiser glided easily over it, a big man with a panther step. Finally he stood in the doorway of the old nursery-schoolroom, its hunting scene wallpaper showing faintly in the light from the breached window. He moved silently across the open space, toes nudging aside the shards of broken glass, and saw quite clearly the figure bent over the parapet. Bruiser stepped to one side of the window to wait.

He heard the sound of exertion and whispered conversation as a second person came onto the roof. They clambered into the room. Bruiser said clearly: 'Stand exactly where you are or I shall shoot.'

The plump one gave a terrified squeal and wheeled round, endeavouring to climb back over the sill. Bruiser took one step forward and felled him with a single disabling chop to the side of the neck. Teddy went down like lead. The second figure yelled, 'Christ!' and made for the doorway in panic.

Lenny scampered into what had been a tweeny's room, grabbed a chair and was about to hurl it through the locked window when the light went on and he froze, hypnotized by the small black hole at the end of the weapon being pointed steadily at his mid-section. For several seconds Lenny's terror emerged as an incomprehensible babble. Then he managed to articulate to the implacable figure confronting him in royal blue pyjamas: 'Please, mister, there's no need for that. I'm not going to do anything – honest. I ain't got a shooter.'

Bruiser said, 'Replace that chair on the floor slowly.' Lenny obeyed instantly. 'Now face the wall.'

Lenny turned reluctantly. 'What you going to do? Look, I'm not going to give you no bother.'

'You most certainly are not,' said Bruiser, stepping forward and laying Lenny out just as he had Teddy.

Bruiser's mind never worked better than when he was involved in physical action. These two would start to come round in about five minutes and there could be others.

He raced back into the nursery and, without turning on the

light, rummaged in the toy cupboard. He emerged with two skipping ropes. The first he used to hogtie the plump intruder, binding Teddy's hands behind his back and to his drawn-up legs. Then he pinioned Lenny in the same manner, and moved out of reach the housebreaking implements, protruding from a custom-made, canvas holdall strapped round his waist.

Bruiser stepped across the broken glass and eased himself out onto the roof. He felt the dangling rope, which was slack: no one else was coming up the wall. He peered over: nothing was moving below and no unaccountable shapes were showing against the light of the gravel. Bruiser tightened the cord of his pyjamas and shoved the Browning into his waistband. Then he went over the top, grasping the rope and reaching the ground in four spectacular arcs, kicking himself outward from the wall and abseiling down, ignoring the ropeburns he collected on the descent.

He landed in a crouch, automatic in hand. No opposition. He made a cautious circuit of the house, moved outward to the shrub line that enclosed Moxmanton on three sides, completed a second circuit, checked the lawn, breathed deeply and allowed his adrenaline to subside. Then he remembered Lucius. The only light coming from the house was the one he had switched on in the tweeny's room: Lucius must have slept through the whole damn show. Bruiser returned to the rope, brushed off the sharp gravel stones that were embedded in the soles of his feet, and went up twice as fast as Lenny could ever have managed. He hauled it up after him and went to collect his trophies.

Lucius started out of a deep sleep when his name was bellowed from outside the room. He groped for the light and his wristwatch. Christ, it was only 1 a.m. Was Bruiser drunk?

'Frankel!' Bruiser was using his best parade-ground voice. Lucius hurried across the carpet, realized he was naked, went back to grab his trousers and opened his bedroom door to an astonishing sight.

'I've caught me a brace of tykes!' Bruiser beamed ferociously. Two dazed, trussed figures, heads weaving back and forth, sat at his bare feet.

'My God!' was all Lucius could find to say.

'Bloody cat burglars,' elaborated Bruiser. He gave Lucius a brisk résumé of the events of the past fifteen minutes. By now Lucius was thinking furiously. He was worried.

'Bruiser, are you sure they're burglars? Could they have been breaking in for other purposes?'

'Other purposes?' echoed Bruiser, baffled.

'Yes, come to check on us. Detectives? Inland Revenue?' Lucius knew he sounded paranoid but his long-nurtured criminal plans had made him edgy.

Bruiser voiced Lucius's confusion. 'You're talking bloody nonsense. We've bagged a sticky-fingered pair of jailbirds. Haven't we?' He yanked up Teddy's head by the curly hair and shouted the last interrogatory remark into his face.

'Yes, sir. Sorry, sir,' mumbled poor Teddy pathetically. 'But we didn't want no violence, sir. Nothing like that, on my mother's life.'

'Don't swear away something that isn't yours to dispose of, you horrible little man,' said Bruiser. And to Lucius: 'Come on, help me get them downstairs and I'll call the police.'

The word 'police' concentrated Lucius's racing thoughts. 'No, Bruiser!' he exclaimed, with a vehemence that halted his host.

Lucius went to the night-stand and slipped into his shirt and shoes. 'We need time to think – and I want to talk to you with those two out of earshot. Let's bung them in the cellar for a while.' Teddy and Lenny exchanged alarmed looks.

'We ought to make that call,' Bruiser insisted. 'What's going on?' A suspicion formed. 'Do you know these people?'

'Christ, no!' said Lucius. 'But, please, just trust me for a while.'

They each took a prisoner by the shoulders and dragged them to the cellar entrance. By now, the pair were panic-stricken. 'Here,' said Lenny, having recovered some of his spirit, 'what are you doing with us? This ain't right. We're not police. It's nothing personal our coming here, if that's what you're thinking.'

'Just shut your mouth and wait until you're spoken to,' said Bruiser, hoisting Lenny onto his shoulder, flicking on the light switch and carrying him down the stone steps. Both boys gazed around wildly as they were brought unceremoniously into what looked like a dungeon and deposited on the flagstone floor. They watched helplessly as the barred gate clanked shut and was locked from the far side. Their captors disappeared upstairs, leaving the lights on.

'Blimey O'Reilly,' said Teddy, in the sudden silence. 'Why ain't they calling the law? That big one looks half fucking mad to me.'

But Lenny wasn't listening. 'Here, we've forgotten all about Jessie,' he said.

Lucius made Bruiser sit at the pantry table. He said, 'I'm going to make a surprising suggestion to you. Let's keep them down there.'

'Yes, that's surprising,' said Bruiser drily.

'Not for long – maybe a week or so.' Bruiser's eyebrows went up. 'If we hand them over to the police, what'll they get? They won't spend more than twelve months inside. And it'll be a dreadful waste. We can make use of those two. But if you call the police now, we'll both have to make statements and our names will be linked on the records. It'll spoil everything I've been planning.'

'Ah, yes,' said Bruiser. 'This mysterious plan of yours that's going to make us all rich. I think the time has come for you to do some straight talking, don't you?'

Lucius said, accurately, 'You've never shown much interest before – and we must have Rolly Ponsford and Dickie Biggs-Salter in on the action.' He laid a hand on Bruiser's knotted forearm. 'Let's meet here next weekend and I'll present the whole plan.' He nodded towards the cellar. 'And, meantime, we'll give those two the option to spend a few days cooped up down there or be handed over for a certain term of imprisonment. They don't look like first offenders to me so I'm betting they'll agree.'

As the cellar door opened Lenny and Teddy broke apart with a start. They'd managed to roll alongside each other and Lenny was attempting to pick Teddy's knots. They were both relieved to see that the big lummox with the posh voice had

58

put away his gun. The smooth, dark one was speaking. 'We've just had a discussion about your fate,' he began. 'We can hand you over to the police now and you'll both go to prison.' Lucius watched their faces closely. They both looked glum and he knew he had sized them up correctly. 'However,' he paused for effect, 'there is an alternative. You can remain in the cellar for a few days while we consider whether or not we're able to put a certain proposition to you.'

Teddy looked wary. 'What sort of proposition?'

'A business proposition that would – er – make use of your talents.'

Teddy felt relief flood through him. 'You mean it's something not straight up?' He was on more familiar ground now.

'That, at the moment, is not for you to know,' said Lucius gravely. 'But what I can promise you is that, if you elect not to be handed over to the police, your term of imprisonment here will last a week at the most.'

'And then?' asked Teddy, uncertainly.

'And then my friend and I will either take you into lucrative employment or send you on your way.'

Teddy said, 'Either way you promise not to hurt us?'

'I promise,' Lucius smiled, 'provided you do as you're told.'

'What about him?' Lenny broke in, indicating Bruiser. 'My head's still ringing.'

'If you behave yourselves here,' said Lucius, 'we shall consider you've paid your penalty. You shall have food and drink, of course, and,' he glanced at Bruiser, 'toilet facilities will be made available.'

Bruiser was looking coldly at Lenny. 'You must have had transport to get here and carry your loot away. Where is it? And are there any more like you skulking in the undergrowth?'

Lenny and Teddy looked worriedly at each other. Jessie was their last link with the outside. Bruiser drew his Browning once more and aimed it directly at Lenny's head. 'Never mind what else has been said, it only counts if you give honest answers.'

'Look, mister,' Teddy pleaded, 'there's a van outside but there's only my girlfriend in it. Couldn't you just let her go? We'll explain we're staying with you for a few days' rest in the country.'

'You'll have a permanent rest in the country if you continue to take me for a fool,' said Bruiser grimly. 'Now where is she?'

Sweating, Teddy told him: the Triggs first law of survival decreed that you don't mess with a man with a gun.

Bruiser slipped upstairs to get shoes and zip on a tracksuit. Lucius waited until the sound of him had faded into the distance. Then, in his deepest, most reassuring voice, he said, 'I know it's difficult for you to think so now, but this could turn out to be a lucky day for the pair of you – and perhaps for your girlfriend, too. No great harm has been done by your break-in and I'm sure I can persuade my friend – it's his house, you know – to wipe the slate clean.'

Lenny suddenly had a bad thought. 'Here, it's not kinky, is it, this thing you want us to do? I mean, what with the girl being brought into it, and all . . .' His voice trailed off.

Lucius's laugh was easy and dismissive. 'No, it's nothing kinky. Just something that could set you all up for life. Think about it.'

Ten minutes later, Bruiser returned, hustling a tearful Jessie before him. She was crying. 'Honest, I only came along for the ride. I didn't know what they were up to.'

Bruiser frisked her thoroughly, disregarding her protestations of innocence and her sex as his large hands moved over her breasts and into her crotch. 'All right,' he told her, 'you can untie those two now.'

Bruiser and Lucius went back up to the servants' quarters and dragged down three old mattresses and some blankets. Bruiser also found a chemical lavatory that had once accompanied Moxmanton house parties on shoots.

Jessie was snivelling quietly. The two men's hands were dirty because, despite Lucius's reassurances, they had spent their few minutes alone scratching in vain for a way out.

Through the bars, Lucius handed them some sheets of paper and three ballpoint pens. He said, 'When I return in the morning I expect to find that each of you has written down full particulars about yourselves. I want names, addresses, phone numbers, occupations – and the same for your parents or next of kin. It is also essential that each of you lists the number of

60

times you've been in trouble with the police, what the charges were and the sentences handed out.'

Jessie said, 'I ain't never been in trouble with the police.'

'Very well, then. Just write that down. Because I want it all on paper. If you've lied – and my friend with the gun will be making a thorough check – we shall have that lie in black-and-white and you must take the consequences.'

The threat hung in the air. Lucius looked around the cellar, which was cool rather than cold. The weather outside had been mild, but heating would be needed here at the year's end. 'I'd advise you,' he said, 'to keep yourselves fit with regular exercise.' He had brought with him a stout chain and heavy brass padlock.

Now he wrapped it around the bars of the grille and secured the gate to it. The upstairs door closed after him with a heavy thud.

When he had gone, Teddy said dismally, 'Did either of you tell anybody where we were going?'

'Tell anybody?' Lenny yelped indignantly. 'All you told us was that we'd be screwing a big house in a park. What was there to tell?'

'I didn't tell nobody neither,' said Teddy. 'We might as well have disappeared through a hole in the ground.'

'We have disappeared through a hole in the ground, you silly sod,' said Jessie, drawing a blanket around her hunched shoulders. 'Here, give me that paper and pen. Let's do what the good-looking git says. I reckon it's going to be our only way out of here.' She used the back of her hand to wipe the tears from her red eyes and began to write.

Next morning, after taking the trio coffee and sandwiches, Lucius studied the smudged, scrawled sheets. When he read the addresses he realized that they and he had all emerged from the same social stratum: the birthplaces of himself, Teddy and Lenny were less than half a mile apart. Lucius did not attempt to suppress a fastidious shudder. There but for the grace of God . . . Before he had collected the sheets, he said, 'At the bottom of your paper I want you to answer the question: Who knows you are here?' The three had glanced quickly at each other, but Lucius said firmly, 'You'll each write without consulting the others.' Now he confirmed that each had answered, 'No one' or 'None'.

He would have to see about that.

Upstairs Bruiser said, 'I'd better stay here and keep them occupied until the weekend. I've also got to round up Dickie and Rolly.' He added slowly, 'I can't help feeling that, in some way, I've committed myself to this scheme of yours.' He cocked his head towards the cellar door. 'It's the high jump already, if we get found out. Unlawful detention without trial, I believe is what they call it.'

Lucius said, 'I want to get back to town to check as many of the details in these sheets as I can without causing suspicion. It's vital we know exactly who we're dealing with.'

'In that case,' said Bruiser, 'you can take their van. I don't want the gardeners finding it here. Park it somewhere else and leave it.'

Lucius wore surgical gloves for the ride and decided that, as he had come up to town from the south-east, he would take the van across the Thames and park it near a main-line railway station as if the owner had gone off on a journey northwards. He abandoned it in a street behind King's Cross.

From his office above the club, Lucius rang the number Teddy Triggs had supplied. It was the same as Jessie Moss's. No reply.

Then he rang the number Teddy had given for his parents. 'Hello?' Lucius put on a Welsh voice. 'Sorry to be bothering you. Is that Mrs Triggs? I'm a friend of Teddy and I'm trying to get hold of him.' Teddy's mother gave the number he'd already tried.

'I've just rung there.'

'Then give it a couple of hours, son. He won't be far away.' No note of concern.

On Lenny's phone – he still had a room at his parents' – Lucius got Mr Belcher. 'He didn't come home last night, but you never know with Lenny, out all night or all week. Give him a bell later in the day.'

Lucius did not ring back. But that evening he carefully telephoned each of the clubs Jessie had listed as her stripping venues. The Welsh voice again: 'A message from Jessie Moss. Sorry, she won't be in for a few days. Nasty case of flu.' The manager had joked, 'Try camphorated oil on her chest, Taff. A bottle for each tit should do the trick.'

On the line from Moxmanton House that evening, Bruiser had been gratifyingly circumspect. 'The canaries have settled down. D'you know what's keeping them quiet? They're watching the butler's television through the bars of their cage. I've run a cable and aerial extension down the steps.'

Lucius climbed, satisfied, into his own bed. The weekend would either put paid to his great dream or see the launch of an enterprise that would stagger the world.

Chapter Ten

In London's clubland Lucius Frankel was a charmed, mysterious figure. He operated a small, elegant establishment in South Audley Street, Mayfair, for the sons and daughters of the aristocracy, the occasional royal, film-star fugitives from the paparazzi and those youth-oriented men of all ages who control the destinies of the major movie-distribution companies. Among London's glitterati it was widely believed that he had come from Brazil and he was happy to foster this conceit.

He was, in fact, the offspring of a Portuguese seaman and a south London state registered nurse. His father had been a passing fancy and soon disappeared. Nevertheless Lucius, whose real name was Leslie Franks, enjoyed a happy childhood in the grimy, busy streets of Bermondsey, and the devotion of an efficient, loving mother.

He was a bright boy whose academic talent came into perspective after he won a place at Alleyn's, which sent its quota of sixth formers to the universities but was principally devoted to turning out the type of respectable work-oriented young men who would be a credit for the next forty years to the banking and insurance institutions of the City.

The person who saved Leslie Franks from this humdrum fate was the school's founder, Edward Alleyn, dead these past three hundred and seventy years. Alleyn, and we have this on the authority of Ben Jonson, had been the finest actor in the age of Shakespeare and in recognition of this stirring past, the school had always felt it important to foster dramatic talent. Thus Leslie Franks's own aspirations were given every encouragement. He was a slim, handsome youth, with raven-black hair swept back from a noble profile and forehead. When he left Alleyn's, he looked splendid, moved wonderfully, spoke richly and could act barely. He changed his name to Lucius Frankel because when he joined Equity he discovered that his own name was already used by another performer.

With considerable difficulty, Lucius obtained dogsbody work in repertory companies. He made tea, operated the tabs, did walk-ons and one-line parts. He had an ear for dialect and, indeed, received his only favourable notice for the Welsh accent with which he invested Fluellen in *Henry V*.

However, women were always eager to console him and take the edge off his continuing professional disappointments.

Later, he bought a mind-reading act from a cabaret performer. He did not ask why the man was selling his professional secrets. He soon found out. The act depended upon his having an accomplice – a scantily clad girl was recommended – who moved among the audience while he remained on stage. The girl would borrow items from people's pockets and ask the man to identify them. He could also provide the dates on coins held up fifty feet away. Lucius recruited a girl and put her through a gruelling training in the verbal codes and body signals by which she secretly fed him the information he needed to give the illusion of extra-sensory powers. The act was polished but somewhat hackneyed. The problem was that each girl left him after one season of working the summer shows and northern clubs, and he was faced with the wearying task of training yet another.

Lucius was standing at this low ebb when overnight he became an entrepreneur. Hunched over a drink in the cocktail bar of an hotel in Great Yarmouth, he found himself listening to the conversation of four men at a neighbouring table. They were telling dirty stories.

The grey-suited one with the Rotary badge in his lapel was saying, 'And what about the chap who makes the sticks of seaside rock with Great Yarmouth in pink letters running through the middle?'

The others waited.

'The boss comes to the factory and says, "Buggins, it's disgusting the way you pick your nose on the job. So it's the boot on Friday." And that's how after Buggins had been paid off, the boss found he had half a ton of seaside rock on his hands that said Bollocks all the way through.'

The three listeners howled and even Lucius's fine-drawn mouth twitched.

He thought nothing further of the vulgar story until that night when he was in bed in his digs – he had long since been unable to afford hotel rooms on his tours. He sat upright abruptly in the dark and said, 'Why not? Why sodding not?'

The girl at his side awakened, and said: 'Come on then, darling. I'm not stopping you.'

'No, no. I wasn't thinking of that,' said Lucius, staying the hand that was sliding along his thigh. 'I've just had a marvellous idea.'

The next morning he went to where sticks of rock were manufactured.

'You want me to do what?' said the boss.

'Make me two thousand sticks of rock with Bollocks running through the centre.'

The boss took a step back, the picture of an exasperated man indulging an idiot. 'Look, we'll make you rock for any town you care to name. But a swearword? I mean, I don't know if it's legal. Have you thought about that?'

'If it's not, you won't feel the heat. I'll take two thousand sticks off your hands in one bulk order. There'll be nothing to implicate you.'

The boss pondered. 'It'll cost you fifteen hundred quid. Cash. In advance.'

Lucius took a short lease on a lock-up garage and accepted delivery of the rock, each stick individually wrapped and stacked in cardboard boxes. The order had eaten up two-thirds of his savings. He had a jobbing printer produce gummed labels on which the story he had overheard at the hotel bar was retold under the heading 'The Rock-maker's Revenge'. Lucius spent a day sticking them onto the sticks and then, a single box under his arm, went in search of a willing shopkeeper. He found one who would take the box as a gift and place it on display 'in the interests of market research'. The shopkeeper also accepted an inducement of fifty pounds in cash.

Lucius checked next day that the Rock-maker's Revenge was on display and then, anonymously, called the police. Was this disgusting sweetmeat another nail in the coffin of the country's moral values?

A uniformed sergeant was sent to investigate, and, a week later, the shopkeeper was before the magistrates accused of selling an obscene article.

Meanwhile Lucius had been on the telephone to the newspapers. As a result, the court was crowded with irreverent representatives of the tabloid national press, eager for a bizarre story. The magistrates, all local worthies whose livelihood depended upon the influx of easy-going holiday-makers, were more than anxious not to give the town a name for prissiness. It was the shopkeeper's solicitor who handed them their lifeline: 'Your worships, the box containing these sticks of rock was kept at all times behind the counter and was available only to those customers who my client could be reasonably certain were over the age of eighteen.' This was a bare-faced lie but the bench clutched at it. The charge was dismissed.

The national newspapers gave the case of the 'Rock-maker's Revenge' joyous coverage and even the more serious publications made a small obeisance to the Silly Season and printed a tongue-in-cheek account of the hearing.

Within a week the rock-making factory was on overtime, while Lucius dealt with a rush of orders from novelty shops and resorts throughout Britain.

By the end of the season he had made thirty thousand pounds and resolved never again to slide into penury. He used the money to launch a small drinking club in Windsor, which became popular with young officers from the nearby Victoria Barracks, the men who guarded the Queen when she was in residence at the Castle.

Quite early on, three young blades had clumped in noisily demanding membership, which he had been happy to confer on the spot, dispensing with the joining fee. Lucius did this with smooth charm, brushing aside with a small conspiratorial smile the bothersome formalities. Bruiser, Rolly and Dickie were agreed. This fellow seemed a good sort. As a club owner, Lucius had presence and displayed discretion. He refused to have journalists as members. His protective efforts on behalf of his members were widely appreciated and when he took the gamble on the South Audley Street premises in London he carried with him a great measure of member loyalty. For men of Bruiser's station, Buckingham's was an establishment in which to meet other gentlemen, while Lucius's place was, as Bruiser put it, 'Where you can get one bit between your teeth and another between some filly's legs.' Lucius managed not to wince.

His manner was never obsequious, neither was it presumptuous. His acceptance by his social betters was a process of gradual absorption: an invitation to a cocktail party, a challenge to a game of squash, the occasional weekend in the country, for which he took a hurried course of riding lessons from stables near Rotten Row. He was amusing and a good man to make up the numbers at table. He appeared to know everyone who was anyone.

The only set-back had been his failure to obtain a casino licence: that was where the real money was. And the more he witnessed of the life led by the well-born, the more he yearned for their financial standing.

Lucius waited and watched. One day a grander version of the Rock-maker's Revenge would present itself. He had only to be ready to seize the moment when it came.

Men like Bruiser, Rolly and Dickie intrigued him: to the outside world they presented a commanding face, authoritarian, severe. Their assumption of their social worth and superiority was unquestioning. Their world was a closed order, a matrix of school friendships intended to last a man's natural span, of land and gentry and old families with ancient wealth and influence. The trio had performed dangerous military service and possessed a breath-taking ruthlessness, he thought, yet their blond, boyish looks betrayed no uncertainties or trauma; they seemed untouched by sorrow, undriven by anything as vulgar as ambition. Insouciance was all. The pose was magnificent.

Chapter Eleven

Detective Inspector Walter Fisk preferred Saturday morning in his office to any other time of the working week. The CID room was long, and several frosted-glass partitions had been installed to provide small areas of privacy for the more senior officers at Stone's End Street station. Fisk occupied one. The back walls had originally been cream-coloured but the economies recently forced upon the Metropolitan Police had meant that they were now a depressing beige. Not that Fisk noticed. An aesthetic sense was of no use to a thief-catcher, which is what he was. He had not become a copper from any consuming need to right wrongs, or to rid the world of evil-doing. Even at eighteen he'd seen the true lures: the bolthole from grey, routine, industrial life, the possibilities for excitement, the comradeship and pride in belonging to a body of men from which the weedy and the inadequate had already been sifted. Fisk relished his life among this physical élite. And he was reasonably certain he would reach the rank of superintendent in his early forties. He knew how to play his cards right.

The detritus of his workload bore heavily upon his steel-edged desk but Detective Inspector Walter Fisk ploughed on without complaint. Strictly speaking, there were few Saturday mornings when he was needed in the office but that's when the telephones stopped ringing and he could get a headlock on his paperwork.

At thirty-three, Fisk smoked too much, was thin and sandy-haired but possessed a sinewy charm. His eyes projected a piercing blue and he wished they didn't. He'd rather have had sleepier eyes that disguised his questioning intelligence, just as he would have preferred a better-padded frame. His own theory was that people tended to confide in roly-poly men. When he played the interrogation game, he was automatically cast as cold and relentless while his stout sergeant, who entered later bearing cigarettes and tea, played the warm, sympathetic role. Fisk never stopped being amazed at how the punters continued to fall for such a dumb act.

Just after 11 a.m. his internal telephone buzzed. 'Balls,' he said.

The station sergeant's jack downstairs said, 'Excuse me, sir, but there's a Mrs Martha Triggs asking for you. Won't talk to me or the skipper.'

Triggs? The correct full name and the previous were effortlessly retrieved from his subconscious. He remembered how he'd put an end to the piss-balling-about by taking that print off the drinking glass. Mrs Martha Triggs? He had a picture of a robust, dyed-blonde saying, after Teddy had gone down: 'Fair's fair. My boy says you always treated him right.'

'Put Mrs Triggs in the interview room,' he said. 'I'll be down.'

He found her twisting the strap on her shoulder-bag. Fisk went into a mild, affable routine. 'Hello, Mrs Triggs. What brings you here?'

'I'm not sure,' she said hesitantly. 'I'm not sure I ought to be here at all. But if anything's happened to Teddy, I thought it best to get the bad news now, rather than wait for one of your blokes to come knocking on the door.'

'Bad news?' said Fisk, waiting for specifics.

'He and his girl haven't been home since Tuesday.'

'Can you take a guess at where they are?' he asked, deliberately planting a suggestion that he nursed knowledge he was not yet ready to impart.

'Oh, Christ!' said Mrs Triggs, taking the hook. 'Has the little bleeder got himself in trouble again? It's no life in the nick, is it? I keep telling him that.'

'Well,' said Fisk, 'I haven't got him or his girl in here. Could be he's been naughty off the manor.'

Mrs Triggs tightened visibly. 'D'you mean you don't have any news for me?'

'Not yet,' said Fisk, keeping the hook in her ample flank. 'But first, perhaps you'd better tell me your side of the story?'

70

Mrs Triggs shifted. She decided she had to speak up, Mr Fisk was a decent bloke; for a copper, that is. She said, 'I last saw him and Jessie on Tuesday. He was cleaning the windscreen on his van and I said, "Going somewhere?" And he said, "Back tomorrow." Then he laughed and said, "Just going down hopping." Well, I just took it as a joke he made because he didn't want to tell me the truth. You know what the little sod's like. I mean, it's not even hopping time, is it? And no one goes any more, anyway.'

Walter Fisk kept his bafflement hidden. He had been born in Snainton, Yorkshire. ''Oppin'?' he said, echoing Mrs Triggs's cockney disregard of the aspirate and the final G. Mrs Triggs explained patiently.

Fisk said, 'He must have meant he was going for a ride in the country – or for a holiday.'

'He'd hardly be going on holiday without telling his mum, would he?' said Mrs Triggs.

Fisk thrust his hands deeply into the pockets of his woollen cardigan, which he wore because he thought it gave him a reassuring, professorial image, and pursed his lips. 'Hang about,' he said finally. 'I'll be right back.'

In the station office he made a quick check of the Occurrences Book and had brief conversations with both the duty sergeant and the collater.

Returning swiftly to the interview room, he said, 'We've had no notification that they or their vehicle have been in an accident and no notification from any other authority that they're in any kind of trouble.'

Mrs Triggs relaxed visibly. 'But it's still not right going off like that without a word, is it?'

'Maybe not,' said Fisk. 'But they're both adults and it's a free country. I have to ask you formally, do you have any reason to believe that there's been foul play?'

Mrs Triggs started. 'Blimey, I didn't say that!'

'In that case,' said Fisk, 'we're dealing here with two missing adult persons. My suggestion to you is that you give it a couple of days before officially reporting them missing although, in the meantime, I'll be glad to have a few inquiries made. How does that sound?'

Mrs Triggs clutched gratefully at the policeman's offer.

He told her, 'There's probably nothing in it. But ring me if they turn up. You wouldn't want me to waste my time if they're back home, would you?'

Walter Fisk's curiosity had been only moderately stirred. Teddy Triggs was a minor villain and his girlfriend unknown to him; the chances were they had shacked up somewhere and were financing their out-of-town sojourn with a hand-out from the local social-security office. The fucking kids were all at it, these days.

But Fisk went through the motions. He instigated a request for information that first went up to Scotland Yard and was then propagated throughout the United Kingdom through the police national computer.

Late that same evening he was at home, watching snooker on television, when the telephone rang to give him the only morsel of information that had turned up.

Teddy Triggs's van had first been ticketed for illegal parking in Copenhagen Street, behind King's Cross station, and had been towed subsequently to the pound. All this had taken place two days previously.

Fisk brooded for a while, then telephoned King's Cross CID. Would they take a look at the van? They would.

A young detective constable called him at home on Sunday morning when Fisk was still in bed. Walter sighed and extracted himself from his wife's sulking embrace. She flounced furiously off the mattress.

'The van was found unlocked,' said the young DC. 'But a meter maid took possession of the keys that had been left on the driver's seat.'

'Very odd,' said Fisk.

'Yes, sir.'

'Anything interesting inside?'

'Some cheap musical instruments in the back and a small portable public-address system. On the floor on the passenger side was a cassette player with earphones. The tape had played through to the end.'

'Music cassette?'

'Yes, sir. The Police, actually.'

'Hilarious,' said Fisk drily. 'Any signs of a struggle?'

'Nothing like that, sir. Apart from the keys, nothing untoward at all.'

The young officer had not ventured far enough into the van to discover Teddy's secret storage compartment. He said, 'I didn't disturb anything, sir, in case you wanted SOCO called in.'

'No, no. Not at this stage. I'm not even sure we have a crime here. Just leave the vehicle in the pound with the usual Keep Off notice on it and I'll get back to you.'

Fisk, now the sole occupant of his marital bed, rolled over and gazed thoughtfully at the ceiling. What was that little bugger Teddy Triggs's game?

Chapter Twelve

Teddy and his companions had recovered some of their natural bounce. They demanded and got a pack of playing cards, and Bruiser had even conceded a bucket of hot water, in which the imprisoned trio had carried out primitive ablutions.

'How much bleeding longer is this going on for?' demanded Teddy.

'Don't take that tone with me,' said Bruiser, shortly. 'Just think yourself lucky you're not on the way to trial and a long stay on Dartmoor.'

Bruiser had not been able to get his little band together until Sunday evening. Dickie Biggs-Salter had been saddled with a weekend duty and raced up in his old MGB on a four-hour break. Bruiser took him and Rolly to view the cellar inmates.

They hooted. 'Bloody marvellous!' chortled Rolly. 'It's a damn fitting punishment, if ever I saw it.'

Jessie, Teddy and Lenny gazed sullenly up the stone staircase at their captors. They'd been watching the Sunday service on television for the sake of something to do.

Jessie crossed her arms angrily in front of her splendid bosom, turned her back and walked to the far end of the underground prison. Those upper-class gits made her feel like a performing dog.

Upstairs, Lucius laid out his photographs and notes, and set up a video screen. He had taken over Constanza's drawing room and had checked that the inner shutters were latched, the brocade curtains drawn. Bruiser kept his own counsel but both Rolly and Dickie were raucously sceptical. 'Pray silence for Professor Moriarty, the Napoleon of Crime,' announced

Rolly, lolling sideways, his cavalry twill-covered legs hooked over one of Constanza's button-back chaises longues.

'Gentlemen, if I may have your attention . . .' said Lucius, unperturbed.

'Can it,' said Bruiser, grinning. 'Lucius really does have something to say. Otherwise I wouldn't have gone this far. We've already taken a devilish risk keeping those tykes downstairs. Now simmer down and let the dog see the bone.'

Lucius pressed the Play button and the Queen of the Earth television programme flashed onto the screen.

He played it through to the accompaniment of catcalls from Rolly and Dickie. He and the waiters at his club knew the sound well and a special blend of tact and imperviousness was required to handle the likes of this pair at the end of a boisterous, uninhibited evening. Lucius noticed that Bruiser was watching thoughtfully, not joining in the baying at all.

'My word, look at the shanks on that one!' whistled Dickie as the Finnish Queen of last year took careful neat steps down from a rostrum. The measurements of feminine beauty against the anatomical splendours of equine thoroughbreds was a characteristic unique to Dickie's social class. The horses frequently came off best.

'You'll observe,' said Lucius, 'that for much of the time the girls travel around in small groups, usually in hired limousines. All fifty are together for only specific events. Obviously the final is one such event but, in the week leading up to the big night, they are together at a Lord Mayor's banquet,' he froze the frame at the scene in the Guildhall, 'and again for a luncheon that has become known as the Ecology Fast.' Lucius stopped at a scene inside the Great Hall at the Grosvenor House Hotel in Park Lane. The pictures showed a smiling Duke of Edinburgh, surrounded by a bevy of queens, most of them as tall as he was in their five-inch stilettos.

'The occasion raises huge sums for His Royal Highness's pet charities. A queen presides at each of fifty large tables and the guests vie with each other to bid for their services as dance partners at the post-final ball.'

Lucius reversed the tape, which skidded back to the camera coverage immediately preceding the Ecology Fast. The sequence showed two single-deck coaches from which the girls, in national costume, were alighting. The scene lacked the elegance of their earlier entrances.

The queens ducked awkwardly to negotiate the doorways in their finery and elaborate head-dresses. Stepping out with them were a number of older women in ordinary clothes, who fussed over the girls, tidying their hairdos and headdresses as they waved and smiled and crossed the Park Lane pavement to make their entrance into the hotel. In a measured voice, Lucius said, 'The women in civvies are the chaperones. One is allotted to every two girls. As you can see, they mingle with the girls in the two coaches, but next September, when the contest will be held during the last week of the month, changes will be made. The practice of making the girls put on their headgear before setting out for the Grosvenor House is to be abandoned. In the past, a number of hats have been damaged on the coach ride and, anyway, the whole procedure is awkward. Next September the chaperones will travel ahead in coach number one, carrying the hats. The girls will follow in the second coach and put on their hats in an anteroom before going into the lunch. Incidentally, the Prince of Wales will be principal speaker this year and will accept the donations for his ecology interests.'

Bruiser asked, 'How do you know about the new arrangement, Lucius? We're talking of an event best part of half a year away.'

Lucius said, 'Point taken, Bruiser. Perhaps you'd allow me to answer that later.'

Bruiser grunted and Lucius resumed his commentary. 'Certain measures are taken each year to protect the girls from over-enthusiastic admirers, from gropers and photographers and a number of fanatics who make bets that they can bed certain of them. There have occasionally been anonymous threats to harm the girls but nothing alarming has ever happened. For some years, security arrangements have been the responsibility of a firm called Watchmen of London. This is Britain so, of course, their men are not allowed to carry firearms. They do, however, have concealed eight-inch truncheons and two-way personal radios that keep them in constant communication with a central control room at the hotel where the girls stay throughout their week in England. A minimum of two Watchmen always accompanies each party of girls that leaves the hotel on sightseeing and shopping tours, and one always rides in each coach on journeys such as we've just seen to the Grosvenor House or wherever.'

Lucius tossed a number of colour photographs onto the table. 'Here are the Watchmen, all conveniently identifiable in their navy-blue battledress and peaked caps. Those in the crash helmets are confined to armoured-car money deliveries to banks.' He produced another set. 'Here we have pictures of the Colonel Blood Inn that has just been built on the site of old wharves on the Bermondsey bank of the Thames opposite the Tower of London. It's twenty-two storeys high and is named after the gentleman who, in the seventeenth century, almost succeeded in carrying off the Crown Jewels from the Tower.'

Rolly stirred restlessly. 'Get on with it, Lucius. We've not come here for a blasted history lesson.'

God, if only I didn't need that brute, thought Lucius, holding himself in. 'Sorry, Rolly. I've thought about this so much and done so much research that I get carried away.' He took up his theme again. 'The management of the Colonel Blood Inn have arranged a block-booking deal with the organizers, and this September the girls and their chaperones will be accommodated on the twentieth and twenty-first floors of the hotel, immediately below the penthouse restaurant. These floors will be guarded by the Watchmen, who will vet all visitors.'

Lucius paused and sipped a glass of Sancerre, which Bruiser had provided from a couple of cases that had survived the cellar clear-out. This moment of solicitude had revealed something to him; he was as certain as he could be that Bruiser wanted to be convinced. He told them what he had learned about the vast sums of money that accrued to charity as a result of the global contest.

Then he said calmly, 'Gentlemen, we live in sour times. Our backgrounds are very different but, without being presumptuous, I think it is true to say that each of us has a financial problem. You are facing financial meltdown and I –' a wry smile '– I have damned myself by acquiring a taste for a lifestyle that can be mine only by seizing the moment.' He tapped the folder. 'Here, I believe I've found that moment. At first, I toyed with the idea of kidnapping just one of these girls, a contestant from one of the rich Western nations, perhaps the girl from the United States. The Americans are a sentimental people and I could see no difficulty in extracting a ransom from them – after all, think of the billions they released a few years back to get their embassy hostages out of Iran. But I had to confess to myself that I have no experience of the kind of physical action this operation would require. I have no knowledge of weapons, nor am I certain that I could handle a violent situation. A certain military discipline and courage seemed called for.'

Dickie and Rolly exchanged knowing grins. 'Know what you mean, Lucius,' said Dickie. 'Lots of chaps prefer the service corps. No shame in that. Someone's got to keep the inkwells filled.'

'I'm glad you understand,' said Lucius, responding with a set face to this banter. 'In the circumstances, it was natural that my thoughts should turn to you three.' He wound himself up for the ego massage. 'Right from the start in Windsor I've always liked you all. I think you know that. I've often wished I possessed your freewheeling high spirits. And once I realized that you had the resource and bravery to carry out a clean-cut kidnapping, my plans began to expand. Why stop at one girl? Or two? Why not scoop up the entire fifty? It would be a crime so outlandish as to be beyond the wildest fears of those whose task it is to protect them.'

The trio were listening keenly now. Lucius said, 'There's another aspect. Apart from the material rewards, what an indescribable satisfaction one would feel in pulling off a coup that would go into the history books, an achievement that people would remember into the twenty-first century. Somehow, that seemed important to me.'

'Paths of glory lead but to the grave, old boy,' Dickie said, unmoved. 'Best to keep things straightforward. Do it because you have to or because there's a bob or two in it at the end of the day.'

But Bruiser was studying Lucius with something approaching respect. What was it he had once said to the others? . . . Let's live the life of conquistadors, that was it. In all the years since, he'd done little but acquire a reputation as a white-tie hooligan and here, by God, stood this man from nowhere, dreaming his bold dream and, though afraid, daring to take the first steps towards its realization.

Bruiser's head came up sharply. 'What was that?' The noise occurred again: a distant jangling. 'Someone's hanging on the front-door bellpull,' he said, on his feet in an instant and in command. 'Dickie, go through to the kitchen, disconnect the lead to the cellar television, keep the inmates quiet and shut the cellar door. Rolly, you and Lucius stay put.'

Dickie slipped out of the sitting room ahead of Bruiser, who padded silently across the black marble of the hall floor. He could hear feet crunching gravel as someone moved away from the house. Bruiser yanked open one of the double doors. Outside, the blue-uniformed figure gazing up at the first-floor window was visibly startled.

'Good grief, it's you, Bob,' said Bruiser. 'I thought I was about to repel burglars.'

'And I thought the same, Sir Brewster,' said Bob Malley, the village constable.

'Was there something you wanted?'

'No, sir. I was doing the usual check when I spotted an upstairs light. I hadn't realized you were still in residence.'

Had he been to the side of the house and spotted the parked cars? From the gloom of the doorway Bruiser looked into the policeman's fresh, open face. 'I didn't hear you go round the house.'

'Oh, I hadn't got that far, sir. Look, you can see the light from here.' Malley pointed upwards at Lucius's window.

'So you can,' said Bruiser. 'Sorry I've alarmed you. I'm hoping to spend a little more time at Moxmanton House in the future. London is becoming somewhat tedious.'

'Well, remember to let me know when you arrive and leave and I'll continue keeping my eyes open for you,' said Malley.

'Most thoughtful of you, Bob,' said Bruiser. 'Be lost without you. G'night.'

Bruiser strolled to the kitchen to fetch Dickie. If Lucius's show went ahead, he'd have to be punctilious about reporting his movements to PC Bob Malley, whose commendable sense of duty could otherwise become awkward.

'I daresay everyone could do with coffee and a sandwich, including the downstairs mob,' he said to Dickie. 'All this talk is making me hungry.' The two men began to slice the bread.

Presently, returned to their conspiratorial huddle, Rolly said to Lucius, 'It's all very fanciful, old boy, but I can't see the bookies quoting any sort of odds on such a stunt. It has to be a non-starter. Even if we worked the miracle and lifted fifty girls from the centre of London, we'd be running a bloody holiday hotel to cater for them while the best brains in the police and intelligence services of the world would be combining forces to descend on us like ten tons of hot manure.'

'You're certainly correct about the likely reaction,' said Lucius. 'I find it thrilling. Don't you? But we shall have the advantage of prior planning, surprise and audacity. The key to success is in a plan where we kidnap the girls so skilfully that, for a while, it will not appear to be a kidnapping at all. We can give ourselves this respite by putting into operation lessons learned from wartime disinformation activities – make the enemy believe in the non-existent, delude him at every turn, match our powers of deception against his powers of deduction. And, as for the holiday hotel, we have one right under our feet, only forty miles from London, totally secluded, totally secure. You could house far more than fifty in that cellar – and keep them undetected for as long as it takes.

'The plan I have in mind falls into six stages. One, the purchase of stores and equipment, with reconnoitring and rehearsal. Two, the operation to secure the girls and stow them safely away. Three, the largely psychological campaign to bring reluctant authorities round to the point of conceding our ransom demands. Four, the complex exercise to get possession of money without leaving a trail. This will be the most dangerous stage because we shall have lost the element of surprise. Five, the release of the girls into the world without providing a trail back to ourselves, and six, there'll be the necessity to handle discreetly the vast sums that should then be in our possession.'

Lucius gazed at each of his languid listeners in turn.

'In the case of the present company, there should be little problem. We are accustomed to high standards of living. No eyebrows would be raised if each of us acquired a Rolls-Royce tomorrow. None of us would be compelled even to leave the country to enjoy our secret wealth. However, a problem will arise over the three people at present enjoying Bruiser's hospitality downstairs. The dilemma is that my plan calls for the assistance, in secondary roles, of petty crooks. The girl could also have a useful function, primarily as a matron for the girls. But, of course, they are basically rabble. The two men own up to criminal records, they lack the discipline to keep their mouths shut or to spend their money with restraint. They would undoubtedly fall into the hands of the police at some stage and that would mean jeopardy for us. We need them for my plan, but we have to accept now that they pose a problem that will need a solution later.'

Lucius stopped talking. He allowed the implication of what he was saying to sink into the silence of the room.

Finally, it was Dickie Biggs-Salter who said, 'I hadn't realized what a cold johnny you can be, Lucius. I'd been wondering when you'd get to the rough stuff.'

He leaned forward and stared directly into Lucius's eyes. 'What you're saying, dear boy, is that we need a Final Solution. There's to be sticky red stuff all over the carpet.'

Lucius studied the three set faces. 'Yes. I can't see how we can do it without encountering opposition that will compel us to kill.'

'Tell us about not being able to make omelettes without breaking eggs,' said Rolly Ponsford drily.

Lucius rounded on him with uncharacteristic ferocity. 'Dammit, Rolly! I want you to have an appreciation of every likelihood from the start. No one is going to make us rich for life unless we display an unshakeable ruthlessness. Yes, there could well be sticky red stuff on the carpets. And, before we're finished, some of it may come from us or from the girls. There are no guarantees of safe conduct.'

'Calm down, Lucius,' said Bruiser. 'Rolly has every right to ask. It's a poor commander who doesn't take his likely casualty rate into account.'

Lucius looked fatigued. 'Let's turn to a pleasanter subject for a moment – the money. With fifty girls in our possession, there is no need to demand greedy, impossible sums. I'd propose that we would graduate the demands on a scale that takes into account the status of the country concerned. You would not expect to demand the same sum from, say, Costa Rica as you would from Germany. But an average of half a million US dollars per girl should be a reasonable target.'

Lucius forestalled their mental arithmetic. He smiled. 'That amounts to twenty-five million dollars, to be split into five equal shares.'

Dickie whistled but Bruiser said, 'Steady on. Five shares? We're only four.'

'We have a partner,' said Lucius, shortly. 'I was going to say a silent partner but, in fact, we shall be relying on this partner saying a great deal. Bruiser, you asked me earlier how I know so much about the details of next September's contest. We have someone on the inside, a mole, if you like, who I have sworn to maintain as an unnamed figure. But from this person I call the Source we shall be kept updated on every movement that might be of use to us. I must tell you adamantly that the Source is vital to our success and demands a fifth share in return for a constant flow of information.'

'You mean, we do the business and this Source character makes a few telephone calls?' said Dickie.

'One phone call, from either Moscow or Washington, can destroy the world. All we want to do is shake it a little – but for that there's a price to be paid,' said Lucius. 'Anyway, it's something for you to talk over among yourselves.' He took out a sheaf of correspondence and said, 'But before I leave you alone to mull things over, I want to show you, if I may, how to simplify the apparently impossible task of kidnapping fifty girls in one go. Look here.'

Lucius began passing round copies of letters. He said, 'I approached the problem by putting the picture of fifty individual beauty queens out of my mind. I began to think in terms of a *coachload* of girls. Capture the coach and you capture the girls in one pretty package. The video film will have shown you that they have never before been together in a single coach but, as I've explained – and here I'm relying on the Source's information – that will not be the case this year. For the first time they will be shepherded handily into one coach. Here's what I've already done . . .'

Chapter Thirteen

Letter to Lady Nancy Cornmorris, Chairwoman, Queen of the Earth Charity Committee

Dear Lady Cornmorris,

I am sure that, even this early in the year, your committee is busy on its plans for the final of the Queen of the Earth competition that raises such admirable sums for deserving causes.

May I be permitted to make my own modest contribution?

If you are so disposed, I am willing to provide two fifty-four-seater coaches of the most modern design and comfort for the transportation of the young ladies who will be taking part in the contest. The two vehicles would be made available by me for the entire period of the London visit, together with drivers in appropriate livery, and my firm would remain responsible for all matters concerning insurance, fuel and servicing. There would be no charge on your committee for any part of this arrangement.

As you will see from the letterhead, my company, Regal Roadways, is in the business of specialist travel. We are a newish concern and if you and your committee would grant me the right to use in future, as publicity material, the fact that we conveyed the Queens in Regal Roadways style, then I would be happy, in addition, to donate £5,000 to the charity.

May I hope to hear from you soon?

Your respectfully,

Robert Ainsworth

Managing Director

Letter to Robert Ainsworth from Lady Nancy Cornmorris

My dear Mr Ainsworth,
I am in receipt of your kind offer which I have passed to our Organizing Secretary, Mr Arthur Emblem. I trust you will hear from him shortly.
　　Yours truly,
　　Nancy Cornmorris

Letter to Robert Ainsworth from Arthur Emblem

Dear Mr Ainsworth,
Lady Cornmorris has passed your letter to me and, I must say, yours appears to be a most generous offer. Regarding the use of the contest in your publicity material, the committee would have no objection to this, provided the material was confined to brochures and posters. They do not feel a £5,000 donation would justify them giving permission for widespread television publicity, for instance.
　　If this limitation is agreeable to you, please let me know before the end of the month. I would, of course, need to inspect the vehicles that you propose making available to us and this would need to take place quite soon before all transportation arrangements are finalized.
　　Yours sincerely,
　　Arthur Emblem

Letter to Arthur Emblem from Robert Ainsworth

Dear Mr Emblem,
I am delighted that Regal Roadways may be of service. Your committee's limitation on publicity is quite understandable and I agree to this proviso.
　　I shall be in touch shortly to arrange for the inspection that you require. In the meantime, I have pleasure in enclosing Regal Roadways' cheque for £5,000, a donation to the cause that I promised in my original letter to Lady Cornmorris.
　　Best wishes,
　　Robert Ainsworth

Lucius waited until they had all read the correspondence. He said, 'I thought the request to exploit the contest for publicity purposes was a necessary touch. They would have been suspicious if they were getting something for nothing. Needless to say, Robert Ainsworth and Regal Roadways exist only on those sheets of paper. The company headquarters is an accommodation address, where they also take telephone messages, off Broad Street, Birmingham, and the company's local bank account was opened with forged references and a bundle of ready money. What is very real are the two late-model Volvo coaches sitting in a rented garage at Deptford in south-east London awaiting the inspection of Mr Arthur Emblem. A six-month lease on these two models has already cost the Source and me more than forty thousand. Which brings me to an important matter. The project requires more "seed" money. If you gentlemen are in, then a contribution of twenty thousand minimum will be required from each of you. It is a minute sum to set alongside the prospect of five million dollars a head, don't you think?'

Lucius spent another hour setting out his ideas for their inspection. Then Bruiser said, 'Why don't you buzz off, Lucius, while we talk amongst ourselves? Dickie has to leave soon and we must decide before he goes.'

Lucius felt obliged to give them a dignified little bow before withdrawing to his room.

'Well, well, well,' drawled Dickie, after the door had closed behind him. 'Who'd have credited our Lucius with such a devious mind?'

'You have to admit,' said Bruiser, judiciously, 'not only has he worked out a meticulous plan but he has committed himself in the most positive way. Insinuating those coaches into the proceedings is a brilliant trump card.'

'You don't suppose,' said Rolly, 'that all this is merely an elaborate con trick to part us from twenty thousand apiece? After all, as far as we're concerned, those coaches still exist only on paper.'

'Not a chance,' said Bruiser, pouring everyone a whisky. 'You can see with your own eyes the excitement's eating him up. And we wouldn't be parting with any money until we'd seen the coaches for ourselves.'

The trio picked away at Lucius Frankel's dream for the best part of an hour. A sticking point was the prospect of blood-letting.

'Why is it that killing people seems such an attractive idea to those who've only ever experienced it via the cinema screen?' asked Dickie. 'The first time I put a hole in a chap I was off my fodder for a week. Lucius seems rather over-keen, if you ask my opinion.'

'I'm inclined to agree,' said Bruiser. 'But as it's our good selves Lucius is expecting to handle the rough stuff, it is we who shall exercise the proper restraints.'

'Shall exercise?' repeated Rolly, cocking an eyebrow. 'Bruiser, I think you've already put yourself among the ayes. So it's up to me or Dickie if there's to be a black ball.'

They argued on. Finally Bruiser said, 'Dammit, I'm in, shit or bust. Anything's better than this poverty-stricken half-life we've been leading.'

'*Moi aussi*,' said Dickie, raising a deceptively limp hand. 'How about it, Rolly?'

Their companion looked from one to the other. 'Oh dear, I should never have let go of nurse. I think you bastards are about to lead me into something worse. All right. Make it unanimous and . . .' holding out his glass '. . . make it a large one with a splash of soda.'

They laughed.

Chapter Fourteen

Bruiser's two comrades had gone and Lucius, jumpy with euphoria, paced the overstuffed drawing room. The trio from the cellar stood uneasily before him, a sorry spectacle in their soiled clothes. Bruiser had made them carry up the thunderbox and empty the contents down the servants' hall lavatory pan. A chemical aroma still lingered on them.

'It's all over now,' said Lucius. He placed three bundles of crisp new banknotes on the table and said, 'Take one.' Hesitantly, they obeyed, wondering what was to come next.

Lucius said authoritatively, 'You've wiped the slate clean. We consider that you've been sufficiently punished for the break-in.'

Jessie wanted to tell them that, as a first offender, she'd have suffered nothing worse than a spell of probation but thought it wiser to show caution.

'You'll find you have five hundred pounds each,' Lucius lectured, 'which is really intended to convince you that we're serious. We want your services and total loyalty for the next six months or so and, in return, there's a strong possibility that you'll all end up rich.'

Teddy was the first to speak. 'How rich is rich, mister?'

'I was thinking in terms of three deposits of a hundred and fifty thousand pounds in secret bank accounts in say, Geneva, from which you would each derive a legal annual income of something like fifteen thousand, depending on the state of the money market, of course. These payments would continue for life.'

Teddy looked incredulous. 'Are you asking us to believe that before the end of this year you'd be in a position to give us four hundred and fifty grand? All respects to you, sir, but we're not just off the banana boat.'

'Not give,' said Lucius. 'You would earn the money.'

It was Lenny's turn to scoff. 'Who would we have to murder?'

'*You* would not have to murder anyone.'

Bruiser silently poured large brandies for the two young men and a stiff vodka-tonic for Jessie.

'Look,' said Lucius, 'I know we've put you through a rather frightening hoop this past week but it has only gone to demonstrate to you that we make our own rules which, if you abide by them, will bring their reward.'

He looked at his Piaget watchface. 'It's coming up to midnight. Far too late to return you to London so you can have baths and sleep and talk over our proposition. You'll be in a much better state in the morning to think clearly. Then I'll run you up to town and show you where I left your van.'

The trio were in and out of each other's rooms half the night, treading softly as people do in strange houses. Finally, it was three packages of crisp notes that swung the verdict.

'Speaks louder than words,' Teddy summed up. 'What we got to lose by stringing along?'

'That big one's got a shooter, remember, and we've never before got ourselves mixed up in that sort of caper,' said Lenny.

'Teddy's right,' Jessie said. 'We're not so bloody brilliant that we can afford to miss this one. Let's give 'em a trial run.'

The discussion the next morning with Lucius, as regards their ultimate function, was wrapped in mystery.

Teddy said eventually, 'D'you mean that for the next few months all we're expected to do is clean out that cellar, move the wine racks to the upstairs rooms, and shop around for war-surplus items and tinned food?'

'Using cash for payments,' agreed Lucius. 'And you'll drive two coaches, help me with certain modifications to the chassis and do a spot of play-acting.'

It was mid-afternoon before he returned the three to London. He cruised slowly along Copenhagen Street, King's Cross, while the three of them car-spotted from the windows of his Alfa. The van had gone.

'Nicked or towed away,' said Teddy accurately. He slipped into a phone booth to discover which.

Lucius dropped them off near the car pound and headed for South Audley Street, experiencing a radiant sense of excitement. It was really going to happen!

That night he made a full report to the Source, who said, 'Time to take a back seat at the club, Lucius. You won't be able to handle everything yourself. You must learn to delegate.'

'I've already sold Windsor to raise our seed money so I must hold on to South Audley Street – if only as a respectable cover. I must be seen to have an income. For me to be without visible means of support would lead to awkward questions.'

The following day he invited his manager up to the leather-walled office for a Pernod. 'Maurice, I want you to take a bigger hand in running the club for a while. I'll be preoccupied with some business plans.'

'Anything you say,' said Maurice, in his neo-French accent; he had been born and raised in Muswell Hill, north London.

'One thing,' said Lucius, his gaze and tone heavy with meaning, 'I shan't expect the takings to fall by more than seven and a half per cent. Do you read me?'

Maurice gave a tight bow. 'I read you with exquisite clarity, sir,' he said, and silently withdrew.

Chapter Fifteen

The same detective constable who had telephoned him at home on Sunday was again on the line to Walter Fisk. 'King's Cross CID here, sir. I've just got the local car pound on another line. The owner has turned up to recover his van.'

'The owner?'

'Yes, sir. Edward Samuel Triggs. He's proved his identity and ownership.'

'Is he alone?'

'No, sir. He's with his girl, name of Jessica Moss, and a friend, Leonard Arthur Belcher. They say they decided to dump the van and go off on a train trip instead. There's nothing that doesn't appear to be kosher, sir.'

'Oh, isn't there?' said Fisk, frustrated. 'Then you'd better tell the pound they can release the van to bloody Edward Samuel Triggs. I'll put a toe up his arse the next time I see him for causing us all that bother.'

But Fisk was still curious. 'Ring me back and tell me how Triggs pays his fine and tow-away fee.'

Fifteen minutes later he received the answer. 'From a bundle of mint-fresh fivers, sir.'

'The conniving little bastard,' Fisk muttered half to himself. 'He's been at it somewhere along the line. He's definitely due for that toe up the arse.'

At Moxmanton, one of Lucius's early moves was to install a make-up room with an illuminated mirror, a ladderback chair, a range of hairpieces, pan-sticks, colouring powders and small prosthetic pieces, reviving skills he hadn't used since the days of his mind-reading act.

He insisted that Teddy diet and Lenny stuff himself with

carbohydrates. Teddy had been instructed to allow his short, curly hair to grow and Lucius had given the protesting Lenny a short back and sides.

Hair and eyebrow tinting followed and Lucius subtly changed their cheeklines by clipping small plastic pads to their upper molars. 'This is all for your own good,' he said. 'You wouldn't want people to identify you later from photographs.'

Then, dressed in grey uniforms with sharp peaked caps, the two had been sent off, a well-rehearsed scenario drilled into them, to dazzle Mr Emblem, organizing secretary of the Queen of the Earth committee.

Mr Emblem came out onto the pavement in Belgrave Square with the Queen of the Earth publicity officer, Alan Jay Jaffe, to witness the pride of the Regal Roadways' fleet perform a drive-past. The two coaches, silver flanks burnished and smoke-tinted one-way windows glinting, made a splendid sight as they came to rest at the kerbside. The two officials climbed aboard to make a closer inspection.

Teddy, proving himself the better actor, actually gave them a snappy salute as they stepped inside.

Later, Alan Jay Jaffe said to his colleague, 'It's a fantastic offer. You'd be mad not to take it. I'd write an acceptance letter before they change their minds, if I were you.' And that's what Arthur Emblem had done.

Neither man had asked to inspect the luggage compartments beneath the floors of the coaches. If they had opened the ones in Teddy's vehicle and wriggled inside, they might have spotted a curious conversion that had never occurred to the coach-makers.

From Bruiser, Lucius learned an interesting fact about Rolly Ponsford. 'You asked about sailing experience, Lucius. Well, here's your man. Knows all about sailing does our Rolly because, once upon a time, the Royal Marines moved him into an interesting little outfit called the Special Boat Squadron. Got up to all sorts of undercover japes with explosives on behalf of HM Government, didn't you, Rolly?'

'Mum's the word, Bruiser!' Rolly was laughing.

In the past Lucius had picked up passing references to

the SBS. This hush-hush organization had been much more successful at keeping out of the headlines than its land-based counterpart, the Special Air Service. The rumour was that the SBS used to conduct a highly effective ferryboat run in and out of the old USSR. So it fell to Rolly to make the river escape into a credible operation, which took him almost two months. Finally, he considered he had done the best he could. He called a meeting of the principals at Moxmanton House, where he hung from a Japanese screen – an antique of some value – a long narrow map of the Thames and its environs.

'Right,' said Rolly, rapping for attention with a telescopic aerial detached from a portable radio. Lucius was impressed to see how purposeful he had become: gone was the languid sceptic.

'I think we've all agreed with Lucius that to attempt to drive a coachload of unwilling girls out of London in broad daylight is madness. An airlift isn't possible in such a built-up area and the numbers involved are too great.'

Rolly waved his pointer and went on crisply. 'We're left with conveyance by water. If we can discreetly transport our haul from central London to a disembarkation point down-river, bringing us close to the M2, we shall be that much nearer pulling this thing off. First, my assumption must be that the coach has fallen into our hands and departed, without raising any alarm, from the Colonel Blood Inn, and has crossed Tower Bridge onto the north bank of the river without challenge.'

Dickie raised a hand like a pupil in class seeking to be excused. 'Don't want to interrupt, old boy, but haven't you forgotten something?'

Rolly cocked his head in interrogation.

'That blasted bridge,' said Dickie. 'Its arms go up to let ships into the Pool of London. Road traffic comes to a standstill. Awkward if we came to a halt with fifty screaming bints on our hands.'

'We'd be extremely out of luck if that happened to us,' said Rolly. 'And if it did, I'd be inclined to call it a day there and then. Very bad medicine indeed. In fact, the bridge only opens once a week on average. I've checked – and I'd certainly check

again on the morning of our effort. The prospect of fifty screaming bints does not appeal.' He looked at Lucius. 'I think we
ought to settle here and now on our D-Day. Are we agreed
that it should be the day the queens set out for their luncheon
at the Grosvenor House Hotel, Thursday the twenty-ninth of
September?'

'Yes,' said Lucius. 'They'll all be in that one coach. So that
day at noon, it is.'

Rolly turned back to the map. 'I've traced a route for the
coach that takes account of one-way systems and, in moderate
to medium traffic, you should be able to drive a vehicle of that
size from the Colonel Blood Inn to here . . .' the pointer
stabbed at an area of inlets and interlinked blue rectangles
marking a dock network '. . . in thirty minutes.'

Rolly went on: 'Embarkation will take place between twelve-
thirty and thirteen hundred hours from a point within the con-
fines of the Captain Cook Docks.'

Bruiser was about to interrupt but Rolly forestalled him.

'I know what you're going to say, Bruiser. How're we supposed to get away with this sort of show in daylight? Well, just
look at these photographs.'

The prints revealed a vast acreage of desolation, of silent
quays, mouldering, wrecked red-brick Victorian office buildings and abandoned warehouses. 'Later, of course, we shall go
over all this ground on foot but what you're looking at is the
last major Docklands site waiting for the developers and a
return of the property boom. The salient point here is that the
Captain Cook Docks are totally depopulated. Even the dock
police run no regular patrols. It's pretty pointless guarding
property that's waiting for the bulldozer.'

Rolly circulated another photograph of a pair of imposing
iron gates.

'This was the East Entrance to the old dock, now chained
and padlocked. At the appropriate time I intend putting a pair
of boltcutters on that chain and replacing it with a chain and
padlock of our own. The coach will be driven through this gate
down to the quays.'

Another photograph showed mossy timber buttresses that
marked the two sides of the channel linking the Thames proper

to the heart of the dock complex. A heavy cable was strung across it, but Rolly assured them that it could easily be removed.

He handed Bruiser another set of photographs. They showed, from a number of angles, a battle-green, blunt-bowed vessel.

'Gaze upon her with affection,' said Rolly, 'because she's the girl for us. You're looking at the ferryboat *Freda*, which provides a summer service across the river in the St Clement Reach from the Kent side to the Essex north bank. At the end of the second week of September, the *Freda* goes into dock until the beginning of the following year's holiday season. She's an Avon class coastal lighter, with twin diesels, a nine-knot maximum speed and has a hundred-ton displacement fully laden. With an overall length a fraction over seventy-two feet, she is capable of transporting a Centurion tank and is more than able to accommodate our coach. The ramp is powered. The official complement is six although all essential functions aboard are capable of being handled by an energetic crew of two. Any questions, so far?'

Lucius asked, 'Are you planning to steal her?'

'Definitely not,' said Rolly. 'The Thames from London Bridge to the Estuary is the closest watched fifty-one mile stretch of river on earth. Apart from the boat patrols of the Port of London Authority and of the Metropolitan Police River Division, we have to contend with an efficient twenty-four-hour radar survey operated by the PLA downstream of Greenwich Naval College. We have to appear to be on a legitimate voyage and our vessel cannot be hot property. We have to do what Lucius did with his coaches. Hire it!'

'Is that feasible?' asked Bruiser.

'Yes, I think so. I've already made a tentative call to the operators of the *Freda*, posing as Regal Roadways, and they're willing to give us a week's hire for two thousand pounds plus crew wages. I've told them we'd crew the thing ourselves and they're happy about this provided they have a written undertaking for their insurance people that we do not intend to remove the vessel from the administrative area of the Port of London Authority. I said this would be satisfactory because we want to give a party of water conservationists a closer look at the Thames.'

They pondered for a while upon the map and the photographs, then Bruiser said softly: 'All right, Rolly, you've taken us for a ride down the river. Now show us where the mines are lurking.'

Rolly gave Bruiser a you-win grin and cleared his throat. 'Of course it would be a bloody miracle if this operation turned out to be plain sailing.

'The reason the *Freda* owners are so blasé about letting us provide our own crew is because they know that at all times we're obliged to have a PLA river pilot aboard. It's extremely irritating.'

'So what's the drill?'

'The drill is,' said Rolly carefully, 'that the river pilot has to be allowed aboard and permitted to confirm his presence by ship's radio to the Navigation Service. He must then be neutralized. The two-pilot system on the river presents us with a further limitation. Our disembarkation point on the Kent shore has to be west of Gravesend or we'd have to pick up a sea-pilot.'

Bruiser looked gloomy. 'Christ, Rolly, things are becoming hellishly tricky. Remember old Clausewitz? "Always try to outdo the enemy in simplicity."'

'Actually, I've put nothing up on the blackboard yet that can't be countered. But I've been saving the lulu till last.' Rolly suddenly beamed at everyone. 'No one has asked me how we get a coachload of bints aboard the *Freda*.'

Lucius volunteered as comic feed. 'All right, Rolly, I'll ask. What's wrong with lowering the boat's drawbridge, which you said yourself is power-operated, and then driving the coach on board?'

'Nothing wrong at all, old boy,' said Rolly, 'if you have a roll-on roll-off concrete ramp onto which the *Freda* can lower *its* flap.' He went on, 'To my mind we now come to the major embarkation obstacle. We are damned fortunate that the Captain Cook dock area is so close to the Colonel Blood Inn and so conveniently unoccupied. The drawback is the roll-on roll-off ramp. It's at the boundary of the dock network and overlooked by three tower blocks of council flats. From that location we'd have an audience of a hundred nosy parkers.'

'So what's the solution?' asked Bruiser.

'A crane to lift the coach and female contents from one of the secluded wharfs at the centre of the dockyard and lower it into the vessel.'

Dickie Biggs-Salter was exasperated. 'Why can't we leave the bloody coach where it is and just take the girls?'

'No, no!' Lucius broke in. 'It's essential that the coach disappears completely so that no one can begin to guess at the route we've taken out of London – or even if we've left London at all. In any case, herding fifty hysterical girls on foot would be too much for our tiny group.'

'All right, then,' said Rolly, 'let's get back to the crane. 'He held up a photograph of what looked like a huge tractor painted vivid yellow. 'This is what they call a crawler crane. It moves on its own giant caterpillar tracks under diesel power and it can raise a forty-ton load.'

'How do we get it to the right quayside?' asked Bruiser.

'We don't. We take the *Freda* to it. At the moment the crawler is sitting on the side of the central basin inside the dockyard, screened by disused spice and ivory warehouses. It's been left in position to load the dumper barges when the demolition contractors move into the docks.'

'Who've we got to work it?' asked Dickie.

'At the moment, no one. I'm afraid cranes are outside my own field of specialization so we have to find ourselves a crane driver. Our little Cockney friend Teddy Triggs has a father who once was a docker so I've asked Teddy to cast around for a likely name – all without causing any suspicion, naturally.'

'Jesus!' said Lucius, leaping up. 'The more people involved, the slacker our security. Precedent doesn't inspire confidence.'

'Precedent?' queried Bruiser.

'Yes, the Great Train Robbery. The robbers' operation had the scope of our own, but they almost hit disaster before they'd even forced their way into the mail-coach. They'd recruited an old man who'd once been a train driver. When they set him down on the footplate, he either wouldn't or couldn't move the train and that's why they had to force the wounded driver to do the job.'

'Then propose an alternative,' said Bruiser. Lucius shrugged.

Bruiser turned to Rolly. 'Well done so far, old chap. Keep at it.' He felt a sense of returning to a long-lost command.

Chapter Sixteen

Bruiser and Rolly waited with some impatience on a bench in front of the grimy hulk of the National Theatre. 'The little devil's late,' grunted Bruiser. 'I'm not having sloppy time-keeping. We're dancing to the clock on this one.'

Teddy Triggs hove into sight along the embankment. He was wearing an expensive soft leather jacket. 'Look, he's already spending his money on flash,' said Rolly.

'Please be on time in future,' said Bruiser, as Teddy smiled in greeting.

'Blimey, it's only ten minutes and there's a lot of traffic about.'

'On time or on a fizzer,' said Bruiser severely.

'What's a fizzer?' asked Teddy, baffled. Bruiser shot him a look of deep distaste. In Teddy, he could see an unanswerable case for bringing back National Service.

Teddy whined, 'I've been slogging my guts out finding the right geezer for you and I think I've got the one you want. He's staying at the spike in Bermondsey. His old woman slung him out.'

It was Bruiser's turn to be baffled. 'Spike?'

'Yes, the Salvation Army kiphouse. He used to drive a crane on the old Dreadnought wharf at Woolwich but he got the heave-ho for nicking. He could use a quid or two.'

On Sunday morning, as the first sightseeing boats of the day were setting out from Westminster to Greenwich, Bruiser and Rolly, in their hired cabin cruiser, pulled into Nancy's Steps hard by London Bridge and took on board a shambling man of about fifty-five. He had a two-day growth of beard and was wearing overalls, as if anticipating a day's work. When he had stepped gingerly over the gunwale his pale head came up and both men could see he had a cloudy eye.

His name was Frank Simpson, but he said, 'Call me Marble. Everyone else does. It's on account of the wonky eye. Looks like a glass marble, see? Nothing's sacred,' he added, not uncheerfully.

'Well, Marble,' said Bruiser, 'can you be trusted to keep your mouth shut?'

'No question,' said Marble, bracing himself as the boat pulled into the down-river stream on the right-hand side of the Thames.

The river run from London Bridge, passing under Tower Bridge's twin bascules, to the entrance of the defunct Captain Cook Docks, took forty minutes. The lifeless smells of the wastelands assailed their nostrils as the low-slung craft nosed into the channel under the cable that Rolly had photographed. The cabin cruiser putt-putted along, the bow pushing aside the floating litter, leaving a short-lived cleared channel in its wake. The whole dockyard seemed to be in the embrace of a deep melancholia.

They spotted the crawler crane as soon as Rolly flipped the wheel and brought them into the central basin. He tied a line to a wall ring and they all clambered up the slimy stone steps for a closer inspection.

The sliding door to the driver's cabin was not locked and Rolly began immediately to dismantle the control panel and hot-wire the starter motor. Marble said: 'These levers control the slewing of the jib and the luffing – moving it up and down. The braking is done with the foot pedal.'

'Can you operate it?' asked Bruiser.

'No doubt about it. I've played with bigger buggers than this. Start her up.'

Rolly brought the wires together and the engine coughed, spluttered and roared into life. Marble let the engine run for a few seconds, then he eased off, pushed into gear and the caterpillar tracks began to churn forward.

'Now reverse to the exact spot in which you found it,' Bruiser ordered.

Marble complied and began testing the luff and slew of the

100

jib. 'It's sound enough but a spot of grease wouldn't do any harm. What's this all about?'

Bruiser told him as much as was necessary. Marble summed up: 'So you'll pay me five hundred notes to load a sixteen-ton coach onto a boat?'

'That's it,' said Bruiser.

Marble studied the pair, the light of speculation livening his one good eye. 'I'm not touching anything to do with drugs.'

'You won't have to.'

'But you're not going to kid me this is all on the up-and-up, are you?'

'No, we're not.'

'In that case, I think the job's worth a grand. You'll be paying for real expert help. It's not everyone who can work those crawler cranes. And if I get caught, it's the end of my career.'

'Agreed,' said Bruiser. 'A thousand it is.' Marble wished he'd asked for two.

Bruiser handed him £250 and said, 'There'll be no more until the job's done. Then you get the rest in cash on the spot. Meanwhile, if you so much as breathe a word of this, even in your prayers, your "career", as you call it, will be abruptly terminated.'

Marble experienced a chill in his innards. 'Look, mate, there's no point in putting the shits up me like that. I'll do the job – and no questions asked,' he said, his milky eye blinking nervously.

Bruiser handed him a slip of paper with the dimensions of the coach and Rolly read out the carrying capacity of the *Freda*. He added, 'The coach has to be loaded with the driver's cabin facing the ramp.'

Marble walked to the edge of the quay and back to the crane. He said, 'Your best bet is to draw it up here in front of the crane . . .' With his heel he traced two marks fifteen paces apart on the dusty concrete. 'I pick up and raise the load five feet to clear those iron bollards at the dock edge, track forward and lower onto the deck. Shouldn't take more than twenty minutes if the vessel's moored between my marks.' Rolly took out a stick of chalk and duplicated Marble's guidelines on the stone rim of the basin.

Suddenly, Marble was all business. He rubbed his hands briskly and said: 'Let's go and find a spreader.'

'Spreader?' asked Bruiser.

'You don't think you lift a bloody great load like that by just shoving a hook through a hole in the roof, do you? There'll be a transit shed around here somewhere with the tackle in it.'

Marble was correct. From a small, broken-windowed brick building, he fished out a pair of ten foot wooden beams with long hawsers attached and four claw-like iron wheel-grabs. 'On the day,' said Marble, 'you'll save time if you have this lot already hanging from the jib.'

They delivered Marble back to Nancy's Steps. Afterwards Rolly said, 'Can we trust him?'

'I doubt it,' said Bruiser. 'He's another of life's chancers. He's going to need frightening.'

'In this land,' said Rolly softly, 'the one-eyed man shall not be king.'

Chapter Seventeen

A strange perversion of *esprit de corps* gripped the four group leaders as they faced, analysed and, in theory, overcame the problems that arose in their plotting to rip the fabric of a civilized society. Ethical and moral considerations had been muscularly faced, challenged and rejected in the interests of the greater personal good.

No such self-examination stirred in either Teddy Triggs or Lenny Belcher. All self-doubt was cured by further injections of money.

As Lucius explained, 'It's to keep them from temptation. If they go off and commit some petty offence, they're stupid enough to get themselves caught and we don't want that.'

Over the weeks, Lucius watched closely as the excitement of the great game built between Bruiser and his two friends. When he judged the moment ripe, he told them about the gas.

'You want to gas the girls?' exclaimed Dickie. 'I dare say you'll be asking us to raid Porton Down next!'

'No,' Lucius said levelly, 'that will not be necessary.' He explained that his mother was an operating-theatre sister approaching retirement and how he had acquired a knowledge of the anaesthetics most commonly used in British hospitals. He tapped a blue-jacketed book in front of him: *A Synopsis of Anaesthesia* by J. Alfred Lee and R. S. Atkinson. 'It's a medical bible,' said Lucius. 'And if we put them to sleep, we won't need guards with guns.'

He went on: 'If their initial fright turns to mass hysteria, no amount of weaponry is going to prevent them running wild. Hysteria is infectious and, if they make a simultaneous attempt to run for it, each would flee with one thought in mind: "I'm going to be the lucky one to escape unharmed." It's human nature.'

Bruiser said: 'We three have our Service sidearms. Aren't they enough?'

'No,' said Lucius bluntly. 'Your Browning automatics will be useful although I think each of you will ultimately need a more substantial weapon to overcome any massed opposition. Large guns are very hypnotic – when you face their muzzles.'

He drove the trio to Deptford, opened the luggage hold beneath one coach and showed them the network of copper tubing that he, Teddy and Lenny had installed beneath the floor. 'One of the advantages of this vehicle,' Lucius said, 'is that the air-conditioning system runs separately from the main engine. We've made a conversion that transfers the operating switches from the driver's dashboard to this under-floor space. Now, if we clip the appropriate containers to the pipes we'll be able to introduce an anaesthetic into the coach atmosphere.'

'. . . and bloody-well end up with fifty beautiful corpses on our hands,' completed Rolly, turning away in disgust.

'Not true,' said Lucius. 'You'll observe that the conduit pipes end in rubber self-linking sections. This is to overcome the difficulty of connecting particular containers of anaesthetic gases to general-purpose tubing. In hospital operating theatres this is impossible because each type of gas cylinder has its individual outlet valve, connector yoke and flow meter. In other words, anaesthetists cannot make the mistake of incorrect linkages. The parts simply would not fit together.

'Now, just think of the advantage to us of being able to sedate all fifty girls and keep them sedated during the hours of greatest danger when we are trying to evacuate them from the London area. A gun guard becomes unnecessary, freeing hands that will be needed for other vital work.'

Lucius turned to Dickie. 'As Bruiser will be in overall charge of the removal operation and Rolly preoccupied with getting the *Freda* down-river, it will inevitably fall to you to take charge of this stage.'

'Shit and derision,' said Dickie, his face darkening. 'Stinks was never a strong suit for me at school.'

'Don't worry,' said Lucius. 'I'm preparing a detailed instruction sheet. We'll be using a gas in everyday use in children's hospitals, cyclopropane. A couple of whiffs is enough to cause unconsciousness and, if the concentration is kept low, it won't irritate the lungs and set up coughing. All the coach's windows and other apertures will be sealed before we seize the girls, and after the driver, Triggs, has delivered them to the dock and climbed out, we switch it on.

'Cyclopropane is odourless and induction does not have to be continuous. Once they're asleep, we'll need to top them up when they show signs of revival. If we do it this way they may be kept under for up to four hours without harmful effects. The coach can also be ventilated from time to time to prevent a build-up of carbon dioxide to more than five per cent of the controlled atmosphere. Go above this level and we would begin to cause them distress. Thirty per cent, for instance, would put them into a coma. But, handled properly, healthy girls such as these should make a fast recovery without side effects. That's why they use this stuff on children.'

His three listeners brooded. 'It's a damn fanciful notion,' said Dickie. 'If I cock up, we'd be left with a coffin-ship on our hands.'

Bruiser said, 'Lucius is right, though. In those few hours, we're going to need all the free hands we can muster. But remember, we are not gassing badgers here.'

Teddy and Lenny slumped moodily in the driver's cab of their rickety van, watching the flow of traffic in and out of the medical gases plant. All the time their eyes wandered, seeking out the orange cylinders of liquid cyclopropane and larger cylinders of oxygen, with black casings and white shoulders.

'What's this all about, then?' asked Lenny plaintively. 'I don't like being kept in the dark.'

Over three days, he and Teddy had followed ten five-ton trucks and had finally established the regularity of orange cylinder deliveries to Great Ormond Street Hospital for Sick Children in central London. Then Bruiser and Rolly took over.

On the following Wednesday, a deliveryman making his normal central London run, was surprised to be waved down by a white-coated man, a row of pens and a chrome-cased thermometer displayed in his breast pocket at the corner of Lamb's Conduit Street.

'Dr Phipps,' said the figure, by way of explanation. 'There's a porters' dispute on. I'll have to guide you round to a different delivery gate.'

'I can't cross any union picket line,' said the driver.

'The question doesn't arise,' said Dr Phipps, climbing into the passenger seat. 'The strikers are allowing essential supplies through. Just take the next turning on the left and I'll set your course.'

Six hours later, a Lufthansa counter clerk, returning to her Mercedes in the short-term car park at Heathrow airport, found a man lying on her back seat. He was bound hand and foot, gagged, blindfolded and had rubber plugs in his ears. All he was able to tell the police was that before he had been deprived of speech, sight and hearing he had heard a Welsh voice say, 'Black and white, and orange containers only.'

Sure enough, when the police found the abducted driver's truck, abandoned alongside a gravel pit at Chertsey in Surrey, they discovered that all twenty ten-inch cylinders of cyclopropane had been removed, plus four fifty-seven-inch cylinders of oxygen. A consignment of nitrous oxide in blue cylinders had been left untouched.

The hijack made a single paragraph in the evening paper. Police stated they were following certain lines of inquiry. In other words, they were stumped. There was no black market in medical gases so what was the game?

Bruiser, Rolly and Dickie met to discuss weaponry.

Bruiser said, 'Can we agree that we need to supplement our existing artillery with a submachine gun apiece?' His companions nodded. 'Then it seems to me,' said Bruiser, addressing Dickie Biggs-Salter, 'that you'll be the one doing the shopping. What does the battalion have in the armoury, Dickie?'

'Usual issue, the West German Heckler and Koch HK5s. Plenty of those about. Though it'll be tricky lifting three. Better let me see if I can work something out.'

A week later Dickie called at Bruiser's flat, carrying a cricket bag. Out of it, onto the floor, clattered three Hecklers. Bruiser was dumbfounded.

'Don't get over-excited,' said Dickie, 'but I have been rather clever. It occurred to me to take a look at the Earl's Court toy and hobby fair. And look what I've found. Apparently, the world is full of replica-collectors.'

'Good try,' said Bruiser, 'but we need weapons that fire.'

'Yes,' said Dickie. 'But if I'm to steal three from the armoury there's going to be a gap that the quartermaster can't miss when he takes his weekly inventory. If I can substitute these for the real thing, it'll hold off the hounds until the next large-scale exercise when the trick, if not the culprit, is bound to be rumbled.'

Two weeks later, Dickie Biggs-Salter was able to report that his name had gone up on the orderly officers' roster. He agreed that Saturday night when the Tel-el-Kebir Lines in the charming Cotswold town of Abbots Malmsey were at their most depopulated, would be a propitious time to make the attempt.

On the afternoon of the day, Dickie played a vigorous game of squash with his duty field officer whom, tactlessly, he left beaten. Dickie slipped his racquet into his long bag and applied the miniature padlock to the zip-pull.

Strolling with his superior to the mess for a bracer, Dickie said, 'Shan't be a sec, sir,' and right-wheeled into the guard-room. He dumped his bag in the corner of the guard commander's cubicle and told the white-belted regimental policeman, 'I'm orderly officer tonight. I'll pick the bag up later.'

Dickie mounted the guard detail at 6 p.m., relieving the daytime regimental police, and left the guard corporal to get on with it. He returned at precisely 8.57. The outside sentry barked: 'Orderly officer approaching, corporal!'

The NCO was not best pleased. He put down his Stephen King paperback and fastened his belt. Fucking officers. You'd think they'd have something better to do on a Saturday night. His six squaddies began straightening up and resignedly retying their bootlaces. Dickie bounded in enthusiastically. 'Right, corporal, armoury inspection!'

'Suh!' shouted the unhappy man, reaching for his key to

unlock the glass-fronted cupboard in which the principal keys for the entire camp dangled on rows of cup hooks. He took down the armoury bunch. This brick building, since the Provisional IRA raids on military installations in the seventies, had been situated immediately at the rear of the guardhouse.

Wordlessly, the corporal unlocked the steel door, handed Dickie the inventory and stood aside for him to enter. The light from the naked bulbs revealed the stacks of ammunition boxes, the rows of standard-issue Belgian SLRs and the Hecklers, glistening under their light film of oil. They were racked in three rows, padlocked chains running through the trigger guards. Dickie glanced at the inventory. There should be ninety.

Just then, way out in the darkness, Rolly and Bruiser began throwing thunderflashes over the perimeter walls, which were being patrolled at that time by two armed private soldiers.

'Good God! What was that?' said Dickie. A second explosion sounded distantly. 'Corporal,' he said decisively, 'there's some funny business going on. Leave the gateman in place and take the off-duty men with you.'

Dickie put his boot to the kick-open metal clasp on a case of 7.62 rounds and handed the startled man a cardboard container of fifty. 'Five rounds per man,' ordered Dickie.

Suddenly the frozen corporal jerked into life and trotted towards the armoury door.

'Corporal!' bellowed Dickie. 'You've forgotten to give me the keys. We can't leave the place unlocked. I'll be right after you when I've made a phone call.'

Dickie listened for a few moments as the man yelled his orders and the guard went charging off. He could still hear faint explosions. Bruiser and Rolly were working well.

Dickie searched swiftly through the key bunch and sprang up the ladder to the highest weapon rack. He opened the padlock, jumped down, carried the ladder swiftly to the other end of the rack and pulled out the link chain from the trigger guards along the entire line. He came down with three Hecklers, raced through to the guardroom and collected his bag. Once he had placed them alongside their genuine fellows the three replicas looked perfect in the low light.

Teetering on the ladder rungs, Dickie spent a minute rethreading the chain through the row of trigger guards. He hopped down the ladder to his bag, extracted a thin blanket from it and wrapped up the three weapons, to prevent clatter in carrying. Then he threw in six magazines and six 50-round boxes of ammunition.

'Bingo!' he grunted, zipping the bag and snapping shut the small brass padlock. He hoped that none of the men had returned to the guardroom.

He extinguished the armoury lights, locked the door and hauled his bag back to where it had lain since the afternoon. He could hear shouts outside but no one had returned.

Trying to control his breathing, he picked up the direct line to the duty field officer, who was at his quarters in Abbots Malmsey. 'Sorry to intrude, sir. Thought you ought to know. There's a spot of bother along the camp perimeter. Sounds like fireworks but just to be sure I've called out the guard.'

'Want me down there?'

'Seems a pity to blight the evening, sir. Let me take a quick look and I'll phone again with a situationer.'

'Right! But if you're more than fifteen minutes, Dickie, I'll be on my way.'

Dickie ran out to a Jeep, shouting to the solitary sentry, 'Don't move from the spot and challenge everyone!' He set out after his guard corporal. He took a hand from the wheel to look at his watch. Not bad. He'd accomplished the switch in six minutes.

In the dark, at the furthermost reaches of the camp, he found a baffled squad. 'Must have been a bunch of drunks chucking bangers, sir. We can't find any damage.'

'Well,' roared Dickie, 'if it's anyone from the camp I want their bloody names!'

An hour later the fuss was over, the duty field officer reassured and the corporal back in his guardhouse in possession of his keys.

Dickie picked up his bag, as effortlessly as he could, and said, 'You won't hear from me again tonight – unless we have any more of that blasted nonsense outside.'

He had to walk with his haul all the way to his MGB in the

officers' car park. Since the IRA unpleasantness, private cars had not been allowed to park willy-nilly about the camp.

The guard corporal was left thoroughly out of sorts. The incident meant that he would be obliged to submit a detailed written report. Christ, what a drag. He suddenly remembered the five rounds he had issued to each man. Returning the refilled box to the armoury, he was so preoccupied with the bureaucratic nuisance to come that he failed to notice that the ladder against the weapon racks had unaccountably moved from one end to the other.

Chapter Eighteen

Dickie was the hero of the hour and the two thunderflash throwers carried him off to Sandown Park for a day's racing. Lucius had declined an invitation to join them, although they were all in need of relaxation after the tension of the past weeks. He explained politely that he did not feel it wise to be seen with them in so public a place.

The trio enjoyed a boisterous afternoon. They flung their caps high into the stand, yelling, 'Hoorah!' as a horse named Kidnap came home at eleven to one. Dickie had a tenner on its nose, a wager prompted by superstition rather than racing form.

Indeed, most of the omens were good. Rolly and Lucius had combined to form a search team to crack the final problem of their stage one planning. They had located a suitable site on the Kent side of the Thames where the queens could be securely disembarked from the *Freda* before the final leg of their journey to Moxmanton House.

The disused Svensk paper mill near Northfleet was the answer. It had a wharf, at which barges of esparto grass had once been unloaded, and a series of large, echoing sheds, capable of hiding a fleet of vehicles. Rolly took soundings and pronounced that the *Freda* would have no difficulty in making fast to the wharf.

'There's one hurdle,' he said. 'The transfer must be after dark. Traffic on this stretch of the river is heavy because of Tilbury docks on the other bank. It would take only a curious deck officer on a passing ship to put a glass on us and we'd be rumbled.'

Lucius did a rapid mental sum. 'That means we have to keep them undetected on the water for at least six hours.'

'Can't be avoided,' said Rolly.

'We won't be able to keep them anaesthetized for that long. It's far too dangerous,' Lucius remonstrated.

'You'll gain one advantage, anyway, by letting them come round,' Rolly pointed out. 'You'll be able to walk them off the *Freda* rather than have us waste precious time carrying each sleeping beauty ashore.'

Rolly took out a memo card and jotted down some figures. 'We have a distance of twenty-two sea miles to cover from the Captain Cook Docks to the disembarkation point. For much of the first hour the tide will be running against us and, if my calculations based on past September wind and tide charts are accurate, we'll be making something like five to six knots. Then, with the ebb, we should gain about two knots for the remainder of the dash down-river.'

'That sounds more like a crawl than a dash,' said Lucius.

'Then get yourself a hydrofoil,' Rolly said. 'In any event, there's a ten-knot speed limit.'

'All right,' said Lucius. 'So what time does that bring us opposite the paper mill?'

'Some time after four p.m.,' said Rolly.

'When's lighting up time?'

'Seven fifteen – and that's when we boys and girls come out to play.'

'Jesus!' breathed Lucius. 'The whole operation will be at a standstill for more than three hours.'

'There's no way round it, I'm afraid.'

Lucius began to take all the morning newspapers and to clip the items concerning the progress of the Queen of the Earth preliminary contests. Brief conversations with the Source, using only the Kew telephone, fleshed out his knowledge. The usual upsets, scandals and partisan rows were reported in the press; so far, the selection process had caused riots in Manila and Lima and the burning down of a stadium in Trinidad.

On the day that the fifty finalists left Kennedy Airport for London, where Teddy Triggs and Lenny Belcher were preparing to meet them with the Regal Roadways' coaches, Professor Hugo Menniken of the Department of Computer Sciences at Rice University, Houston, Texas, issued his prediction of the winner. His conclusion was that the world's taste had turned from the over-tall, blonde, wide-mouthed beauties who had swept up the honours in the past few years. This would be the year of the petite, demure girl. Therefore the winner would be ebony-haired Sunoo Khushlani, the queen from India, with the girls from Egypt and Austria as her ladies-in-waiting.

The professor was soon to learn that he had overlooked a programming factor or two.

For the last hour of the flight above the Atlantic, the lines for the lavatories had been long as the girls repaired their make-up in preparation for the photographic exposure to come. The chaperones fussed over their charges' day clothes and the queen from Norway, an outgoing drama student named Maiken Grenske, charged scattily along the gangway shouting, 'Make way for a lip-glossed has-been!' Her physical attributes ran closely along the lines damned out-of-hand by Professor Menniken. So, too, did those of the queens from Germany, Sweden and, against national type, Brazil. Before boarding, they had combined their indignation to fax him his come-uppance. Their message read: 'Standing where we are, we cannot tell you what we did with your print-out, sitting where we were.'

Contrary to popular belief, girls thrown together in the highly competitive atmosphere of an international beauty competition do not instantly fall to bitching and clawing at their rivals. Most are far from home and they tend to cling to each other. They also experience a period of embattled togetherness in the face of the ever-present legion of male gropers, buttock patters, squeezers, and out-and-out queen-fuckers. A week in the queen business is a long, exhausting time and leaves little energy for spleen and advantage-seeking within the group.

Some girls remain reserved out of stage-fright or shyness but in this collection of international beauties only the queen from France, Mathilde de Montméja, had not entered into the spirit of girls-together-in-adversity. There was an air of apartness about her, a watchfulness that the others dismissed as a manifestation of adolescent jealousy. Everyone knew how haughty the French could be.

In terminal three at Heathrow, the media had massed. 'Smile tho' your hearts be aching, girls,' sang out the queen from the United States, Prentiss Decker, a green-eyed copper-head, who had interrupted her studies to plunge into this carnival. Even if she did not carry off a cash prize, Prentiss did not plan to end up a loser: she could see the commercial possibilities of a fast paperback book, her story of the whole crazy, freaked-out event from the inside. Prentiss was a journalism major at Columbia University.

Both Teddy and Lenny stepped back hastily behind the bellowing, elbowing, cursing ranks of news photographers and television men. They had been briefed about the danger of getting themselves photographed even on the periphery of camera lenses.

'Blimey, what a right bunch of tearaways,' said Teddy genially. He'd never seen a Fleet Street pack in action before.

The chaperones, the Watchmen, the bodyguards and the organizers' publicity man, Alan Jay Jaffe, ushered, cajoled and shepherded the girls towards the exit where the coaches waited.

The queen from Jamaica, Frenchy Bonaventure, was the group genius is captivating photographers. She wore a flimsy yellow dress with a slit up one side that opened to a startling extent every time she took a long forward step.

Spirits and bosoms high, this year's loveliest girls in the world set out on their London odyssey. Through the tinted windows of the coaches, the view was rosy – and one way. At traffic lights the convoy rated barely a glance from other drivers. Up front, in his uniform, Teddy kept his eyes on the road and the lid on his natural ebullience. 'Talk to people only when you have to. Remain respectful and in the background. Don't give anyone cause to remember either your appearance or accent,' Lucius had said.

Only one detail marred Teddy's *sangfroid*. He, Lenny and Jessie had at last been given a revelatory talk concerning their objective. They'd all thought the toffs had gone potty but, at the same time, they felt flattered to be included in the big-time.

Try as they might, they couldn't think of a crime that had ever come bigger – not even the Great Train Robbery.

During the briefing, Teddy had been led to expect that the Watchman would be the only other male aboard his coach. Yet at the airport another swarthy young man in civilian clothes had sat himself silently beside the Watchman in the seat next to the door, and a similar type had walked towards the rear and placed himself alongside one of the six-foot blondes. Teddy had been about to say something when he remembered the constraint imposed upon him by Lucius. Let the toffs sort it out.

Teddy's happy coachload glided in under the *porte cochère* of the Colonel Blood Inn to wild enthusiasm from the waiting crowd. The girls were cheered as they made a sleek progress to the lifts. Bustling around them, uttering cries of delight, was an elegant, fashionably slim woman of a certain age, her pale, ash-blonde hair exquisitely coiffed. 'My dears, you all look so wonderful – even after those unending hours on a plane! I don't know how on earth you do it.' This was the organizing chairwoman, Lady Cornmorris.

Despite her apparent middle age, she still had remarkably fine, arched brows, untouched by pouching, and an uncreased ruby mouth of startling sensuality. For a short time, in girlhood, she had been an actress.

The girls listened, fascinated, to her very English prattle. Prentiss Decker raised an amused eyebrow, and received in return an acknowledging grin from the Canadian queen, Mirabelle Montcalm, a descendant of the hapless French soldier who had lost the country to the British in the course of a single morning's fighting.

Lucius impatiently paced his office until 9 p.m., an agreed time when the Source would endeavour to be on the other end of the line at Kew. 'There were two unknown men on the coach,' said Lucius savagely. 'Who the fuck are they?'

The Source sounded flustered. 'There's been a sudden change in the security plan. The Israeli government threatened to withdraw their girl, Rebecca Engelman, unless she was allowed her personal bodyguard. They're afraid there might be some attempt to harm her by the Palestinians. The two men are air marshals seconded from El Al airline. They refuse to leave her side.'

Lucius punched the top of his desk, sending a stab of pain up his arm. 'Damn! It's two more to cope with.'

'Even worse,' came the Source's fretful voice over the phone. 'They both have tiny revolvers strapped to their waists.'

'*What?* That's illegal in Britain.'

'I know. But the authorities are turning a blind eye. They don't want any recriminations from Israel if anything bad should happen.'

Lucius's emergency meeting with Bruiser was brief. 'Those Israelis are mad death-or-glory boys. If you go aboard that coach waving your guns, they'll take their chance on a shoot-out. The operation will be an abortion from the word go.'

Bruiser said, 'It's damn serious. Seems to me there's no soft option. We just have to arrange it so that the Israeli girl can't join the others for lunch on D-Day. If she doesn't appear on parade, neither will her minders.'

'The first step,' he told Lucius, 'is for the Source to supply us with a complete briefing on the girl's habits. We have only five days in which to sort this out.'

The response from the Source was not reassuring. One of Rebecca's escorts even went along to the hotel kitchens to watch her meals being prepared.

While these hidden moves in Lucius Frankel's great game were taking place, the queens had taken over the headlines in the popular press. The event had become much more than the simple bathing-beauty parade of earlier years: the girls' outings, witticisms, bookmakers' odds, likes, dislikes, romances and other attendant trivia filled columns of newsprint. Lucius particularly studied one photograph that showed a stout official of the Israeli fruit growers' association presenting Rebecca Engelman with a single orange from the groves of Galilee. The caption implied that Rebecca's blooming good looks and health were directly attributable to her daily intake of orange juice.

Lucius made a 9 p.m. call to the Source. 'Find out if she's really drinking the stuff and where it's kept.'

The reply came the following evening. The oranges were

squeezed under supervision in the hotel kitchens and the jug kept chilled in the refrigerator in her room. Rebecca liked a glass at breakfast-time.

Lucius's mother was surprised to find her son on her doorstep before she set out for the hospital. He was not normally an early riser.

He looked worried, and that disturbed her.

Leslie – or Lucius, as she had finally schooled herself to call him – took her hands, which, he noticed, were beginning to show liver spots. 'Mum, I'm going to ask you for something that'll upset you.'

She waited.

'I'm on the verge of pulling off a business deal that'll provide an old-age pension for both of us. But I have a rival who I've got to put out of commission. Nothing violent, you understand. I just have to find a means of keeping him away from the negotiating table while I seal the bargain.'

'What's that got to do with me, son?' Mrs Franks looked at the fob watch clipped to her uniform. She was going to be late.

'I'm having a breakfast conference with this character and I need an emetic to slip into his orange juice – nothing serious, just a little something to put him out of action for a few hours.'

'Are you asking me to get you something to upset someone's stomach?' Mrs Franks stared at her son.

'That's it,' he said eagerly, ignoring the obvious disapproval. 'Just a little emetic.'

'Well, it wouldn't work,' she said firmly.

'Why not?'

'I don't know of any emetic that isn't salty. If you doctored a glass of orange juice, this business rival would only spit it out.'

Lucius clutched her desperately. 'Mum, you know I wouldn't ask this if it weren't a crisis. I haven't told you everything. If I don't pull off this deal, I'm ruined.'

Mrs Franks looked into her handsome son's face. The lines of strain were there. She said, reluctantly, 'You'd better come back this evening. I'll see what can be done.'

When she returned home Lucius was on the doorstep of her

small south London flat. She found that even more disturbing but it reinforced her decision. Her concern for her own blood allowed her to breach an ethical code by which she had abided throughout a long, worthy nursing career.

She showed him a glass phial containing a trace of white powder. 'This is white arsenic. Give a person a large enough dose and they'll die a horrible death in hours. However, there's no chance of that. There's just enough here to lace a carton of orange juice. It has little taste so this poor man you have to keep out of the way won't gag on it.'

Lucius held the phial up to the light. 'How will it affect him?'

'Will it be drunk on a full stomach?'

Lucius thought of the girls' flab-free waists and their perpetual dieting. 'No, only a light meal. This chap's trying to lose some weight.'

'Well, he'll certainly achieve that if he swallows this,' said his mother drily. 'About an hour after he's had it, he'll feel a burning pain in his throat and stomach and he'll vomit. None of the symptoms will be severe because the dose isn't big enough. But they'll be enough to put your man to bed in need of tender loving care.'

'Perfect,' whispered Lucius. 'But will it arouse suspicion?'

'Not unless the orange juice is analysed. By the time a doctor gets to his bedside – and you know how long that takes these days – the signs should indicate mild gastric upset. Unless the man drinks another glass of it, he'll be out of bed in twenty-four hours.'

Lucius kissed her on both cheeks. 'Mum, you've saved my bacon. I can't thank you enough.'

'Just don't get yourself into any trouble, that's all. I don't enjoy doing this sort of thing.'

The Source was horrified. 'You know I can't involve myself in direct action. You'll have to get someone else to do it.'

'There *is* no one else. You're the only one of us with legitimate access to the guarded floors. Unless you get into the Israeli girl's room some time on Wednesday evening and spike her juice it's all off.'

'But I'm expected to be with the rest of the party at the Lord Mayor's Guildhall dinner . . .'

They argued back and forth. 'You've already broken our arrangement that we shouldn't meet during this period of danger,' reproached the Source.

Lucius resolutely pressed the phial into the Source's hand.

Unwillingly, the Source said, finally, 'Each day the girls receive a great many bouquets of flowers at the hotel. They're checked by Security and arranged in the rooms while they're out at evening functions. I have no master keys so the only opportunity I can see of gaining entry is in the wake of the maids.'

'I'll make sure that on Wednesday, Miss Rebecca Engelman receives an avalanche of magnificent floral tributes from unknown admirers. Arranging them in vases will occupy the maid for half an hour. The rest is up to you,' said Lucius.

Late on Wednesday evening, 28 September, Teddy Triggs and Lenny Belcher were sitting, bored, in their empty coaches out-side London's ancient Guildhall, waiting to complete the last chore of the evening – to return to the Colonel Blood Inn the fifty queens and their long train of attendants.

For Jessie Moss the evening meant business as usual. She stood on a tiny stage, near-naked, in a peach spotlight that enhanced her skin tone, in the Hot Shot club in Lisle Street, Soho, flourishing a scourge more usually found in the pos-session of hardline members of the Catholic priesthood.

On the previous evening she had fulfilled a different and most unusual role for which she had been thoroughly rehearsed, and tomorrow she would be on call again. Yesterday the toffs had made her climb into some grotty clothes that, as she put it, 'showed my lot', had wrapped her in a raincoat and driven her to Dover. They'd all sat for more than an hour in the dark, watching the ferries unload. Jessie had become bored. They wouldn't even let her put the radio on.

Then they'd fallen in behind a blue refrigerated juggernaut with the name of a Paris abattoir painted on its sides. The vehicle headed for London, presumably bound for Smithfield meat market. On a quiet stretch of road between Canterbury and Faversham the big toff put his foot down hard and roared a couple of miles ahead of the meat lorry. Here Jessie had been deprived of her raincoat and tipped out into the dark to do her stuff.

Daniel Rosay, up front of a massive tonnage of Charollais beef, jammed on his brakes as a girl lurched into his headlight beam. She wore a dress that had been ripped apart. Daniel could clearly see her bikini pants, suspender belt and one magnificent breast. Her shoulder and brassière straps had been torn down.

Daniel worked to explicit instructions about unscheduled stops on the road but his natural French gallantry, not to mention the agreeably erotic sight, brought him to an abrupt halt.

'Help me! Help me!' screamed the distressed girl at his cabin window.

Daniel opened the door and she scrambled in gratefully. Then she did a strange thing. She reached across, pulled out his ignition key and threw it into the road. It was caught by a man wearing a ski-mask over his face, who was pointing a pistol at him.

'Merde! Qu'est-ce que j'ai foutu!' he groaned as plugs were pressed into his ears, a mask taped over his eyes and ropes secured his hands and feet.

Lucius felt in serious need of a drink but decided against it. The call did not come until 11 p.m. The Source's shaky voice said, 'It's done. Let's hope she doesn't suddenly develop a taste for grapefruit.'

Lucius cut off his caller and dialled Moxmanton House. 'It's done,' he relayed. 'It'll be mid-morning before we know if we're under starter's orders.' He was beginning to sound like Bruiser and friends.

At last Lucius permitted himself a brandy and rolled into bed, setting his quartz alarm for 5 a.m. He had to have opened the make-up room at Moxmanton House by seven.

Rebecca Engelman began to feel seedy at ten thirty on Thursday. Her throat burned hot and unpleasant and, a minute later, her stomach began to sway inside her body. She rushed to the bathroom, gagged and deposited her breakfast in the washbasin.

One of her guards came through on the run. Gentlemanly delicacy at the door of a lady's boudoir was not in his repertoire.

He found Rebecca in a sorry mess, spittle dripping from her lovely mouth, her glowing tan dulled. He plunged for the telephone. 'I'll get the house doctor.'

But Rebecca followed him frantically, waving her arms. 'No, no! I'll be all right.'

'You're ill.'

'It's nothing serious.'

He still had his hand on the phone.

'Dammit! Listen to me!' shouted the girl. 'Just get me into bed. All I need is rest. Don't mollycoddle me!' There was an odd expression on her strained face that the guard could not fathom.

Chapter Nineteen

The drill for getting the Queen of the Earth contestants and their helpers out of the hotel without first having to run a time-consuming gauntlet of the crowd in the lobby was simple.

Lifts took the large party from their floors straight down to the underground car park where Regal Roadways' twin coaches were waiting.

'Chaperones first!' shouted Arthur Emblem and Alan Jay Jaffe, shepherding the women along the corridors. On their way out, several girls looked in to commiserate with Rebecca who was wanly sitting up in bed.

The chaperones carried a weird assortment of hats and head-dresses, incorporating wax, fruit, pearls, diamanté, mirror fragments, semi-precious stones, real and artificial flowers, tinsel, metal foil and, in the case of the exquisite little girl representing Thailand, a valuable tapered crown of gold leaf, a replica of one reputed to have been worn by the consort of Rama, the first King of Siam, as she floated in majesty down the Chao Phya river.

There was also a peacock-feather fan. The queen from Holland asked if that wasn't unlucky. No one seemed to know.

Arthur Emblem made the last tick on his checklist and said to Lenny Belcher, 'Right. All present and correct. Off you go!' All the chaperones and a Watchman were aboard.

Lenny moved slowly up the car park's corkscrew ramp and, behind him, Teddy advanced his coach to take Lenny's place opposite the lift doors.

In chattering groups, the forty-nine queens began to file out in their bizarre collection of national costumes. Prentiss Decker had opted for the Uncle Sam look, consisting of a stars-and-stripes corselet that allowed her to show her legs, with a top hat and tailcoat.

'Pretty gross,' she said, 'but if I don't wear it they'll think back home that I've turned communist.'

Mathilde de Montméja, too, had expressed distaste for the cliché Marianne costume of her country. She acidly suggested going to the Grosvenor House luncheon dressed as a *tricoteuse*, one of the gnarled crones who sat knitting and cackling as the heads dropped from the blade of the guillotine. This had not been received with favour by her French sponsors but they finally agreed upon a sleek Givenchy day dress in silk that clung lovingly to her body. Mathilde liked getting her own way.

The Kikuyu, the queen from Kenya, climbed into the coach scantily draped in a fake zebra skin, her black skin powdered with red ochre. Row after row of coloured beads drew attention to the slender stem of her neck.

Amid this exotica, the queen who represented the United Kingdom, Fran Pilkington, a doctor's daughter from Basingstoke, felt positively frumpy. Against her better judgement, she'd allowed her sponsors to garb her as Britannia. Her trident, shield and helmet had gone ahead on the first coach.

Lenny was already on his way on the half-hour cross-town journey in lunchtime London. It was all right for him; he had only to deliver his charges in a perfectly ordinary way. Teddy felt envious. His stomach had a clamp on it, his hands tingled and his tongue registered the taste of old brass in his mouth.

'Come on, come on, come on!' a voice inside him screamed. At last, the Watchman, an impassive, well-built thirty-year-old, brought up the rear, nodded to Teddy and said, 'Let's be off.' The El Al guards had remained with Rebecca.

Teddy hit the switch and the door hissed shut. He turned the starter, released the handbrake and moved off. He heard the Watchman murmur into his handset to the control room on the twenty-first floor, 'Coach Two. All passengers on board and starting out.'

Teddy went as slowly up the ramp as he dared without stalling. He could feel the Watchman's eyes on him. He felt sticky under the arms. They were running late: it was 12.22 p.m.

The coach crawled round the bend and Teddy saw daylight ahead. He also saw the two toffs step out from the shadows.

Bruiser was wearing horn-rims with clear lenses and Dickie a sharp beard. They were dressed in the pearl-grey uniform of Colonel Blood Inn porters. They stepped forward, laughing and waving. Each carried a fancy headpiece of ludicrous size. Bruiser's looked like a giant dunce's cap in silver lamé.

The Watchman half rose from his seat as Teddy applied the footbrake. 'What's going on?'

'Looks like a couple of the girls' hats got left behind,' said Teddy.

The impassive Watchman was out of his seat with a restraining hand on Teddy's shoulder. 'Just a minute.' He half turned to face the girls. 'Can I see the hands of the owners of those hats?' No response. He peered through the window suspiciously.

Teddy shuffled in his seat. The two toffs were now at the door, loudly demanding admittance. Teddy shook his shoulder free – it was now or bloody well never – and punched the door release. 'For Chrissake,' he said, 'we're late already.'

'Now hold on a—' Bruiser took the steps in one bound. The damn fool Watchman was already raising his two-way radio to his mouth. His eyes jerked open at Bruiser's single blow to his neck and he fell back into his seat. His radio clattered to the floor, where it was scooped up by Dickie Biggs-Salter as he came in hard behind Bruiser.

Bruiser cursed. He hoped he'd not done permanent damage but the chopping blow to the fellow's vagal nerve had surely disrupted the heart rhythm.

The girls in the front seats were already screaming.

'Get the door closed and get going!' Bruiser shouted at Teddy, who swallowed and began to do the job for which these powerful men had trained him so thoroughly. The door closed and the coach roared forward, turning towards Tower Bridge.

Bruiser and Dickie began to bellow in unison at the girls. In close combat, hideous screams and shouts often give an infantryman a surprise advantage, even in modern warfare. Bruiser and Dickie now practised their craft, paralysing the girls with fear. Then, simultaneously, they tossed away the hats,

124

ripped the wrappings to reveal the gleaming Hecklers and made a show of cocking them. Most of the girls flung themselves in terror out of the firing line. Three fell prostrate into the gangway and the Catholics crossed themselves and appealed to the Virgin for succour.

Hanna Hansen, the German queen, tried to clamber forward over the seat but was pulled back hard by Prentiss Decker. 'Do you want to lose your ass?' she hissed. 'Let's see what these guys want.'

Teddy's hands, wet with sweat, slipped on the wheel, but he was already heading into the Docklands. The tinted windows revealed none of the drama going on inside. The noise from the girls had subsided to a low crying and whimpering.

'That's better,' roared Bruiser. 'Now listen to me carefully because your lives depend on it.' At this there was another outbreak of sobbing.

He instructed, 'Keep your heads down. Don't try to look at us and don't try anything foolish. The emergency exit at the rear is sealed so there is no way out of the coach except under the muzzle of my gun.' He went on, 'In our machine guns, my friend and I have enough bullets to shoot you all but we don't want to use them. It is not our intention to kill you. To make you feel less frightened, I'm going to tell you exactly what is happening. We are kidnapping you and holding you to ransom. So, you see, it is in our best interest to keep you alive.'

Bruiser did not expect a reply, neither did he get one. A number of the girls had assumed a shocked, foetal position and had their hands pressed over their ears.

Teddy took a corner and Bruiser put out his hand to steady the unconscious Watchman. He and Dickie exchanged a wordless look.

There was no way back now. What had he become? Bruiser looked down. He was gripping the Heckler so tightly that his bones showed.

Teddy muttered, over his shoulder, 'Gates coming up!' Bruiser bent to look ahead as the coach raced down the depopulated approach and pulled up at the Captain Cook Docks' East Entrance. Teddy kept the engine throbbing as Dickie jumped out and went ahead. He fitted a key to Rolly's padlock, tugged the chain aside and swung open the gates. Teddy edged through and Dickie closed the gates.

The abductors and their victims sped down the inner dock access road. It was 12.50 p.m.

Bruiser could feel his neck hair bristling. Peering ahead, between the buildings, he waited for his first glimpse of the *Freda*. If Rolly had failed to make the rendezvous, what price a fall-back plan? His wide shoulders relaxed as the ferry's wheelhouse came into sight. His spirits rose markedly as he spotted Marble standing on a caterpillar track, agitated but definitely on parade. The show was going to get off the ground. The spreader hung disjointedly from the crane jib, waiting to wrap itself around a $25,000,000 load.

Teddy rolled the coach forward until it came to rest between the chalk marks, then cut the engine.

Bruiser faced the cowering girls again. 'Now pay attention and stop that bloody caterwauling. We're getting out and leaving you inside the coach. But we'll be immediately outside with our guns so keep down and out of view. In a few minutes you'll feel the coach being lifted and placed aboard a ship. Don't be afraid. This is a perfectly safe manoeuvre.'

Prentiss Decker was gripped by dismay. These guys weren't a bunch of blundering terrorists. The accents were wrong for a start. They really had themselves a back-up organization.

As the door opened, the rich smells of the river flooded in and Teddy took his first good look at the Watchman. 'Christ, guv, has he croaked?'

'Don't worry about that now,' said Bruiser. But Teddy was worrying. Murder? No one had said anything about murder. What had he got himself into?

He and Bruiser heaved the Watchman down the coach steps and onto the quayside. Bruiser banged the man's chest and slapped his face. He gave a groan and colour began to suffuse his cheeks.

'Thank God,' said Teddy fervently.

Bruiser's stomach unknotted but, impassive, he grunted, 'That's better.' He looked around, pondering. 'I don't think we can leave him here. We'll have to take him with the girls, so let's hog-tie and blindfold him before he comes round and sees too much.' He called to Rolly, 'Where's the pilot?' Rolly grinned and cocked a thumb over his shoulder at the wheelhouse. 'Safely tucked up. I took him aboard as per regulations at Tower Pier, let him confirm his presence aboard to the Thames Navigation Service. Then I put him to bed before he could appreciate that the crane chappie and I were the only crew aboard.'

Marble, like Teddy, was having a crisis of conscience. 'Here, I ain't getting mixed up in any heavy stuff,' he quavered.

Bruiser swung round. Marble was dancing nervously on his crane. There was only one possible response. Bruiser drew the Browning from the back of his belt, where it had been concealed by the porter's uniform, and levelled it straight at the narrow space between Marble's eyes. 'Shut your fucking mouth and get on with the job for which you are being paid.'

Marble scuttled into his cabin for protection and a few moments later the crane began to creep forward.

Dickie came panting up with the orange cylinder that Rolly had unloaded onto the dockside. The trussed Watchman was bundled back into the coach. Bruiser slammed the door shut and opened the luggage compartment. The two men rapidly fitted the rubber cuffs over the cylinder valves and connecting tubes. Dickie consulted his operating instructions briefly, switched on the air-conditioning, dextrously twisting the valve until it was fully open. The needle on the flow meter flicked forward as the gas entered the system. 'Good,' he said. They shut the compartment doors and stood up.

Marble had the crane in position. Rolly leaped off the *Freda* and the four men, Bruiser, Rolly, Dickie and Teddy Triggs, each took up a position at a coach wheel. The jib luffed downwards and the four men took hold of the grabs and guided them towards the tyres. Bruiser shouted, 'Everyone in position?' He registered three affirmatives, then nodded up at Marble whose worried face could be dimly perceived through the grimy cabin window. The hawser began to tighten and the coach to creak as the jib rose.

Bruiser raced round to the other side. 'Dickie, where's the Watchman's two-way radio?' Dickie drew the apparatus from a pocket.

Bruiser placed a hand at the back of Teddy's neck and hooked him close. 'You heard the Watchman speak, so do the best you can with his accent and pass the message. The airwaves will distort the tone.'

Teddy's throat was suddenly clogged with phlegm. He hawked manically. He'd never been so scared in his life. Bruiser's hand pressed on the back of his neck. An encouragement? Teddy wanted to think so.

He opened his mouth to speak but only the sound of flaking rust emerged. Bruiser tightened his grip. Teddy tried again. 'Hello, Control Room. Hello, Control Room.'

Bruiser snarled, 'Press the transmit button, you fool!'

Teddy tried once more, endeavouring to keep his voice as flat and as colourless as that of the Watchman.

'Coach Two here,' he managed.

The tiny speaker rustled and then the voice of the security controller came through clearly: 'Go ahead, Coach Two.'

Teddy cleared his throat. 'We've got brake-fluid trouble and we've had to pull over.'

The mike rustled. 'Is it serious, Coach Two? Do you need back-up transport?'

'The driver doesn't think so. He's working on it now,' said Teddy. 'I'll advise further in a few minutes, but you'd better warn them at the Grosvenor House that we'll be a little late.'

Bruiser was mouthing the words with him. They'd rehearsed them often enough together, having decided that Bruiser's brass-bound Etonian boom would be a giveaway even on a bad radio link.

Bruiser slapped him on the back. 'Well done. He's bought it. Now let's get this aviary stowed aboard.'

It was 1.10 p.m. when, if the day had gone well, the coachload of queens would have been five minutes from its destination, the Grosvenor House Hotel.

Instead, at this point, Marble had lifted the coach high enough to clear the bollards at the water's edge and had crept his machine forward so that the load was poised over the *Freda*'s hold, the driver's cabin pointing towards the ramp as specified.

Marble juggled with his levers and brake – the light autumn breeze was disturbing the load's balance. He leaned sideways out of his cabin and shouted to Bruiser, 'You'll have to steady it.'

Two of the men in grey uniforms stepped agilely onto the rim of the steel hull and reached up to help.

Inside the coach, the girls squealed as they felt the floor bucking and losing touch with the ground. They held tightly to the seat supports. Prentiss was disgusted with herself. Fright had made her feel giddy.

She could hear the lugubrious voice of the queen from Belgium, strangely far away. What was she saying? Something about smelling sweet? Prentiss's head began to buzz. She put up a hand, palm flat against the cool window, to steady herself. Then she slowly subsided, her hand squeaking against the pane as it slid down and fell limply into her lap.

Chapter Twenty

The huge round tables under the glinting chandeliers in the Great Room at the Grosvenor House Hotel made a picture of great splendour for the television cameras mounted on silk-draped scaffolding above the heads of the rich and famous now assembling.

The tables were filling up although the single gilt chair, or 'throne' as it was being called for the day, at each remained tantalizingly vacant. There was much merry speculation among the guests as they located their name cards and took their places. Which table would get which queen?

Up in the gallery overlooking the magnificent hall, a select number of top-tablers took a pre-luncheon aperitif. An attentive and deferential group stood listening to the Prince of Wales. The guest of honour was holding court

Lady Cornmorris tried not to let HRH, who was in the middle of an amusing yarn about his underwater encounter with a giant turtle in the Galapagos Islands, see her consulting her watch. The royal party could not take its place at table until the girls had made their entrance.

Just then she saw Arthur Emblem scurrying across the carpet towards her. He was wringing his hands, an ominous sign.

Lady Cornmorris excused herself from the royal presence.

'It's really too, too bad!' said the organizing secretary, reaching her side. 'The coach is delayed by some fault.'

Lady Cornmorris took his arm and moved him deftly away from royal earshot. It simply wasn't done to involve them in the minutiae of daily life.

'How long are they going to be?' she whispered.

'We're waiting for a call,' said Emblem.

The couple crossed to an ante-room where the supervising Watchman stood holding his radio.

'Well?'

'No word yet, madam.'

Police constables Blakey and Laxton, the crew of patrol car Hotel Five from H District, were beginning to feel peckish. 'Give it another thirty minutes, shall we?' said Laxton, the driver. 'Right,' grunted his observer, whose eyes flicked constantly from the passing scene to the receding townscape that he could also see in the extra rear-view mirror. They both had an ear cocked to the monotonous code-wrapped broadcasting from Scotland Yard's information room. They were on listening watch but nothing was coming up with their name on it. This section of dockland had lost its nefarious charm since the great blight of Britain's economic decline in the seventies. They were passing through a bleak landscape of dead buildings and corrugated iron curtains.

'Hold your horses a minute,' said Blakey abruptly. The patrol car came to a gentle halt.

'Would you back up to the iron gates we just passed?' PC Laxton went into reverse.

'A fraction more.' The Ford Mondeo inched backwards.

'Now there's a funny thing,' said Blakey. 'Take a look way over there between the two warehouses.'

Laxton twisted in his seat, hampered by his belt. Through the bars on the gate they could both see in the distance the top of a yellow crane jib. 'It's moving,' said Blakey.

'So?'

'When did you last hear of any activity in these docks?'

PC Blakey unclipped his safety belt and stepped out of the car. He crossed to the gate and looked at the chain. The padlock was new. He turned wordlessly to his driver, holding it up and working the open hasp like a mandible.

'The gate's been unlocked.' He gave a push and the twin gates obligingly swung open.

'Let's take a butcher's,' said PC Blakey, slipping back into his seat. 'I could use a breath of fresh air.'

★   ★   ★

In the wheelhouse, Rolly was the first to spot distant movement. He adjusted his binoculars and rushed to the rail. 'There's a police car coming up fast,' he shouted to Bruiser.

Bruiser's mind went into cold, clear race. He swiftly appraised each man. The Hecklers were aboard and stowed, and the Brownings out of sight.

'Keep lowering the coach,' he bellowed at Marble. And to Dickie he said quietly, 'Take the off-side.'

PC Laxton slowed up as they came to the frozen tableau of the dangling coach and three uniformed men on the dockside. Two of the men moved towards them smiling. Laxton said, 'Rum. Very rum.' He prided himself on his nose for villainy.

'Hello,' greeted Bruiser expansively, his hands casually stuffed into the pockets under his porter's tunic. 'What's the trouble?'

'Should there be any?' inquired PC Laxton. 'What are you people doing here?' The man's upper-class accent did not seem to fit his flunkey's uniform.

Bruiser did not take his eyes off PC Laxton for a moment. 'Doing? As you can see we're loading that coach onto that ferry.'

PC Blakey's eyes were taking in everything and he felt uneasy that the two men had approached on either side of the patrol car. They both had their hands in their pockets in the same easy manner. PC Blakey looked beyond them to the third man. His hands were clutched in front of him. And in the pale lemon sun of late September the policeman could see that his hands displayed an odd sheen. They were encased in transparent surgical gloves. The policeman experienced a moment of chill.

PC Blakey tried to reach unobtrusively for his radio. 'No, don't do that,' said the brilliantly smiling man at his open window. An automatic was rising in his right hand and he abruptly shouted, 'Bruiser!' the smile falling away.

PC Blakey hit his partner hard on the shoulder. 'DRIVE!' he screamed.

PC Laxton went into action. The Mondeo leaped forward between the two men in pearl-grey uniforms, almost brushing them, and screeched along the desolate edge of the basin.

Bruiser barked a command. The two men alongside the

Freda dropped to one knee. 'The tyres,' was all Bruiser said.

Both men took careful two-handed aim and began to squeeze off rounds as calmly and accurately as if they had been on the regimental range.

Both rear tyres on the Mondeo shredded. PC Laxton tried to hold his hurtling vehicle on the narrow feed-road between the water and the blank wall of a storage shed but it began to veer and sway. The gunbursts sent the dock's birds soaring aloft in an alarmed flurry.

The Mondeo now had a volition of its own and Laxton, trying desperately to keep his wheels from the water's edge, over-compensated. The patrol car slewed into a warehouse wall, crumpling the bonnet and throwing both officers against the windscreen. They'd undone their seatbelts back at the gates.

The Old Etonians were upon them in seconds, dragging the dazed uniformed men from the vehicle and ripping out their radio equipment.

'Blindfold them,' snapped Bruiser. Rolly came racing down from the *Freda*'s deck with ropes and gags.

Bruiser knew he had to keep a grip and think out the implications of this cock-up. Then he said, 'We're not taking any more aboard the Skylark, but we can't just let these fellows go free to blow the whistle!'

He looked at the sky. 'If a helicopter flew over now our goose would be cooked. We'll have to push the car into the warehouse and stow these two in it. If they're not found in a couple of days, we can telephone their whereabouts.' Then to Rolly: 'You'd bloody well better make sure you do your best sailor's knots.'

The three men's preoccupation with the battered policemen was suddenly broken by a crashing sound. The *Freda* bucked violently at its moorings and a sheet of water, sandwiched between the hull and the dock wall, splashed up and over the side.

'What the hell . . .' said Dickie, turning. Marble had dropped the coach the remaining two feet onto the deck plates. The *Freda* bumped heavily against her fenders. The crane driver was taking to his heels, his arms windmilling wildly as he strove to put as much distance as possible between himself and the dock.

'Damn, he's lost his bottle. Put a burst over his head,' said Bruiser. Rolly obliged.

Marble's reaction to the rounds whizzing overhead was dramatic. He gave a strangled cry, toppled forward and was still.

'Christ, you've hit him,' said Bruiser.

'Not a chance,' said Rolly, affronted at the slur on his marksmanship.

Bruiser ran the fifty yards to the crane driver and turned him over. His eyes were open and fluid trickled from his contorted mouth.

'Get up, you stupid bugger,' said Bruiser. But Marble remained inert. Quieter now, Bruiser said, 'Are you all right, old chap?' but he was already feeling for Marble's pulse.

While Rolly tended his gas cylinders, Bruiser and Dickie worked desperately on Marble. Finally, Dickie panting, said, 'It's no use.' Marble had turned an unnerving yellow. 'I've never seen a man die of fright before.'

Bruiser gazed down grimly. 'A most unexpected casualty,' he said.

He looked at the ashen-faced Teddy. Useless. He turned back to Dickie. 'Get the body wrapped in tarpaulins and aboard.' Bruiser looked around. 'And take one of those.' He pointed to the crane's pile of counter-weights.

He said to Rolly, 'Give me the key to the East Entrance. I'm going to lock up. While I'm gone, try to move the crane back to its original parking space.'

'Jesus, Bruiser, it's going to take fifteen minutes for you to get to the gate and back,' objected Dickie.

'Can't be helped. We must cover our tracks. If anyone spots us now, we've had it.'

He set out, sprinting furiously. Then he halted for a moment to shout back: 'Dickie, Triggs's second message is overdue. Make sure he sends it right away, will you?'

Teddy barely suppressed a whimper. 'You've got to do it, Triggs,' said Dickie. He handed over the Watchman's radio.

Teddy pressed the button and said, 'Come in, Control. Coach Two here.' The speaker immediately crackled angrily.

134

'Christ, Coach Two! They're going bananas at the Grosvenor House. What the hell are you playing at?'

'Sorry, Control,' said Teddy, trying to steady his voice. 'We thought we could do the repairs but we can't. We're stuck in Stamford Street, Blackfriars. Could you ask the Grosvenor House supervisor to despatch Coach One to give us a lift? We could try for taxis but there aren't many in this area.'

The controller in his eyrie in the Colonel Blood Inn exploded. 'Have you lost your senses, Coach Two? Don't you dare put those girls on the street to catch taxis. They'll be mobbed or worse. I'll have Coach One on its way like greased lightning.'

'Thanks, Control,' said Teddy. 'We'll be waiting.'

Bruiser got back as Dickie finished trussing the policemen. They balanced Marble in his tarpaulins on the side of the *Freda* together with a cast-iron weight from the crane. Only Dickie's hand was stopping the grisly bundle from toppling over into the water. He'd made Teddy recover as many cartridge cases as he could find along the dockside. Bruiser went into the warehouse and inspected the patrol car and its immobilized occupants. He was satisfied. They'd live.

'Right! Everyone on board,' ordered Bruiser, casting off aft. He scrambled on as Rolly hauled in the forward rope and took his place on the bridge. They were under way at last, with the eerily silent cargo. The *Freda* drifted out to mid-basin and Bruiser nodded at Dickie, who placed a hand under his bundle and shoved. The body bounced once against the side and was rapidly dragged down into the depths. The time was 1.32 p.m.

Bruiser climbed up to the wheelhouse, ignoring the pilot who was blindfolded, bound, made deaf with rubber earplugs and stretched along the deck. 'Time to give Mastermind a tinkle on the mobile,' he said briefly.

Lucius sat at his desk above the club. In the past twenty minutes he had smoked four cigarettes. Jessie Moss sat across from him, looking resentful: he'd refused to let her smoke a joint to ease her tension.

Lucius fairly leaped as his mobile trilled. He wanted to shout, 'You're half an hour late, you bastards!' but they had agreed on as little air traffic as possible. The agony of not knowing was making him ill.

'Leader speaking. Slight snag now ironed out. We're on the way – I say again – on the way.'

An onrush of weakness flooded Lucius's frame. 'Understood,' he said.

'Roger and out,' said Bruiser. The transmission had taken eight seconds.

Bruiser broke the connection and glanced down at the prone, but clearly breathing, figure of the pilot. 'He all right?' he asked.

'No problem. I didn't even need to hit him,' said Rolly, who was holding the wheel with one hand and fiddling with the VHF dial with the other. 'I'm setting the ship's wireless on channel fourteen, which will give us the Navigation Service's half-hourly broadcasts as far down-river as Woolwich. It'll be channel twelve the rest of the way.'

Teddy Triggs had been sent below to the engine room. Bruiser and Dickie now climbed onto the roof of the coach and walked its length, pulling a wide, green canvas sheet behind them. The nature of the *Freda*'s cargo could no longer be seen by the casual observer.

Dickie took a torch and went down into marine green twilight to inspect his charges. He clambered onto the coach and shone his lamp through the driver's screen onto the girls in the front seats. They were slumped, semi-comatose. Eyes were half open and he could see limb movement. The Watchman, he noted, was in a similar condition.

'A touch more Chanel No. 5, I think,' he murmured to himself. He opened the luggage-hold doors, saw that the flow meter needle had fallen back and began to exchange the empty cylinder for a full one.

At the mouth of the Captain Cook Dock main channel, Bruiser said, 'I'd like to close the door behind us.'

'Right,' said Rolly, bringing the vessel into the side. Bruiser ran a restraining line to a stanchion and loped back along the embankment.

He knelt, gathered in the cable that normally barred the entrance, and dropped the end link over the wall hook. He stood up, dusting off his surgical gloves. Had he forgotten anything? He thought not. Although, in Marble's case, he was trying.

He cast off again and the *Freda* broke out into the Thames. Rolly steered across the river to the south side to join the eastbound fairway. It was 1.43 p.m. He checked the water's surface. They were in the slack before the tide turned in their favour. Thank God, he thought, for a small mercy. The blunt nose of the *Freda* dug deeper into the grey surface as Rolly took the engines up to six knots.

Chapter Twenty-one

Anger and recrimination reigned at the Grosvenor House Hotel. The control room at the Colonel Blood Inn had broken the news to the luncheon organizers that Coach Two was *hors de combat*.

Lenny Belcher was summoned peremptorily to Arthur Emblem's presence as, standing quietly within calling distance, he had known he would be. In their agitation, no one found it odd that the driver, having delivered his passengers, had not taken himself off for his own lunch with the dozens of other drivers and chauffeurs.

'Stamford Street? Know it well,' said Lenny cheerfully. 'But it'll take me thirty minutes in the traffic to get there and back.'

Lady Cornmorris uttered a small, well-bred cry of distress, and the organizing secretary began again to wring his hands. Lenny scooted off, leaving her ladyship in deep argument with the catering manager.

'I simply cannot hold the first course any longer,' the manager said vehemently. 'The whole meal will be ruined.' Behind them, they could hear the rising sounds of a dissatisfied, impatient assembly.

Lady Cornmorris put a hand to her wonderfully contoured cheek. 'It simply isn't protocol for people to arrive after His Royal Highness has taken his seat at the table.'

'Then you'll just have to explain and apologize to him,' said the manager insistently.

Prince Charles was good-humoured tolerance personified. 'Let's go down, announce me and I'll pour a little soothing oil over them,' he suggested.

The entrance of the Prince was greeted with ironic cheers.

138

He took his place at the top table as the waiters filed in and began to place food on the plates. 'Pray silence!' demanded the crimson-coated toastmaster, introducing the Heir. The room fell quiet.

The toastmaster ran through HRH's impressive range of titles and the Prince sprang to his feet, one hand in jacket pocket. 'My lords, ladies and gentlemen,' he began, beaming around, 'you all doubtless have a vivid recollection of King Louis the Eighteenth once saying: *L'exactitude est la politesse des rois.*' At this there was laughter, a great deal of it uncertain from the non-linguists.

Prince Charles went on: 'Or, put another way, "Punctuality is the politeness of kings."' HRH paused for just the right length of time to allow the joke to sink in. Then he added: 'However, it is perhaps significant that His Majesty had nothing to say about the punctuality of Queens!'

The room broke into a roar of rueful cheering. HRH had restored the room's good humour. Lady Cornmorris gushed gratefully at him.

Lenny did everything by the book, as instructed. He took his coach to Stamford Street, found a public telephone and called Lucius, who questioned him closely. Were the Queen of the Earth organizers alarmed? Had they contacted the police for assistance?

'They're more pissed-off than alarmed,' said Lenny. 'At the moment they're just leaving it to me to bring the girls in.'

'Excellent,' said Lucius. 'Make your call back to the Grosvenor House Hotel in precisely ten minutes. Tell them you can't find the other coach. Then volunteer to make another comb-out of the route. They'll accept.'

Lenny telephoned the hotel on cue and was put through to an ante-room. Arthur Emblem, who picked up the call, was more exasperated than alarmed. Lucius had guessed correctly. 'Yes, take another look – and, for God's sake, hurry!'

The Watchman in the control room at the Inn had just reported that he could no longer raise Coach Two by radio. He was told to keep trying.

* * *

The bombshell call from a Welshman reached Lady Corn-morris, summoned from the top table in high dudgeon at 2 p.m., at which time the catering manager had ordered the serving of the main course.

While her ladyship was storming towards the phone the pirate crew on the *Freda* saw the Limehouse Basin come into view.

Lady Cornmorris's shriek could be heard out in the hall. 'What did you just say?' Arthur Emblem and Alan Jay Jaffe rushed anxiously to her side.

The two officials craned their necks until their ears were almost as close to the instrument as Lady Cornmorris's skilfully painted mouth.

'I thought I ought to ring in case you were worried,' said Lucius, keeping his tone light and youthful. 'I'm Glyn Owain, chairman of the Rag Week committee at London University, raising money for student charities. We want you to go back into the lunch and appeal to your fifty tables to raise ten pounds a table in aid of our fund.'

Lady Cornmorris opened her mouth to interrupt, but her caller hardly paused to draw breath. 'It's a bargain, really. The moment you've collected the money, we'll return your beauty queens.'

'What the devil are you saying, Mr Owen?' Lady Cornmorris struggled to keep her voice under control.

'It's Owain, not Owen,' said Lucius. He was beginning to enjoy his role as disinformation officer.

'I don't care what your wretched name is,' said Lady Cornmorris. 'Are you saying that you have my girls with you?'

'That's right. We invited them to afternoon tea and they were happy to come.'

'*Invited?*' she screamed. 'You've kidnapped them. You've abducted them, their security guard and their coach. Do you call that invited?'

'Oh, come on, be reasonable,' said Lucius. 'We're all working in a good cause. When we explained what we were up to, the girls cheered and came along. We've even arranged an after-noon disco for them. Listen.'

Lucius nodded at Jessie who turned the volume knob on the stereo. Lucius held up the handset six feet away from the speakers.

Lady Cornmorris could faintly hear the rumbling beat. 'You're raving mad, young man! Do you realize I have four hundred people sitting here, including a member of the Royal Family? This afternoon we intended to raise more than twenty thousand pounds for charity work – not your pathetic five hundred. You've ruined an hour-long television programme coverage of the luncheon, you've ruined my day and now I shall do my best to ruin you and your cretinous friends. I'm putting the whole thing in the hands of lawyers with instructions to issue writs to recover punitive damages.' Lady Cornmorris shook with rage.

At the mention of writs, Alan Jay Jaffe, the organization's fixer and trouble-shooter, laid a cautioning hand on Lady Cornmorris's arm and asked for the phone. She held it out to him at arm's length, as if it were a snake.

'Now, look here, Mr Owain. I'm the public-relations officer. Can't I appeal to you to be reasonable and get those girls to Grosvenor House before the end of lunch? I'm sure we can find five hundred pounds without bothering our guests, although you'll have to take your chances afterwards. Lady Cornmorris isn't joking about issuing a writ for damages. You've been very clever in spiriting the girls away like this, but sometimes one can be too clever by half. Some of the girls must have been frightened by your actions and there are bound to be repercussions.'

'Absolutely untrue!' said Lucius. 'The girls are having a grand time, although I must admit we've had to sit on your driver and bodyguard.'

'So they at least will have a case for suing you for technical assault. Why don't you get everyone back here as fast as you can, before you land yourself in even deeper trouble?'

Lucius fell silent for a moment. Then he said, 'I'm trying to work it out. I don't think it's going to be possible to round them up and get them to the Grosvenor House in time for lunch.'

'Where are you?' asked Jaffe, sighing.

'Somewhere in north London,' said Lucius carefully. 'You wouldn't expect me to say more than that, would you?'

'I suppose not,' said the public-relations man, resigned. 'Are you able to get them into their coach and return them to the Colonel Blood Inn?'

'What about the five hundred pounds?'

'Don't be silly, Mr Owain. How long do you think you can hold fifty-one people before we set the police on you?'

'Long enough to muck up this evening's reception in White-hall,' said Lucius, throwing in a small laugh of satisfaction.

Weary now, Jaffe said, 'Mr Owain, if you're a student of English history, you will know that a foolish monarch once lost his head there. I think you're well on the way towards losing yours.'

'I'll take my chances, Mr Jaffe. Now what about the five hundred pounds?'

Jaffe saw no further purpose in this dialogue. 'All right, Mr Owain. Five hundred it is, but I wouldn't bet twopence on your chances of getting away with this.'

Lady Cornmorris snatched back the telephone. 'Dammit, Alan, we shouldn't be wasting breath on this little yob!'

She said into the mouthpiece, 'Now listen to me, you – you –' Lady Cornmorris bit back the epithet. 'Let me speak to one of the girls.'

'You'll have to hold on for a while,' said Lucius. He placed the receiver on his desk and sat back, watching the sweep hand of his watch. The disco music still thumped from the stereo so that Lady Cornmorris, pacing furiously, knew she had not been cut off.

Lucius allowed a full minute to pass, then nodded at Jessie. She took the phone. She said timidly, 'Hello?'

Lady Cornmorris halted in her track. 'Who is that?'

'Maria Clavijo Encina,' said Jessie, speaking in the accent that she had rehearsed.

'Maria?' queried Lady Cornmorris vaguely.

'*Sí*, the girl from Spain,' said Jessie.

'Oh, yes, my dear. Of course. Are you all right?'

'Yes. All right,' said Jessie.

'And the other girls?'

'Yes. All right, too. The university students have been naughty boys, yes?'

'Very naughty boys,' said Lady Cornmorris, with feeling. 'Now, you are to tell the girls that they must return to the Colonel Blood Inn immediately.'

'They are dancing but, okay, I tell them right away.'

'Maria,' said Lady Cornmorris severely, 'I insist that you emphasize to the girls that they will all be in breach of their contracts unless they stop encouraging the foolishness of these wicked boys.'

'Foolishness? Excuse me. I don't know what is this foolishness.'

'Oh, never mind,' said Lady Cornmorris, defeated. 'Put me back to that scoundrel.'

Lucius said, 'We'll give them a cup of tea and a bun and then deliver them to the doorstep. Have the five hundred ready.' He cut off before Lady Cornmorris could shout her objections.

She leaned against the moiré silk wall of the ante-room. 'My God, those little swine have wrecked the whole thing. What am I to say to His Royal Highness?'

Chapter Twenty-two

'Damn!' said Rolly. 'I thought we'd got the nag over the last jump.' He was listening intently to the 2 p.m. broadcast to mariners on the VHF.

'What's up?' asked Bruiser.

'The PLA are giving the Thames barrier a test run at two thirty. We can't expect this old barge to get us to Woolwich in time to pass through, so it means yet another delay.'

Rolly touched the heavily breathing pilot with his foot. 'This chap must know all about it but I'm afraid I didn't give him much opportunity to speak.'

'How long?'

Rolly shrugged. 'I suppose if the rehearsal goes smoothly, they'll lower immediately.'

'And what time are we likely to be under way again?'

'Can't be before three thirty,' said Rolly.

'Let's hope,' said Bruiser, 'that Mastermind, sitting safely on his elegant bottom, is giving an award-winning performance. Before the balloon goes up, we need every delaying trick in his repertoire.'

Lucius looked at Jessie Moss. 'I'm impressed. You were very convincing.'

She said, 'You weren't so bad yourself. Can I have my smoke now? I've almost wet myself with nerves.'

'Of course,' said Lucius. 'Then we must sit out the next few hours until Sir Brewster phones.'

Jessie studied him. He gave her the willies but he was the cleverest bastard she'd ever met. And he didn't seem to be as much of a bloody fascist as the other toffs.

* * *

144

At 3 p.m., while a thoroughly unsatisfactory event was coming to a chaotic end at the Grosvenor House and the disgruntled guests were dispersing, the dispatcher responsible for H District in the Information Room at New Scotland Yard was having problems of his own. Twice in the past hour he had put out general calls for assistance, to which any patrol car on listening watch in the relevant area had a duty to respond. On neither occasion had Hotel Five been among the cars responding. He made a note on his pad.

The *Freda* had nosed along, passing Elizabethan inns and historic sites such as Execution Dock, where pirates had once dangled helplessly in chains while the tides washed over them. The Greenwich naval college slid by to starboard, as she crossed the zero meridian. Then she slowed to a dead stop. Ahead were eight other craft, stationary in the fairway, facing nine great piers topped by concrete cowls. Between these piers the gates of the Woolwich Barrier resolutely barred their progress.

Down in the hold all was quiet. Dickie had shut off the gas some way back along the river and, with his torch, now watched his fifty helpless charges floating in fitful oblivion.

Rolly trained his binoculars on a new building at the southern end of the Barrier. Eighty feet up, an observation window ran the length of the roof: behind it lay the Barrier Control Station, manned round the clock by marine officers of the Port of London Authority.

'Smile,' said Rolly. 'We're being watched. From now on, until we reach the disembarkation point, we shall also be under radar surveillance.'

'And I daresay there's an anti-terrorist unit patrolling the Barrier,' said Bruiser.

'Yes,' said Rolly. 'We can't afford any more shooting.'

Bruiser contemplated his boots. He said, 'You're right. So far it's been much worse than I ever envisaged. I don't mind so much about the crane driver. But the other three chaps were only doing their duty. I'm sorry we've hurt them.'

He stared out through the wheelhouse windscreen. Then he fished a silver hip flask from under his jacket. 'I think we need a snort,' he said, handing it to Rolly.

Both men took a long swig, then Rolly bent down and put the flask to the blindfolded pilot's lips. Alarmed, the man averted his head. Rolly loosened the bandage holding the plugs in his ears and said, 'It's only brandy, you idiot. Good for *mal de mer*.' The pinioned man swallowed gratefully.

Rolly straightened and said to Bruiser, 'No more bang-bangs.'

'Yes, that's the way I see it. Lucius thinks we're all playing parts in a cowboy film and that, after the day's work, all the casualties get up and go home to a good dinner. He would've learned a lesson if he'd been with us two hours ago. Those coppers were quite knocked about.'

My God, thought Bruiser, was that all it was? Two hours ago?

By 3.30 p.m. the Information Room dispatcher had tried in vain three more times to raise patrol car Hotel Five. He reported this to the duty inspector who authorized a check on the frequency. The Yard's radio engineers reported that they could detect no fault.

The inspector, following a set procedure, informed the chief superintendent at Hotel Five's home base, the Limehouse police station, who directed staff to check local hospitals and other likely points at which the crew of the missing Mondeo might have stopped.

As yet, no one was more than slightly curious as to their whereabouts.

Rolly's prediction proved correct. The river authority, not wishing a head of water to build up behind the raised barrier, had begun to lower the steel gates at 3.12 p.m. Thirty minutes later, on radio instructions from the control station, the *Freda*, in line astern of other waiting craft, passed without incident through Span D.

Rolly said, 'We have fourteen sea miles to disembarkation. We should be there in two hours.'

At 4.40 p.m. Rolly registered Dartford Creek passing to starboard and told Bruiser, 'You'll be pleased to know we've just sailed beyond the Metropolitan Police administrative area.'

Bruiser recalled Lucius giving them an interminable lecture about the mistakes made by the police during their hunt for the Great Train Robbers: the search had spread outwards from the scene-of-crime, rather than from a far-flung circumference inwards. Would the limit of the hue-and-cry end here? Bruiser was doubtful.

He went down the ladder into the hold, looked in on Teddy Triggs, skulking among the thumping diesels, and found Dickie replacing another spent gas cylinder.

Bruiser nodded towards the coach. 'How are they?'

'Resting peacefully. I'm only giving them an extra whiff when they start to stir,' he reported.

'All right, Dickie, I think they've had enough of that muck. We've already made ourselves one dead 'un. Get your blindfolds and ropes ready, then pump in the oxygen and bring them round.'

While the forty-nine queens surfaced from four lost hours, distress signals were going out elsewhere.

The search for Hotel Five was now under the direction of the H District commander from his headquarters at Leman Street.

At the Colonel Blood Inn confusion and outrage predominated. The evening papers were already carrying light-hearted accounts of how London University students had wafted away the forty-nine beauties and spoiled the Prince of Wales's lunch. A group of reporters and three television crews waited under the Inn's *porte cochère* for the girls' return and the sequel to the story.

At 5.04, by the clock on the wall of Scotland Yard's Information Room, an irate call was registered from a Mr Arthur Emblem.

The duty inspector listened courteously and suggested that perhaps this was a civil matter and best settled between the parties. 'It is not a civil matter,' shouted agitated Mr Emblem. 'This is a kidnapping in broad daylight from the streets of London!'

The duty inspector was not convinced: the idea was too absurd. Nevertheless, the apparent involvement of royalty in the matter made him send a patrol car to the Senate House of London University in Bloomsbury.

The crew found the imposing building strangely quiet. They asked for the man in charge.

Lord Lavington, vice-chancellor, scientist and world authority on radio waves, was sitting in his modest oak-panelled office on the first floor, gazing out at the rear end of the British Museum and trying to find inspiration for a speech he was to give to a symposium of astronomers. His secretary had gone home. It was an apologetic porter who tapped on his door and introduced two uniformed policemen, caps tucked under their left arms.

Lord Lavington listened, amused, to the tale they had to tell. 'I think, gentlemen,' he said, 'that someone is wasting your time. For a start, our students are not due back for another two weeks. Therefore a Rag Week escapade is hardly possible. And, anyway, Rag Week usually takes place in the spring.'

The two patrolmen were inclined to withdraw there and then. But the driver hazarded one last question. 'Is there any way we can check the present whereabouts of a student named Glyn Owain, sir?'

'Not tonight, there isn't. We have forty thousand internal students and a further twenty-two thousand externals. They study at fifty-five colleges and institutions that stretch from Surrey and throughout London to a marine-biology station on the Firth of Clyde in Scotland. Indeed. We also have an institute in Paris. So you may readily appreciate the immensity of the task – even if this scamp exists.'

The *Freda* was tied up at the wharf of the papermaking works. Rolly had informed the Navigation Service by radio that he had to pull out of the fairway while an engine fault was remedied. An offer of assistance was declined with thanks.

The ferryboat sat a tantalizing hundred yards from the hijacked juggernaut concealed in a vast abandoned shed. But there was no way until dark that a long line of spectacularly garbed girls wearing blindfolds could be transferred to it without being seen from the river.

Bruiser jumped ashore and strolled over to inspect the great vehicle. The hijacked meat, still frozen, had been dumped against a wall. Bruiser was reminded of disinterred human corpses. He closed his eyes briefly.

148

He trod through the puddles around the open rear doors: the refrigeration unit had been switched off soon after they had snatched the vehicle and the driver deposited in the cellar at Moxmanton. Bruiser climbed in and carried away a paraffin heater that had been burning for the past twenty hours to dry out the interior. He returned and reached up to let a carcass hook take his weight. It did not buckle. Sixty such hooks ran in three lines from the front to the back of this giant refrigerator on wheels.

He glanced at his watch: 6.15 p.m.

By seven o'clock Lady Cornmorris was being attended by the hotel doctor for hysteria, the two Israeli air marshals had locked their charge in her room and the police had at last conceded that the joke had gone too far.

University administrators were being summoned to their offices all over London to check files for a student named Glyn Owain. A description of the coach and its licence number had been circulated throughout the Metropolitan Police area.

Lucius's voice rose to a shriek. 'You did *what*? You've ruined everything!'

Bruiser said, 'Control yourself and listen to me. For a start, those bobbies aren't going to be telling tales to anyone for at least the next couple of days. And then what? It won't matter a tinker's cuss that they'll lead the hunt to the dock. As for identifying us, they had a quick glimpse from inside their car of me and Dickie and, perhaps, young Triggs. We were all disguised. I see no problem. In fact, one problem we might have had, that wretched Marble fellow, has conveniently removed himself from our list of worries.'

Lucius fumed impotently. He disconnected the call and Jessie watched his face working stressfully. He sat staring at his desk, black hair falling forward. Finally, he said, 'I'll drive us down to the house – but a little later than I anticipated. You wait here and lay off those bloody joints or you'll be too zonked to work. I'm going out but I should be back in a couple of hours to pick you up.'

He peered out at the Mayfair skyline. It was darkening.

Chapter Twenty-three

At 7.20 p.m. Bruiser judged the dusk deep enough to begin the transfer. One by one the weeping girls were led blindfolded to the juggernaut. Airline sleeping masks had been taped over their eyes and ear plugs were held secure by headbands.

The girls stumbled on their high heels, swore and prayed. 'Fuck you!' said Prentiss Decker recklessly, as she felt hands on her arms. Lucius had bought high-quality soft rope for the bindings but even so, the girls cried out in pain and fear as they were lifted bodily and the rope links between their wrists placed over the hooks, leaving them dangling off the floor. Shoes fell with a clatter and several began to complain of cramp in the arms.

Lenny had now arrived and he joined the others in the transfer, making no answer to the victims' pleas. Lenny felt bad at this pitiable close-up view of his handiwork. He wished he'd never become involved.

Dickie relayed restraining ropes along the lines of dangling legs, a strangely erotic sight, to prevent the girls swinging wildly once the juggernaut started moving, then climbed into the meat compartment and pulled the doors shut. He knew he'd have to keep ventilating the interior during the eighteen-mile dash to their final destination. In the dim interior light he felt awe at their achievement. Here he now stood, master of forty-nine of the most beautiful girls in the world.

A pasha's dream of paradise . . . Dickie pulled himself together. Enough of these randy meanderings. A warning from Bruiser, uttered during the planning, came back to him. 'I don't want to catch anyone sexually harassing the captives. Everything is going to be done strictly according to Geneva. We are not a rabble.' Dickie sat down beside the *Freda*'s pilot and the Watchman, imprisoned in a world without sight or sound.

Shortly before 8 p.m. Bruiser swung up into the driver's cabin and said to Lenny at the wheel, 'Let's get going.'

Rolly Ponsford and Teddy Triggs, standing by the old Ford Escort in which Lenny had arrived, watched the juggernaut lumber off into the gloom and the tail lights come on as the vehicle turned on to the main road.

'Right,' said Rolly, 'let's wrap up this little lot.' He changed swiftly into a wetsuit and the two men climbed back aboard the *Freda*. Rolly, masquerading as the pilot, radioed the Navigation Service to report the completion of repairs: the *Freda* would now complete her journey across to the Essex side and to her home berth. Would the pilot need a pick-up launch to get him home?

'No thanks,' said Rolly. 'The owners are giving me a lift.'

He and Teddy uncovered the coach and stowed the green canvas, together with all the gas cylinders, inside the now empty vehicle. Dickie handed Teddy a pickaxe and said, 'Nip up on the roof and hack a line of holes through the ceiling.'

Teddy protested. 'It's a bit unnecessary, ain't it?' He'd grown quite fond of his magnificent vehicle.

'Just do it,' said Rolly. 'You'll see why.'

While Teddy did as he was told, Dickie knelt at the centre of the coach interior and carefully arranged a two-ounce cone of plastic in the aisle. It would be just enough explosive to blow out a section of the undercarriage.

Up top, he switched on the *Freda*'s running lights and Teddy cast off. Rolly moved the craft out slowly into the now empty fairway, suspended between the twinkling lights of the Kent and Essex banks, and put the craft into reverse at barely half a knot so that the river now batted against the stern, leaving the forward ramp in the wake.

During the voyage down-river he had linked the coach's rear fender by two stout ropes to stanchions on the *Freda*. Rolly put Teddy's hands on the wheel and ordered, 'Just keep her steady as she goes. I'll be back.'

Rolly went swiftly forward and activated the ramp winches, bringing down the flap until the ship's wake broke over it. Then he climbed into the coach, leaving the door open. He switched on and gave the engine plenty of revs. Then he ran down the centre aisle, consulted his watch, plunged the detonator into the plastic cone and set the clock.

'Blimey O'Reilly!' whispered Teddy, as the coach began to move and he realized the toff's intention.

Rolly gave the engine a last massive rev, jammed down his foot and the coach flew forward onto the ramp, hanging out over the water.

The front wheels cleared the edge and the *Freda* bucked wildly at the abrupt redistribution of weight. Teddy clung grimly to the wheel.

Rolly accelerated again, gave a triumphant war-cry as he felt the powered rear wheels take off from the ramp. He killed the engine as the coach hit the river hard. The retaining ropes snaked out after it, taking it immediately into a slow tow. On the Navigation Service radar screens, the *Freda* and its load would still be represented by a single blip.

Rolly hauled himself onto the roof, ran to the rear and went hand-over-hand along one of the taut ropes, his body in water, until he could pull himself up onto the ramp. Dripping and puffing, he gazed back with satisfaction at his work. His watch said there were forty seconds to go. He looked around the empty deck. The unorthodox manoeuvre had caused the *Freda* to ship some water, but the pumps would take care of that.

The soft crump of the explosion came on time and for a moment the coach's interior was a blinding box of light. Then it began to settle fast. Rolly unhitched the ropes, which slithered across the deck and joined the coach in the water. The vehicle was swallowed greedily, air pushed out through the open door and the pickaxe holes in the roof as the water rose up through her ruptured bowels. There would be no air bubble trapped in the ceiling to hold her afloat. Then Rolly winched the ramp shut and strolled along to the wheel-house.

Twenty minutes later he reported to the Navigation Service that the *Freda* was tied and made safe for the night. He and Teddy launched a rubber dinghy to recross the river to their car on the Kent side. The Navigation Service had queried nothing.

    ★ ★ ★

The juggernaut was turning from a deserted country lane into the main gates of Moxmanton House. Bruiser frowned. The gates were unmanned, although Lucius and the slut should have been there ahead of them.

Lenny ran back to close the gates and Dickie, jumping down from the juggernaut, exclaimed jubilantly, 'We've done it! We've done it!'

Bruiser cut him short. 'Save the victory parade until later. I want this vehicle emptied and out of here in double-quick time.'

They were backing the vehicle to the kitchen side of the house when Lucius and Jessie finally arrived. Lucius looked strained but he then observed what he had wrought and felt godlike.

The queens came off their hooks confused and cowed. Blindly they flexed their arms to restore circulation. When the last had been lifted to the ground, Bruiser went to the front, guided the still-roped hands of the second girl onto the waist of the first and so on down the row until they resembled a grotesque conga line.

Then the men, joined by an amazed Jessie Moss, led the line through the kitchen and pantry until the leading girl, Stefania Moreno, the Italian queen, felt the cooler air of the cellar on her face. Hands guided her forward and onto a step. Then another. And another. The girls edged slowly down into their prison.

Outside, there was an autumn chill in the air, made pungent by sulphur from a nearby Kentish oasthouse drying the year's hop crop.

Bruiser checked the inside of the juggernaut, gathered up an armful of dropped shoes, and stood aside as the trussed driver was brought up from the cellar and placed alongside the river pilot and Watchman.

'Get out of that uniform and get going,' Bruiser ordered Lenny. He slapped the juggernaut's side. 'And after you've dumped this thing, don't forget to open a rear door otherwise these three won't have enough air to survive the night.'

Bruiser turned to Lucius and handed him a rake. 'When Belcher has gone, I want you to rake the gravel from the main gate to the kitchen. This bloody thing will have made trenches in the drive.'

Lucius's first impulse was to protest at the imposition of this menial chore but Bruiser was looking purposeful. The godlike moment evaporated.

Fifteen minutes later, apart from a man inexplicably raking gravel, the outside aspect of an unlit Moxmanton House presented a picture of English country serenity. It was 9.40 p.m., little more than nine hours after the queens had set out in such high spirits to lunch with a prince.

At 10 p.m. policewomen were dispatched to sit at home with the waiting wives of the crew of Hotel Five.

An hour later the ground-floor press bureau at New Scotland Yard was jammed with crime reporters whose inquiries over the past few hours had been as fruitless as those of the police. What was Scotland Yard holding back?

On the hour, the Assistant Commissioner (Crime), a balding man who was counting the days to his pension, took the stand and cleared his throat. 'Ladies and gentlemen,' he began, not meaning it. 'Scotland Yard wishes to appeal through you to the public to help trace these vehicles.' The cameras zoomed in on the photographs he was holding of the missing coach and Hotel Five's Mondeo.

This was the first inkling that the reporters had had that there was a link between the two. 'What's the connection?' shouted the *Sun* man.

'We're not certain,' said the AC, 'but we think it too much of a coincidence that these two vehicles should disappear at around the same time. Widespread inquiries have gone on all evening and are still going on, but we've been unable to confirm the story of the student prank that the organizers of the Queen of the Earth contest were told about eight hours ago. On the contrary, our inquiries indicate that this explanation for the girls' disappearance is a fabrication. If our assumptions are correct, we feel it entirely possible that the crew of Hotel Five accidentally stumbled upon the truth and have been somehow neutralized.'

The word 'neutralized' fell on a silent room. Then

pandemonium broke out. Finally, one reporter managed to bawl a question louder than his confreres: 'Are we dealing here with a real kidnapping – of forty-nine girls, two policemen, the coach driver and the security guard?' He sounded incredulous.

'I'd hesitate to use the word kidnap,' said the AC. 'Let us say "temporarily detained". Kidnapping such a large group hardly seems a likelihood.'

'Terrorists wouldn't hesitate because of large numbers,' yelled the *Daily Mail* man. 'The more hostages, the better for them.'

This was an aspect that the AC had hoped to avoid. 'We have no indications that a terrorist group is involved although, of course, this cannot be ruled out. But, so far, the usual messages claiming responsibility have not been received. Our minds are open.'

'Which means they're blank,' muttered a BBC woman cynically.

The AC gathered up his notes to leave but she called out, 'How on earth can two highly visible vehicles such as these disappear from the heart of London and not leave a trace?'

'How on earth indeed?' said the AC grimly.

Upstairs, the commander of the anti-terrorist squad was already setting out to find an answer to that question, with the aid of Special Branch and the security services. And the Home Secretary had just persuaded the Prime Minister to authorize a precautionary measure.

The battalion adjutant at the Duke of York's barracks in Chelsea was tracked down to his club and alerted to receive midnight visitors. A company of the Special Air Service 22nd Regiment was already on its way in closed trucks from Hereford, together with their arcane equipment.

But those were not matters to be disclosed as yet to the media.

In London, Scotland Yard's puzzled statement landed conveniently in the middle of the ITN television news bulletin. The BBC interrupted its programmes, as did European stations. In New York, the first news flashes were heard on car radios by homeward-bound commuters and were being analysed within the hour on the early-evening news shows. 'We still don't know if we have a backfiring practical joke or an ongoing diabolical crime here,' summed up Dan Rather of CBS. 'We shall bring you further news as it breaks.'

The mayor of the tiny township of Bloomsbury in Queensland in northern-most Australia, off the Great Barrier Reef, was hampered by no such caution. Citizens greeting the morning found the flags on public buildings already at half-mast in sympathy for the unknown fate of their most famous daughter, Helly Harris. This lovely eighteen-year-old Queensland girl was Australia's torch holder now residing at Moxmanton House, Medsham, Kent, England.

'Those bloody Poms couldn't organize a bunk-up in a brothel,' was his honour's pithy opinion.

Chapter Twenty-four

The girls eddied into a sightless group in the centre of the long cellar, relieved that they were still together. Under the black masks the mouths of some were set firm. Others emitted sobs or the mewing sounds of wounded animals. Jessie Moss experienced a deep satisfaction at the humiliation of these toffee-nosed cows who, a few hours earlier, had thought they were God's Gift, so high-and-bloody-mighty.

She decided she was going to enjoy the next few days. She sauntered close and laughed at one stupid bitch. In the hurly-burly of getting them out of the juggernaut and down into the cellar, one girl's *décolletage* had become disarranged and her right breast had dropped out, a pale, brown-peaked mound set dramatically against blue-black silk. Jessie walked over, lifted the soft flesh and weighed it in her hand. She laughed again. She was sure the nipple was tingling in her palm. She stared hard at the girl. She'd remember her. Then she roughly tugged Mathilde de Montméja's neckline straight and dropped the breast back inside. Mathilde said nothing.

Bruiser came bounding down the steps with Lucius. 'Get your helmet on,' he said. He selected one of the bigger, more capable-looking girls, who was wearing a Bavarian oompah-band outfit, and pulled her to one side. He unknotted her rope, removed the bandage, earplugs and mask.

Hanna Hansen winced in the first light she had seen for ten hours and began automatically to massage her wrists as she faced her captors. There were three – a male and a female dressed in black overalls and a larger man in a grey uniform. She thought he was probably one of the two who had seized the coach. All three wore motorcyclists' crash helmets with mirrored visors that gave them the frightening aspect of one-eyed giant insects.

The large man raised his visor half an inch and held out a plastic dustbin liner. Through the aperture, he said, 'Untie your friends and put the ropes, masks and plugs into the bag.' Her eyes were readjusting. She could now see the submachine gun dangling from his wide shoulder.

Hanna began furiously to free the other girls, hugging and kissing the inconsolable and putting them to help free the others. She handed Bruiser the filled bag and said calmly, 'I know the driver is one of you but where is the man who was guarding us? Is he dead?'

Bruiser replied, 'Step back with the others. You are here to obey my orders, not to ask questions.' The icy dismissal was the douche that awoke her.

Hanna lunged forward in anger, preparing to smash her tormentor's mirrored face, but before her fist could land against his visor, an object touched her shoulder. Hanna screamed and reeled back. The woman was standing, legs astride, holding in front of her a long pole. In shock, Hanna reverted to her native German. 'Was ist das?'

The English girl, Fran, answered fearfully, 'It's an electric cattle prod.'

Bruiser said levelly, 'Let's have no more of that nonsense. From now on misbehaviour will be severely punished. There's still a lot to do before you all bed down for the night, so let's get on with it.'

Bruiser brought up his gun and waved it in an arc. The girls in the first rank cringed. 'I want you all to move down to the other end of the cellar,' he said.

The queen from Korea started to collapse and even Hanna trembled. A painting she had once seen was suddenly vividly before her: Tsar Nicholas and his family, bullets from the Cheka's rifles thudding into their toppling bodies in the cellar at Ekaterinburg.

Bruiser saw their fear. 'Don't worry. All that's going to happen is that you will step forward one at a time, place all your jewellery, watches and clothes, apart from your knickers, in plastic bags and be body-searched by Nanny here.'

Jessie stepped forward with a pile of black plastic dustbin liners.

'I'm not wearing any knickers,' wailed Mirabelle Montcalm who, in the absence of a truly national Canadian garment, had opted for a body-hugging cocktail dress displaying a discreet maple leaf motif.

'That's tough,' said Bruiser, 'but you will be issued with other clothes afterwards. No more arguments. Let's move!'

The girls stepped forward one at a time, some hesitantly, some crying, some boldly. 'Legs apart, arms raised,' snapped Jessie.

The two men watching felt themselves hardening as the clothes and jewellery came off and were dropped into the bags.

Teresa Flanagan, the queen from Ireland with a face as soft and lovely as a Derry spring, started to weep as Jessie began to tug at her diamond ring. 'For mercy's sake, miss. That's my engagement ring. I've only just been given it. Please don't take it away.'

Bruiser interrupted. 'Put it in the bag. You'll be wearing it again – if you do as you're told. We are not here to steal baubles.'

Jessie became conscious of a rising excitement that was part sexual and part joy at the immense power she had acquired. Even compelling the girls to take off their stilettos, cutting them down to size, became a form of arousal. She looked down at the front of her overalls. The fabric did not betray the aching rigidity of the nipples beneath.

The pale girl glided forward, one feather step deliberately set down in front of the other as if she were on a cat-walk. Mathilde stripped elegantly and posed, looking straight ahead without expression, legs astride and arms raised. Jessie stretched wide the band of her silk panties and inspected her pubis and the tight cleft of her buttocks before muttering, 'Get back with the others.'

Before surrendering her watch, Prentiss Decker checked the time. They'd now been missing for eleven hours. She remembered the coach being lifted. She'd risked a peek at the ship's deck before the sweet smell had reached her nostrils and robbed her of her senses. Eleven hours! Time enough, she

pondered glumly, for the whole damn circus to have been transported out of England. Why else would these bastards need a
boat? Were they in France? Holland? Belgium?

The big guy was addressing the naked assembly again. 'You'll
each take one of these boiler suits, a pair of espadrilles, plastic
fork and spoon, a paper beaker and plate. There are three
chemical loos in the alcove at the far end, mattresses for each
of you, plus two blankets. You're going to be here for some time
so it is in your own interest to make yourselves as comfortable as
possible and to organize yourselves so that you do not begin
to wear upon each other in a confined space.' Bruiser's voice
issued in a muffled boom from the black crescent slit of his
partially raised visor. 'Naturally,' he went on drily, 'you will all
be thinking of escape. But let me assure you that that is not
possible. Even in the unlikely event of your breaking out of the
place, you would be shot down instantly. That is fair warning.
I hope you will take heed of it.'

The band of three withdrew behind the iron grille and the
girls watched as the gate was locked and chained. Prentiss
called out, 'None of us has had any food since breakfast.'

'When you've collected your kit, we're bringing down hot
soup and coffee. You will not starve,' said Bruiser. The three
disappeared and the upper door slammed shut.

The morning newspaper headlines screamed: VANISHED
ALL BUT ONE', the *Express*; THE MISSING PRIDE OF
QUEENS, *Daily Telegraph*; WHO'S GOT 'EM? *Daily Mail*,
WORLD'S GREATEST VANISHING TRICK, the *Mirror*.

Variations on these themes rolled off the presses around the
globe. In many cases a neat parallel was drawn with the story
of the Pied Piper of Hamelin, with Rebecca Engelman cast as
the crippled child who could not keep up with the other children as they were lured away. A front page picture showed her
being comforted by a distraught Lady Cornmorris.

But, as yet, the press, like Scotland Yard, were still unsure
if they were dealing with comedy or tragedy.

At first light the search for the missing vehicles and their
occupants had become a nationwide effort. At 8 a.m. an ice-
cream salesman, collecting his van from a municipal car park

160

on the sea front at Birchington, on the south-eastern tip of England, provided the first break. He noticed the parked juggernaut overshadowing his own vehicle and became curious at the sight of the heavy rear door standing ajar. The salesman placed a tentative finger against the edge and eased it open. The light of a bright morning flooded in, illuminating the bizarre spectacle of three trussed and gagged men lying on the floor.

The river pilot was able to gasp out his story to the Birchington constabulary, and Tower Bridge was on everyone's lips.

Jugs of coffee with rolls and butter were brought down the cellar stairs at 7.30 a.m. The girls formed a line and were served through the bars.

They were a sorry-looking, bedraggled group after a night of little sleep and some hysteria. Yesterday's skilfully applied make-up was caked and smudged, the lip-gloss worn away. Sunoo Khushlani was crying gently and scrambling across the flagstones looking for her plastic *bindiya*, the red dot Hindu women wear in the centre of their foreheads. It used to have religious meaning but modern Indian maidens have for years used it as a beauty spot.

The girls' mattresses were strung along the cellar from end-to-end in a disorderly row. Already the Roman Catholics had formed a prayer group and were hard at their devotions in one of the alcoves.

Prentiss said impatiently to Hanna, 'We're all bright girls. We have to start thinking our way out of here. Praying is the last resort of the helpless.'

When the kidnappers had gone, Prentiss stood in the centre of the room and clapped her hands for attention. 'Ladies,' she said, 'we need to talk.' The forty-eight flip-flopped across in their espadrilles until they formed a loose circle round her.

Prentiss said, 'We're in the shit. We can't afford to believe those people when they say they won't harm us. What happens if they don't get the ransom money?' She did not wait for an answer.

'As I see it, we have to fall back on our own talents. I don't think we can just sit on our fannies waiting for a handsome cop to come to the rescue. These guys are brilliantly organized. They could even be smarter than the police.'

Prentiss drew a breath. 'Spread out so that you each face a section of the wall. Go over every inch of stone and brick. We must be sure they don't have this place bugged. After that, let's play pick-a-back and examine the ceiling in the same way.'

A couple of girls began to smile and the defeated mood of the group began to lift at the imposition of targets and physical activity. Immaculate, long, painted fingernails probed mortar and plaster. Prentiss herself concentrated on the grilles covering the ventilation shafts at the far end of the cellar. Hanna gave her a leg up so that she could apply an eye to the interstices. Prentiss came down plucking a strand of cobweb from an eyelash. 'They're definitely vents. I can feel the air flowing but it's too dark to see if there are mikes on the other side of the grilles. We'll just have to do all our important talking at the other end of the room.'

The girls swarmed over the walls and held each other up close to the light fittings, but they found nothing.

Prentiss moved briskly to keep the girls on an up mood. 'Right! What do we know about these people?' She turned to the British girl. 'Fran, this is your country. Tell us what you think.'

Fran Pilkington said, slowly, 'Well, first, I was surprised at how posh some of them sound.' She stopped while 'posh' was translated in half a dozen languages. 'The big one and the other one we saw in the hotel jacket seem to have had a good education. The woman called Nanny and our driver both have Cockney accents. They're much more the type I'd expect to be involved in something like this. And there was another man, tallish and slim, who watched us while they made us take our clothes off. He hasn't yet said enough for me to have any opinion.'

'Thanks, Fran,' said Prentiss. 'I reckon the big guy in charge is military. My dad was navy and I was brought up on bases. Men in authority have a particular way of speaking. I'd say we're in the hands of a bunch of former military men – mercenaries, perhaps – and the Cockneys are the gofers. You'll note that the Cockneys don't have guns, only a cattle prod. What I gather from my ventures into political science is that the gentry have the hand-made sporting guns and the peasants make do with the pitchforks.'

That raised a few smiles.

She ticked off another fact. 'We know we've made a journey on the Thames, but we don't know how far we came.' She looked around at their prison. 'I'm not an expert on architecture but I'd say we're locked in some sort of medieval dungeon.'

'Oh no! Much later,' broke in Tilly Jo Evans, a fey ash-blonde sprite from New Zealand, who so far had said little. 'Oh, excuse me,' she said nervously, 'I didn't want to interrupt but I'm studying architecture for my degree.'

She knelt and placed her hand flat upon the floor. 'These stones are not worn enough to be medieval. More like eighteenth century. I'd say we're in a stately home,' she said. 'Just look at the size of this cellar. Once upon a time, they must have stored enough wine down here to get a whole town drunk.'

The Italian girl, Stefania Moreno, folded her arms and turned away, her long black hair swirling. 'What is the point of these games? It's all guesswork.' She pouted.

'Honey,' said Prentiss, 'the good Lord gave us brains to use so let's not disappoint him. Know thine enemy – and one day we may get a chance to cap him with our knowledge. Okay?'

Greet Stoll of Holland had her hand raised. 'Did anyone notice a strange smell as we were carried from the van that brought us here?'

'I'm not sure how you say it in English but it smelled like *schwefel*,' said Hanna Hansen.

'Sulphur,' translated Greet, quietly. 'Are we near a chemical plant?'

'A stately home near a chemical plant? It doesn't sound kosher,' said Prentiss. 'A garden bonfire, perhaps? It is the fall, after all. Anyway, let's file sulphur away for future reference.'

'It's also the smell of Hell,' said Maiken Grenske in her plodding English.

'Honey,' said Prentiss, tiredly, 'I'd just as soon you kept that tidbit under your hairdo.'

The girls' animated chatter tailed off as the top door opened and the slim, silent mystery man came down the steps unarmed but flanked by two helmeted men carrying guns. The gate was unchained and the three advanced into the cellar.

'I want the American girl to come forward,' said the slim man.

'Welsh,' Fran Pilkington muttered immediately. 'He sounds like a character in a Dylan Thomas play.'

Upstairs, Lucius had made his preparations and told the others, 'We ought to begin with the American. The representative of the most powerful nation on earth will create the largest stir.'

Prentiss Decker froze. Why her? What was happening? She experienced a moment of heartsink, knowing there was no place to hide, but she stepped forward. 'Well, what do you want?'

No one replied. They took her beyond the iron grille, rechained the gate, placed a mask over her eyes and steered her upstairs.

Chapter Twenty-five

The Chief Constable of Kent swiftly extended an invitation to an outside force and by 9.30 a.m. cars and helicopters were ferrying members of the anti-terrorist squad and an augmented Scotland Yard scene-of-crime team of forensic scientists and fingerprint experts into sleepy Birchington.

Close behind them panted the reporters, the forerunners of a legion descending upon London from the farthest ends of the globe. The Concorde and jumbo flights from New York were jammed with media stars and television crews, summoned by agitated London bureaux. The *Paris Match* team flew in by private Lear jet to Biggin Hill and, finding themselves on the right side of the great metropolitan sprawl, were among the first of the international circus to reach Birchington.

Affronted at being kept by the British police at a distance from the juggernaut in which they felt a proprietorial interest, the Frenchmen fell back upon their formidable ingenuity. The celebrated *Paris Match* war photographer, Marcel Danzinger, sprinted along the pavements of the town centre until he found a fashionable ladies' shoe store where he purchased a glistening pair of red evening shoes with six-inch stiletto heels. His heart-jerking photograph of a single red shoe, heel broken by some unseen agency, abandoned mutely on the gravel car park, with the juggernaut forming the background, was later to win him an international prize – and to waste a great deal of police time. They, naïve fellows, had threatened Marcel with prosecution for withholding vital evidence until the resourceful ways of modern journalism were whispered to them.

However, the action did not remain in Birchington for long.

From a bed in the local hospital where he, the Watchman and the juggernaut driver had been taken suffering from shock, the river pilot put detectives on the trail of the ferryboat *Freda*.

'I might have been blind and deaf,' he told them, 'but you can take it from me the *Freda* headed downstream. The Thames smells different below and above the Pool of London – and the bastards didn't think to bung up my nostrils.'

The *Freda* was found moored in its usual berth on the Essex bank. A regular member of the crew, washing down the deck, was startled to have two burly men in plainclothes take a run at him and snatch the hose-pipe from his hands. They looked at each other in dismay. If there had been any clues to the fate of the girls and their coach, they had just been sluiced into the river. 'The guv'nor's going to go ballistic,' said one.

Nevertheless, the police began to feel that progress was being made. The two Thames Navigation Service radar operators, who had shared the responsibility of getting the *Freda* safely down-river, gave a precise commentary on the ferryboat's movements of the previous day. Consequently, the papermill was pinpointed and the beef discovered.

The French juggernaut driver supplied a vague description of the hijack girl but the Watchman was still incoherent. Were the boat and the empty juggernaut with its sinister rows of meat hooks just a blind? The pilot said he had caught a whiff of perfume on a section of the road journey after he had been carried off the *Freda*. He could have been sharing his plight with the girls. But had he been spoofed? The gang had pulled off an outstanding deception yesterday. They were not to be regarded as natural blunderers.

These and other questions were being asked at noon by a man with an exhausted face and a pressing headache. He sat with his back to the marble fireplace in the Cabinet Room at Number 10, Downing Street, exasperated in the extreme at this unseemly drama.

Attending this meeting of the Cabinet Emergencies Committee were the Foreign Secretary, the Home Secretary, the Defence Minister with his military advisers, the head of MI5, and Sir Travers Horder, the Metropolitan Police Commissioner, widely known as Old Law and Horder.

The Prime Minister was saying, 'This is all so embarrassing. A few minutes ago I took a call from the President of the United

States – and you all know how international terrorism gets him going. He's offering us the CIA and any of their specialized equipment we may require. Two senior officers are flying to London today and they'll be joining the head of station in Grosvenor Square early this evening. Naturally, I've thanked the President while at the same time making it clear that we're trying to weed our own garden.' The security and police chiefs stared impassively at their blotters. 'We shall look complete idiots if we fail to sort out this shambles for ourselves.'

The Prime Minister looked around the table with, for him, an unusually cynical expression. 'The President says that, even though an American national is at risk here, he'll back me all the way if I refuse to have any truck with the abductors' demands. This is also the gist of messages I have received from both the German Chancellor and the President of France.'

The Foreign Secretary smoothly inserted himself into the proceedings. 'Prime Minister, I have to inform you that since nine this morning I have received representations from every foreign mission in London with a direct interest in the outcome. And I regret to say that not a few were sharply critical of the security arrangements.'

'I hope you put a flea in their ears,' said the Prime Minister sharply. 'The United Kingdom is not an armed camp with its citizens subject to curfew.' He directed a cool glance at the Police Commissioner, a man appointed during his predecessor's time. 'What has happened is a unique act of terrorism. It may require from us, of course, a massive act of courage. We shall negotiate, but we will not submit to demands from the kidnappers.'

The Prime Minister turned once again to the Commissioner who, he could see, was trying hard to conceal his dislike. 'What news do you have for us, Commissioner?'

Sir Travers, his voice a rumble, said, 'We still await the terrorists' demands, Prime Minister. It is unusual for so long a period to go by without the perpetrators at least claiming the criminal act as their own. We can only speculate that, with such a large number of victims on their hands, they are having difficulty in handling them. Unfortunately, the hours that elapsed before the disappearance of the coach could be confirmed as a crime make the search area vast. They may still be in central London or even out of the country. At this moment a road-block operation is in progress from John O'Groats to Land's End. All outward bound vessels still in home waters are being stopped and searched. Here and now I would make application to you for the assistance of the military, civil-defence personnel and the Territorial Army. Until we find the perpetrators, we can't contain them.'

The Prime Minister passed on to the head of MI5, Britain's spy-catching secret service. 'We've been in close consultation with Special Branch,' said the Director General, 'and the odd fact that emerges is that there is no odd fact. We have two IRA cells under full-time surveillance and we can categorically state that they are not involved. The Palestinians in this country are dormant, as are the Moluccans, the Red Brigade and the remnants of the Baader Meinhoff gang. We have no knowledge of any terror group with a current grudge against Her Majesty's government deep-seated enough to warrant such an outrageous act.'

An aide from the Cabinet Office had entered and was advancing down the room to murmur into the Prime Minister's ear.

The PM held up a hand, palm outward. 'My apologies, but I'm told the Commissioner has a vital telephone call.'

The aide plugged the telephone into a wall socket and placed it in front of Sir Travers. All eyes rested on him. The Commissioner relished his moment. He listened, replaced the receiver and said, 'They've made contact.'

Prentiss Decker tried to register as much information as she could despite her restricted senses. She silently counted her steps, including a flight of twenty-four upwards from the ground floor which, judging by the hard, slapping noise her espadrilles made, were either stone or marble. Perhaps Tilly Jo Evans had hit the bullseye with her stately-home theory.

Invisible hands steered her forward and she heard a door close behind her. Then she was made to duck her head. The Welsh voice said, 'Stand where you are.' They had not bothered to tape her mask this time and, below the rim where it touched her cheeks, she was suddenly aware of a harsh line of brilliant light.

The mask came off with a jerk and Prentiss was left blinking in the dazzle of two arc lights. When her eyes had adjusted she saw that she was inside a blue, family-sized tent. The interior was airless and, as she had not felt fresh air on her face while she was being brought to this place, she deduced that it had been erected within a room.

Beyond the arc lights stood three shadowy figures in their helmets. One, judging by the chest bulge, was Nanny. A fourth, the Welshman, was fiddling with the jacks on a cable linking a tripod-mounted video camera. She could see the built-in condenser microphone. They were shooting vision and sound. Prentiss almost screamed with excitement: she needed time to think. She sank to the floor with a low moan. 'Please let me have some water. I'm feeling weird.'

Nanny swore, unzipped the tent flap and went out. There was nothing to be seen through the flap: the outer room was in darkness.

By the time Prentiss had allowed her captors to revive her and lift her back to her feet, she had decided what to do. She felt her first tremor of hope. But there was an appalling risk.

The Welshman cut into her frantic interior debate. 'I'm going to video-record you,' he said. 'First, you will hold up this news-paper while I zoom in and establish the date.'

He placed the *Express* between her fingertips, the headline, VANISHED – ALL BUT ONE, facing towards the lens. A warm relief flooded Prentiss. The world was still out there, caring and reacting.

'Then,' he went on, 'I shall put you in focus while you read off these cards.'

A stack of idiot boards, the kidnappers' message blocked out in three-inch letters in Magic Marker, was propped against the tripod.

'After you've put down the newspaper, you will keep your hands at your sides and make no arm movements of any kind. Is that understood?'

Prentiss nodded.

'And, of course, you will not deviate by as much as a syllable from what is on the cards. If you do, the video will be rewound and we shall start again. You will also be severely punished. Is that understood?'

Prentiss nodded again. God, I'm going to look a wreck, she thought.

The Welshman said, 'Begin when you see the red light on the top of the camera.' He trained the lens at her upper body and brought the *Express* into focus, with Prentiss's delectable nose and eyes clearly visible above the edge of the paper. Then, obediently, she let her arms drop to her sides and began to read the message:

'This is communication Number One from the Colonel Blood Raiding Group.' The name had been Lucius's idea.

'As you can see, I am alive and being treated well – as are my sister captives. Our captors wish first of all to issue an assurance to the governments of the countries from which we come: the morning newspapers and Scotland Yard are not correct. Our captors are not terrorists. They have no political motives whatsoever. They are a group of people who have banded together to raise a sum of money. Once they have it, they promise to release us unharmed. They are realistic enough to appreciate that, from that moment, there will be an open season in the hunt to track them down and recover the money. They accept this is an inevitable risk arising from their actions.'

Prentiss came to the end of a card and watched Nanny slip it from the front to the back of the pile.

Prentiss continued: 'The ransom money must be assembled in London in a basket of currencies that may include US dollars, sterling, Deutschmarks, Swiss and French francs. The notes must not be sequential and must not be of extraordinary denomination. In value they must come no lower than the equivalent of a hundred-dollar bill or any higher than the equivalent of a thousand-dollar bill.

'The sums demanded are based on the prosperity of the countries involved and it is of no concern to our captors whether the money is provided from official funds or by subscription from members of the public who have sympathy for the peril we face.'

Nanny changed the card again.

'I will now read off, country by country, the sums demanded: United States of America, two million dollars, West Germany, one million dollars, United Kingdom, one million dollars, France, one million dollars . . .'

Lucius watched through his viewfinder as the grave-faced girl worked down the list, her rapidly blinking eyes betraying her nervousness when Jessie changed the cards. Lucius checked the recorder. The tape wound inexorably onward.

Oddly, there had been no wild exhilaration among the kidnappers the previous night once the cellar door had slammed on the girls. Lucius had, without Bruiser's permission, helped himself to two bottles of Dom Perignon and rushed into the dining room, shouting, 'Marvellous! Marvellous! Let's celebrate!'

Rolly had arrived and they were slumped in Constanza's overstuffed chairs. Bruiser, Rolly and Dickie gazed up sourly. Bruiser turned to Teddy Triggs. 'Cut along to the kitchen with your friend and give yourselves a drink. We have some business to talk over here.'

Teddy and Jessie retired, deflated. Bruiser peeled off his porter's jacket and said, 'All the uniforms must be burned in the morning, the buttons taken a long way and dropped into a drain.' He turned to Lucius and added, 'I should imagine that by now half-a-million men are looking for us.'

Lucius had put down the champagne and poured himself a large Scotch instead. He listened while Bruiser sketched in the story of Marble's death and the fate of Hotel Five. Later Bruiser had quartered them all in upstairs bedrooms, with a firm injunction to keep the shutters closed. The house was to appear sparsely occupied. Triggs was left on a camp bed outside the cellar door and armed with the cattle prod. Bruiser also gave him a whistle. 'Use this if there's a panic. I'll leave my bedroom door open . . .' Lucius had closed his own door but remained in his clothes throughout the long night.

The American girl was coming to the end of her recital of ransom demands . . . 'the island of Aruba: four hundred thousand dollars.'

Prentiss paused because there was a gap on the card. Then she added, 'Our captors appreciate that transferring these sums to London must take a week – and that is the length of time they are allowing you. Arrangements for delivery will be communicated later. Failure to comply with these demands will, it hardly needs saying, result in terrible consequences for me and the other girls.'

Prentiss hesitated minutely on 'consequences' and then finished tonelessly. Lucius switched off the camera and said, 'Stay exactly where you are.' He hit the fast forward button and the video-tape spun madly until he pressed stop.

'What you've read out was for public consumption,' he told Prentiss. 'Now comes the private message to the police.'

The red light came on again and Prentiss read the short paragraph from a fresh card. 'All communications should be inserted in the personal column of the London *Times* and be signed "Lord Grey".'

Concocting the messages earlier, Dickie Biggs-Salter had objected: 'They won't see your little postscript after the tape runs blank.'

Lucius had explained, commendably keeping a patronizing note out of his voice: 'Every inch of that tape will be under intense examination in the national police laboratory before the day is out. They won't miss a thing.'

Lucius Frankel was wrong He hadn't reckoned with the American girl, Prentiss Decker.

Sir Travers Horder finished his recital to the Cabinet Emergencies Committee, referring to the notes he had made with his thin gold pen.

'Well, that's something of a relief,' said the Foreign Secretary, a pragmatic man. 'At least we're not dealing with a bunch of fanatics. If you can talk money with a chap, you can also talk sense.'

The Prime Minister was pondering. 'Did you notice that the poor girl refers only to "*my sister captives*". There's no mention of the policemen. I don't like that.'

He thrust out his chin. 'Anyway, that message is manifestly an attempt to whip up public sympathy as a prelude to the

172

money-raising exercise. Well, these scoundrels will get no quarter from me. The government will not be a party to ransom payments.'

He turned to the Home Secretary. 'Obviously, you may now stand down the anti-terrorist squad and hand over the responsibility for finding these impudent devils to regular CID officers. Meanwhile, the details of that video-tape will not be published. I'm not going to give the swine that satisfaction.' The PM thumped the table with his fist.

Always a cautionary sign, thought the Foreign Secretary, glumly. He said, 'Prime Minister, I do have a difficulty. I'm faced with forty-eight friendly powers offering assistance and demanding to be put in the picture. I simply have to throw them a bone before the day is out.'

The PM suggested, with a touch of malice, 'Why don't you put up the Commissioner here to sprinkle bromide in their early-evening cocktails? Just keep the *corps diplomatique* from under foot while his men are given room to work. Let's try to lower the temperature for a few days.'

The Home Secretary asked the Commissioner, 'Who will you put in charge?'

But before the Commissioner could reply, the PM said crisply, 'Surely, it has to be Ringrose.'

'Commander Ringrose is on annual leave, sir,' said the Commissioner, hardly able to contain his fury at his prerogative being usurped. 'He has able deputies.'

'Commissioner,' said the PM patiently, 'this is no time to be fielding the second eleven. Both the Home Secretary and I will have to go down to the House of Commons soon and answer Members' questions on this matter. We shall be able to shut up the honourable members all the more effectively if we can say that the Ringer has assumed charge of the investigation. He commands an enormous amount of public respect, you know. It's for your final decision, of course, but I'd suggest you find him and tell him to put away his bucket and spade and come home.'

The Prime Minister stood up to terminate the discussion. Gathering up his spectacle-case and notes, he said suddenly, 'By the way, how did the video-cassette reach you?'

'An anonymous male with a Welsh accent telephoned Lambeth Palace,' said the Commissioner, 'and an aide to the Archbishop of Canterbury went to the neighbouring graveyard and discovered it concealed behind Captain Bligh of the *Bounty*'s tomb.'

The PM exited, shaking his head. He turned back with an afterthought. 'Why don't you all go out of the front door together? It'll please the photographers, and our overseas friends will get the idea that we're doing something.' There was nothing lacking in the PM's nose for public relations.

His colleagues stumped out obediently. The Foreign Secretary put a consoling arm round the Commissioner's shoulder. 'I'm sorry the PM stood you in a corner, Travers, but he's right about Ringrose, you know. Good man to have on your side.'

'It's not that,' wailed the Commissioner. 'The bloody man's on holiday in Corsica.'

'My dear chap,' soothed the Foreign Secretary, 'just send me over the details and I'll have the PM give Jacques Chirac a ring.'

Tom Ringrose's successes as a murder investigator had rapidly come to the attention of the popular press – and so had his nickname. There were two theories as to how he had acquired his sobriquet. The first was that it was a corruption of his surname, the second that criminals dreaded his ring on their doorbells. Neither was true, although the wrongdoers' dread was real enough.

Ringer has another meaning: a person who substitutes one object for a fake. As a detective sergeant, Tom Ringrose had once, in a moment of compassion, risked his job. A civilian store detective had brought into the station a plump, snivelling girl of seventeen and laid a charge that she had shoplifted a bottle of liquid make-up. Ringrose had looked at the jar, then at the girl, and said, 'Do you have to lay a charge? You've already frightened her out of her wits.'

'Sorry,' said the store detective. 'I don't make the rules. It's company policy to prosecute all offenders.'

Ringrose handed him a statement form to complete and strolled into the CID secretary's cubicle. Suddenly galvanized, he slipped the secretary a ten-pound note and sent her out for a replica of the stolen jar. When she returned, Ringrose scuffed the label and poured half the contents into a handful of paper tissues. The store detective was still writing when Ringrose made the switch.

Some time later, he said, 'Half a mo'! Is this a new jar?'

'Of course it is – she lifted it straight off the counter.'

The girl began to blub harder.

Ringrose unscrewed the cap. 'This is a used bottle.' He looked askance at the store detective. 'Christ, you've pinched a kid for "stealing" her own make-up.'

He'd ushered out the shaken store detective and taken the girl into his office. 'Now I know you did it, and you know you did it.' The girl nodded dumbly. 'I want your promise that you'll never do anything wicked again.'

The girl nodded once more. Ringrose handed her the liquid make-up jar and a handkerchief to dry her eyes. Then he kissed her right in the middle of the port-wine stain that disfigured half of her face and saw her out into the busy high street.

The Mystère-Falcon taxied onto the apron at Northolt where Ringrose could see his personal aide, Detective Inspector Lionel Firth, waiting by the car. He did not have to look to know that the dazzlingly efficient Firth would already have the rear seat upholstered in statements.

Ringrose gave his wife and daughters an apologetic hug and saw them into an RAF car to take them home.

His own car turned out of the aerodrome's main gate. The driver put his foot down and the siren on. 'Turn that thing off, would you, driver? I can't hear myself think,' said Commander Ringrose. He hated fuss.

Firth, a dark-eyed whippet who'd barely made the five foot eight minimum-height qualification for the Metropolitan Police, was saying, 'This one's a real cow, guv'nor. We've been turning over all the regular firms since last night but all we have so far is zero feedback. I think we're up against a whole new outfit, possibly Continental.'

Ringrose speedread the statements and summaries as the car hurtled towards London.

'They want us to sign ourselves "Lord Grey"? Is that the lights-of-Europe-are-going-out Lord Grey?'

'I don't think so,' said Lionel. 'I've discovered another. He's a character in Shakespeare's *Richard the Third*. The kidnap gang appear to be feeding us rather a good line from the Bard about themselves. It goes, "A knot you are of damned blood-suckers." Cheeky buggers.'

'Cheeky *educated* buggers,' corrected his commander. 'Let's go directly to the Colonel Blood Inn. There's a question bothering me.'

Commander Ringrose said to Rebecca Engelman, 'Now, I know my men have asked you questions until you're dizzy but please don't be cross with me if I ask you a couple more.'

He was alone with her. He could hear her bodyguards arguing with Firth outside in the corridor. He took her hand – she was a wonderful-looking girl, despite the red-rimmed eyes. He said softly, 'Now you're an intelligent lass, Rebecca, and I'm sure that it has occurred to you that these criminals could not have pulled off this remarkable feat without some help from inside. And I'm sure you're also intelligent enough to know that you, the only girl left unscathed, must raise certain suspicions.' He held her hand tighter. 'Now, tell me really why you wouldn't have the doctor called when you were sick yesterday morning?''

'I've already said. I didn't think it necessary,' said Rebecca fearfully.

Ringrose shook his head kindly. 'No, Rebecca, that's a fib. You were very sick but you were afraid of the doctor.'

'Oh God!' Her head dropped until her brow was touching the back of Ringrose's hand. The confession came in a rush. 'I think I'm pregnant. I was sick again this morning.'

At last she looked honestly into his soft brown eyes. 'I've been secretly married for the past year. If the Queen of the Earth organizers got to know, I'd be disqualified. It's a contest for single girls.'

Sick a second time? Yesterday's nausea had to have been deliberately induced to get her personal gunslingers out of the way.

Ringrose's mind ranged over the possibilities. Was Rebecca confusing pregnancy symptoms with a planned poisoning? Five minutes later he called in Firth and opened the door of the refrigerator. 'Have that jug examined and the rest of the orange juice analysed,' he said.

It was the only breakfast utensil that had not been cleared away on two successive days.

Chapter Twenty-six

The inquiries of the Birmingham Police had quickly established the hollow nature of Regal Roadways. Only fifteen pounds remained in the firm's account and a cheque issued to the owners of the ferryboat *Freda* had just bounced.

Ringrose examined the correspondence brought to him from the Queen of the Earth's Belgrave Square headquarters. The original letter from the non-existent managing director, Robert Ainsworth, bore a comment from Lady Cornmorris scribbled in the margin: 'This offer sounds too good to be true! N.C.' Ringrose smiled grimly.

There were a number of internal memos in the file and it was clearly established therein that the fateful decision to accept the two coaches for free had been made by Arthur Emblem and Alan Jay Jaffe.

Within five hours of touching down at Northolt, Commander Ringrose had made out his list and one of his senior officers was on the way to the Home Office, to which the Home Secretary returned from a dinner engagement to sign a number of phone surveillance orders. They were immediately put into operation by a secret department operating from British Telecom's centre in Newgate Street in the City of London.

There was only one non-issue item of furniture in Commander Ringrose's office: a black leather Eames chair with footrest that Helen had bought him for his forty-fifth birthday. He'd sat down with a bump when he learned the price. But this had become his thinking chair. After a long, eventful day, Ringrose stretched himself on it and began to use it for its primary purpose.

Firth remained next door within calling distance. Two miles away the presses were turning with the first editions of next morning's papers. 'The Ringer Takes Charge' was the most popular headline.

Ringrose was still wearing his vacation clothes: a policeman had been dispatched to his home to raid his wardrobe.

He had earlier seen the video-tape, which had already been scrutinized by police engineers, scientists and a psychologist. His heart went out to the American lass, enunciating the kidnappers' demands into the camera with barely a falter. He imagined Prentiss Decker as one of his own daughters and a rare fury twisted his gut. God knows what the bastards were doing to her and the others. But Ringrose had to put such emotive speculation out of his mind. What did he have to show so far?

The tape had yielded little in the way of physical evidence. It was of the two-hour type, manufactured in millions. The psychologist's report told him what he had just deduced for himself but without the jargon: whoever had composed the ransom message was a person of education, able to marshal thoughts and communicate directly with some knowledge of the financial world – 'basket of currencies' was not a term in general usage. The Captain Blood gang were also in a confident – not to say cocksure – mood. Their operation to seize the girls must have gone well, as indicated by the tone of supreme insouciance concerning the 'open season in the hunt to track them down'.

The word 'educated' came up again as he pored over the river pilot's statement. The brandy his abductors had given him was 'of the best'. And the man feeding it to him had said it was good for *mal de mer*. Most people would have said 'sea sickness'.

Ringrose barely gave a glance to the E-Fit sketches, prepared by Yard artists from witnesses' descriptions of the two coach drivers, the 'distressed' girl on the Dover Road and the man on the bridge of the *Freda* who had welcomed the pilot aboard at the Tower.

He'd have the prints released to the media in the morning but he doubted that the likenesses any longer resembled the kidnappers' true appearances. He was not about to underestimate the buggers.

Ringrose had in his mind three versions of the telephone conversations between 'Glyn Owain' and the Grosvenor House Hotel: those of Lady Cornmorris, Alan Jay Jaffe and Arthur Emblem. Two statements agreed on one small detail that indicated the extent of the gang's inside knowledge. Jaffe had introduced himself on the telephone only as the 'public relations officer'. But later, in the negotiations to have the girls returned, 'Glyn Owain' had addressed Jaffe by his name.

By now, too, on the first day of his investigation, he was as sure as he could be of the method used by the abductors to subdue and carry off at least fifty healthy young people. The Welsh male voice and the unusual business with the ear-plugs had provided the indicators that linked the crime with the hitherto inexplicable hijacking of a vanload of medical gases.

Ringrose permitted himself a low whistle when he read the print-out from the computer that had done the detective work and made the connection. The kidnappers were damnably stylish.

Ringrose had also sorted through a score of claims to have spotted the missing coach. Some were plainly mistaken, some had merely seen the second coach on its to-ing and fro-ing. He extracted only one that he regarded as reliable.

The flow of vehicles in and out of central London is controlled by a series of television cameras, positioned at strategic road junctions, and a computer that operates the traffic lights. This automatic traffic system is supervised from the central communications complex at the Yard. A young constable who had been monitoring screens on the day of the snatch had come forward to say that on the Tower Hill cameras he had seen the coach cross the bridge from south to north at some time between noon and 1 p.m.

During traffic surveys, the views from the monitor screens are sometimes video-taped. But not that day. Ringrose sighed. But he believed the constable: the boy had noted the coach because of its sleek appearance.

Ringrose placed a red-ink circle on the map. It embraced a vast tract of the riverside east of Tower Bridge and north of the river. Whatever had happened to the coach and Hotel Five had happened somewhere there. He would have the search beefed up at dawn.

He had one other overnight preparation to make. Firth entered with a cup of thickly brewed tea. Ringrose said, 'Lionel, I want you to telephone the Lord Mayor of London – get him out of bed if you have to. He threw a dinner for the girls and the Queen of the Earth organization on the evening prior to the kidnapping. Through him I want you to track down every photographer who took pictures at the event. I've attended some of those Guildhall dinners myself and there's always at least one official cameraman taking pictures at the reception and of the groups at the tables. I want every roll of film printed up in the order the photographs were taken, and I want every photograph marked with the approximate time it was taken.'

'The Lord Mayor's going to love me, rousing him at this time of night.'

'Just tell him the Prime Minister presents his compliments,' said Ringrose drily.

Indeed, the Prime Minister had presented his compliments: 'Commander,' he'd said, 'I want you to know my prayers are with you – and, more than that, my active concern. Just remember, if you encounter any hindrance from whatever quarter, you have my full authority backing you. And I'm always within distance of a telephone if you should need my personal intervention.'

Ringrose had hung up thinking that Old Law and Horder would have apoplexy if he should ever find out how he had been circumvented.

It was 1 a.m. Ringrose slipped off his sandals and transferred himself to his camp bed and slept the sleep of the righteous. You didn't solve major crimes by turning yourself into a zombie.

Chapter Twenty-seven

Sir Travers Horder, arriving in his official limousine, was appalled. There must have been eighty cameramen who leaped forward as he alighted and as many journalists hurling questions at him in a variety of tongues and accents. He was accustomed to being treated with more respect for his high office. In any case, a news blackout had been placed on the investigation. Sir Travers forced his way, white-lipped, through the unseemly throng.

Inside the Yard, his press bureau chief was haggard from twenty-four hours of continuous harassment. 'I'm sorry, sir,' he told the Commissioner, 'but they're going to have to be told something very soon. Hostile stories are already appearing abroad and it's not going to get any better. As of nine this morning I have had four hundred and eighty applications for press accreditation and every plane is bringing in more media people. The big hotels are filling up. You'll appreciate that this is the most dramatic crime to hit the country since the Yorkshire Ripper murders.'

'Four hundred and eighty?' Sir Travers sat back in his chair and pondered. 'All right. Get as many of them as you can into the fifth-floor briefing room and I'll come along at eleven. And try to get them to behave, would you? And if Commander Ringrose is in the building, would you please have him step this way.'

The two hundred lucky pressmen crammed into the briefing room raised an ironic cheer as the Commissioner made an entrance in his splendid blue silver-buttoned uniform. He'd considered carrying his swagger cane but thought better of it.

The Commissioner took the oak lectern and raised his hands

in a mute appeal for silence. 'Where's the Ringer?' shouted an impudent voice.

The Commissioner glared. 'I am speaking to you because, as I'm sure you will understand, Commander Ringrose has other things on his mind. It is inevitable that many of our inquiries must take place secretly but I can tell you that the police forces of this country have combined to mount the largest search operation ever seen in war or peace time. Moors, forests, caves, mines, quarries, remote buildings, abandoned airfields and other military installations, in fact buildings anywhere in town or country large enough to conceal the kidnap victims are being combed.'

'So it is a kidnapping?' asked a totally bald man from *Stern* magazine.

'Yes,' said the Commissioner. 'It's a non-political criminal act associated in no way with any terror organization.'

The room exploded into hubbub.

'Commissioner,' said the *Times*, bellowing above the maelstrom, 'have they made contact and have they identified themselves?'

'Yes, they have made contact. No, they have not identified themselves beyond giving us a code-name.'

Now all the reporters were scribbling furiously. 'We have their word, and their word only, that the girls are safe and well. They have made no mention of the missing men and we're trying to make contact again for further information on that point.'

'Sir!' It was a middle-aged man with clipped grey hair and gold-rimmed half-moon spectacles, his manicured hand raised. 'Yes, Mr Wallace?'

Everyone knew Murray Wallace, the veteran correspondent of the *New York Times*.

'May we know what demands the kidnappers are making for the safe return of the hostages?'

'The demand is for money. The motive is profit. But beyond that I am not at liberty to go.'

'Why not?' shouted a score of voices.

The Commissioner raised his hands again for order. 'Representatives of all the concerned governments are being called to a meeting at Lancaster House this afternoon where the Prime Minister will make the British government's position known and when he will give full details of the nature of the demands. It is a matter of international courtesy that the heads of state of the forty-eight other countries involved should be given the news first.'

The British crime reporters groaned loudly. The *Daily Mail*'s crime man summed up their dilemma: 'The diplomatic and lobby correspondents are going to beat us to the fucking story.'

The three Cockneys were gathered round the butler's television set. Even the normally sacrosanct Saturday afternoon sporting fixtures were being interrupted to bring live to viewers the Prime Minister at Lancaster House, a traditional conference centre for diplomats accredited to the Court of St James.

As a sop to growing public concern, Whitehall officials had also permitted entry to the meeting to the tearful group of the missing girls' relatives who, for the past twenty-four hours, had been streaming through Heathrow airport and taking up vigil at the Colonel Blood Inn as guests of the Queen of the Earth organizers.

The three looked at each other uneasily as television news cameras revealed the extent of the hunt in progress. Troops had been called in to aid the civil authorities and Britain, as portrayed on the screens, was beginning to look as if it was under martial law.

Endless pictures of roadblocks and vehicle checks followed shots of long lines of men beating across moorland and through wooded areas. There was news, too, of communities every-where raising weekend search parties of civilian volunteers. Teddy Triggs said, 'Blimey, I hope that idea don't catch on round here.'

He, Lenny and Jessie were becoming fretful at being confined inside a dark musty house. Before anyone could go out on an errand, the big toff who owned the place reconnoitred his own grounds. Twice already they'd been delayed because gardeners were outside raking the first of the season's fallen leaves. They were resentful, too, at the imposition of unaccustomed labour. It was Teddy and Lenny, sweating under their helmets, who had to haul the stinking chemical lavatories upstairs and empty the contents. And Jessie had become the cook. She listlessly stirred catering-sized cans of soup in huge copper pots and warmed sheets of frozen ravioli in the microwave.

The toffs had dumped boxes of apples in the kitchen, picked from local orchards. Each girl was to have one a day. The big guy was most insistent on that. Even in prison those cows were pampered. Jessie felt aggrieved.

She and the others were even more aggrieved when the Prime Minister's conference was over. They'd watched a document being handed to each diplomat, watched the PM talking to anxious groups of relatives and even giving the unhappy mother of Frenchy Bonaventure a comforting hug. They watched him make a fighting speech and then watched and listened grimly as the commentator, having got his hands on the document, read out the kidnappers' demands. Jessie had told them what was coming.

The commentator worked down the country-by-country list and said, 'If my arithmetic is correct, the total being demanded is twenty-five million dollars, or in excess of sixteen million pounds sterling. You've just heard the Prime Minister say that the government will have no part in raising such a sum.'

'Those greedy sods!' exclaimed Jessie. 'We're getting peanuts compared to that.'

In the sitting room, Lucius Frankel turned in a cold fury to face the others. 'He's deliberately withholding the video-tape. He knows that once the plight of the girls is brought home so vividly on television they'll just have to cave in and find the money.' He thought for a moment. 'All right, if that's how they want to play it, here's what we do . . .'

Bruiser, Rolly and Dickie had to agree. It meant a colossal effort for the remainder of the weekend but Lucius's counter-attack was damned clever.

Prentiss Decker had nursed her secret for something like twenty-four hours. She ached to tell the other girls but she was also loath to raise a hope that might be extinguished. And there were so many girls. Could they all keep a secret?

She looked around: the television millions would hardly recognize them as proud beauties now. They'd been fed and watered like farmyard animals but no washing facilities had been made available. She'd appealed to Nanny who had laughed unpleasantly and jabbed the cattle prod at her. Prentiss fell backwards to escape the brain-jarring sting.

They had made yet another minute examination of their prison, had rejected the air shafts as being too narrow to admit even the slimmest body, and had finally concluded that the only exit was through the cellar door.

A numbing lassitude had set in, broken only by sounds of petty squabbles. Here Monika Dahlberg from Sweden had proved a heroine. Back home in Gothenburg, the giant blonde was an aerobics instructor and now she was bullying girls out of their depression and organizing them into classes. Whenever she had a dozen lined up, she ordered them out of their baggy boiler suits and began to put them through their paces. Prentiss had joined a workout group and afterwards felt energized. Monika and Juvenal were right. *Mens sana in corpore sano.*

They all needed to remain alert and in physical trim. Perhaps a chance might come that they could seize . . .

At the other end of the cellar, the Roman Catholics softly muttered their fervent prayers in their do-it-yourself chapel. The queen from Mexico, Caterina Rosario, had removed one of her coral-pink plastic fingernails and was using it to shape a crucifix by chipping away at old, crusted whitewash on the alcove wall. And this was the focus for all their entreaties.

The Swiss girl, Vera Lankermeyer, a vivid redhead, had revealed herself as a skilled tap-dancer and was demonstrating a time-step to a small knot of interested queens. Time was passing and morale was keeping up.

Prentiss felt proud: they weren't going to fall to pieces. She laughed when Fran Pilkington, brought up on too many late-night television war movies, walked across to her and said, 'Don't you think we ought to elect an escape officer?'

Prentiss had already made her first bid for freedom but that, still, was her secret. Later, after the girls had been taken upstairs one by one, she wished she had shared her knowledge sooner.

186

Chapter Twenty-eight

There is a somnolent quality about Victoria Street on Sunday mornings. Small knots of tourists and the faithful drift towards Anglican service at Westminster Abbey at the eastern end and to Roman Catholic Mass at the over-elaborate Victorian-Byzantine cathedral several hundred yards westward. At each, prayers of intercession for the kidnap victims were said.

There was, however, one group thronging the fast-food cafés of Victoria Street whose thoughts were on anything but divine intervention: the ladies and gentlemen of the world's media.

Just off Victoria Street, Scotland Yard was under siege. Every exit had now been subjected to press surveillance for more than forty-eight hours, with the comings and goings of senior police officers recorded and photographed and futile attempts made to extract progress reports from them as they went about their inquiries.

At 11 a.m. a white van advertising a firm of carpet cleaners drew up at a side entrance and three men in workmen's nylon coats manhandled a foam-making machine into the building. The Central Intelligence Agency's head of London station and his two Langley colleagues had made an unremarked arrival.

The Commissioner's briefing to Ringrose had been succinct. 'Our political masters want a show of cordiality and co-operation. Give these chaps a run-through of what we know, but they're not to see the video-tape. This crime has taken place on our pitch and we're going to solve it. We don't want a bunch of bloody cowboys swaggering in and taking the credit.'

Ringrose was embarrassed. The CIA head was an old friend and they had helped each other in the past, most notably on the Pan-Am hostess slayings.

'Tom,' said Jake Bishop, 'I want you to meet Paul Zaentz

and Parker Dodsworth. We're here to help in any way we can.'

Ringrose was well aware of Zaentz and Dodsworth's dazzling intellectual and field achievements. He shook hands warmly and introduced them to his aide. For an hour he conscientiously reviewed the evidence, while Firth fetched files. Ringrose said, 'We're dealing with a group of highly sophisticated people, possibly international in origin, and it is on that likelihood that you could perhaps best concentrate your resources. Our own security services are, of course, already making extensive overseas checks themselves.'

'Do we get to see the video-tape?' asked Bishop.

Ringrose tried not to look evasive. 'It's still being examined in the laboratory, I'm afraid.' The three men briefly exchanged glances.

'But this is noteworthy.' Ringrose handed over a photograph of Prentiss Decker holding up a copy of Friday's *Express*. Her eyelids were closed. 'This is an electronically enhanced picture taken from a single frame at the beginning of the tape. After she had shown the newspaper to the camera to establish the date, she made no gestures for the remainder of her recital, which she was apparently reading from an off-camera idiot board.' He took a pencil and made a circle on the glossy. 'Those three tiny black stars under the paper's masthead indicate that this copy of the paper was circulated in London and the Home Counties. For a while, what with employment of the ferryboat and finding the juggernaut at a coastal resort, we could not dismiss the possibility that they had been wafted out of the country, but your girl must have been filmed holding that paper some time after 7 a.m. on Friday, which is about the earliest time the kidnappers could have bought, or had delivered, a copy of that three-star edition. If they had made it as far as the continent, the girl would be holding a one-star.' Ringrose put down his pencil. 'My gut tells me they're in Britain.'

The three CIA agents carried their carpet-cleaning machine back across the pavement and drove away in silence. 'I think we've been politely put on the back burner,' said Parker Dodsworth, finally.

'Yeah,' said Bishop. 'Tom's been got at. He's too honest a

188

cop. And Marlon Brando he ain't. Did you see his neck flush when I asked about the tape?'

The three laughed.

Bishop said: 'We'll sit it out. You just have to remember that the Brits have been made to look inept in the eyes of the world and there's a lot of national pride now riding on Tom Ringrose's ability to bring off a brilliant salvage job.'

The first of the girls taken upstairs to the tent was Stefania Moreno. She went blindfolded and terrified.

'Why me? What you going to do?' Her voice broke.

When the blindfold was whipped off, the video camera and the impassive line of helmets faced her. She shuddered.

As he had with Prentiss Decker, Lucius drilled her insistently on how to behave once the red light came on. Brutally, he added, 'We may have to kill you, Stefania. The British are not co-operating. Your only hope is to read this appeal to your own people.'

The girl fell wailing to her knees, but Lucius went on relentlessly, 'Tears won't save you so stand up and do as you're told.'

He nodded to Jessie, who stepped forward and dragged the half-fainting girl to her feet. She held up the first idiot card. Lucius had debated with the others the advantages of allowing the girls to use their own languages – the impact of the message on their fellow countrymen would be all the more powerful. But they risked a girl slipping in a personal message. Finally, they'd agreed that English would be spoken, with only the French and German speakers allowed to use their own languages, which the three old Etonians could monitor confidently.

Stefania held up that day's *Sunday Telegraph* and began brokenly in English. Lucius, centring her in the view-finder, was satisfied. She looked and sounded as if she was on the verge of a nervous breakdown. There could be no doubt of the reaction of her warm-hearted countrymen as opposed to the cold, implacable English, if they could get the tape shown on Italian television.

Stefania read: 'This is communication number two from the Colonel Blood Raiding Group. My name is Stefania Moreno and I direct my heartfelt appeal to my fellow Italians at this time of great danger for myself and my friends.

'We are horrified to learn how callously the British government has abandoned us to our deaths. They have suppressed the first video-tape that our captors allowed us to make and have refused financial negotiations with the people holding us. Meanwhile, the British blunder along, hoping to uncover our hiding place. Doesn't it occur to them that while they nurse their pride they are playing with our lives?'

Stefania's voice went shrill in her distress. 'A week from now none of us will exist unless our captors' demands are met. Please, please, please make the British show some mercy. Our time is running out.'

Lucius could not have wished for better from Sophia Loren.

'Take her back downstairs and bring up the next girl,' he said, gloved hands lifting the cassette from the recorder and replacing it with another. This had been an idea of genius.

The procession of girls to the tent continued throughout the morning and into the afternoon. After three days underground, they were bedraggled, sallow-skinned and, in some cases, Lucius noted fastidiously, giving off a pungent body odour. What a fragile commodity beauty was.

Jessie Moss steered Mathilde de Montméja upstairs without the usual coarse sneers. 'Watch your feet,' she said gruffly, although Mathilde could see nothing. 'There are five more steps to go.'

Mathilde turned towards the sound of her voice and murmured, 'Nanny, I'm getting so unclean down there with the other girls. I think you're probably a kind person. Would you let me have a bath? You could keep my hands tied and watch me so that you may be sure I'm not trying to escape. Just a bath . . . Please . . .'

They had stood silently on the stairs for a few seconds, then Mathilde felt Jessie's hand, quite gently, on her arm. 'It's not possible,' she said, 'the way things are.'

The day's drive to video-record all forty-nine girls came to a halt on the forty-third. Hanna Hansen stood tall and defiant. She scattered the pages of the *Sunday Telegraph* on the tent's built-in groundsheet and folded her arms. 'You can do what you like. The dignity of my country demands that I do not co-operate. That is all I have to say.'

Lucius Frankel exploded. 'You'll obey orders like the rest. Isn't obeying orders what your country has always been good at?' Hanna stood silent, refusing to be goaded.

Lucius snatched the cattle prod from Jessie, switched it on and jabbed angrily at Hanna. She jumped from side to side to escape the live metal disc at the tip of the pole. Suddenly an espadrille strap snapped, her ankle gave way and she fell backwards into the canvas wall, her weight pushing the tent into a parallelogram. Lucius loomed over her and pressed the prod against her ankle. Hanna howled, scrambling to her knees and tucking her ankles beneath her.

Lucius handed the prod to Jessie, panting. 'That's the second time you've stepped out of line,' he said. 'Now you'll be punished.' She remained kneeling, her head down.

Lucius unzipped the tent flap and was absent for five minutes. The others turned their mirrored visors towards the kneeling girl and waited.

Hanna tried to make her mind a prophylactic blank and to control her trembling. What had that sadistic bastard in mind now?

Lucius Frankel returned. In his hands he carried two items he had purchased in a Soho sex shop from a display of 'love restraints'. Anyone of lesser imagination would have called them manacles.

'Stand her up,' he said coldly. Jessie and Dickie Biggs-Salter hauled Hanna to her feet, which Lucius immediately locked into shackles joined by a twenty-four-inch steel rod that would force her to swing her legs in half-circles, one before the other like a cripple. He then pulled her hands behind her back and clamped chain-linked manacles to her wrists.

'Right,' he said to Jessie. 'Now go down and fetch the Dutch girl. We'll put her alongside this cow and she can read the message in German for her.'

Lucius raised his visor a fraction so that Hanna could not mishear what was being said to her. 'If you interrupt,' he hissed, 'I'll have you held down while I ram this electric pole right up your cunt. Do you understand?'

Hanna understood all right. She made no further protest while an apprehensive Greet Stoll stumbled through her message in German. Afterwards, they laid Hanna face downwards on the floor while they video-recorded the remaining girls. Lucius Frankel surveyed the stack of cassettes with satisfaction. Hanna heard him say, 'That little package should blow the British government sky high.' Then he ushered the others in the group outside the tent. She could hear him muttering in the room beyond.

Lucius was saying, 'We have to make an example of her. If she gets away with it, we'll have a mutiny on our hands and it's simply not practicable to keep them sedated all the time.'

'An example?' queried Bruiser. 'We're not going in for an execution,' he added firmly.

'I wasn't thinking of an execution but we must demonstrate to the rest of the queens the least they can expect in the way of punishment if they start rampaging,' said Lucius. He made his proposal.

Bruiser stood with pursed lips, pondering for a while and then said, 'Yes, I can go along with that. She'll not like it – as I can painfully testify.' Bruiser went off to find an object that, ever since he could remember, had hung on a hook in a cupboard in the attic nursery.

Prentiss Decker was furious with herself. She banged her fist against the unyielding wall of her prison, breaking the skin on her knuckles.

Some of the others gathered around her. 'What's wrong, Prentiss?' asked Mirabelle Montcalm.

'Mirabelle,' said Prentiss, groaning, 'I've been the biggest lame-brain of all time. I've just let slip the best chance we've had yet of getting ourselves out of here.'

Mirabelle whispered, 'What are you saying?'

Prentiss leaned her forehead against the cold stone. 'If only I'd known they were going to make all of us record a video message, I could have rehearsed everyone.'

Mirabelle put a consoling arm on Prentiss's shoulder, but before she could get some sense from the American girl, she heard the upstairs door open. They all looked upward.

192

The helmeted gang were leading an ashen-faced Hanna down the steps. Several girls cried out in fear when they saw the iron rod keeping Hanna's feet wide apart.

The sinister black-garbed group reached the bottom of the steps but no one moved to unchain the gate.

The girls clustered closer. The man with the Welsh accent unlocked the manacles. Hanna began to massage her freed wrists but her arms were grabbed and tightly held. Nanny stepped in front of her and when Hanna saw what she was doing she started to struggle.

The man took her under her elbows and lifted her off the ground. Nanny unbuttoned Hanna's boilersuit then the men dragged it off over her arms. She was naked but for her lavender briefs.

Hanna was carried forward until her contorted face was thrust against the bars of the grille. Her breasts protruded through to the other side as her arms were hauled above her head and her manacles reapplied, the chain threaded through the bars. In this position, she dangled helplessly, in full view of the other girls.

Nanny moved forward again and gave Hanna's briefs a hard yank that bared her buttocks. The big kidnapper handed something to Nanny, which was when the girls began to scream.

The gang proceeded as if they had heard nothing. They stood back to give Nanny room. She measured her distance, raised her right arm in a wide sweep and brought down the cane that had once disciplined the infant Bruiser. It landed across the exquisite globes of Hanna Hansen's backside.

For a second Hanna went rigid and bit back a cry. After the second blow she appeared to be trying to squeeze between the bars. Nanny's arm was raised again but the appalled queens rushed forward, thrusting their arms between the bars, trying to ward off the cane.

The Welshman had the cattle prod in his hands and now he used it. Girls cried out and retreated as the prod buzzed, transmitting its sting.

The Welshman cleared the protective hands from round Hanna. Girls wept and clutched the fiery spots where the twelve-volt prod had caught them. Ignoring their distress, the

Welshman said to Nanny, 'She's had two strokes. Now give her the rest.'

Jessie set to with a will. On the fifth vicious stroke she extracted her first involuntary cry from the phlegmatic German girl. Purple weals leaped to the surface of her tanned skin in a criss-cross pattern.

It'll be a long time before this bitch wears a bikini bottom again, thought Jessie. On the sixth stroke, she drew blood. Transfixed and elated, she went rigid, her eyes rolled and her mouth opened to emit the sound of a dry rattle. Jessie had had a massive orgasm.

Automatically she raised her aching arm to deliver a seventh rapturous blow but it was stayed by Bruiser.

'That's enough,' he said, lowering her arm. 'I know we said ten but I think the girl has fainted.'

Jessie pulled away angrily, frustrated.

From his vantage point at the head of the steps, Dickie Biggs-Salter murmured to Rolly Ponsford: 'My God, Rolly, that brought back painful memories of nursery days. I felt every last stroke. My arse is positively *aching*. She's a real Whiplash Willa, that Moss girl. I think the Jerry is in dire need of some ointment. I'll pop upstairs and see what I can find.'

Hanna's shackles were removed and she slumped to the floor. Lucius unchained the iron gate and, on hands and knees, Hanna crawled over the threshold. Saliva dripped from her sagging mouth but she refused to weep.

The sound of the gate slamming rang through the huge cellar. The girls gazed steadily at him with undisguised hatred.

'She was asked to perform a simple task and has been punished because she refused. It is the least any of you can expect in similar circumstances,' the Welshman said, and turned away.

Another of the helmeted men tossed in a plastic bottle of calamine lotion. 'Best I could find,' he said gruffly. The kidnappers retreated up the steps and shut the door, leaving the queens to their anger and fear.

Jessie was the spokeswoman in the Cockneys' confrontation with Lucius. Lenny had urged caution: he had been physically sick with terror at the thought of retribution to come when

194

Teddy had described Marble's heart attack and the overpowering of the policemen at the Captain Cook Docks.

Jessie had received the news calmly. 'You two silly gits didn't think they were going to pay us a fortune just to drive a couple of coaches and do some impersonations, did you?'

'No,' Teddy muttered, 'but I didn't think I'd be mixed up with a bunch of violent nutters, neither. Look at old Marble. I got him into this and now the poor bugger has got eels coming out of his eye sockets.'

She made that point to Lucius: 'You didn't tell us we was going to get mixed up in rough stuff. If you had, we'd have run a bloody mile. But now we're in it up to our necks and we want better treatment.'

'Better treatment?' asked Lucius quietly.

'Yes,' said Jessie. 'You stand to make twenty-five million dollars and you're palming us off with a tip. It just ain't fair.'

'Not fair? We're proposing to give each of you more money than you'll ever otherwise see in your lives. This operation took brains, many months of planning and the investment of a fortune – none of which required any contribution from you. All you've had to do is obey a few simple orders, some of which,' Lucius added drily, 'I think you found enjoyable in the execution.'

The three were facing him in Bruiser's library. They stood awkwardly in a pool of light from a green-shaded lamp. The shelves of books soared into the shadows near the ceiling.

Jessie said, 'Well, it's not over yet and we've still got to do your dirty work. We're the ones getting all the toe-rag jobs. I'm fed up working in the kitchen, never knowing when the filth might walk through the door. And the boys might as well be back in the nick, having to do all that slopping out every morning. Why can't those lazy bitches empty their own crap? We're not their bloody servants.'

Lucius said patiently, 'If we did that, we'd have to take off their blindfolds and let them into other parts of the house. The less they know, the safer for us. As it is, they can't even be sure that they're still in England.'

'All right,' said Jessie, 'but it doesn't alter the fact that we're being shortchanged.'

'Just tell me what you've decided among yourselves,' said Lucius.

'A million pounds split three ways,' said Jessie promptly.

Teddy and Lenny swapped nervous glances.

'Is that all?' said Lucius. 'And what if my colleagues and I say no?'

Jessie had anticipated that question. 'Then we'll have to reconsider our position,' she said.

'And we shall have to think over what you have said,' Lucius replied.

Chapter Twenty-nine

Commander Tom Ringrose watched the walls of the main office of the Serious Crime Squad being covered with a series of eight-by-ten photographs.

Firth had unearthed two photographers who had covered the Guildhall dinner on the eve of the kidnapping. Between them, they had exposed 680 frames of negative film which had been developed, and kept in time sequence, by Yard technicians.

The first set had been taken as each guest was received by the Lord Mayor and Lady Mayoress. The second showed casual knots of guests, glasses in hand, chatting at the champagne reception that preceded dinner. The third consisted of formal shots of individual tables with everyone staring fixedly at the cameras.

With the aid of the photographers and a City *chef du protocol*, Firth's men were now inking in the approximate time at which each picture had been taken and setting about the task of identifying each of the three hundred guests.

Ringrose spent all of Sunday afternoon moving from picture to picture. By tea time he had made an interesting discovery.

He was on his Eames chair taking his first celebratory sip of tea when he received a telephone call that brought a beam to his drawn face.

Later, snatching a few hours at home, hot dinner and a bath, Helen said, 'How's it going?'

She was surprised when her husband replied, 'An inch at a time, but I think I've got one of the sods in my sights.'

Hanna lay on her front while the Argentinian, Eva Ravignini, a student nurse from Bahia Blanca, dabbed calamine lotion across the fiery welts. She had a touch like the kiss of swansdown but Hanna could not hold back a prolonged wince. She felt nauseous and throbbing waves of bone-deep ache racked her from thigh to chest. Eva had shouted up the steps at the closed door for hot water to clean Hanna's wounds, but the kidnappers had not returned.

Prentiss Decker, kneeling at Hanna's head, stroked her hair and whispered, brokenly: 'I'm so sorry, Hanna. I could have prevented this.'

Hanna made a negative movement from the neck up. 'No, Prentiss, my family has always had a pig-headed streak.'

'But, I could Hanna, I could!' Prentiss's voice was low and intense. 'You would have made their video recording if I had shown you a way beforehand of getting a signal to the outside world.'

Hanna turned her head to look up at the American girl. 'You're dreaming. How could that be possible? They would not allow any movements or any departure from their printed cards. What chance did that leave?'

'Just one,' said Prentiss. 'And I've already taken it.'

Hanna looked incredulous. 'Prentiss, this has to be a joke. Please stop.'

'No, Hanna, no! I'm telling you I've already sent one message to the outside world.' Prentiss stood up. 'Girls,' she said, 'I want you all to gather close so that I don't have to raise my voice.'

The queens, curious, gathered round her in a tight cordon. 'Does anyone do a piercing whistle?' The Bermudian, Alison Outerbridge, placed two fingers to her mouth and gave a shrill blast. The other girls cheered.

'Marvellous!' said Prentiss. 'Alison, stand guard at the gate. Watch the upstairs door carefully. If it opens by so much as a whisker, sound the alarm.'

In a low voice she told them of retired Admiral Jeremiah Denton of the United States Navy. 'You know my daddy was a Navy man, stationed at Norfolk, Virginia. He was there at the same time as Jerry Denton who was our great hero.'

'What had he done?' asked Fran Pilkington.

'Got himself shot down during the Vietnam war and captured by the North Vietnamese,' said Prentiss. 'He became the most senior United States officer they had in captivity. The admiral – he was then a captain – took an apathetic bunch of POWs by the collar, instilled discipline and raised their morale by ridding them of the sense of shame they felt at having been captured.'

'Fine,' said Fran. 'I can see the parallels with our own shitty situation. But, with all due respect, Prentiss, so what?'

'There is another parallel that I have not yet mentioned. One day the Viets hauled him out of the prison camp that was known as the Hanoi Zoo. Captain Denton had been chained and tortured but they wanted him to appear in front of the cameras of a Japanese television team to say how humanely he was being treated. Now the Captain was tough – every bit as tough as you, Hanna – and you might have expected that he'd refuse to lend himself to this propaganda exercise. But he went willingly and made the statement his captors demanded. He had an ace to play. He knew the Morse Code.'

'Morse?' queried Fran. 'I don't understand. You need an electric tapper to transmit Morse, don't you? And I'm sure the Vietnamese were not stupid enough to let him tap with his fingers in front of a camera.'

'No, they weren't that stupid,' said Prentiss, 'but they were stupid all the same. *All the time he was speaking their propaganda message, Captain Denton used his eyelids to blink out in Morse Code the fact that he had been tortured.*'

'Did anyone in America cotton on?'

'You bet your sweet ass they did. It was a secret that the intelligence guys kept for years after Jerry Denton was repatriated to the US and was awarded the Navy Cross.'

'Okay, Prentiss,' said Mirabelle Montcalm, 'it's an uplifting story but how does it help us? Do you think those bastards upstairs are going to provide a Morse Code manual for our bedtime reading?'

'They don't have to,' said Prentiss, softly producing her bombshell. 'My daddy once took a radio-telegraphy course. And guess who was the cute little girl who used to hold Daddy's manual and prompt him when he learned Morse?'

In the silence that followed, Mirabelle whispered, 'Jeeeeeezus! Are you saying you know it?'

'Better than Daddy himself,' said Prentiss. 'Kids learn faster than adults.'

Mirabelle grabbed her by the shoulders. 'And you've sent a message, haven't you?'

'Guilty,' said Prentiss, but she waved down the excited cries until they were listening again. 'Don't let's get over-hopeful about this. It is the reason why, until now, I've held my tongue, which has proved to be just about the dumbest thing I ever did.

'When they took me upstairs to deliver their first communication, I was bowled over. When I saw the video camera, I flipped. I had to pretend to faint to give myself time to think. The story of Captain Denton came back to me straight away, like an arrow between the eyes. But the problem was: what message should I try to transmit? I didn't want to say anything banal like "We're all unharmed." In any case, words to that effect were already contained in the message they wanted me to read. No, I needed to transmit a clue to this location. In fact, it is devilishly difficult to read aloud and simultaneously send Morse by blinking. I made a false start, screwed up completely and then slowed down my reading so that, when I took long pauses to draw breath, my actions seemed natural. That's when I sent the message – during the pauses.'

The queens were hushed. 'Prentiss, the suspense is killing us. For God's sake – what message did you send?' Mirabelle wrung her slim hands.

'Well, it wasn't much, but it was a beginning that should alert the outside world to my ploy. I transmitted the only solid clue we have. "Sulphur in air."'

Prentiss shrugged at their disappointment. 'There were other choices. I could have transmitted "*Mercenaries Query*", or "*Victorian Cellar Query*". It just seemed to me that the sulphur smell was something the police could get their noses into. When I was upstairs again an hour ago, I tried to include the Victorian Cellar clue but the message they'd prepared for each of us was so short that I got only as far as VICT before it was over and they shut down the camera.'

200

Prentiss shook her head. 'Just think how effective it would have been if we girls could have agreed on a simple message of up to forty-nine letters. Then I could have schooled each of you with a single letter that you could confidently repeat during each pause.

'Today, the gang didn't call us up in any order. The running order, if they repeat the exercise, remains immaterial because even if we go upstairs in the order in which we've memorized the message, it'll be a jumble of single letters when the police randomly place the received cassettes alongside each other. But their experts – cryptographers with computers, perhaps – will switch the letters around and make sense of what we've sent. I'd say we have twenty-four hours or more before they come for us again – if they do – but it's time enough to start a crash course in Morse Code.'

'Excuse me,' said the small voice of Vera Lankermeyer. 'It would be tragic, yes, if the world has forgotten Captain Denton? The war happened a long time ago. Everyone expects us to flutter our eyes. We do it all the time in front of the competition judges. Who will be looking into them for anything but – how do you say it? – a come-hither look?'

'Honey,' said Prentiss indulgently, 'the way we are right now, the only look we're capable of giving a guy will say go-yonder rather than come-hither. So just leave your Swiss caution hanging on an Alp and let's get our cute asses into gear.'

Commander Tom Ringrose had been awarded priority use of the family bathroom. 'Stay out until your father's finished,' Helen had told the girls firmly.

If by nothing else, Helen's edict would confirm the gravity of the situation. To get in before his daughters performed their mysterious and interminable *toilettes* was a rare privilege for the *paterfamilias*.

As he shaved, Ringrose tried not to dwell on the grey shadows spreading from his eye sockets down his cheeks. He had just finished and was sniffing the aroma of bacon floating up the stairs, when the telephone rang. It was 7.10 on Tuesday 4 October.

He and Firth had decided to alternate the dog watch. Firth

wasted no words. 'Guv'nor, the car's on the way. The foot-by-foot search reached the Captain Cook Docks this morning. The supervising officer called out the owners' agent to have the gates unlocked at dawn. His key didn't fit the padlock on the main East Entrance. Someone switched locks recently.'

'All right, Lionel. Have the gates opened and muster the largest body of footmen possible plus a scene-of-crime team. But don't make any move until I get there.' He shouted down the stairs, 'Put that bacon between two slices, would you, love?'

The hot sandwich in his hand, he told his driver, 'This time you can use the siren – and don't spare the horses.'

'Yes, sir!' said his man, as he swung the car to the wrong side of the commuter-jammed road and began to bully the oncoming traffic to one side. Ringrose tried not to look.

Police coaches, a control van, a mobile canteen, at least three hundred uniformed policemen and a large body of journalists already thronged the access road as Ringrose's car nosed up to the dock gates.

Journalists were protesting at being held back, especially the Americans, who were accustomed to flashing their police-issued shields and being allowed to pass most barriers.

Ringrose walked over and said courteously, 'Good morning, ladies and gentlemen.' The questions came at him in a dense barrage.

'All we know is that someone has gone to the trouble of substituting the padlock on that gate over there. The lock and chain are already on the way for forensic examination. This operation is being mounted to make a detailed search of several hundred acres of waterways and abandoned warehouses. It's going to be a long wait.'

By 8.30 the number of mustered men had risen to eight hundred. No Metropolitan policeman ever regarded himself as off-duty when the lives of colleagues are at stake.

Ringrose and Firth studied the tarmac dock road but there was nothing to be learned. The weather had been dry for a week and there were no tell-tale tyre markings.

Ringrose said, 'Let's you and me take a walk down to the river entrance. If this is where they spirited away a coach and a patrol car, they'll have brought the ferryboat through into one of the inner basins.'

As they walked, a feral cat ran spitting across their path. When Ringrose heard a clatter he looked up: the camera-laden press helicopters were beginning to arrive.

The pale mark in the green moss clinging to the timber baulks above the wall hook stood out distinctively. Experimentally, Ringrose took hold of the rope attached to the cable barring the river entrance and pulled the cable-end off the hook. As it came loose it swung against the moss. Ringrose raised it six inches and the end followed exactly the pale marking. 'Someone's been here,' he said.

They followed the main channel inward. If the water had been recently disturbed, it was impossible to detect. The tides since the kidnapping would have resurfaced the channel with flotsam.

Ringrose looked ahead and stopped. The yellow jib of a crane protruded above a two-storey structure. He gripped Firth's arm. 'Come on.'

The two detectives studied the crawler-crane's caterpillar tracks and the ground. Even a child could see that the machine had recently been moved forward. 'Could it take the load?' Ringrose mused.

'It's a big bugger. Pending the arrival of an expert, I'd say yes,' said Lionel. He nipped up onto a track and, without touching anything, peered into the cabin. 'There's a couple of screws missing from the control panel. They've been pulled out recently.'

'Hot-wired?'

'Most likely,' said Firth. He clambered down.

Ringrose circled the giant machine again, now examining its super-structure. He halted abruptly. The heavy metal bars that formed the crane's counterweight were stacked in a neat block but the last bar in the top row was missing, revealed by the less-weathered sides of the neighbouring bars.

Chapter Thirty

The Prime Minister had called a meeting of the Cabinet Emergencies Committee for Tuesday afternoon, when the queens had spent their fifth night in captivity. The British government had been deeply rattled by the critical newspaper reports now flooding in from British embassies around the world.

The media clamour was rising.

The lack of results had concentrated the world-wide official reaction to the ransom demands.

A handful of island states, on the lower end of the ransom scale, had decided to make the cash available from contingency funds, confident that the renowned Scotland Yard would hunt down the kidnappers and recover the money.

The industrial nations of the West, following the British lead, announced that there would be no ransom money from public funds, but large amounts of currency might be moved to London from private sources . . .

Thus in the oblique way of bureaucracies, the green light was given for an appeal to public generosity without compromising the official position.

The Queen of the Earth organizers called a press conference at the Colonel Blood Inn at noon. Flanked by anxious parents and a hastily recruited appeals committee, Lady Nancy Cornmorris made an impassioned plea to newspapers to begin a gigantic ransom-raising operation.

'Time is desperately short,' she said, to a bank of television cameras and heads bent over notebooks, 'and we must plead with the kidnappers to show some mercy and give us a breathing space. We cannot assemble such a vast sum overnight. We must collect on behalf of *all* the girls.'

Within an hour of the live telecast, boards of directors up

and down the country were voting donations, humbler collections were organized on factory floors and tin collecting-boxes appeared in corner shops and supermarkets. The Charity Commissioners averted their gaze. To point out the illegality of such *ad hoc* arrangements would have brought public scorn on their heads. With so many young lives at stake it was no time for legalistic quibbling.

None of this was lost on the Prime Minister.

The Metropolitan Police Commissioner was glowering because, through the Home Secretary, he had been ordered to bring Commander Tom Ringrose with him. But Ringrose was late.

The Prime Minister, fidgeting, listened to the negative reports of the security services. Ringrose's chair remained empty. Finally, he asked, 'What's keeping him?'

'He was making an early morning sweep of some dockland . . .' began the Commissioner but stopped when a soft-footed cabinet official placed a telephone in front of him.

The Commissioner listened and gazed stonily across the table at the Prime Minister.

'Lionel, come and look at this,' said Ringrose. His assistant studied the place where the crane's counterweight had been.

'Sweet Christ,' said Firth. 'A weight for a body?'

They walked to the basin's edge and studied the unrevealing surface. They noticed the fresh chalk marks. Ringrose paced out the distance between them. 'It's almost exactly the length of the coach. We need frogmen, grappling and lifting gear and a team to go over the crane and the ground surrounding this basin – and we want them pronto.'

While they waited, the two detectives examined the overlooking warehouses. Only one set of roll-back gates was open. They noticed the newly chipped brickwork alongside the entrance, the flakes of paint and the oil stain on the ground. There was a similar oil stain inside the building and a considerable number of scuffed footmarks in the dust.

The search yielded a single 9mm cartridge case and a considerable quantity of vulcanized rubber from shredded car tyres. Ringrose examined those items wordlessly and allowed the scientific officers to take over.

He walked forward with outstretched hand as a car arrived and a small, vague man with a high-domed forehead, on which was perched a totally unsuitable Homburg, climbed out accompanied by his girl assistant.

'I always feel a damn sight better when you're around, Professor,' said Ringrose, and they shook hands warmly. Franklyn Dart, Professor of Forensic Medicine at Guy's Hospital, was the only man in Britain who could justifiably claim that he had solved more murders than Tom Ringrose – but, then, he'd been at it longer.

The elderly pathologist listened, head cocked, to Ringrose's brief recital of his fears. Then, disregarding his immaculate pinstripe trousers, he knelt in the dust and began to cover the area like a manic washerwoman.

The frogmen were arriving with their rubber dinghies as the Professor made his first find. He gave a shout and Ringrose came over to watch him scrape a dried substance from the stone paving and deposit it in a glass phial. 'It's some sort of animal fluid and it contains a little blood,' said Professor Dart.

Ringrose sat on a bollard watching the frogmen rolling over the dinghy sides in their wetsuits and dragging their lights down into the murk. They were about thirty feet out when one surfaced with his arm raised and started to swim towards him. Ringrose stood up, dusting the seat of his pants, wanting to be sick.

He bent over to catch the breathless man's words, although the stricken expression on his face said it all. 'Sorry, sir. It's Hotel Five right enough.'

'Anyone inside?'

'At least two bodies, sir.'

Ringrose said to Firth, 'How long before the PLA floating crane arrives?'

Ninety minutes later, the roof of Hotel Five broke surface, rank water cascading from every aperture. The onlookers tried not to examine too closely the bloated, obscene objects hogtied in the front seats. A young Limehouse constable standing near

Ringrose started to sob as the crane deposited its grisly load on the side of the basin. They could all see the rear tyres hanging in ribbons.

'My God,' said Firth. 'That's the shooting of a marksman. There isn't a single bullet in the chassis.'

Ringrose steeled himself and looked inside. He said to Firth, 'Keep the frogmen at it. I want that iron bar found.' He turned away, leaving the car for a few minutes to Professor Dart, the ballistics experts and the police photographers.

An hour later the tarpaulin bundle, with the third corpse, was brought dripping to the dockside. Ringrose waited patiently while the wrapping, the iron bar and the rope knots were examined and photographed, and the decomposing contents carefully exposed. Ringrose's brow knitted. Who was this middle-aged man in the blue overalls with no apparent injury?

In the mortuary, the clothes were peeled off and the pockets ransacked for any lead to the third man's identity. There was nothing.

Ringrose was back in his office, studying the wad of forensic reports that the day's gruesome discoveries had brought, when Professor Dart called.

He came directly to the point. 'Constables Laxton and Blakey were both drowned like unwanted kittens in a sack. Their facial wounds were only superficial, caused when their car struck the warehouse wall. I'd say they died on the evening of the day they disappeared.'

The professor drew breath. 'The same timescale is also true of the unidentified man. He was well nourished, in his mid-fifties and the dried fluid scraping is his. He lay dying on the spot where I took it. The interesting aspect of his death is that it was natural. He was suffering from degenerative heart disease. The excitement must have been too much for him.'

'Do you have any other crumb for me?' Ringrose sounded desperate.

'Could be,' said the Professor. 'The dead man's most distinguishing feature is that he has a posterior cortical cataract in his left eye.' Ringrose scribbled furiously.

*　　*　　*

Within thirty minutes Ringrose and Firth were in the car heading across Westminster Bridge to South London. The missing persons computer file had coughed up the name of Frank Reginald Simpson, aged fifty-six, unemployed and reported absent after failing to appear for five nights at a Salvation Army hostel in Bermondsey. His personal possessions, plus £200 in new banknotes, were being minded by the major in charge. The outstanding feature of the circulated description of Frank Reginald Simpson was that he had a clouded left eye.

The inmates of the hostel lined up to be questioned by a team from Ringrose's squad about Frank Simpson, who otherwise answered to the name Marble.

His estranged wife, interrupted in her early-evening viewing of her favourite television serial and betraying no discernible grief, viewed and confirmed the identity of the remains, sniffed and said she hoped she'd be given a lift back home in time for the late-night film. She also told the police that Marble's last known job had been as a dockside crane driver.

Ringrose began the dog watch that night on the camp bed in his office. Three deaths in less than half a day. His insides felt hollow. Those poor girls. Beside him lay the copy of that morning's *Times* in which he had placed a personal message signed 'Lord Grey'. It read: 'Time is not enough. What news of the menfolk?'

He had had his answer.

The zoom cameras mounted in the helicopters gave an all-too-graphic view of the raising of Hotel Five. Rolly said, 'What the blazes . . .' But Bruiser, eyes bulging incredulously, knew the truth instantly.

He hurled himself across the room at Lucius. 'You murdering bastard! There's no way that patrol car could have ended up in the water unless someone pushed it!' he roared.

Lucius tried to fend off the onslaught but Bruiser had him by the throat. 'So that's why you were late leaving London, you shit,' said Dickie. 'You crept down there and did those poor, helpless buggers in. You were supposed to telephone their whereabouts.'

Through his fear, Lucius's anger blazed. 'All right, I admit it. But I was only doing the job you didn't have the guts to finish yourselves. You may think they weren't a threat but how could you be sure? For God's sake, they *saw* you. That made them threat enough.'

Bruiser said, 'You cold-blooded swine. You've made us all party to murder.' He clenched his fist and felled Lucius with a single blow to the chin.

The three old Etonians stood over his unconscious figure.

'That's torn it,' said Rolly.

Ringrose sat with some awe in the graceful, pillared Cabinet Room, not a little embarrassed as the Prime Minister ruthlessly bypassed his Commissioner and turned to him.

He outlined his tactics but felt no qualms at omitting his primary suspicion. It was a suspicion he could, as yet, only thinly defend. If he were to make premature charges that they considered preposterous, their confidence in him would slip rapidly away.

He said, '*When* we catch up with these people, I think we shall find that the nucleus of the group is far removed from the traditional criminal fraternity. These people are educated, they're excellent shots, with great organizing ability and sufficient original funds to have mounted a costly operation. They are of an élite, an officer class. I can say that with some confidence because, over the past few days, we have eliminated every other possibility. There isn't a known criminal outfit of any size that hasn't been raided by my men.'

'But what about the blackguard who operated the crane? He hardly fits into your officer-class theory,' pointed out the Prime Minister.

'No, sir. But officers need their non-commissioned help and I believe this man Simpson was one of these. My inquiries show that, until his disappearance last Thursday, he had slept every night at the Salvation Army hostel since he and his wife parted company six months ago. If he were a principal in the preparation of this crime I would have expected him to be staying elsewhere with other leading members of the gang. In the weeks preceding the kidnapping he received just three telephone calls at the hostel and they were all from the same man, who spoke with a Cockney accent. Naturally, intensive inquiries are in progress to seek out all his known associates.'

'Where do we stand in the search for the missing coach?'

'We can now be certain that it was loaded onto the ferryboat *Freda* at the Captain Cook Docks,' said Ringrose, 'but we cannot swear that it wasn't unloaded again before the vessel came under radar surveillance at the Woolwich Barrier. It was definitely *not* unloaded at the paper-mill because it doesn't have a crane or a roll-off facility. However, the girls were unloaded there. Their fingerprints are sufficiently numerous on the juggernaut's hooks to prove this point. We made the comparison with prints taken from their rooms at the Colonel Blood Inn.'

The discussion moved on to a proposal from the Defence Minister that extraordinary powers of search and detention be taken under the Defence of the Realm Act.

'Not bloody likely,' said the Prime Minister inelegantly. 'Let's move on to what is politically possible.'

Ringrose had a suggestion. Sir Travers Horder looked daggers but the Prime Minister said, 'Commander?'

He chose his words gingerly. 'I think you'll agree, sir, that although your unyielding stance as a government is the only proper one, this may well be misinterpreted in certain quarters as heartless. I believe, therefore, it would be in our interests if the ransom-raising operation were placed in semi-official hands. This act would head off criticism that the government is gambling with the lives of forty-nine young girls. I need hardly add that should a tragedy occur the reaction from abroad would be hostile, no matter how misguided.'

The Commissioner snorted. 'Ringrose, I really think you're stepping beyond the bounds of a serving police officer into the political arena.'

'No,' said the Prime Minister, 'let him finish. What do you suggest, Commander?'

Ringrose said, 'Ask the Lord Mayor of London to take command of the appeal, using City corporation staff and volunteers from the City banks to process the money into the currencies and denominations demanded by the kidnappers. It would be in the tradition of wartime lord mayors who placed giant barometers outside the Mansion House to show the progress of national savings and personally led the drive. In this instance, it will be an international drive through which the Lord Mayor may make direct money-raising appeals to the municipal leaders of the world's capitals. However it is done, I am concerned to take the operation out of the hands of the Queen of the Earth organizers.'

'It's subtle, I grant you that,' said the Prime Minister. 'The government can stand aside and have no truck with murderers yet the ransom drive would still have an official air about it.' He flashed Ringrose a sharp look. 'But what was that about it being in *all* our interests? Why should our political difficulties concern you?'

'Because,' said Ringrose, 'I want the Lord Mayor to lie about the volume of contributions coming in.'

The Prime Minister's eyebrows shot up. 'I certainly think that remark needs an explanation.'

'My guess,' went on Ringrose, 'is that contributions will arrive rapidly by computer from all around the world. If it's left to the Queen of the Earth organizers, they'll be announcing triumphantly that they've hit their target by the end of the week.' He shook his head. 'That won't do for me. I'm playing for every extra hour I can get. This crime has been elaborately constructed. Unravelling it is going to be time-consuming. I'm not underestimating my opponents. So, although the ransom may flood in, I want the Lord Mayor to slow down the count. I don't want the mercury in that big barometer outside the Mansion House to rise too fast. It's money the gang's after so, while they can still see the mercury going up, no matter how slowly, they'll not harm the girls.'

'It's risky,' said the Prime Minister. 'Both for the girls and the government. If it should ever leak that there existed such collusion between us and the Lord Mayor . . .'

'Sir, I think you could always lay the blame for any delay at the door of innumerate bungling bureaucrats,' Ringrose suggested.

'Commander,' said the Prime Minister, 'you have a subtle train of thought.'

Everyone joined in the brief murmur of approval, except the Commissioner.

'I propose we go along with Commander Ringrose's suggestion,' said the Prime Minister. He looked around the table for signs of dissent. There were none. 'I'll talk to the Lord Mayor directly,' he said briskly.

Lucius Frankel, nursing his resentment and a bruised jaw, spent much of the day holed up at Moxmanton House, duplicating the video recordings made by the girls. He turned out the American's tape for each of the three major US television networks and one for the *New York Times*. As the French government had total power of veto over all television broadcasts within its frontiers, he made a duplicate of Mathilde de Montméja's appeal for *Figaro*. In Britain, tapes of Fran Pilkington were destined for the BBC and Independent Television News plus a copy for *The Times*.

Lucius wanted global saturation coverage and he worked his way slowly through *Willing's Press Guide* and a stack of television-industry reference books.

He ended up with eighty tapes, all stowed inside the rear seat of his car. It would be a cruel irony if he should be uncovered at a routine road-check on the way to London.

He set out on Tuesday morning. The fine weather of the previous few days was fading and the first chill of autumn nipped at the flesh. Overnight, they'd had to run a cable down the cellar steps and plug in a blow-heater. The girls were huddling near the iron grille to keep warm.

In the privacy of his garage, Lucius opened the car seat and transferred the video tapes into a large hold-all.

An hour later, a bearded man presented the visiting card of a public-relations company to a dispatch clerk at the Zip-Fast Courier Service and paid £400 in cash for the same-day delivery of eighty packages in the central London area.

'It'll take three drivers four hours,' said the clerk.

'Fine,' said Lucius, in his Fluellen voice. 'It's the beginning of a big charity appeal for those less fortunate than ourselves.' He couldn't resist the joke.

'Nice one,' said the clerk.

By mid-afternoon, while the Prime Minister was suborning the Lord Mayor of London at Number 10, Downing Street, British Telecom experienced a sudden rush to book satellite-television links to an extensive number of reception stations round the world, while in newspaperland and the West End of London, media people could be observed acting in an erratic, excitable manner.

Murray Wallace of the *New York Times* was not a man who indulged in common expletives. Sitting in his office in Buckingham Gate, Westminster, he held up a Polaroid photograph, accompanying a video tape. It showed Prentiss Decker, in her prison garb, wearing an expression disdainful of her captors.

'Ho-ly sheeeeit!' said Murray Wallace. He startled his nearby colleagues with a mighty roar. 'Where's the damn video player?'

He pressed the cassette home, juggled furiously when it would not click neatly into position and began to swear like a drunken sailor.

His Scottish secretary said, 'Och, Mr Wallace, ye're beating the wee thing to death.' She took the cassette gently from his frantic fingers and showed him how. A few moments later he was watching Prentiss stolidly deliver her short message. Then he rewound the tape and played it again.

He said to his secretary, 'Miss McIntyre, get me Mr Art Decker at the Colonel Blood Inn.'

Prentiss's father, an athletic, steel-haired man with a Florida tan – in his retirement from the Navy he had founded a pleasure fishing-craft company in Key West – listened on the telephone to Murray Wallace, grabbed his jacket and was in the London bureau within twenty-five minutes. He allowed himself to be photographed watching his only daughter on the television screen. At one point he opened his mouth to say something, changed his mind and clamped it shut again. Three times he asked for the tape to be rerun.

The *Times* staff looked at each other understandingly; it must be an emotional moment for him.

It was, but not for the reason they thought. Art Decker gave Murray some appropriate quotes for his front-page story and said, abruptly, 'I have to get back to the Inn to telephone Prentiss's mother,' shook hands warmly all round and couldn't get down to street level fast enough. 'There's an extra ten bucks in it for you if you can break the speed record to the American Embassy in Grosvenor Square,' he told his cabbie.

'What's that in real money, Yank?' said the fellow, putting his foot down.

Lucius Frankel had cause to be gratified. The media, although generally co-operative with the police, were tempted beyond endurance by the unexpected shower of exclusive video tapes. Self-interest won the battle over conscience. By the time Ringrose's men had taken possession of all eighty, many had been handled so thoughtlessly that any hope of finding original fingerprints was gone. Not one recipient would surrender the original before copies had been made: journalism is too ruthless a game for self-denial.

'Blood Group Stage TV Show' was the banner in the late-afternoon edition of the London *Evening Standard*.

Pandora's box was open. Neither the director-general of the BBC nor the Independent Broadcasting Authority saw any point in banning Fran Pilkington's poignant image from British screens. She made great television – as did the other girls around the world – and gave to the appeal fund the psychological shot it needed. The promises of contributions turned into a tide.

The Prime Minister watched the early-evening news and was furious. The short video message, slandering the British government, was going round the world and he had been checkmated. These devils were not missing a trick; he was profoundly grateful that he had agreed to Commander Ringrose's idea. At least the major criticism of government indifference was sidestepped.

Detective Inspector Lionel Firth popped his head round the door. Ringrose envied his chipper look, although Firth was, as always, giving him his all. The two men were now working a sixteen-hour day.

They'd just persuaded all the water supply authorities to take special readings of all water meters to see if any unexplained increases in water consumption could be detected. Ringrose had reasoned that, if the Blood Group were allowing the girls any sort of decent bathing and lavatory facilities, a considerable usage of water must be involved.

214

He'd gone somewhat cool on the theory since viewing the unwashed appearances of the girls on the eighty tapes but nothing ventured meant no one nicked.

'I've got Jake Bishop on the blower. Insists on speaking to you,' said Firth.

Ringrose sighed and put down the wad of telephone-surveillance transcripts dumped on his desk by a detective sergeant from SO11, the Yard's Criminal Intelligence Unit.

He picked up the phone. 'The US cavalry's on its way, Tom. Boy, have I got good news for you.' The CIA man sounded gleeful.

'I won't pretend I don't need some. What's up?'

Bishop dropped his voice. 'I'm on my way round with my back-up team and a mystery guest. Have Prentiss Decker's first tape ready, Tom. We're going to play at I'll show-you-mine-if-you-show-me-yours. And, relax, pal. At last we're in business.'

Ringrose had always admired Americans' perennial optimism. They invariably saw the world as a can-do place and he knew Jake was no Company bullshit artist. 'All right, Colonel,' he said, entering into the spirit. 'But you'd better make it fast. I've got the wagons circled down here.'

When Bishop bustled in, he was accompanied by Zaentz and Dodsworth, both looking like card players who had acquired an edge. With them was a tanned figure that Ringrose recognized from television interviews as Prentiss Decker's father.

'Okay, Mr Decker,' said Bishop, dropping into the Eames chair. 'Tell the great and good Commander about your little girl's special talent.'

Ringrose had to stop his jaw dropping as Art Decker related his own struggle for proficiency in the Morse Code and of the Vietnam exploits of Captain Denton.

Ringrose said, 'I had dossiers prepared on each of the girls. There's no mention of your daughter's knowledge of Morse.'

'Why should there be?' said Art Decker. 'She's not just a dumb Barbie doll, you know, Commander. She probably hasn't given it a thought in years, yet here she is dredging up an old skill like a pro.'

'All right, Mr Decker. Let's see it in action.' Ringrose sat the American in front of the video system installed in his office after the kidnapping. Communication number two from the Colonel Blood Raiding Group was already in the slot. Ringrose pressed the button and a numbered lead-in flashed onto the screen followed by the image of Prentiss holding up the newspaper.

'Now watch her eyes!' said Art Decker, pulling his chair closer.

Indeed Ringrose could see that Prentiss was blinking madly as if dazzled by the lights.

'Di . . . di . . . di . . . dah – a Vee,' said Art Decker.

'Di . . . di – an Eye.'

When she vanished from the screen, Ringrose said, 'So what do we have? VICT?'

'That's it, Commander,' said Art Decker. 'Prentiss must have been cut off before she could complete the message. There aren't that many words in the dictionary beginning VICT. There's victim, victor – D'you think she was trying to tell us something about the victims? The dead men. Remember, they hadn't been found when she recorded that message on Sunday. Or maybe one of the bastards is called Victor.'

'It's possible,' said Ringrose. 'Anyway, Mr Decker, I'm impressed by your daughter's bravery and resourcefulness. We'll have to examine all the possibilities. But, more importantly, you should look at the longer message we had from the kidnappers – it contained the original ransom demand. I think you might need this pad and pen.'

Ringrose handed him the writing implements while Firth changed the tape. The CIA men huddled up to Art Decker.

Relief warmed Ringrose as Prentiss's upper torso, partly hidden by a copy of the *Express* she was holding up to the camera, came on the screen. Instantly she started blinking. What a girl! She'd been on to the Denton dodge from the outset. Art Decker began to scribble.

Prentiss blinked and talked . . . talked and blinked. Ringrose stood hypnotized.

The tape reached the point at which Ringrose had noted in earlier viewings that Prentiss had slowed her delivery. He'd assumed it was because the off-camera prompt was becoming difficult to read.

The tape reached the end of the main message and Firth pressed the fast forward button until he got to the secondary message. But Art Decker shook his head. 'There's nothing there.'

He asked for the whole tape to be run again. In all, Art Decker watched his daughter's performance six times.

Then he turned to the tense group and said to Ringrose, 'Commander, my little girl got herself into a bit of a tangle in the beginning of that message. After a while, she began to shape up and she started over. And by the end of the main section she'd finished saying to us everything she intended. She made no attempt to add anything to that itsy-bitsy piece further along the tape. Christ! I'm proud of her.'

Art Decker's eyes were brimming. He handed Ringrose a piece of notepaper. 'I'd swear that this is what she wants us to know.'

Ringrose looked down. Prentiss Decker's Morse signal read: SULPHUR IN AIR.

The others peered over his shoulder.

'Could they be holed up near a chemical works?' asked Dodsworth.

'Some kind of laboratory?' suggested Zaentz.

'Jesus,' said Bishop, 'the kid may not even be identifying the smell correctly. It could be any kind of industrial pollution.'

Ringrose asked Art Decker, 'Any chance she added a question-mark to the message?'

He shook his head. 'Absolutely not.'

'She could even be referring to the fumes from an anthracite-burning stove,' said Ringrose. 'We'll alert local forces to the possibility of the prison being in an area of serious air pollution but it's not much of a peg to hang on, is it?'

After his early euphoria, Ringrose experienced a let-down. 'One thing's for sure,' he said. The others looked at him. 'We must give the Blood Group every encouragement to send more tapes.'

He turned once again to Art Decker. 'I'm afraid, Mr Decker, that you're in for a long night. I have another seventy-nine taped messages that I'd like you to vet. It's a slender chance but your daughter might have passed some of her heaven-sent know-how to the other girls.'

Chapter Thirty-one

The understanding between the Scotland Yard Commander and an American beauty he had never met might have been telepathic. Wrapped in their blankets the queens had, after long, whispered debate, agreed upon a message that, if opportunity arose, they would attempt to transmit in eyeball Morse.

'If those creeps upstairs stay true to form, they'll have us holding up the day's newspapers first. That'll be the moment to blink. If they get suspicious, you've got grit in your eye!'

Prentiss was trying hard to keep everyone upbeat and busy. They had been in captivity for five days, and but for the regularity of the primitive feeding arrangements, they would have lost their grip on time.

Had her first message been picked up? Prentiss tried to adhere to the principles of positive thinking. She had 'auditioned' each girl for telegraphic suitability. Hanna Hansen, nursing her battered buttocks, had been eliminated immediately. 'They'll smell a rat, Hanna, if you suddenly cave in and start performing for them.'

Prentiss could afford to 'lose' six girls because the agreed message was forty-three letters long: POSH MERCENARIES QUERY. WE IN VAST VICTORIAN CELLAR.

A couple of queens could not master the precise timing of the blinks. Donna Rosario, the exquisite Chilean queen, stuck her neck forward like a tortoise and blinked so deliberately that her head nodded in harmony with each eye movement. 'My God, you look like you're keeping time with a band!' said Prentiss. Donna sat crestfallen among the rejects.

Prentiss had broken down the message alphabetically. She began to separate the queens into groups: several to do individual letters, two to do V, four to master the dot-dash of A, six to learn E – child's play. Prentiss showed them how to stand wide-eyed and unblinking and then make one deliberate, fast closure of the eyelid to telegraph a single dot. The two girls for T had a similarly easy time – just one long 'berlink' to represent a single dash.

Lucius Frankel slammed the TV cabinet doors. He was put out by the Lord Mayor's statement on the late news that he was taking control of the ransom-raising operation.

'All seems tickety-boo to me,' grunted Bruiser. 'No skin off your noses. They can have Old Nick himself putting the money together for all I care.'

'Yes,' said Dickie Biggs-Salter, sniffing at a brandy balloon. 'After a bad start out of the gate, we seem to be hitting a patch of decent going. I do believe I'm due to come into a sizeable inheritance from a rich uncle quite soon.'

His friends chuckled. Lucius said, 'Everything certainly appears secure at this end. Ringrose is floundering. He'll be hoping to get his break during the transfer of the ransom. So tomorrow we must shift to London to begin our preparations to make sure he's disappointed.'

Rolly Ponsford had a bucket of boiling water and an oil-can standing in the fireplace. With wadding and a pull-through, he concentrated on cleaning their arsenal of weapons. 'A pity there's blood on the money,' he murmured.

Helly Harris, the dashing, hip-swinging Australian, had set herself a target of a thousand paces, running on the spot. A handful of the other girls drifting, bored, around their prison, joined her.

'Yer know,' said Helly in a breathless twang, 'there's one line of attack we haven't considered yet.'

Prentiss Decker, jogging alongside, crooked an eyebrow into a question mark.

'Sex, of course,' said Helly. 'Holy Christ, just look at us. We're meant to be the hottest pieces of ass on the planet. How come we haven't tried to fuck our way out of here? These guys may not let us go even if they get the money. So, I've been thinking, better bed than dead. It might be worth flashing one of the bastards something shocking. One of them must have a dong he hasn't exercised since he started behaving like Ned Kelly. Get him going and he might make a mistake.'

'But they must be waiting for one of us to try,' agreed Prentiss. 'It's a bit obvious – you must have noticed how clinical they were the day they snatched us and put us through that striptease.'

'I bet the insides of those helmets were steamed up, though,' Helly puffed. 'I wouldn't dismiss the idea altogether.'

Mathilde de Montméja was leaning against the stonework, listening intently to the conversation. She murmured lazily, 'Perhaps you are examining the problem from an incorrect angle. Perhaps there is a strategy that they have overlooked. The men may be, as you say, watching each other for any sign of awakening sexual interest in us. They do not come into the cellar unaccompanied. The guardians guard each other at all times. But what of the *gardienne*?'

'How's that, Mathilde?' said Helly.

'Who is safeguarding Nanny from seduction?' asked Mathilde.

'Hey, sweetheart!' said Helly, stopping abruptly. 'That's a very rude thought.'

Mathilde shrugged. 'Australia is perhaps not a comfortable country for sophisticated people. There are those in older civilizations of other persuasions.'

Helly made a coarse gesture with her forearm.

Prentiss said, 'I noticed Nanny gave you more time than she did the rest of us, Mathilde. Would you make a pass at her?'

'Poof!' said Mathilde, shrugging again. 'I make no secret: making love to a woman is to my taste. Women are my preference.'

'No kidding!' said Prentiss, thoughtfully.

'Different strokes for different folks,' said Helly.

'It is my privilege,' said Mathilde, coolly. 'I think Nanny is already interested in me. We shall see.'

'She wouldn't dare come on to you while the men are around,' said Prentiss. 'How will you handle it if she finds a way?'

'I've asked her to take me upstairs for a bath,' said Mathilde. 'I think I shall then kill her.'

All the girls stopped exercising. There was a silence in which they stared at the French girl.

'How do you think you would manage that?' asked Prentiss finally.

'Upstairs there must be something I could use as a weapon if she liberates my hands from those barbaric handcuffs.'

Mathilde could not have sounded more matter-of-fact if she had been discussing her dressmaker. She said, 'I am very practical. I think they intend to kill us when they get the money. I believe the guard on the coach is already dead so they have nothing more to lose.' She made a swinging motion with her hands as if she were holding a machine gun. 'Bub-bub-bub-bub-bub-bub. It would all be over quite soon. No more witnesses. All dead.'

'Can it,' said Prentiss. 'You're upsetting some of the girls.' She took Mathilde's slim arm and steered her away from the gathering. 'Look here, honey, we have to give your plan careful thought. The repercussions would be awful if you screwed up. At this stage we're not entirely without prospects so let's put Operation Sappho on ice, huh? Trying to kill them is only going to ease their way to killing us, but even for the most unmitigated bastard, murdering forty-nine people requires a big mental leap into a state where conscience doesn't exist.'

Prentiss stayed in earnest conversation with the French girl until the afternoon apple ration arrived. The girls sauntered into a ragged line and were each handed two green, bruised windfalls by one of the Cockney kidnappers.

Presently, Prentiss received a visit from Wanda Dahlberg, the honey-haired queen from Denmark, a student of mathematics who, before the kidnapping, had been destined for an overseas three-year course at the University of Pennsylvania.

'I don't want to be Cassandra,' said Wanda, whose English was almost totally free of an alien accent, 'but you'd better look at this.' She took Prentiss over to a wall where she had spent the last hour scratching at grubby whitewash. A series of equations disfigured the flat surface.

Prentiss looked questioningly at her. 'I've been doing some

figuring. Even if we succeed in signalling your message of forty-three letters and they were fed into a Cray computer, the result would be an almost unimaginable number of permutations, including a colossal number of words, the further permutations of which will leave the police totally baffled. I'm speaking of a figure in the order of one plus sixty noughts.' Wanda placed a hand on Prentiss's arm. 'Sorry,' she said.

Prentiss felt the energy draining down through her body and onto the cold flagstones. She stared at Wanda's wall calculations without really seeing them. 'So unless I can train the girls to deliver whole words we're sunk?'

'That's about it,' said Wanda. 'Unless you do the message yourself.'

'I'll only be able to do that in the course of delivering a long communication from the kidnappers. We have no reason to hope that they'll be so obliging.'

Prentiss felt like screaming. She placed her hands flat against the wall and began to breathe deeply to calm herself. Idly, she focused on Wanda's scratch marks. In some places, more whitewash had flaked from the wall than the girl had intended. 'What's that?' asked Prentiss, pointing to a raw area. The whitewash had covered some graffiti. Prentiss could see the letters 'ER' carefully scratched into the underlying brickwork in Gothic lettering complete with decorative serifs. Curious, she began to chip at the white covering, following the line of the old markings. Revealed finally was the work of some long-ago idler. The legend read: PETER LINDEN 5.9.1940.

'We're not the only ones to have spent some time in this hole,' she said. 'Look at this – it goes back to May of 1940.'
'No,' said Wanda. 'That's how an American would write the date. Here in Europe we put the day first. It's really the fifth of September, 1940.'

'Excuse me. I forgot,' said Prentiss. She said slowly: 'You know, Wanda, this might be the best clue to our whereabouts we've yet had. Just suppose I could pass that piece of graffiti to the outside? The police could track down Peter Linden and ask him where he was on the fifth of September nineteen forty – and we win through.'

'It's more than half a lifetime ago,' said Wanda dubiously.

'Peter Linden may be long dead. Or,' she jabbed a thumb ceilingwards, 'he may be one of those upstairs.'

'Hell,' said Prentiss. 'The message we've rehearsed is aborted. This is worth a try.'

'Yes,' agreed Wanda, 'it is.' Her precise mind had been busy, 'The message PETER LINDEN WAS HERE 5 9 40' consists of eighteen letters and four numerals. It's half the length of the message you were hoping to send. That should give you more of a chance.'

'I make it the equivalent of five words,' said Prentiss. A fair amateur should be able to transmit that in less than thirty seconds.' She shook herself. Think positive. The refrain of an old song floated out of nowhere . . . 'You pick yourself up, dust yourself off and start all over again.'

'Listen, ladies,' Prentiss shouted. 'We're going back to the drawing board . . .'

Chapter Thirty-two

On Thursday, 6 October, one week after the mass kidnapping, a new message above the signature of Lord Grey appeared in *The Times* personal column.

It read: 'Deal agreed. Before completion sample of undamaged goods needed as evidence of good faith.'

Commander Tom Ringrose craved more video tapes.

He was a policeman of wide-ranging experience but no other officer in British history had commanded a task force of such complexity and vastness. *Time* magazine's cover story that morning made riveting reading, even for him.

Time had concluded that the Scotland Yard commander was now directing two-thirds of the Metropolitan Police CID – 1,900 experienced detectives – and, through the other chief constables of England, Wales and Scotland, had access to a vast provincial back-up.

The Prime Minister had cleared the Ringer's path: heads would roll, he made clear, if the Commander was thwarted in any way by interdepartmental or intercounty demarcation squabbles, such as those that had marred the hunt for the Great Train Robbers and the Yorkshire Ripper. He wasn't going to tolerate it. He had forty-eight heads of state on his back.

Ringrose himself viewed this cornucopia of manpower with some alarm.

With Lionel Firth's assistance, he had devised a series of daily conferences through which his orders and suggestions filtered down to the men on the ground and through which he obtained a feed-back.

Ringrose reflected grimly that, despite this massive deployment of detectives, the break that might solve the case could well come from an unarmed bobby on the beat. This had been the outcome in the hunts for the Ripper and the Black Panther. Two policemen were dead and there wasn't a copper in the country not thirsting for retribution.

Ringrose's own thoughts had focused on one anomaly in the avalanche of information provided for his personal assessment. He had approached it from every conceivable angle, worrying at it obsessively. Ringrose was no fan of detective stories – did plumbers read books about plumbing for entertainment? – but he could not reject Conan Doyle's Theory of Elimination: 'When you have eliminated the impossible, whatever remains, however improbable, must be the truth.'

The time had come to see if the dictum of Sherlock Holmes stood up to twentieth-century circumstances.

Since the death of her husband in a cross-Atlantic yacht race, Lady Nancy Cornmorris had lived in a top-floor apartment of a post-war block in Palace Court, Bayswater, a few steps from Kensington Gardens and the Round Pond where she was wont to stroll, watching the model ships on the dappled water and the kite-fliers on the nearby mound.

Despite her high profile in public, her private life was solitary. Her husband's estate had been shockingly small and, in widowhood, her style of living had been adjusted accordingly.

In fact, there was now an observer – or, more accurately, a small corps of observers – of this way of life. Since day two of the investigation, the post office had placed an intercept on her mail, which was being examined by Ringrose's men and then resealed and forwarded. The Home Secretary had signed a tap order for her telephone and the hall porter at her apartment block had suddenly acquired round-the-clock assistants. An electronic listening device had been installed in the pelmet above her living-room curtains and a fellow to it in a light-fitting in the only bedroom. The use of directional listening devices had not proved feasible. These work via a laser beam trained on the glass windows. The pane imperceptibly vibrates and carries speech from the target room along the laser, to be decoded. The drawback to this ingenuity is that it does not work on double glazing. Lady Cornmorris's windows were double-glazed.

Nevertheless, the team monitoring her ladyship's life was reasonably satisfied with their arrangements as, indeed, were similar teams assigned to the activities of Arthur Emblem and Alan Jay Jaffe.

Between them, this trio had admitted the Trojan Horse in the shape of Regal Roadways. Ringrose had never let that fact stray far from a central place in his deliberations.

He had Lady Cornmorris picked up as she left Palace Court for her Belgrave Square office. She accompanied the two detectives graciously, a woman anxious to help. They took her to the police station in Ladbroke Grove, where her arrival would pass unnoticed by the media army. She was placed in a bare interview room, furnished only with a plain table, two chairs and a mirror.

Lady Cornmorris gazed hard at the mirror. She was not a fool. She knew what it was for. A policewoman who needed to lose at least twenty pounds stood impassively by the door.

Ringrose studied her from the other side of the observation mirror. She was wearing a well-cut two-piece suit in bitter chocolate, with a black silk scarf camouflaging time's treacherous touch on her throat. Coolly she crossed her black-stockinged legs. The most detailed account of her life was in Ringrose's hands plus the recent observation reports. She'd had no unusual contacts or telephone calls either at home or at the office. The dog watch had recorded sounds of restless nights but this could be attributed to anxiety over the missing queens and the disastrous financial flop of the contest. Each night, Lady Cornmorris had slept alone.

Ringrose walked in and took the seat facing her without saying good morning.

'Lady Cornmorris,' he began, with no preamble, 'you are here this morning to clear up certain matters that have been puzzling me. May I rely on your total co-operation in this?'

'But, of course, Commander.' Nancy Cornmorris fought a desire to shift nervously in her chair. This was a different Ringrose from the solicitous figure who had led her gently through her version of events within three hours of his arrival from Corsica. This man was cold, suppressing hostility with difficulty.

226

He said, 'I have been studying old newsreels of past Queen of the Earth contests and it is clear that this year the travel arrangements were different. You've always employed two coaches but in previous years the girls and their chaperones travelled together so that in both coaches you had a mix of the two.' He leaned forward, his knuckles resting on the table edge. 'Rather convenient for the kidnappers that the girls were all concentrated in the one coach this year, would you not say, Lady Cornmorris?'

She returned his gaze steadily. 'Distressingly convenient, Commander.'

'How did it come about?' he demanded.

'As I remember, it was something to do with having the chaperones go ahead separately with the queens' headdresses.' She waved a hand vaguely.

'*As you remember!*' mimicked Tom Ringrose rudely.

'I've not come here to be mocked,' she said.

Ringrose brushed aside her indignation. 'You *should* remember because the changeover was made at your instigation. I have signed statements here from three people who witnessed you throw a tantrum because some of the girls' headdresses were damaged last year when they wore them in the coach.'

'I think I was entitled,' said Lady Cornmorris. 'Having the girls put the headdresses on before arrival at the Grosvenor House was clumsy. Much better that they should be safeguarded beforehand by the chaperones.'

'Fine!' said Ringrose. 'Perhaps a tantrum was justified. My problem is that you did not have the tantrum, as one might expect, in the full flood of temper as the girls alighted from the coach with their battered headgear. *You waited six months and had it at Belgrave Square.*'

Lady Cornmorris instinctively moved back her elegant head as Ringrose's voice rose to a bellow. 'I shan't tolerate this for one more moment!' she gasped, pushing back her chair.

'Policewoman!' shouted Ringrose. 'Put Lady Cornmorris back in her seat.'

The Brünnhilde stomped smartly forward and pressed the woman firmly back into place. Lady Cornmorris screamed in disbelief. 'You thug!' she said.

'Bugger that!' said Ringrose. 'You waited six months to have a tantrum because you needed to jolt Arthur Emblem into changing the coach arrangements.'

'It was he who suggested putting all the girls together in one coach,' Lady Cornmorris cried.

'Oh, so you do remember!' said Ringrose. 'Yes, you're quite right. It was Arthur Emblem. But, after your well-acted tantrum, it was just one of the number of suggestions he made to you to overcome the headdress problem. You let him talk on until he came up with the suggestion you wanted to hear. And then you said, "That sounds the best idea yet, Arthur."'

Ringrose tried to imitate her higher-pitched voice. He wanted her truly outraged and rattled.

'I don't recollect the discussion proceeding like that,' she said. She was now pale under her blusher.

'No, you wouldn't, would you?' said Ringrose. 'But three other people do recollect it *exactly* like that – Emblem, his secretary and Alan Jaffe. Your mistake was to have the tantrum in the first place. People tend to remember vivid dramas of that nature – and the events leading to them. But for that outburst everyone might have forgotten exactly who proposed what. After all, it was six months ago. But you were once an actress and you couldn't resist giving an old skill an airing.'

Lady Cornmorris surrendered to her urge to twist in her chair. 'All this is monstrous,' she said. 'You're drawing disgraceful conclusions from trivial findings.'

'Oh, don't run away with the idea that my case ends there.' Ringrose banged his folder on the table. 'Let's move on to the second trivial happening. Cast your mind back to the telephone conversation you had on the day of the kidnapping with the man calling himself Glyn Owain.'

The pressure was off her. 'Very well – if it will help,' she said, trying to settle herself.

'You asked to speak to one of the girls?'

'Yes, and they brought the Spanish girl to the telephone.'

'You had quite a conversation with her, according to your two colleagues who were at your elbow. She was almost certainly an impostor, yet you immediately accepted her at voice-value. You'd met and chatted to all the girls previously, hadn't you?'

'Yes, yes,' said Cornmorris impatiently. 'But the only one I'd known well was the British contender Fran Pilkington. How could you expect me to recognize any one of them from a telephone conversation in those trying conditions?'

Ringrose ignored her question. 'Tell me, Lady Cornmorris, what does the Spanish word *tontería* mean in English?'

'It means "foolishness".'

'Yes. You see, you answered that question without hesitation. Since the last time I spoke to you I've learned that, during your late husband's diplomatic service, you were stationed for two years in Madrid. Your Spanish is excellent, is it not?'

'Yes, as a matter of fact it is. But what has this . . .'

'. . . got to do with you?' Ringrose stuck his head forward and lowered his voice to a near whisper. '*Tontería* has everything to do with you. It's what you have been, isn't it, Lady Cornmorris. Foolish. *Tontería is the word that you should have used to the so-called Spanish girl in that telephone call. When she asked what "foolish" meant in Spanish you said "never mind". The reason you said that, instead of explaining the one word "tontería", was because you were play-acting again.*'

Ringrose's voice resumed its normal level. He sat back and said affably, 'I've taken a private wager with myself. When I catch up with that female accomplice of yours, I bet I find that she can't speak a word of Spanish. You knew that – and that's why you didn't keep up the charade. You really should have had someone else write you a more convincing script.'

'Accomplice?' Lady Cornmorris's eyes were wide in shock. 'I can't believe you're saying these things to me.'

'Oh, I'm saying them all right,' said Ringrose. 'And there's some more.' He drew out his set of photographs and placed them face down on the table. 'Now, tell me, where were you on the eve of the kidnapping?'

'At the Guildhall, at the Lord Mayor's dinner with the rest of the Queen of the Earth party, of course.'

Ringrose made no comment. He turned up the first of his photographs that showed a scene in the Guildhall, with the

Lord Mayor and Lady Mayoress in their high-backed chairs at the centre of the long top table.

'There, you see!' said Lady Cornmorris, triumphantly. She placed a perfectly painted coral-pink nail on a figure fourth down from the Lady Mayoress. 'That's me!'

'So it is,' said Ringrose. 'That picture was taken at approximately the pudding stage. The bread plates have been cleared away and the wine waiters are distributing the liqueurs before the speeches begin. Your plate is clean because your waiter says you refused the pudding. Watching your figure, I expect?'

'Yes, that's correct,' agreed Lady Cornmorris, subdued.

Ringrose turned up his next picture. This revealed the same top table from a different angle with herself inclined over her plate, raising a forkful of food and making a remark to a neighbour.

'This photograph was taken at approximately eight thirty, during the main course,' said Ringrose. He cleared the two prints from the table and began to lay out the rest of the photographs as if he were playing patience.

'Now here's an intriguing thing,' he said. Lady Cornmorris watched, hypnotized, as the pictures were laid out in reverse time order, down through the beginning of the meal to the cocktail party preceding the dinner to the official handshake greeting by the Lord Mayor and Lady Mayoress.

'For instance,' said Ringrose, 'look at this picture of everyone standing to say grace. It is unusual for one fact: you're not in it. And look at the rest of these pictures. Neither are you in any of the others.' He took a pencil and positioned the point on one panoramic view. 'Here is one taken at eight fifteen. There's a gap where you should be sitting and enjoying your smoked salmon.'

Lady Cornmorris made a tiny sound of exasperation. 'I don't see why you should make such a fuss. I'm not in those photographs for one simple reason. I had trouble starting my car and missed the beginning of the meal.'

'That's what you told the Lady Mayoress,' said Ringrose. 'Tell me more.'

'Well,' said Lady Cornmorris, shrugging, 'I'd been at the Colonel Blood Inn all day. I drove home to bathe and change for dinner. My car would not start – damp plugs – I walked down to the Bayswater Road and hailed a taxi that took me to the Guildhall.'

'Damp plugs, my arse!' said Ringrose. 'The weather had been fine and dry for days. There was nothing wrong with your car. You're a member of the AA yet you did not summon them. Neither did you seek aid from your own garage nor any other garage in the Bayswater area.' He leaned forward again, his elbows thumping the table. 'In the London Metropolitan area there are 21,784 licensed taxi drivers, of whom 6,467 were plying for hire on the evening of Wednesday, the twenty-eighth of September. In the past five days my men have spoken to every last one of them. They found eighty-four who took fares to the Guildhall for the dinner but not one picked up a fare in the early evening in the Bayswater Road who gave the Guildhall as the destination. And, although each of those 6,467 drivers was shown a set of six fine photographic studies of you, not one claimed you as a customer. And I think you'd agree, Lady Cornmorris, you're not a woman whose looks people forget in a hurry.'

She was severely rattled now. Her luscious mouth, with the wide, velvet upper lip, opened and closed several times. Finally she said, 'Someone is playing fast and loose with you. Of course my car would not start. Perhaps the trouble was a piece of grit in the works. At any rate, next morning it had dislodged itself and the car was working perfectly. As for the taxi, please don't saddle me with the blame for some wretched taxi driver who lacks either memory or eyes. In any case, where is all this taxi nonsense taking us?'

Ringrose said, 'It is taking us to the Colonel Blood Inn, where between seven thirty and eight on the Wednesday evening, when you were supposedly having difficulties with your car and the chambermaids were arranging admirers' bouquets of flowers in the queens' rooms. It's rather odd, don't you feel, that the Israeli girl had three times as many admirers as any of the others? Her maid tells me she spent at least fifteen minutes in Rebecca Engelman's room arranging a huge mass of blooms. She tells me that the door behind her was open all the time and she cannot swear that nobody sneaked in.'

'I don't understand,' said Lady Cornmorris, fearfully. 'Why should anyone want to sneak in?'

'To spike Rebecca's orange juice,' said Ringrose. 'To pour just enough of an arsenic substance into a jug in her refrigerator to make her sick the next morning thus keeping her and, more importantly, her two bodyguards, off the coach that went missing. It would have been most inconvenient, would it not, Lady Cornmorris, if your co-conspirators-and-murderers had become engaged in an exchange of gunfire with these trained pistol shots? Your people are good only for killing unarmed policemen.'

'Are you accusing me?' she cried.

'Oh, yes,' said Tom Ringrose agreeably. 'You dressed early for the Lord Mayor's dinner, lingered on at the Colonel Blood Inn, poisoned the orange juice after most people had left for the Guildhall and then you followed on, arriving just in time for the main course.'

Lady Cornmorris slumped sideways in a dead faint.

'Pick her up and get her some smelling salts,' Ringrose ordered impassively. He sat watching as the policewoman loosened Lady Cornmorris's scarf and rubbed her wrists.

She came round groggily, then realizing where she was, drew herself up and spat at him, 'These are disgraceful fabrications. I demand to see my lawyer.'

'Who's stopping you?' said Ringrose.

'Then give me the telephone.'

'I don't see that we owe you a call on police funds. Make the call from your own place.'

Lady Cornmorris's eyes widened. 'Do you mean, after all that, you're not detaining me or proffering charges?'

'No, I'm letting you return home for now. I just wanted you to know that I know. Soon you will come to me of your own volition and tell me everything because I don't believe that you meant to get mixed up in the slaughter of innocent people. I know your personal life has not been easy since your husband's untimely death and I understand how the promise of a large sum of money in return for a modicum of work, normally unworthy of you, would have seemed to be the answer to all your financial worries.' Ringrose nodded. 'You'll come to me all right, and when you help me, I'll see what I can do to help you.'

Lady Cornmorris flinched. She could no longer hold eye contact with this chilling, omniscient man. He'd pieced the story together perfectly.

Tom Ringrose and Lionel Firth watched from a window as the policewoman helped her down the steps into the station yard where a car waited to return her home. Something terrible had happened to her face. In daylight it was suddenly pouched and seamed.

Ringrose said, 'It's not just greed, you know. It's not just because she's supporting a life-style without money. She's doing this for a man, someone evil. That's who she must lead us to. Lionel, I'll have severed heads on poles on London Bridge if the surveillance team loses her over the next few days.'

'Guv'nor,' said Lionel with feeling, 'she has more people shadowing her at this moment than the President of the United States.'

From her apartment, Lady Cornmorris made no attempt to telephone her lawyer. The clandestine voice-activated tape recorder began turning only once when Lady Cornmorris left a brief message at her office to say she was unwell and would not be in.

From their listening van, parked in Palace Court, Ringrose's men could hear her pacing the floor, saying, 'Oh, God! Oh, God!' and making a smacking sound. In her anguish, she was smashing one small fist into the palm of the other hand.

In mid-afternoon she emerged from the apartment, well wrapped against the chill, and walked to the public telephone box at the corner of the road. She opened the door and hesitated on the threshold.

'Go on! Go on!' she was silently urged from the observation van. Every public telephone within a thousand-yard radius of Palace Court had been tapped.

Her watchers held their breath for as long as she held the door. She let her arm drop. She'd changed her mind.

She crossed Bayswater Road, entered the broadwalk of Kensington Gardens and, head down, made for the Round Pond.

She looked exactly what she was: a woman gravely disturbed.

In all she made six circuits of the water, heedless of the south-westerly breeze breaking up the slate surface. Then her head came up. Now, with more purpose in her stride, she pressed on across the park to the Kensington High Street side.

She found a telephone box off Kensington Square. 'Shit! Shit! Shit!' cursed her watchers. The box was outside the tapping radius. They bustled into position to train a parabolic directional microphone upon the box. This instrument had been developed in the United States so that, from a spot high in a football stand, a team coach could eavesdrop on rival players planning their moves on the pitch below.

However, London telephone boxes muffle a great deal of sound, and Lady Cornmorris spoke low, cupping the receiver and her mouth with a gloved hand.

'The only thing the lads can tell us,' said Firth later, 'is that she dialled an out-of-town number of eleven digits.'

Ringrose sat on his Eames chair eating a canteen corned-beef sandwich. 'Keep the ring tight around her,' he said, 'and add that blasted telephone box to the tap list. She may be a creature of habit.'

It was a good try. But she wasn't.

Lucius Frankel dropped the receiver back into the cradle, his mind racing. 'So, all is revealed,' drawled Bruiser, who had answered the phone. 'The Source is a female.'

An intense voice had said, 'Please get me Lucius Frankel at once.'

'Who is that?' Bruiser had inquired.

'Just tell him it's the Source,' said the woman urgently.

Without a word, Bruiser handed the receiver to Lucius and watched his face. His features went from surprise to concentration to alarm to total absorption.

'Christ, we agreed you weren't to telephone here,' said Lucius, panicked.

'I know, I know, darling,' said Lady Cornmorris. 'But the worst possible thing has happened. That man Ringrose knows *everything*. Oh, why did you have to kill those policemen? I simply *had* to call.'

At this Lucius suddenly experienced difficulty in breathing. He managed to say, 'Where are you telephoning from?'

'Don't worry, darling. I'm in a call box. I'm not stupid. I know they must be watching me.'

'*Watching* you!' Lucius echoed. 'Christ, they'll be doing more than just watching you if Ringrose really knows everything.'

He let her pour out her story. But, as bad as Nancy Cornmorris's news was, Lucius felt a measure of relief.

'Now listen carefully,' he said. 'All right, Ringrose has been clever. He has intelligence and has analysed what must have happened on the night of the Guildhall dinner. But you mustn't blame yourself. The Israelis simply had to be neutralized. We all appreciated that there was a risk involved. He has made the correct deductions – but that's all they are. He certainly doesn't have enough to charge you. Otherwise he wouldn't have let you walk out of the police station.'

Lucius did not believe this. Ringrose was quite devious enough to have released her in the hope that she'd break cover and lead the hunt straight to the lair. But he said, 'The important thing is to keep a tight grip on yourself. Go home and try to remain calm. I think we must assume that they're listening in to your telephone, and that in all likelihood your flat is bugged. So act normally, as if you suspect nothing.'

Nancy Cornmorris broke in shakily, 'Please, please, Lucius, I must see you. I need you to hold me and tell me everything's going to be all right. I can't keep up this front much longer on my own.'

She's on the point of falling apart, thought Lucius. He'd have to move fast if disaster was to be headed off.

Soothingly he said, 'We're almost there. I'll come to see you by the usual route. Make sure your television is switched on loudly by 8 p.m. and leave it on. Put your door on the single lock and, when I come in, for goodness sake don't say a word. Remember, they'll almost certainly be listening. Then you can leave the rest to me.'

He sounded so purposeful. Nancy Cornmorris pushed open the door of the telephone box, the other hand at her throat to curb its fluttering. He was coming! Oh, how she needed him. No one, not even her husband, had possessed her totally. And, merciful Lord, what she had allowed herself to do for love!

Bruiser said, 'Trouble?'

Lucius said, 'Yes, but it's something I'll need to handle myself. It means getting up to town fast.'

From Moxmanton Lucius drove directly to his home in South Audley Street. He unlocked one of the leather-fronted cupboards in his office and took out an instrument that he had not expected to use until the dangerous day came when the ransom money was handed over.

Chapter Thirty-three

Lucius had been surprised at the ease with which it was possible to acquire such an article. Inside the Counter-Spy Shop, a charming American salesman had laid out his wares. Among them was a device that looked like a walkie-talkie radio with twin aerials. In fact, this piece of electronic wizardry was a counter-surveillance receiver, capable of picking up any transmission in the AM and FM range. Thus it would be possible to detect the presence of both listening 'bugs' and signal-emitting bleepers.

'With this you can sweep and clean a room or a car in less than thirty minutes,' said the American.

Now Lucius attached the device to his belt and buttoned his top-coat over it.

He reached Palace Court just before 8 p.m. and took a leisurely stroll along the street on the opposite side of the road to Nancy Cornmorris's block. The entrance hall was a blazing rectangle of light in the surrounding autumnal gloom. He'd always avoided drawing attention to his relationship with Nancy. He'd only used that front entrance. There had been one hall porter in attendance. At this hour in the evening should there be two? He thought not. Yet within the box of light he could see two men in porter's uniforms.

Lucius completed his stroll to the end of the road, crossed over to double back along the near side. He found what he was looking for half-way along the road: a plain van with glass panels let into the sides that seemed to have been painted over. He smiled at the authentic touch of the parking warden's ticket in its Cellophane bag under the windscreen wiper. As he passed he could hear the chassis creaking under the weight of its occupants. He looked down into the gutter. Coppers were dirty sods. There was a small heap of ash and cigarette-ends near the tyre. Someone had been emptying the watchers' communal ashtray.

Lucius had seen enough. He continued on until he reached the Bayswater Road, turned left and doubled back along St Petersburg Place, running parallel to Palace Court.

In the van, one of the surveillance squad eased his earphones and said to his colleague, 'She's turned on the telly. ITV's comedy hour. Pity. They've got the Liverpool–Arsenal match on BBC One.'

Since his first exploratory visit via the front door, Lucius had always used the same method to visit Nancy Cornmorris. He remained the invisible friend, lover and conspirator.

Lucius had parked his car outside a block of flats in St Petersburg Place, which backed onto Nancy Cornmorris's building. He climbed into the driver's seat and waited. His vigil lasted only ten minutes. A young couple came arm-in-arm along the road and approached the entrance. Lucius was already sliding out of the car as the man pressed the entryphone button. The trip-lock on the glass doors buzzed and the couple pushed open the door. Lucius was immediately behind them as they stepped inside. 'Good evening,' he said pleasantly. In the lift the young man pressed the fourth-floor button. Lucius pressed the sixth.

He came out silently and moved swiftly along the empty corridor to the flight of steps that led up to the roof fire escape. The door was opened by means of a push bar. Lucius operated it quietly and stepped onto the dark roof. He carefully sited a small wooden wedge so that the door could not self-lock and, skirting the building's central-heating unit, headed softly for the rear. He stopped at a low wall separating the flat roof from Nancy's building. He waited for fifteen minutes in the shadows, listening, watching, every nerve-end on duty. Only the sounds of traffic floated up from the busy streets of Bayswater below. No one else was sharing his nocturnal prowl. The police surveillance was apparently being conducted from ground level. Lucius clambered across and lowered himself gently onto the far side. He moved confidently over the familiar terrain, circling a ventilation shaft.

238

The roof door was similar to the one through which he had just gained access to the rooftops and could only be opened from the inside. But Nancy, in her stockinged feet, had done her job well. The door, her wedge in the jamb, opened easily. Lucius took off his shoes and stuffed them into his coat pockets. Then he slipped silently down the stairs, a phantom caller.

Before leaving South Audley Street he had coated the Chubb key with oil and now he inserted it into Nancy's front-door lock and turned the tumblers noiselessly. He was across the threshold, with the door shut behind him, in one second.

The armed policeman sitting on the stairs between the fifth and sixth floors looked up sharply as he imagined he heard an abrupt increase in the distant volume of Lady Cornmorris's television set. He pulled out the earpiece that kept him in touch with the outside squad and listened. Everything sounded normal. Still . . . he crept up to the sixth floor and peered along the corridor. It was deserted and her ladyship's door was closed. He even gave it a tentative push to be certain. He returned to his lonely post.

She was sitting, unheeding of the television, as he came in. She wore a vermilion wrap, loosely knotted and displaying a deep V to the waist.

She started to see him standing in her living room with a cautionary finger to his lips and leaped into his arms, hugging him so fiercely that he could not breathe. She smothered his face with kisses. One hand held her and the other mechanically stroked her back. He felt hot in her embrace and uncomfortable in his bulky street clothes.

Tonight her physical appearance mercilessly exposed her age. She was making small mewing sounds and he had to prise himself out of her arms and sit her down. He made signs for her to remain still.

Lucius peeled off his coat and unclipped the counter-bug from his belt. She watched wide-eyed as he extended the two probes and clipped earphones to his head. He switched it on and immediately heard a rapid beep-beep-beep-beep. He adopted a grid-pattern search technique, moving slowly in parallel lines, sweeping the floor and furniture. The counter-bug continued its fast beep. Then Lucius started on the walls. The window wall came third on his search sequence. The beeps slowed perceptibly as he scanned slowly along the under-sill radiator. He moved higher and higher until, on a level with the pelmet, the beep came almost to a stop. Lucius took a chair and stood it in front of the closed curtains.

The listening device had been placed on top of the pelmet. It consisted of a metal disk, the size of a tenpenny piece, a two-inch long battery and a wire aerial that gave the device considerable range and definition. He beckoned to Nancy Cornmorris and he helped her up onto the chair to inspect his find. She put out a hand to touch the bug but he shook his head and pulled back her arm.

Lucius completed his sweep of the room and moved on to the bathroom, kitchen and dining area. There were no more surprises. Then he moved silently into the bedroom.

Nancy was showing signs of impatience. After another ten minutes he beckoned her in to show her the bug in the light fitting.

Lucius detached the apparatus and, taking from his pocket a quilted envelope, he gingerly packed it away, sealed the flap and placed it inside the oven. He closed the door on the kitchen, led Nancy by the hand into the bedroom and closed the door.

'This room's clean,' he said, 'but it's as well to keep your voice low.'

He listened for what seemed hours to her outpourings of woe. 'I thought I was being so damn clever letting Arthur and Alan listen in to my conversation with that ghastly girl. I thought they'd make reliable witnesses. That slip-up with the Spanish was so stupid of me. It was small but Ringrose didn't miss it. God! He scares me. I swear he is psychic.

'I knew something was wrong when the Lord Mayor tele-phoned and insisted that he take over the ransom-raising. He even threatened me with the Charity Commissioners.'

She hooked an arm round his neck. 'I'm so sorry, darling. We've lost control of the money.'

Lucius had stretched her out on her antique brass-railed bed. He slid a hand inside her wrap and gently took her left nipple

240

between thumb and forefinger. She gave a little gasp. He said, 'I think we were perhaps being too optimistic. I doubt that, in the long run, the police would have left it to the Queen of the Earth organization to make the handover arrangements.' He added grimly, 'They'll gain no advantage. They'll pay the tribute all the same – and they'll be left looking like clowns.'

'But what about me, darling? Even if they can't arrest me, they'll always *know*. I'll never be able to spend a penny of that money without looking over my shoulder.' Her head turned each way on the pillow in distress.

'Are you certain there's nothing incriminating in this apartment? They must have searched it already and when they really turn nasty you can expect them to tear down the walls,' he said.

'I swear,' said Nancy Cornmorris. 'I've been most careful. The only thing in the place is the key to the flat at Kew. It's in my handbag on my key-ring,' she said.

'You'd better let me have it for now,' he said. His hand worked knowingly over her chest. 'We'll have to live abroad. A long, long way away,' he said.

He looked down at her worn face, stripped of its customary hauteur and now poised between anxiety and urgent lust. She resembled a slim, pale chrysalis lying on the petal of an exotic tropical flower.

'Do it to me, Lucius!' she whispered fiercely.

'Hmmm. You're wearing your suspender belt,' he murmured. And lowering his dark head to lay his lips on her thigh, he began to unclip her dark green stocking.

In the van in Palace Court, the surveillance men suffered the comedy, the ten o'clock news and a late made-for-television movie.

The listener with the earphones said to his mate, 'Christ, I would have thought she'd have more taste than to stay tuned all evening to that shit.'

He could not hear the sounds of Lady Cornmorris preparing for bed because she had still not turned off the set at 2 a.m.

'That's odd,' said the listener. 'She must have fallen asleep watching. I can't say I blame her.'

Twenty minutes later he was still intercepting the early-morning programme on his earphones.

'Perhaps she's taken a couple of Mogadons?' suggested the second man.

'Christ! You don't suppose she could have slipped out under the cover of the noise? If she has, Ringrose'll have our balls for paperweights.'

The listener frantically summoned up the 'hall porter' on the two-way. No, she'd definitely not eluded him. A minute later he and the armed constable on the stairs tiptoed up to Lady Cornmorris's door. It was locked but, with an ear pressed close, they could confirm that the television was still on. They gazed at each other helplessly.

'Do we use our key?' whispered the 'hall porter'.

'Better let the powers-that-be make that decision,' said the other.

At 2.50 a.m. Commander Ringrose was informed of the dilemma. He sat upright on his camp bed. 'Let the officer substituting for the hall porter knock at the door. If she responds, let him tell her there's been a burglary elsewhere in the building and that he's checking each apartment. If there's no response, go in. I'll be waiting for your call back.'

Ringrose put down the telephone. He didn't like it. He picked up the receiver again and made an inquiry. Nancy Cornmorris, he was informed, had neither received nor made any telephone calls since 7.48 that evening.

The hall porter approached her door and tapped, at first softly and then progressively louder. No answer. He walked back along the corridor to the other officer and said, 'You'd better come in, too. Have that shooter ready.' The constable drew his .38 with the two-inch barrel and took off the safety catch. 'Lead on, Macduff.'

The two young officers found Nancy Cornmorris sprawled obscenely on her bed. One stocking was still drawn tautly up her thigh. The other formed a ligature, biting deeply into the ageing throat. Her eyeballs had rolled up so that only the whites were visible under half-closed lids, and her tongue lolled purple from the side of the once lovely mouth. The livid colour was matched by the *petechiae*, the clusters of subcutaneous haemorrhages that marred the frantic face, a sure indication, even without the stocking, of strangulation.

The armed policeman trod on something hidden in the pile of a rug. Her handbag had been opened and the contents emptied on the floor. Her keys were scattered everywhere. He was standing on one.

'Guv'nor, you can't blame yourself,' said Lionel Firth. 'Your first duty was to find the girls. If you'd pulled Nancy Cornmorris in and kept her, there's no knowing how the rest of the gang would have reacted. They might have moved the girls to a different location or even bumped off the lot of 'em and made a run for it.'

Ringrose ran a hand through his greying forelock and said, 'I know. But try telling that to them.' His toe touched the newspapers scattered over the floor of his office. The headlines screamed at the latest outrage and the British press was beginning to adopt the critical tone of much of the foreign reporting.

Beyond supplying the basic facts concerning the finding of the body at the morning media conference, Ringrose had refused to speculate about the reasons for Lady Cornmorris's murder. The crime reporters were now doing the speculation for him and every aspect of the dead woman's life was coming under the fiercest press scrutiny.

Ringrose had been summoned to see the Commissioner who, set-faced, had taken him round to the Home Secretary who, equally set-faced, had taken the pair to Number 10, Downing Street, to give an account of themselves to the Prime Minister.

Ringrose had briefed him on everything he had felt unable to tell the media. He was not feeling too pleased with himself but the Prime Minister said, 'Brace up, Commander. You've lost a skirmish but you haven't yet lost the war. I have to tell you that the ransom money is flowing in.' He smiled thinly. 'I have to consider the political aspects. It's all making it that much harder for the Lord Mayor, but he is so far dragging his feet in the most convincing manner. However, there seems little doubt that the twenty-five million dollars these scoundrels demand will be reached by the middle of next week. The Lord Mayor may be able to lay a smokescreen until the following weekend. But financial journalists can do their sums as well as we can. They'll only have to tot up the amounts collected in individual countries to end up with a truthful result. That's when we may expect awkward questions.'

Chapter Thirty-four

By the time their second week in captivity had begun, Monika Dahlberg was having difficulty coaxing the girls into her aerobics classes. A perilously fatalistic air pervaded the cellar. The girls were exhausted by the long, newsless days and fretful nights.

Despite all Prentiss Decker's ingenious ideas, morale was oozing away. All requests for washing facilities had been brusquely refused, although they were fed regularly, if monotonously, from what they had nicknamed The Kidnap Canteen. The sole drink was now tap water.

Medical problems were arising. Hanna Hansen's weals had festered and, reluctantly, ointment and hot water had been provided for her. Four girls had disintegrated into bouts of hysterical weeping and the queen from Aruba had hurled herself against a wall in an apparent suicide attempt. Girls were now guarding her round the clock. More than a quarter were enduring menstruation, and half a dozen complained of chills. All in all, Eva Ravignini from Argentina, the only girl with any professional nursing experience, was getting all the exercise she needed without resorting to Monika Dahlberg's classes.

Prentiss, like Eva, had been too busy to feel ill and paced their prison like an impatient tigress. It was the second Saturday and their captors had summoned no one to tape a further video message.

Prentiss offered up a silent prayer: 'Peter Linden, whoever you are, please don't be dead. And please may the swine upstairs soon start videoing again.'

Their midday meal revealed a variation in routine. So far at mealtimes, the girls had been made to stand well back from the grille by at least one man armed with a submachine gun. The gate was unlocked and the two Cockneys would enter the cellar carrying the vats. The food would be doled out, the utensils cleared away and the gate relocked. Today the upstairs door opened and Nanny, on her own with no firearm cover, made four journeys down the steps carrying two vats of soup, dry bread and apples. She did not unlock the grille gate but placed the food against the bars. 'You'll have to reach through and help yourselves,' she said, standing well out of reach of hands that throbbed with murderous impulse.

While Mathilde de Montméja stretched her arm through to scoop up a beaker of soup, she gazed steadily into Nanny's blank mirrored visor and silently mouthed one word. 'Please . . .' Nanny made no response.

Nanny waited until the last of the girls had filed past the grille and helpings had been collected for the sick, then wordlessly gathered in the pans, retreated up the steps, leaving the top door ajar to admit the electricity cable for the heater.

King William Street is a short thoroughfare, beginning north of London Bridge and running crookedly through the oldest part of the City until it reaches the Mansion House where the Lord Mayor was organizing the counting of the money in such a way that every banknote was checked no less than five times. It was the opinion among City leaders that the old fool was making an absolute mess of things and ought not to have poked his silly nose in. However, peer group loyalty forbade any public airing of these misgivings.

Three hundred yards away, in King William Street, an incident occurred on Saturday that was not immediately connected with the events that were dominating the world's television newscasts and headlines.

The Colonel Blood Group was of no pressing concern to Bill Beer as he settled down to an afternoon's sports viewing while his wife, Flo, carried on knitting the layette for their first grandchild. Their small, spotless flat was on the rear ground floor of a King William Street office block, of which Bill was the caretaker and Flo the supervisor of a corps of charladies who reported for their office-cleaning chores on five weekdays at 6.30 a.m. and were finished by ten, when the first City workers arrived.

The Beers enjoyed a contented life. The building was not rated by insurance companies as a high security risk, as it housed firms who kept little money on hand. The ground floor was rigged with a burglar alarm and Bill made regular inspections around the building which, at the weekend, was as peaceful as a country cemetery.

All the more puzzling, then, the events of that afternoon.

More people were strolling along King William Street than was usual on a Saturday. Most were sightseers on their way to the Mansion House to join the crowd that cheered the poster artist every time he emerged to paint in another high mark on the towering wooden barometer. There was a special roar of approval when the line rose above the ten-million-dollar line.

At 3 p.m. Bill Beer's door-bell sounded. He turned his back reluctantly on his television set and walked through the corridor to the foyer. Through the one-way spyhole he could see a man in overalls.

'Yes, what is it?' shouted Bill, without opening the door.

'Sorry to bother you, mate. Gas Board,' explained the voice from the other side. 'Have you smelt gas on your premises during the past few hours?'

'No,' said Bill, 'but you'd better hold on.'

Bill Beer crossed to a panel set into the marble wall, unlocked it and threw the switch that killed the alarm system. He took a few deep inhalations of the still but unsullied air. He couldn't smell any gas.

Bill took off the chain, turned the double locks and opened up. The big fellow said, 'Mind if I sniff around? You don't want the happy home to go up.' He was already crossing the threshold.

'Here!' said Bill, trying to put a restraining hand on the man's massive chest. 'Don't you have to show me some identification?'

The big fellow lifted Bill off his feet, swept into the foyer and kicked the door closed.

Bill got out one bellow of fright before a hand the size of a shovel was clamped over his mouth.

'If you don't struggle, you won't get hurt,' said the man. Then there were three distinct raps on the door from the outside. The big man easily held Bill with one arm while he turned the locks and admitted five other men in overalls. Bill now felt real fear.

'You've made a mistake,' he gasped. 'This isn't a bank. There's hardly anything here worth pinching – it's all files and stored documents.'

'Just hold your tongue,' said the big fellow. 'Who else is in the building?'

'Only my wife,' said Bill. 'For God's sake, don't hurt her. We're only working people. We haven't got anything.'

'Shut up,' said Bruiser. 'Show us where she is.'

The intruders had agreed beforehand to do nothing that could link them with the Colonel Blood Group, so there were no weapons, ear plugs, gags or blindfolds for the victims.

Half an hour later, Bill and Flo were lashed with cord to chairs, which in turn were lashed to the legs of the kitchen table.

One of the gang filled two saucepans with fresh tapwater and placed one in front of Flo and the other in front of Bill, a hinged straw in each. The same gang member also broke two chocolate bars into squares and lined them up along the table edge within distance of their tongues.

'If you shout, no one will hear,' said Bruiser. 'The chances are you'll be here until people start arriving on Monday morning. So be thankful that we're leaving some food and drink for you.'

In the Beers' living room, Lucius cut the telephone cable and told Lenny Belcher and Teddy Griggs, 'Go and break into some of the offices and take a few things – petty cash, VDU screens, anything that's portable and has some value. Make the break-in look convincing.'

The rest of the gang headed for the basement, where there was nothing of marketable value.

On Monday when, as Bruiser had predicted, Bill and Flo were discovered – by Flo's charladies – City of London detectives expressed their own puzzlement.

'A real fish-and-chip job,' summed up one to a colleague.

'All they've got away with is Mickey Mouse money and a few bits and pieces of office equipment. Whatever they expected to find, they must have been sadly disappointed.'

He was wrong.

While Bill and Flo's weekend was being disrupted, Jessie found herself temporary mistress of Moxmanton House. The moment had come, Lucius had informed them that morning, to launch the complex exercise in which they would lay their hands on the ransom money without getting caught.

Lucius had taken the men into the dining room to show them his sketches, photographs and maps, while Jessie was sent to prepare the meal for the queens. She felt excluded and demeaned.

Later she watched the men depart for London. Lucius had warned her sternly that she was not to leave the house during the weekend. The shutters must remain locked. She was to answer neither the telephone nor the door. When dishing up the food to the captives, she was not to unlock the cellar grille.

Don't do this, don't do that! Jessie felt like a skivvy. But she'd make those toffee-nosed bastards pay. She'd been watching the television reports of the mounting piles of ransom money as keenly as the rest of them. They weren't going to palm her off with a measly £150,000 out of more than sixteen million! That was the equivalent of a tip that you left on some tart's dressing table.

Jessie mooned around the silent house. She could scarcely comprehend having so much money. What would she buy? Where would she live? Who would she let love her?

Bruiser had allocated to her one of the maids' austere rooms in the attic but now, testing the doors along the first-floor corridor, Jessie came upon Constanza's suite. Inside she flooded the rooms with light. Blimey, this was more the ticket.

While most of Moxmanton House had been maintained in plush, comfortable Victorian order, Constanza had brought her quarters into the twentieth century. White thick-pile carpet covered the floor of the bedroom. A mirrored wall concealed a range of wardrobes and storage cupboards, and cunningly shielded lighting illuminated a built-in dressing table. The chairs and curtains were in modern, lemon-pale fabrics, a colour picked up by the canopy over the four-poster bed.

Jessie wandered through into the marble bathroom. The circular bath sunk into the centre of the floor had a rubber headrest so that the occupant could soak and revel at the same time. Within easy reach was a portable television, a book rack, a CD deck and a marble-shelved cabinet displaying glasses and a range of aperitifs.

Jessie left the lights burning and walked through to what had once been a dressing room. This space Constanza had converted into a small health spa. Exercise bars ran from floor to ceiling against one wall and there was an exercise bicycle, a set of scales, a compact pinewood sauna, some weights and a sunbed with a matching canopy so that one could tan lying inside a sandwich of beneficent, filtered light rays. Jessie's black mood began to dissipate. The men wouldn't be back until Sunday. She might as well make the most of what the house had to offer. She'd go out of her mind just watching television all weekend and feeding those bitches downstairs.

She went back to Constanza's bathroom and rummaged among her bottles. She found a phial of Nina Ricci's L'Air du Temps bath oil. She turned on the hot tap, tilted the Nina Ricci phial and watched the aquamarine liquid fall in a long stream to join the gushing water.

She dropped a CD onto the deck and started to gyrate to the music, unzipping her black jumpsuit as if she were working the act in front of paying customers.

She laughed at her own reflection in the mirror and wriggled the garment in a slow tease down her body. She kicked it off into the corner, made a fast pirouette, took hold of her black satin pants and yanked them down her legs. She slid her hands over her boyish hips: no sign of padding yet – she had become concerned at the calorie-laden food she was compelled to share with her prisoners. Yes, she thought, *my* prisoners!

Jessie ran some cold water and, fishing in the crumpled jumpsuit for the tin she'd had to keep concealed from the others, found a joint. She lit up and slid blissfully into the foam.

Jessie lay floating in balm for a few minutes, her eyes closed, her mind meandering.

Her right elbow was perched on the side of the bath to keep the joint dry, but her left hand began to wander over her breasts. Expertly, she teased each nipple into thrusting life, and let the hand slither leisurely downward over her flawless stomach.

She hadn't realized just how far apart you could spread your legs in these circular baths. The hand moved on, the forefinger seeking out the exact spot. Yes, there it was. Yes, oh, yes. Hmmmmm. Jessie fought to bridle her rising excitement. Easy, easy, easeeeeeee.

She put down the half-smoked joint and dipped her other hand beneath the foam, using it to open herself to the water. Can't stop now. Can't stop . . . can't stop . . . can't stooooooop. NOW!

An hour later Nanny appeared at the head of the cellar steps. The queens all looked up expectantly. Jessie was carrying the metal restraints that had been used on Hanna Hansen, and over her shoulder was slung a submachine gun. She'd fished it out of a chest in the drawing room where it was kept with the other two. She had no idea how to fire the black, glinting thing.

She raised her visor fractionally and shouted, 'Everyone go down to the far end of the cellar!' The girls, lying on their mattresses, climbed slowly to their feet. 'Come on!' shouted Jessie. 'Shift your fat arses!' They began to move away from the steps.

Shuffling painfully with them, Hanna murmured to Prentiss, 'She's on her own and she doesn't have a magazine on that gun. I don't think she knows how to use it. We've never before seen Nanny carrying any weapon, apart from the cattle prod. What do you think?'

'I think you're right,' said Prentiss. 'If she opens the gate I'm going to rush her. God! It's the first glimmer of a chance we've had.'

Hanna measured the distance with her eye. 'It means a fifty-foot sprint.'

'Yes, I can see,' said Prentiss. 'But it's our best shot.'

The queens stood facing Nanny at a distance. 'I want the French girl to step out,' ordered Jessie.

Mathilde de Montméja glanced swiftly at Prentiss and then took three paces forward, her face betraying nothing.

'No,' said Nanny. 'Come right up to the bars and put your arms through.'

Mathilde did as she was told, an arm on either side of a bar. 'No, not like that,' said Nanny impatiently. 'Put both arms through the same gap.'

Mathilde did so and Nanny clapped the manacles on both her small wrists.

'Now bring your head close.' Mathilde obediently inclined her head and Nanny slipped the blindfold over her eyes. She then took the key and unlocked the chain around the gatepost.

Nanny's mirrored visage gazed directly at them as she put the key in the lock. Prentiss tensed.

Nanny reached through the bars and roughly pulled Mathilde in front of the gate, shielding the lock from Prentiss's sight. Then, with a dramatic jerk, she pulled the door towards herself and dragged Mathilde through.

She *had* turned the key. Prentiss took off from a crouch, her lungs shocked at the sudden demand for oxygen. Nanny saw her coming and her curses echoed incomprehensibly inside her helmet. She gave Mathilde a mighty push that sent her stumbling over the bottom stone step and out of her way. Prentiss had covered half the distance and the girls broke into screams of hope and excitement.

The butt of the gun was impeding the swing of the gate and Prentiss's hopes rose. Nanny barely managed to clear the weapon to one side and slam the gate shut as Prentiss laid hands upon the bars. But Nanny still had to turn the key. She desperately jammed her foot against the bottom of the gate but the American girl gritted her teeth and pushed while the others charged down the cellar to her.

Nanny swore, her hand finding the key while her body tried to keep the lock in position so that the tongue could be clicked into place. She could see the girls advancing at a gallop. They were almost upon her. She had one hand on the gate, the other on the key. Suddenly she saw a way. She lowered her head and, with all the strength in her neck and shoulders, smashed the dome of her metal helmet against Prentiss's fingers. The blow sent Prentiss reeling back, insupportable pain throbbing up her arm. Nanny gave a cry of victory and turned the key, snatched it out of the lock and jumping back as a forest of arms shot through the bars and tried to grab at her.

'You cows!' she sobbed in relief. 'You fucking cows! I hope you all die.' She sat down on the stairs, shaking and recovering her breath. They'd almost got her, the rotten bitches. They'd have torn her to ribbons, given half a chance.

She looked at the French girl who was groping her way, confused, up the steps, took her roughly by the neck of the boiler suit and hauled her to the top. She turned back and shouted, 'You can spend the rest of the weekend in darkness for that, you lousy slags!'

Prentiss sat dejected on the floor, watching Nanny push Mathilde ahead of her. Seconds later the cellar was plunged into darkness and the sound of weeping among the queens rose all the louder.

Jessie removed Mathilde's blindfold in Constanza's bedroom. The girl winced at the sudden bright lights. 'What happened?' she asked.

'Some of your bloody friends tried to take liberties, that's what,' said Jessie. 'And all because I was sodding well doing you a favour. It's a bath you want, isn't it?'

'Yes,' said Mathilde gravely. 'I'm sorry for whatever they did. I did not know.'

'No, I suppose you couldn't have.' Jessie sniffed. She raised her hands to unstrap and remove her helmet.

Mathilde raised her hands sharply. 'No, please do not do that. I must not see your face.'

Jessie smiled. A sardonic smile. 'You mean, we'll have to kill you if you see my face and can identify me?'

Mathilde had not even thought of that. But she knew instinctively that she could never summon up the courage to kill another human being unless there existed an impersonality in their relationship. She did not want to see Nanny's face.

Jessie said, 'Don't worry. I've thought of everything.' She

continued to unstrap the helmet and lifted it off to reveal a head concealed in a ski mask. The eye, ear and mouth apertures had been stitched round with lines of rainbow colour. It was an expensive, modish item – Jessie had found it in one of Constanza's drawers. Mathilde saw two speculative green eyes appraising her.

Jessie looked around. 'Now, how shall we do this?' She steered Mathilde to the four-poster and said, 'Lie face upward on that.'

Mathilde swung herself onto the bed and lay back. Jessie took hold of the foot shackles and secured her feet. Mathilde did not resist. Jessie unlocked the manacles round her wrists. 'I can't risk letting you walk around free. You'll have to wear either the foot or hand set.'

'I understand,' said Mathilde, compliantly. 'Do whatever you wish.'

'Yes,' said Jessie, breathing heavily, as she climbed onto the bed and knelt beside the supine girl, 'that's exactly what I will do.'

She unbuttoned Mathilde's boiler suit and pulled it down to her ankles, collecting her pants on the way and dragging them along, too. Jessie's eyes were bright and sharp behind the mask.

'You've got smashing little tits,' she said. 'Now, put your hands together again.' She restored the manacles, but removed the foot shackles and finished stripping off Mathilde's clothes.

Mathilde took in the room, seeking likely weapons. The bed-side lamp, perhaps? The stool? The art-deco bronze on the dressing table? There was not much. Should she wait? Gain this girl's confidence? She'd soon tire of locking and unlocking her chains. Or should she, as the American girl had suggested, put thoughts of murder on hold for now?

Jessie's nose wrinkled. 'You don't half stink. Come 'ere.' She led Mathilde, pale and naked, across the carpet's deep pile.

Ten minutes later, Mathilde was soaking and squeezing a sponge over herself. It was the most wonderful bath she'd ever had in her life. Her hands were free but under water her feet were still joined.

Jessie sat on a stool, watching her. She had brought over a

254

bottle of Constanza's shampoo and now turned a lever in the marble wall. Mathilde looked up as the overhead shower, built into the small crystal light, came into play. The water drilled down over her head and shoulders and she washed out of her long tresses the grease and filth of the past nine days.

Jessie seemed to be absorbing pleasure from Mathilde's enjoyment. 'Want a joint?' asked the Cockney girl. Mathilde looked puzzled. 'Marijuana . . .' said Jessie.

Mathilde understood. 'If you please,' she said.

Jessie lit a joint for each of them and Mathilde lay back, clean again, and puffed contentedly.

After a while, Mathilde said lazily, 'Why don't we go to bed? I've been dying to get my head between your legs.'

'Me first,' said Jessie. And she began to help Mathilde out of the water.

Nanny returned Mathilde to the cellar on Sunday before noon because she was uncertain about the time of the men's return.

In the dark the queens were keeping up their spirits with a sing-song. They broke off to give a heartfelt cheer as the upper door opened and the overhead lights came on.

Jessie had blindfolded and manacled Mathilde again. She led her slowly down the stairs. Prentiss came alert. Should she make another dash? Her knuckles were purple from yesterday's agonizing encounter. But Nanny solved the dilemma for her. 'Everyone get to the far end of the cellar,' she ordered.

To underline her mastery of the situation she produced one of Bruiser's bone-handled cut-throat razors and held it against Mathilde's neck. 'If anyone tries to repeat yesterday's funny business, she'll find herself with a second mouth where her throat used to be.'

Nanny opened the door, pushed Mathilde into the cellar and hastily relocked and chained the gate before reaching through to remove Mathilde's manacles and mask.

Prentiss stepped forward, nursing her throbbing hands. 'We haven't eaten since yesterday. Are we going to get any food?'

'You'll get it when I'm good and ready,' said Nanny. 'And that means at least two hours from now. You've only yourself to blame, you dumb bitch.'

Prentiss did not reply. Nanny stomped up the steps and closed the cellar door.

The girls crowded round Mathilde. 'My God, you smell divine!' said Mirabelle Montcalm.

But abruptly there was an angry eruption and Greet Stoll elbowed through. Before anyone could prevent her, she pounded Mathilde's shoulder with both clenched fists and seized her hair in a vicious grip. Mathilde would have fallen to the ground if the other girls had not been so close.

'You dirty *collaboratrice!*' swore the Dutch girl. 'Typical stinking French – you'd sell your grandmama for a sou. You've gone over to them. You don't fool me with that charade with the razor. You've been sent back here as a spy!'

It took four of them to haul Greet off. Prentiss said, 'For Christ's sake, Greet, don't be such a birdbrain. If we begin fighting among ourselves we can kiss goodbye to everything.'

Greet wiped her mouth. 'I bet she has told them about your Morse Code message. Go on – ask her!'

Prentiss said, 'Why don't we just cool it and let Mathilde tell us what's been going on upstairs?' She turned to the French girl. 'The floor's yours, kiddo.'

Mathilde gave a shrug. 'As you see, I failed to kill her. I failed even to make the attempt. There were no weapons and, in any case, Nanny is cautious. Even in the night she kept me chained to a post of the bed. Before she went to sleep she placed the key to my manacles on the far side of the room. She said that if by some chance I managed to smother her, the men would find me next day still in bed with a corpse. She is very practical.'

Mathilde described Constanza's suite of rooms and her bath to a hushed assembly. Hers was the first news from outside in nine days. Mathilde said, 'The walk to the bedroom took several minutes. We are, indeed, in a large house. The décor is modern but the carved bedroom door is of a greater age. I was not permitted to see further, but as Nanny brought me back here just now I could hear a church bell ringing, perhaps summoning people to Sunday-morning service.'

'Did you learn anything about the men?' asked Prentiss.

Mathilde hesitated. Perhaps they had no real choice but to

face reality. 'Oh, yes, I learned about the men,' she said. 'We are dealing with killers. Nanny says that one member of the gang died and two policemen were murdered in the course of our kidnapping.'

Prentiss shuddered. 'Do you think she was just bullshitting?'

'No, I don't think so,' said Mathilde gravely. 'We were in a position of intimacy at the time. She just wants her share of the money. She's not interested in murder despite her taste for sadism.'

Mathilde looked at Prentiss. 'She was angry with you. She says action such as you attempted yesterday will only get us all killed and there won't be any money for her.'

Each stood silently with her own thoughts.

'Gee, Mathilde, it must have been a hellish night for you,' said Mirabelle, warmly sympathetic to make amends for Greet Stoll's hostility.

'No,' said the French girl honestly. 'I am not a hypocrite. I was bathed and fed and pleasured. I was unable to kill her so I enjoyed *le bon moment*. In return, I have given Nanny intense pleasure also. I think she will want to see me again. Perhaps another opportunity to accomplish something will arise . . .'

Her speculation was taken up from an unexpected source. Khun Varannee Charuvastr, the queen from Thailand, a bashful girl who had endured their ordeal in stoic silence, said, 'I am thinking that next time you visit Nanny you should take these with you.' She reached up to the hair coiled around her small head and to the amazement of everyone withdrew two slender needles, each five inches long, from the dark mass. She said apologetically, 'I was due to wear the steepled golden crown of my country at our lunch with Prince Charles. These pins normally hold it in place.'

'Pins!' said Helly the Aussie. 'They're more like bloody great stilettos. It was brave of you to hang on to them, sweetie.'

'Not brave,' said Khun, seriously. 'I was so afraid when they took all our clothes and possessions I forgot they were in my hair.'

Mathilde de Montméja fingered the two objects thoughtfully. She said to the nurse, Eva, 'What could I do?'

'Push one through an eye socket or up under the skull at the back of the ear into the brain stem, or into the jugular vein.' Mathilde felt sick. 'Anywhere else?'

'The heart, of course.' Eva opened her boiler suit and showed Mathilde the spot, a little off-centre between the third and fourth, or fourth and fifth ribs. 'The important thing is to place two fingers over adjoining ribs and insert the needle between the fingers. That way you avoid striking the bone.'

Upstairs Jessie was opening tins and pouring cold soup into vats when she heard someone at the front door. The sound of the bell echoed eerily in the silent house. Jessie froze, then put down the can and turned off the kitchen lights at the old-fashioned domed switches. She tiptoed into the hall. She could hear above her own rasping breath the sound of someone moving on the gravel. Then there were footsteps. Panicked, she realized that whoever it was had started to walk round to the side of Moxmanton House. Jessie rushed back into the kitchen to confirm that she'd left the door bolts on. She had. Relieved, she flattened herself against the side door.

The footsteps hesitated outside. She jumped as the knob was tested. The caller stood for a few moments before walking back in the direction of the main drive. The sound of gravel crunching underfoot faded away. Then a car engine started up and a vehicle was driven off.

She moved around the house nervously until the men returned in the early evening.

Chapter Thirty-five

Teddy Triggs and Lenny Belcher had an amazing tale for Jessie.

'You've got to hand it to these toffs,' said Teddy. 'They've really got their heads screwed on. I mean, we've lived in south London all our fucking lives and we never knew there was anything like that, did we, Lenny?'

Jessie said impatiently, 'Anything like *what?* Where the hell have you been since yesterday?'

'Seventy-five feet underground. That's where we've been,' said Lenny.

On 4 November 1890 Queen Victoria's son, the Prince of Wales, later to become King Edward VII, declared operational to the cheers of a throng of Cockneys an underground railway which, because of the circular nature of its tunnel, soon became known to Londoners as the Tube. This early line of the City and South London Railway ran in twin tunnels from Stockwell in south London to London Bridge where the tubes passed under the Thames, the riverbed just seven feet above this fine piece of engineering. The line proceeded north for several hundred yards and terminated in the King William Street station, near the Monument.

The railway was an immense success from the moment the Prince of Wales cut the ribbon. Yet, less than ten years later, a three-quarter mile stretch of the line running from Southwark, south of London Bridge, under the river to King William Street was abandoned. Both tunnels and the King William Street Station were sealed off and, for technical reasons, the remainder of the line diverted. The by-passed tunnels and station, nestling in the foundations of an office block, lay forgotten for forty years.

Then the Second World War brought about a brief resurrection when they were used as an air-raid shelter. Cockneys christened it the Deep. Among the thousands who lay on their wire-mesh bunks at night listening to – and feeling – the reverberations of bomb and rocket was the frightened teenage girl who would one day be the mother of Lucius Frankel.

The men gathered their equipment in the lobby of Bill Beer's building and Lucius led the way to the basement. On his advice, they'd all brought gumboots. Lucius held a sketch plan in his gloved hand. 'We're looking for a door that has a musty smell coming from underneath,' he said.

Presently, Bruiser said, 'Does this fit the bill?' He indicated an ordinary timber door secured by a Yale lock. Lucius bent down and sniffed, inserted a screwdriver and levered back the tongue of the lock. They switched on their lamps and stepped inside.

'This is all right,' said Lucius. 'The gale-force wind is London Transport's automatic ventilation system at work. They have to keep it going to prevent a dangerous build-up of foul air.'

To their right was a short passage, blocked by iron bars. Lucius consulted his sketch. 'That must be the old entrance that opened out into Fish Street Hill, alongside the old Billingsgate market.'

He flashed his lamp along another passageway, curving to the left. It was lined with old metal conduit pipes and rusting handrails. They proceeded for twenty-five yards, the passageway dropping all the time, until they came to seven concrete steps that opened into a vertical circular shaft, lined with mildewed cast-iron panels, and gave on to a staircase. They descended another thirty-six steps until, suddenly, they emerged into a forgotten world.

Their lamps revealed another staircase, this time tiled in brown and white squares trimmed with a classical Greek leaf motif. 'This,' said Lucius, 'is the original passenger access to the platforms of the old King William Street station.'

They pushed on, emerging into a twenty-six-feet-wide area that had once contained two platforms and a single track. Posters still clung to the walls. Lucius's torch picked out a 1940

War Finance Campaign appeal and a number of exhortations in the famous Careless Talk Costs Lives series.

They were now faced with the abandoned twin tunnels of the City and South London Railway track, heading south. The intruders selected the right-hand tunnel and began walking, their lights fending off the darkness ahead of them. 'We're seventy-five feet deep,' said Lucius.

The railway track had long since been removed and they were moving through sludge and occasional pools of water. They crunched slowly on until their lights fell upon a solid obstruction – the five-feet-thick concrete wall that would have prevented a tidal wave engulfing sleeping Londoners in their shelter should one of Hermann Goering's bombs have penetrated the mud bed of the Thames and pierced the roof of the tunnel.

A four-foot square hole through the wall was protected by an iron grille. Bruiser took a club hammer from his backpack and swung fiercely at the brass padlock until it fell shattered into the slime at their feet. The grille swung open and Bruiser eased his bulk into the cavity. The far side of the river wall was sealed by a solid, cast-iron floodgate, with four huge wing-nut fasteners. Bruiser twirled them loose and pushed open the heavy gate. The six men crawled through and stood upright.

'Blimey!' said Teddy Triggs, impressed. 'It's like a bleeding Christmas grotto!'

Ahead, receding into the blackness, stretched an inverted alpine range of stalactites, dangling like icicles in a snow god's dwelling and shimmering with phosphorescence. Teddy tried gently to break off a four-foot spike but it shattered in his hand and fell in brittle shards to the floor.

The air was damp here but after walking a few yards they were halted by a thrumming sound. It grew louder. The rays of the lamps caught the whites of their eyes as they glanced sharply at each other. The eerie sound swelled to a crescendo, then began to fade.

'God's teeth!' said Bruiser. Teddy and Lenny were shaking.

'Nothing to worry about,' said Rolly. 'Just a boat passing overhead.'

'Gawd help us!' said Lenny Belcher fervently.

They squelched on for another four minutes, passing under the Thames a few feet to the west of the existing London Bridge. Lucius said, 'Now we come to the bad bit.' The tunnel began to rise and on this incline their path was barred by the southside water barrier, another five-foot concrete wall. This time the river gate built into it presented a blank, unyielding face. It was secured from the far side.

Rolly shone his torch over the metal facing. 'As you can see, it's identical to the gate on the north side of the river and we must assume it's battened down by similar wing-nuts.' He pursed his lips. Then he tapped the centre of the four-feet square gate. 'I'll place a small charge here and blow a hole just large enough to get an arm through. Cast-iron shatters nicely and we should be able to reach the retaining screws.'

Lenny and Teddy shuffled nervously at the cavalier manner in which Rolly handled his cache of plastic explosive. 'Don't wet your knickers,' he said. 'It's as harmless as tapioca until you insert the detonator.'

Rolly built a small grey cone and taped it centrally to the vertical face of the gate. He perched a timer at the side of the tunnel, set it and slid the detonator jack into the cone. Lucius observed closely.

'Let's all take a stroll back under the river. We've got two minutes,' Rolly said calmly.

Teddy and Lenny scampered off. The others, including Lucius, followed swiftly but with dignity. They retreated a hundred and fifty yards and Rolly said, 'Okay, everyone, get down with your backs to the fireworks. And cover your ears.'

The explosion dinned into their skulls and propelled a cloud of dust towards them. Broken stalactites showered down and powdered their heads.

The gale and noise howled past and dissipated. They stood up, shedding debris. 'Right,' said Rolly. 'Let's take a dekko.'

The explosion had punched a jagged hole through the centre of the iron and Bruiser placed an arm inside to fight with the wing-nuts. Finally, he said, 'I've got three, but the explosion must have distorted the thread of the fourth. It'll only move so far. It means another spot of Rolly's *plastique* or a hack-saw.'

They opted for the tedious, but quieter, hacksaw. Bruiser worked the tool through the hole and for over an hour they took turns at guiding the blue steel blade. By the time the recalcitrant nut fell away, all their right arms ached. They were beginning to shiver in the cold and moisture of the under-river atmosphere.

Then Bruiser reached through the iron grille again with his hammer and attacked the padlock. After the twelfth blow it clattered off into the darkness and they clambered through the four-foot opening. They now stood under the south bank of the river Thames, a few yards from the approach to London Bridge.

Thirty feet on, the tunnel was blocked again by a brick wall but set into it was a rusting iron gate of normal height. Lucius's lamp found an ordinary drop-latch at waist level. He lifted it and the gate opened.

Their smiles of relief froze. The moment the door opened they could hear noise somewhere up ahead of them – and voices. 'Kill the lamps,' hissed Bruiser.

They stood in blackness. Yes, voices, but, puzzlingly, they could see no lights, although the tunnel ran straight before them.

They moved forward slowly, Bruiser twenty feet in the lead. Suddenly they saw his lamp flash a message of reassurance. They joined him and he said, 'Look down.'

A vertical vent had been bored through the floor of the tunnel and through the bars that prevented anyone climbing either up or down, they could see lights and hear people.

Lucius was running his torch over his sketch map. 'Of course,' he said, 'it must be one of the platforms of the Northern Line. This tunnel runs directly over London Bridge tube station.'

The way forward was now dry and uncluttered. They stepped up onto a concrete-slab floor. 'It must have been put in when they turned the tunnels into an air-raid shelter,' said Lucius. He played his light on the wall. 'Look, you can still see the bunk numbers stencilled there. This place sheltered thousands – including my mother.'

'Ah, that explains a mystery,' said Dickie Biggs-Salter. 'I've been wondering how you knew this Aladdin's cave even existed. Learned it at your mother's knee, eh?'

'Something like that,' said Lucius.

They came to a junction where the clay had been excavated at right-angles to the tunnel to link the two parallel lines. At this point, fifteen concrete steps, alongside a brackish pool, led upwards.

'Let's have a look up there,' said Lucius. 'We can leave the backpacks here.'

The pumped air of the ventilation system beat at their faces while they climbed up until they came out into an abandoned lift shaft. They continued up and eventually arrived on an iron landing. A nine-foot-high oak door was built into the wall. From the far side they could hear traffic.

Lucius said, 'Shall I take a look?'

Bruiser fingered his Browning and said, 'Go ahead.'

Lucius smoothed his dishevelled hair, turned the latch and poked out his head. He closed the door again, and said, 'There's only a doorstep between us and London Bridge Street on the approach to the station.'

'Christ!' said Dickie Biggs-Salter. 'Then why did we have to go through that performance under the river and bugger about tying up that old couple? We could have got in through this door.'

'It wouldn't have worked,' said Lucius. 'We'd have had to force it in full view of passers-by. Even if we managed to do that without being spotted, the marks of the break-in would have told the police that someone had got down to the old line. Our way was more elaborate but it will baffle them. And we've gained ourselves a bolthole.'

They descended once again to the twin tunnels, picked up their gear and Lucius said, 'We shall now be heading south on a course that follows Borough High Street above our heads.'

They walked for another ten minutes along the right-hand tunnel, occasionally hearing the rumble of trains.

Simultaneously their lights picked out the wall blocking their progress. It was pierced by a wire-covered circular hole. Bending low, they peered through and saw a set of signals and a brilliantly lit station platform floating in the surrounding blackness.

'This is where the old City and South London tunnels were abandoned and sealed off,' said Lucius. 'Those lights are on one of the platforms of the present-day Borough tube station. Just beyond this wall are the electrified tracks.'

They heard a train approaching and Lucius said quickly, 'Put the torches out. If a driver sees them, he'll report unauthorized people in the tunnel.'

They watched a train snake into the distant platform. 'It's south-bound,' said Lucius. 'I think we'll be able to use that information.'

He started to move back down the tunnel, shining his torch upon the curved walls. 'I seem to have missed an opening that should be somewhere along here,' he said.

Then he swore. His torch had revealed a section where the curved cast-iron plates had been removed. The gap had been bricked over.

'What's wrong?' asked Bruiser.

'I was hoping we'd find another unblocked staircase like the one leading up to London Bridge Street. We have to go through this wall. On the far side will be another staircase leading up. It's essential to our plan.'

Bruiser looked dubiously back down the tunnel. 'Then we'll have to wait until they've locked up that tube station and gone home for the night,' he said. 'Even if we use muffled tools, there'll be one hell of a noise – they'll hear it from the platform we've just seen.'

They put down their packs and began to open packets of sandwiches and vacuum flasks of coffee and soup.

'You know, I never could quite grasp the attractions of potholing,' said Rolly Ponsford.

Teddy Triggs produced a pack of cards and he and Lenny opened a ragged game of whist. The three men of military experience all knew the value of snatched sleep and got their heads down on their packs.

Lucius Frankel sat with his back to the curved wall, brain

racing in overdrive as usual, the chess player staying one move ahead of his above-ground opponents.

Tom Ringrose and Lionel Firth were grabbing a rare opportunity for a Sunday-lunchtime pint. They'd arranged to meet Jake Bishop and his two spooks at the Windsor Castle on Campden Hill, a long way from Victoria. Every pub within a wide radius of the Yard was thronged with media people and the Commander was in no mood to take a constant badgering for information.

The truth, he had to admit to himself, was that he had no information worth a damn.

Bishop said, 'What's new, Tom?'

Ringrose gazed into his pint and said, 'They haven't replied to the last advert in *The Times*. We badly need more video from Prentiss Decker.'

'I've got her father standing by and under wraps,' said Bishop. 'I've moved him into a safe house.'

Ringrose said, 'Good. Keep him at Readiness One. I'm afraid the lack of a result is beginning to affect the entire search effort. The momentum's slowing down as we come up against one blank wall after another. We're dealing with highly sophisticated people. I'd go for the mercenary theory, except that they don't seem to fit the mould of mindless, brutish thugs. They're literate and they understand French and German well enough to allow some girls to make their video appeals in their own languages. I think we're dealing with people who've had military experience and a privileged upbringing.'

'People with no criminal history,' suggested Bishop. 'Like Lady Cornmorris.'

'Yes,' Ringrose agreed.

'Anything on the sulphur clue?'

'Nothing. We've had every municipal air-pollution officer in the country guiding our squads to every strong chemical whiff recorded on their pollution charts.'

Ringrose's gaze fell idly on a bine of freshly picked hops that the landlord had strung decoratively over the bar. He said to Firth, 'Have we got oast-houses on the check-list, Lionel? I seem to remember it's the right time of year for drying hops. Don't they give off an acrid smell?'

'Quite right, guv'nor,' said Firth. 'It's caused by the sulphur used to preserve the bright green colour. I had a check run with the Hop Marketing Board at Paddock Wood in Kent. Unfortunately, sulphur was dropped from the process in nineteen eighty.'

Ringrose sighed and turned to Bishop. 'See what I mean? It's your shout, I believe.'

'Shout?' said the American.

'Your turn to buy the bloody drinks,' said Ringrose.

The Northern Line of the London Underground had finally fallen silent at 2 a.m. A maintenance train had passed through the north-bound tunnel at 1.30 a.m. and, thirty minutes later, the platform lights at Borough station had been switched off.

Working with a cloth-muffled hammer, Bruiser began to drive a chisel into the mortar between the bricks. The wall was in good condition and did not yield easily but, by 3.30 a.m. on Sunday, the gang had hacked a large enough gap to admit a man's body. When the chisel first broke through to the other side, they'd been aware of the leak of foul air entombed for fifty years.

Lucius thought of Egyptologists hacking their way into Tutankhamun's secret resting place and standing in awe of the golden mask and sarcophagus. Soon they, too, would be standing before their own treasure.

A broad flight of stairs confronted them and their feet stirred clouds of fine grey dust. When they had climbed about sixty feet, the stairs ended in a concrete wall.

'Shit!' said Dickie Biggs-Salter.

'No, wait,' said Lucius. They were on a landing and he directed his torch to the right-hand wall. Happiness swept him as the light picked out the rusting iron door. It showed two bolts in the closed position but the door had been permanently sealed into the wall with a fillet of cement around the frame.

'During the war,' Lucius said, 'when the authorities decided to open up the two tunnels down below as air-raid shelters, they had to provide suitable entrances. The staircase we are standing on was one of them. They commandeered part of the graveyard that lies against the north wall of St George the

Martyr church in Southwark. They dug down through earth that contained the bones of plague victims, executed murderers, debtors from the old Marshalsea Prison and created this staircase. Then, when the war was over, they built the concrete seal in front of us and restored the outward look of the churchyard. From up top you'd never know, unless you're old enough to remember, that this place ever existed.'

'What about the iron door here?' said Bruiser.

'During the war the crypt of the church was cleared, reinforced and also used as an air-raid shelter. This door was intended as an escape hatch, should the church suffer a direct hit.'

Lucius patted the door affectionately. 'Do you realize what we've achieved?' The others looked at him. 'Once we've broken through here, we'll have created a secret three-quarter-mile escape tunnel, with one exit just south of the Thames at London Bridge station and another north of the Thames in the heart of the City. We shall have the ransom money delivered to St George's church up above and we shall rise up from the earth and spirit it away.' Lucius was exalted.

Teddy Triggs said, 'I've got to hand it to you, Mister. I was christened at St George's and I've never heard a whisper that this bloody great mousehole existed.' Lucius gazed upon him almost with affection.

'Let's get on with it,' said Bruiser. He was as impressed as Triggs: Lucius Frankel was a ceaselessly surprising and – Bruiser's antennae reminded him – dangerous cove.

Bruiser took a narrow-bladed chisel and began to tap out the cement fillet. He cleared the door frame, squeezed fine oil over the bolts and waited while it permeated the rust and joints. Then he tapped lightly, driving the bolts out of their sockets. The door moved a fraction and slowly Bruiser opened it wide on protesting hinges.

They found themselves in a small boiler house, sharing it with a central heating unit and a 500-gallon oil tank. A further door opened directly onto the barrel-vaulted crypt of St George's.

Lucius said, 'We must take off our boots. We mustn't trail dirt into the church.'

In their socks they padded into the crypt. The walls were cream-painted and the space had been converted into a games room for youth organizations.

Bruiser counted the steps up to the ground floor: seventeen. He was always careful about timing.

They emerged into the silent church from under a staircase and entered the nave, their lamps switched off. Street lights through the windows slanted off the painted ceiling with its puff-cheeked cherubs. The stone font stood centrally, facing the main double doors, and to the right was a cupboard-lined vestry. Without torches, they missed the legend on the door of this small room, one of the most celebrated in English literature.

It was here that Charles Dickens had the kindly sexton take down the second volume of the burial register and tenderly place it as a pillow under the weary head of Little Dorrit who, overnight, had been locked out of the nearby Marshalsea debtor's prison.

Bruiser said, 'We've seen enough. It's one hell of a fine plan. Now let's get back down the tunnel and make sure we lock all the doors behind us.'

Lucius Frankel glowed. They were the first words of praise he'd heard since he'd done their dirty work for them and disposed of the coppers.

Chapter Thirty-six

They had to wait until mid-morning, when Sunday pedestrians were about, before they could emerge from the King William Street building and walk away.

They were all back at Moxmanton House by evening. Jessie told Bruiser of the unknown caller, but there appeared to be no harm done.

On Monday, Bruiser strolled into the village to pick up the morning paper. ('Only one,' Lucius had warned. 'You mustn't look too interested in the news.')

He came out of the newsagent's shop and his heart skipped a beat. Bob Malley, the village bobby, was waiting for him. But smiling.

'Sorry to bother you, Sir Brewster,' said Malley, deferentially. 'I called at the house yesterday but you weren't at home.'

Bruiser almost blurted out, 'So it was you,' but he bit his tongue. The young constable said, 'We're having to check all the large properties in the area, sir, and Moxmanton House is on the list.'

'Check? What on earth for?' Bruiser stalled for some fast thinking.

'The missing beauty queens, sir. The powers-that-be think they must be tucked away somewhere in Kent.'

'I see,' said Bruiser. Then, brightening, 'Well, pop up for a drink around midday. I'll have cleared them all out of the house by then.'

They both laughed at Sir Brewster's little joke.

'You said *what?*' exclaimed Lucius, a little later.

'I couldn't tell him to piss off,' said Bruiser. 'We'd have had the whole of the Kent constabulary around our necks. I'll just have to spoof him.'

'We'll need to move all the extra food into the cellar, tidy the room and stay down below while you try to see him off.' Lucius added bleakly, 'Too bad for him if he gets nosy.' He consulted his watch. 'We have an hour.'

The carved front doors of Moxmanton House were wide open when PC Malley drove up at noon in his panda car. Sir Brewster came out onto the steps in old clothes and said, 'Bob, you're just in time to do me a service. Come and give me a hand.'

Sir Brewster led him upstairs. PC Malley could not fail to notice that all the doors were open and that the rooms were empty. 'Giving the place an airing,' Sir Brewster explained.

On the top landing he said, 'Lend me a hand with this picture. It has to go up to London for valuation.'

An ancestral portrait of a mottled eighteenth-century dragoon glared from the wall into the mid-distance. PC Malley helped him carry it to the hall.

'Come on, you've earned a drink,' said Sir Brewster, leading the way into the drawing room before PC Malley could speak. 'Whisky all right?'

He poured and handed the policeman a glass. 'Cheers,' said PC Malley.

'Jolly good,' said Sir Brewster. He was leaning on the weapons chest.

PC Malley cleared his throat to speak but Sir Brewster cut in, 'I'm feeling absolutely hellish about my cellar.'

'I was going to ask you about that, sir.'

'Were you?' said Sir Brewster, looking surprised. 'I thought I'd been frightfully discreet but I suppose you can't stop village gossip.'

PC Malley was perplexed. 'Discreet, sir? I'm afraid I don't understand.'

Sir Brewster leaned forward. 'Clearing up my father's estate. Death duties, that sort of thing . . . I've been quietly selling off my father's stock of rare wines from the cellar to pay the blasted taxman. And, to add to the problems, I've had to call in a professional firm to lay rat bait. The place is infested.'

PC Malley relaxed. 'Rats are often a problem after the

harvest, sir. It's the machines – they chase the rats from the fields. They have to find a home somewhere.'

'But not in Moxmanton House,' Sir Brewster said, grim-faced and proffering the whisky bottle although the policeman had hardly touched his glass. 'Have a top-up.'

'That's very kind of you, sir, but I won't – driving, you know,' said Malley. What the hell? He didn't want rats running over his boots. In his mind, he ticked Moxmanton House off his check-list. Sir Brewster was a gentleman of the old school. No bother there.

At last Bruiser watched him go. 'Sonny boy,' he said to himself, 'you'll never know how close you came to taking the long night's sleep.'

In the cellar the girls had stood for an hour with the gun muzzles trained upon them. The top door opened and the big man came in. Whatever the emergency, it was over.

Prentiss Decker felt the tension ebb from her but, just as quickly, she keyed herself up again. One of the men was shouting for the English girl.

Fran Pilkington ran as far away from the staircase as she could get. 'I won't go! I won't go! They're going to kill me,' she shouted. She threw herself on the floor in an hysterical heap.

Their captors stood nonplussed. Prentiss stepped forward and asked, 'What do you want her for?'

Two of the guns pointed directly at her. The slim man said, 'We want her to tape a video message. That's all.'

Prentiss gave a hopeless shrug. 'Well, you can see the state she's in. Won't one of us do?' Play it cool, she thought desperately. Don't volunteer directly.

The helmets turned uncertainly. Then the slim one beckoned Prentiss. 'You haven't fallen entirely to pieces. You'll do.'

If Prentiss could have leaped for joy at that moment she would have banged her head on the ceiling.

As they escorted her, blindfolded, up the stairs to the tent, she could still hear Fran shrieking. The kid had put on a great performance. They'd all agreed in advance that if anyone but Prentiss was called upstairs, the chosen one would throw herself

272

into a frenzy. It had to be Prentiss: the girl who could now transmit in twenty-eight seconds the Morse message 'Peter Linden was here, 5 9 40.'

The message the gang gave her to read directly to the camera was heartening – up to a point. It showed that the outside world cared, but the threat of ultimate sanction was still hanging over them.

Prentiss blinked heavily in the glare of the floodlights and, as the red light came on, launched into the word 'Peter' . . .

Nanny was holding the idiot cards. 'This is Communication Number Three,' Prentiss read. 'First of all I wish to assure you that on Monday, the tenth of October,' to prove the date, she held up the newspaper Bruiser had bought in the village, 'all forty-nine of us are fit and being properly treated.'

Prentiss paused, peering over the paper and started on 'Linden'.

The kidnappers' message went on, 'Our captors have been impressed by the world response to the ransom appeal and now concede an extension to the deadline until next Saturday, the fifteenth of October. But that will be the absolute limit . . .'

Nanny was muddling the cards. Prentiss swiftly blinked out the Morse for the words 'was' and 'here'. She daren't look up at the helmets to see if they were noticing anything odd in her face.

Nanny finally got the correct card to the front of the pile and Prentiss read on: 'Our captors calculate that twenty-five million dollars in the denominations specified will weigh more than five hundred pounds. The notes will be divided into ten equal lots and packed in ten identical suitcases. No attempt to bug these cases electronically or chemical tampering with the banknotes will be tolerated . . .'

Nanny, smoothly this time, slid the front idiot card to the back. Prentiss pretended to have difficulty reading the continuing message. In the hiatus she telegraphed the day and the month. Only the year remained.

The kidnappers' message went on: 'The cases will be placed in the hands of Commander Thomas Ringrose and he will personally receive instructions for delivery next Saturday. If the total sum is not safely in the hands of our captors by midnight next Saturday, a girl will be executed on each day that then elapses while our captors are kept waiting for the money.'

Nanny now had the last card in her hand. Prentiss blinked furiously . . . She'd made it! Four-oh!

Prentiss could barely contain herself but, if she made any body or hand movement, they'd wipe the tape and make her start all over again.

Standing rigidly, she concluded the gang's third communiqué: 'To demonstrate that this is no bluff, the executions will take place in front of the camera and the video tapes will be widely distributed to world television networks.'

The last had been Lucius's idea; he could imagine the politicians and the granite-faced don't-pay brigade blenching at that prospect.

The round-the-clock surveillance teams had spent a week maintaining a watch on Captain Bligh's tomb. Commander Tom Ringrose was taking no chances. If the Colonel Blood Group had used the tomb once as a message drop, they might use it again. One loiterer, a youth with a shaven head, approached and immediately triggered a tailing operation of immense intricacy. It was called off only when it was discovered that the youth had been guilty of no more than discarding an empty cigarette packet.

This surveillance, like so many of Tom Ringrose's painstaking arrangements, came to nothing.

The Welsh voice informed the Scotland Yard switchboard operator that the third communication from the kidnappers would be found behind the books on the bottom shelf of the detective fiction section at the Westminster public library in Buckingham Palace Road.

Despite the disappointment, Ringrose was marginally mollified after he had run the tape for himself and Firth. The gang were becoming cocky. Detective fiction, indeed! And wanting him to handle the money personally! There was a hint of quixotic jousting in that – a suggestion that the other side wanted to deal only with an opponent worthy of their steel. It was the first time that they had allowed romantic nonsense to stand in the way of their coldly logical moves.

Jake Bishop, his fellow CIA spooks and Prentiss Decker's father arrived at the Yard. Ringrose said, 'Mr Decker, your daughter is blinking her eyes like a lighthouse beacon on this tape. See what you can make of it.'

Art Decker took up his position, with pad and pen, in front of the monitor screen. Watching him, Ringrose felt in bad need of a cigarette but he'd promised himself to kick the habit.

Art Decker was jotting down something. So the darling daughter *was* telegraphing! Ringrose ran the tape four times, the tension in the room becoming barely supportable, until at last Art Decker said, 'Got it!' and ripped the last page from his pad. 'I don't know what the hell it means, but this is what my little girl is saying to you.'

Ringrose and the others craned their necks: 'PETER LINDEN WAS HERE. 5 9 40.'

'Who's this Peter Linden guy? Is he some kind of English celebrity?' asked Paul Zaentz.

'If he is, I've never heard of him,' said Ringrose, thinking.

'And what was he doing on the ninth of May nineteen forty?' asked Bishop.

Firth said, 'Fifth of September, surely.'

'You're forgetting Prentiss is American. She'd transmit the month first,' said Bishop.

'Not necessarily,' said Ringrose, slowly. 'Suppose she were copying faithfully details from a document. Unless it were written by a fellow American, the day would come before the month.' He added, briskly, 'Whatever, we have two dates and one name to work on. Gentlemen, it's a drowning man's straw. Let's grasp it and find Linden – even if the trail leads only to a cemetery.'

Ringrose picked up the telephone and made a direct call to the Prime Minister. He issued instant authority for the police to be given access to the nation's personal tax returns for 1940 and for the computerized records of National Insurance contributions held at Newcastle-upon-Tyne to be examined. Teams were dispatched to ransack the clippings libraries of national newspapers and the British Museum's newspaper and magazine collection.

Within the first twenty-four hours, the search yielded thirty-eight Peter Lindens who had been living in Britain in 1940; nineteen were still alive. Dead or alive, the places where all these Peter Lindens had laid their heads so many years ago were visited, raided or written off. Lawyers' advertisements appeared in the newspapers. If he made contact, Peter Linden would hear something to his advantage.

The most wanted – and elusive – man on earth was Peter Linden.

Meanwhile, the two Langley men had been coaxing Ringrose. Parker Dodsworth told him, with truth, 'We've had infinitely more experience of dealing with kidnapping offences than you British. The Federal Bureau of Investigations in Washington keeps a whole passel of equipment for just such a contingency.' Parker detailed the list, which included a suitcase with a bug and aerial built into the structure so carefully that, even if the fabric lining was ripped out, the doctoring remained undetectable to the eye.

'All right,' said Ringrose. 'We need ten?'

'You've got 'em,' said Parker Dodsworth.

The suitcases were on the next afternoon's Washington–London flight.

Ringrose's first real break since the anomalous behaviour pattern of Nancy Cornmorris, came in an oblique, casual manner, two days into the hunt for Peter Linden when all results had proved negative and Tom's hopes were beginning to evaporate once again.

Lord Lavington, the vice-chancellor of London University, fancied an evening stroll through St James's and a pre-prandial drink at White's club. He and the former academic who was now the Director-General of MI5 swung their rolled umbrellas and strolled along Pall Mall. They had just come from a meeting of the Scientific Intelligence Review Board of which Lord Lavington had long been chairman.

The Director-General was saying, 'I hear you got yourself caught up in this beauty-queen business.'

'For a while,' said Lord Lavington. 'There was some early thought that it was a university prank.'

'Well, that chap Ringrose is going balls-out for a fellow

named Peter Linden, for reasons best known to himself. But I don't believe he's having much luck. The trail goes back to nineteen forty and it's gone cold on him.'

'My God, that's a year engraved on our hearts, Hector.'

'Never forget it, old boy. Never forget it,' agreed the Director-General.

The two friends passed on their way, chuntering amiably to each other.

Later when Lord Lavington was settled in the seat of his taxi on the way home to Dolphin Square, a fragment of memory was suddenly retrieved from some storage lobe in his formidable brain. Lord Lavington frowned, thought, and finally sat bolt upright. He tapped the partition glass with the ferrule of his umbrella.

'Stop!' he shouted. 'I've changed my mind.'

The cabbie looked wearily over his shoulder. These old boys ought not to be allowed out alone at night. 'Where to, then, guv?'

'Take me,' said Lord Lavington, 'to New Scotland Yard.'

Ringrose was in his thinking chair going over every measure he had taken. Had he missed something? He'd just had a call from the Cabinet Secretary to inform him that the ransom money was complete, although the Lord Mayor's barometer still registered only fourteen million dollars. The Saturday delivery was on ... How far could he go without endangering the girls' lives?

Firth interrupted his brooding. 'Lord Lavington's downstairs demanding to see you.'

'Lavington?'

'Yes – you know, the vice-chancellor of London University. He figured in one of the early reports.'

'Oh, yes,' said Ringrose, swinging his legs off the Eames chair, intrigued. 'Waft him up.'

Lord Lavington came directly to the point. 'Commander, I'm told on the best authority that you're turning the country upside down in a search for a man named Peter Linden.'

'That's correct, sir, although I must ask you to keep that information to yourself.'

'Young man,' said Lord Lavington, without annoyance, 'I've spent my entire adult life keeping information to myself. And here's a piece that you might consider more than interesting. I believe you may be looking in the wrong country for Peter Linden.'

'Sit down, sir,' said Ringrose.

Lord Lavington dropped into a chair. 'I'm sure you know that nineteen forty was a ghastly year for Britain, with the Germans on our doorstep across the Channel. I was then a junior scientist working in an intelligence unit from No. 54 Broadway, a stone's throw from here. I was a member of R. V. Jones's team, engaged in a frantic battle of wits with our opposite numbers in Germany. One of our most pressing tasks was to learn all we could about an ingenious apparatus that guided German bombers along short-wave beams to their targets in Britain. Reggie Jones was forever despatching me to various parts of the country to examine the entrails of shot-down enemy aircraft in the hope that we might recover some vital piece of equipment intact.'

He drew a breath. 'I also sat on a number of interrogation boards. A captured member of a bomber crew would be subjected to a rigorous grilling from myself and an officer from the Y Service of Signals Intelligence, while a squadron leader took the chair to see fair play under the rules of the Geneva Convention.' Ringrose started to speak.

Lord Lavington raised a finger. 'Bear with me a little longer. We were not allowed to keep personal diaries so what I'm telling you now is all from memory. Some time in the autumn—'

Ringrose broke in, 'Would the fifth of September of that year mean anything to you?'

'Highly possible,' said Lord Lavington, patting his pot belly reflectively. 'That was just two days before the Luftwaffe began its intensive bombing of London.' He took up his story. 'Anyway, around that time, a Heinkel 111 was brought down by a nightfighter and one of the surviving Germans did not appear to be a conventional member of the crew. When he was taken into custody he was wearing civilian clothes under a flying suit. A theory arose that he was a German scientist, studying their equipment under operational conditions. If this were so, we had hooked ourselves a most valuable fish, and I was sent to give this chap a preliminary once-over. His name,' said Lord Lavington, 'was Peter Linden.' Ringrose felt the hair bristle on his neck.

'The interrogation team was promulgated and I was driven down to play my part. I must say this Linden chap was most indignant. I gather he'd been pushed about a bit and he kept swearing he had no scientific knowledge whatsoever and was, in fact, a war correspondent for *Volkische Beobachter*, a Nazi newspaper, often used as a cover by spies.

'We put this to him rather roughly and he insisted that we examine the press passes and so forth that had been found on him. But, as we pointed out, any fool with a printing machine could produce such documents. We said if he wasn't a scientist, he must be a spy, and if he was a spy he could expect to find himself gazing down the barrels of a dozen rifles one fine morning. Finally, I said to him, "If you are a *bona fide* journalist you must have international contacts among the newspaper fraternity. Write down the names of those you know."

'The fellow dutifully made a list and, when we looked at it, we saw one name that stood out. At some time in the thirties in Berlin he claimed to have met Edward R. Murrow, the American broadcaster. Well, Murrow was in London at that time, covering the Battle of Britain for his radio audience back home. A splendid fellow. Churchill had the highest regard for him.

'So we all sat gazing at this Linden chap while we sent a car round to Murrow's flat in Hallam Street at the back of Broadcasting House. Got the poor devil out of bed actually – he'd been up all night because of the time difference with New York, making his broadcasts home. He looked like death warmed over as we wheeled him in to take a look at Linden.

'Murrow didn't recognize him at first, then Linden began to prod his memory. "Don't you remember Frau Goering's party . . ." That sort of thing. Finally, Murrow took his cigarette from his mouth and said, "Yeah, I've got you now, pal." He turned to us and said, "Relax, gentlemen. He's only one of Goebbels's dancing boys."''

Ringrose said, 'So what happened to Linden?'

'Tossed him back into the water. He was no use to us. I suppose he must have sat out the rest of the war in a POW camp.'

'Lord Lavington,' said Ringrose, 'do you remember where Linden was shot down and first held in custody?'

'I'm afraid I can't help there. I must have been told at the time but I had no reason to remember. It's only the intervention of Ed Murrow that caused this story to stick in my mind.'

'And what about the place of interrogation? It must have been somewhere in the London area. You spoke of sending a car to Hallam Street.'

'No problem there,' said Lord Lavington. 'It was at the Royal Patriotic Schools in Wandsworth. The pupils had been evacuated to the country. MI5 had got their hands on Linden and the building, and they had him locked up there in south-west London.'

'Christ!' said Firth. 'Is the building still standing?'

'It was the last time I drove across Wandsworth Common,' said Lord Lavington. 'Monstrous Victorian Gothic pile. Only a mother could love it.'

Ringrose and his aide exchanged wild-eyed, speculative looks. Could the girls be in *London*?

Ringrose, who hated guns but who had the vision of two bloated corpses in blue uniforms in front of him, said, 'Lionel, round up a party and issue small arms. We're going to Wandsworth.'

At dawn they returned crestfallen to the Yard, and Ringrose arranged a car to take Lord Lavington home. Two hundred men had encircled the turreted edifice that had once been the Royal Patriotic Schools and had moved in warily. They had awoken a number of surprised flat-dwellers, and found a recording centre and a series of craft studios, but no beauty queens, in the large cellars beneath the Victorian structure. The building had caught fire in 1981 and had later been developed for modern usage yet Lord Lavington had shown them the room in which the long-ago interrogation of a frightened German journalist had taken place.

Ringrose stood with Firth in the cellar and groaned. 'It all fits so neatly. Peter Linden was here, there's more than enough room to hide forty-nine girls, and the VICT in Prentiss Decker's second Morse message could so easily be applied to a Victorian building.'

Firth said, 'Is it possible, guv, that the girls were held here? Maybe the Peter Linden message was copied by the American girl from graffiti left by Linden on the wall.'

'What? With all those people living and working upstairs noticing nothing unusual?' said Ringrose. 'But I like the thought about the graffiti, so let's have these walls gone over inch by inch. Although I think we're up the gum tree again.'

He was right.

At the Yard Ringrose and Firth got down on their camp beds to snatch two hours' sleep. 'Who was it who said, "I'll think about it tomorrow?"' asked Ringrose, eyes half closed in exhaustion.

'Scarlett O'Hara in *Gone With the Wind*,' said Firth, an avid cinema buff.

'That just about sums up our present predicament,' said Ringrose. 'Tomorrow we'll think about getting the Bundeskriminalamt in Wiesbaden on the track of Peter Linden. We *must* establish his whereabouts on the fifth of September nineteen forty.'

He pulled a blanket over his head and was asleep in twenty seconds.

Chapter Thirty-seven

The extensive supplies of canned and frozen food collected piecemeal during the summer months were exhausted. Lenny Belcher and Teddy Triggs had been sent out with their van to renew the stock. They'd wanted to cut short this tedious chore by picking up all they needed from a wholesale cash-and-carry depot, but Lucius had been fierce in his opposition to this. 'Anyone buying large quantities of food in this part of the country is automatically going to arouse suspicion,' he said. 'You'll buy from supermarkets in only family-size quantities. Do you understand?'

They had sloped off, contemptuous of his ultra-nervousness. They could not know it but Lucius Frankel was again ahead of those who would seek to destroy him. At Commander Ringrose's suggestion, the Kent Constabulary had quietly mounted a county-wide surveillance of wholesale and retail food shops. Buyers of abnormally large quantities of foodstuffs were having their vehicle numbers noted and checked and, where suspicion arose, a police raid followed.

In the cellars of Moxmanton House, the girls gloomily registered the end of their second week in captivity.

'To think,' said Mirabelle Montcalm, 'just fourteen days ago we were putting on our glad rags and warpaint to have lunch with a prince!'

Prentiss was becoming concerned at the mental condition of some of the girls. The sudden, brutal incarceration was beginning to tell in terms of 'jail fever' or downright claustrophobia. All of them had enjoyed a gregarious social and largely outdoor, sun-worshipping life. The abrupt change was taking a mental toll, no matter what distractions were dangled before them. The 'keep-your-sunny-side-up' programme of cellar activities

– exercises, parlour games, charades, sing-songs, talent contests – staged by Monika Dahlberg and Fran Pilkington, was assuming an increasingly hollow and despairing air.

Some wandered their prison in a trance-like state. Others had developed tics, lip chewing, nail-biting and a manic inability to remain still.

Prentiss had cast herself as group booster. 'Hold on!' she urged the basket cases. 'The ransom money is being handed over two days from now. Any time after that, they'll set us free.'

That same day her optimism was propped up when she was taken upstairs again, this time to make an ordinary tape-recording of ransom hand-over instructions. The audio message was directed at the man mentioned in her last video cassette.

'Please God, don't let Commander Thomas Ringrose foul up,' prayed Prentiss, to a deity she had long neglected.

The German police joined the hunt for Peter Linden at 9 a.m. on Thursday, 13 October, and by noon a search of the MI5 registry had produced two documents relating to him.

The first, a body chit, showed that Peter Linden, aged twenty-eight, a German national, had been transferred from the custody of the Military Police to the Security Service on 7 September 1940. The second, another receipt, confirmed that two days later, on 9 September 1940, Linden had been handed over by MI5 at the Royal Patriotic Schools into the custody of the RAF police. This had been annotated by some MI5 functionary with the words, 'No further interest.'

Neither document indicated Linden's movements of the previous few days nor his destination thereafter.

The two dates supplied indicated that the interrogation board attended by Lord Lavington had most probably taken place on 8 September. The vital question, Where was Linden on the fifth?, remained tantalizingly unanswered.

Ringrose spent an hour on the telephone to the Ministry of Defence and ended up talking to a man with an encyclopaedic mind in the Air Historics section.

He put down the telephone and said to Firth, 'I'm informed

that the most likely place to find Peter Linden's wartime documents, his record as a POW and so on, is at something called the Departmental Records Office at Hayes in Middlesex. We'd better get out there.'

With the siren on, the fourteen-mile journey in heavy traffic took eighteen minutes and twenty seconds. Ringrose and Firth emerged shakily from the Jaguar.

The Departmental Records Office of the Ministry of Defence is situated on a small site alongside a railway line. From the road its two main buildings look like aircraft hangars. In fact, the place was purpose-built pre-war as a Royal Ordnance factory for the manufacture of field guns.

A telephone call from the Ministry of Defence had paved the detectives' way and they were ushered in to meet the executive officer in charge, a quizzical, thin man with tufted grey hair named Charles Bollam. They explained their problem and Bollam made notes.

Finally, he said, 'On the strength of the information available, I can tell you in about five days' time whether or not we hold the material here and, if we do, extract it within two weeks.'

The two detectives stared at him in dismay. 'Two *weeks*?' exclaimed Ringrose. 'We're thinking more on the lines of two *hours*. Mr Bollam, we have the lives of forty-nine women at stake here. Is there nothing you can do?'

Bollam said, unhappily, 'You don't need to tell me. I have daughters of my own. Gentlemen, come with me.'

He led them into one of the hangars. Steel racks stretched upward for three storeys and off into the distance. Cliff-faces of books, box files, manila folders, brown envelopes soared into the roof. A small corps of men and women moved about the gangways and stacks, maintaining, checking, filing and extracting items.

'These people are called the Paper Keepers,' said Bollam. 'The last time they took the trouble to check, they had enough files that, laid end-to-end, would stretch all the way to Brighton and back again – more than one-hundred-and-twenty miles of bumf.'

Ringrose's heart sank further. 'Look, Mr Bollam, we *must*

284

have a go. Would it help if I loaned you fifty police officers to assist in the search?'

'Fifty would be overkill,' said Bollam. 'They'd only get the files in a muddle. Give me twenty-five who've signed the Official Secrets Act and I'll put them to work.'

By 3 p.m. the two sheds at Hayes bustled with activity. At five, Ringrose received a call from Bollam. 'Thought you'd like to know my team just voted to work in shifts around the clock until they've found what you want. They don't like those murdering bastards, either. I'll ring you the moment I have anything.'

He added, almost apologetically, 'My son has just brought his camping gear along to my office. I'll stay here on a bed-roll. Will it matter if I have to ring you during the night?'

'Mr Bollam,' said Ringrose fervently, 'you could ring me even if I was in bed with Helen of Troy.'

Chapter Thirty-eight

The tape recorded by Prentiss Decker on Thursday was recovered the next morning from a crevice under a Barbara Hepworth sculpture at the Tate Gallery, after the usual Welsh-voiced call to the Yard's switchboard. A pity. Ringrose had added crime-fiction library shelves to the Central London surveillance list since the last drop. He was dealing with a mind that did not fall easily into unthinking patterns.

The message, read by Prentiss and addressed to him by the kidnappers, was short and direct: 'Commander Ringrose, you will acquire an open truck and two Day-glo orange suits of the kind worn by road-repair men. The suitcases will be packed as previously instructed and loaded onto the back of the truck. You will guard the money personally and you may have one other officer to drive the truck. Each of you will be dressed in a Day-glo suit. No other law-enforcement officers are to be involved in this operation. If there is any transgression of this condition, the girls will start to die. All police road blocks and other surveillance activity is to be called off, as from midnight tonight, and will not be resumed. We girls cannot be released while there is any danger for our captors. To signify your agreement to all these conditions, insert the word "Understood" over the Lord Grey signature in the personal column of tomorrow's *Times*. If you do not agree, insert the word "Snag". This, however, will not prevent the first girl being executed on Sunday. Stand by your office telephone from noon Saturday. You will be contacted with further instructions.'

'So,' murmured Ringrose, 'we come to the moment in the joust when the lances actually touch.' He felt he was beginning to understand the mind of the shadow with which he had been grappling for the last two weeks.

He turned to Firth. 'Do as they say. Get the advertisement organized for tomorrow.'

'Which word?'

'"Understood", of course,' said Ringrose. 'Then come back here. There's a massive reshuffling of manpower to be accomplished before noon tomorrow.'

On Friday at 7.30 p.m. Gerhardt Fischer, the German *Polizeidirektor* in Wiesbaden, telephoned.

'Hello, Thomas,' he said, in ponderous English. 'When are you going to return our beautiful Hanna to us?'

'Soon, I hope, Herr Direktor,' said Ringrose. 'Sooner still if you have good news for me.'

'Maybe, maybe,' said Fischer. 'Our records show that Peter Linden did indeed work for *Völkische Beobachter*. He escaped military service because the Ministry of Propaganda had him registered in a reserved occupation. We have so far been unable to trace any record of his wartime activities. His disappearance in a bomber was never reported by his own newspaper – too demoralizing, I should say, eh?'

Ringrose could hear Fischer rustling his reports. The German went on, 'Linden surfaced again in Germany in 1946 when he was repatriated as a prisoner-of-war by you British. He had spent most of the war in camps in Canada and told the story that he even survived his prison ship being torpedoed by one of Germany's own U-boats in the north Atlantic.

'Because of his pre-war record as a Nazi, he was picked up on his return here and held for a denazification court hearing but this was merely a formality. In open court he expressed repentance and was released immediately. Remember, he had already spent six years as a prisoner and that was regarded by the court as punishment enough.'

'What happened to him afterwards?' asked Ringrose.

'He tried to find newspaper work in Berlin, Bonn, Hamburg and Munich, but his pre-war record of association with Dr Goebbels hung like – what is the bird? – an albatross around his neck. His post-war life in West Germany seems to have been a bitter disappointment to him and he emigrated to the United States in 1949.'

Ringrose swore silently. 'Is that it, Herr Direktor?'

'That is it, Thomas. You must turn to the Americans for further assistance. I only hope you are not chasing a corpse. Remember, Peter Linden is now a man in his seventies – if he is still alive.'

Ringrose cut the line and dialled Jake Bishop. Bishop listened carefully and said, 'This is one for the FBI. I'll have Langley get the Bureau's ass into gear right away. Linden must have done a powerful lot of lying on his immigration documents to gain admission to the USA. It's never been our policy to welcome ex-Nazis, unless they had some special skill like Werner von Braun, the rocket man.'

Lucius Frankel's stomach churned. Was tomorrow at last to be the day? The day he joined the golden few who bestrode the world, unfettered by considerations of money or morality? He gazed round at the others.

Bruiser, Rolly and Dickie checked their weapons and equipment, their aristocratic faces masked in professional absorption. Did they have the same furnace burning in their guts, he wondered. Could he ever acquire the same enviable *sang-froid*?

The plan was that at 8 a.m. they would buy the *Times* to confirm that the operation was on and then they would reconnoitre the various routes to London to confirm that the roadblocks had been lifted. They would reassemble at ten, pack the Hecklers and set out for their collection day.

As a result of their weekend ordeal Bill and Flo Beer had endured a brief celebrity in the newspapers. At 11 a.m. on Saturday, 15 October, Flo returned home with the weekend shopping. Bill was attempting to choose a certainty from his racing paper. At 11.15 a.m. the telephone rang and Flo answered. She handed the receiver to Bill. 'It's the police again,' she said.

'Sorry to bother you, Mr Beer,' said a cheerful male voice. 'It's Bishopsgate police station here, sir. We've gathered together another bunch of photographs from the rogues' gallery we'd like you to have a glance through.'

'Can't it wait will Monday?' Bill complained.

'We have to push on while the trail's still warm, sir. But if it'll help, I'll send a young detective constable round to your place and you can look at the pictures there.'

'All right,' said Bill, sighing. 'I hope it's not going to take all day.'

'Don't worry, sir, he'll be in and out in fifteen minutes.' Bill grunted cynically. The man from Bishopsgate added, 'The detective constable's name is Maurice Penfold. Be sure you check his name before opening the door. Don't want a repetition of last Saturday, do we, sir?'

'No chance!' said Bill, with feeling.

When the front-door buzzer sounded, he killed the alarm and confirmed that a fresh-faced young man was standing alone on the step. 'Who's that?' said Bill.

'Detective Constable Penfold. I believe you're expecting me.'

'Oh, right!' said Bill, removing the chain.

Seconds later he was gazing pop-eyed down the muzzle of a Browning automatic.

'Oh, no!' said Bill. 'Not again!'

''Fraid so, old boy,' said the figure, as the rest of the familiar gang filed in.

Soon Bill and Flo were leashed once more to their chairs, water and chocolate within reach. 'You,' said Flo, glaring at her spouse with naked contempt, 'are as daft as the day you were born.'

It was a judgement that the hapless caretaker was in no position to dispute.

Ringrose and Firth sat in their Day-glo dungarees watching the clock. Radio experts had wired them both for speech and sound reception. Aerials ran down the insides of their trousers, minute microphones were clipped under the cloth at the neck and each had tiny receiver headphones inserted into their left ears, the leads held down by flesh-coloured plaster. A barber had been called in to reshape their hair-styles and, with a liberal application of fixative, set their locks over their ears.

During the night, radio listening cars and vans had been deployed throughout London and on all exit roads, while the roadblocks themselves had been ostensibly lifted.

A control van would follow the ransom truck at a safe distance. The suitcase bleepers, Bishop had said, would give a powerful signal over a twenty-mile range. Ringrose had a helicopter standing by on the roof of the National Westminster skyscraper in the City. The Prime Minister had insisted that the Special Air Service detachment were placed on alert at the Duke of York's barracks.

If they were called out, Ringrose knew he would have failed. He wanted those girls without a firefight. Firth was packing a .38 in a shoulder holster and Ringrose had issued instructions that any officer in the operation could, at his own discretion, draw a weapon. He would be unarmed but he could not refuse his men the means to protect themselves against armed killers.

Noon. The telephone on his desk did not ring for another five minutes.

The Welsh male voice wasted no time. 'Commander Ringrose, you will take the loaded truck as agreed and park it in full public view near the war memorial at the top of Constitution Hill opposite Apsley House. Look for a litter bin nearby with a yellow cross painted upon it. Remove the contents.'

The line went dead. Ringrose did not stay for the trace report. 'Come on, Lionel. We're on our way,' he said. The two vividly dressed detectives left the Yard in a regulation patrol car to the accompaniment of howling protests from the assembled media mob who were held back.

The flat truck stood under armed guard outside the operations annexe at the Horticultural Halls in Vincent Square. Firth climbed into the driver's seat and Ringrose hauled himself on top of ten neat navy blue suitcases. Not only whores got to sit on fortunes, he thought wickedly. He checked his contact with control. Reception was perfect.

Duke of Wellington Place at Hyde Park Corner marks the conjunction of Piccadilly, Park Lane, Knightsbridge and Grosvenor Place. It is among the busiest road junctions in Britain. Firth nosed the truck into the kerb. Ringrose could already see the yellow cross on the litter bin. He pulled from it a waterproof package and extracted a walkie-talkie radio. As the wrapper fell away the set came to life in his hands.

'Good,' said the Welsh voice. 'Now we can speak nicely to each other.'

Ringrose gazed around. The damned man must have him in sight. The island was overlooked by Apsley House Museum that was also the Duke of Wellington's home, the Inter-Continental and Lanesborough hotels, and, in the distance along Park Lane, the upper storeys of both the Dorchester and Hilton hotels. Tom held the set near to his microphone so that the control wagon could overhear the dialogue.

The voice said, 'I want you to climb back on the truck and open each suitcase in turn, leaving the contents on view for at least ten seconds.'

The cases were on combination locks. Ringrose began to turn the tumblers on the first case. The voice broke in, 'What's the combination?'

'One seven seven six – the same for each case,' said Ringrose. 'Now you tell me how the girls are.'

'The girls are fine. Stop wasting time.'

Ringrose opened the first case, exposing the packed rows of West Germany currency. The next three contained US 100-dollar bills and then came sterling.

From a room high in the tower of the Hilton, Lucius Frankel swept his binoculars over contents and cases, his hand shaking a little. This was a sight long central to his dreams.

Ringrose was now holding up a case of Swiss currency. When he had relocked the last one, Lucius heard him say, 'What now?'

'Stand by,' said Lucius. He packed his walkie-talkie and binoculars into a case and took the lift down to the garage. Everything was in order on the surface yet something nagged at him.

Ringrose sat on the cases for several minutes before the set came to life again. 'Drive to London Bridge and halt in the middle, facing south,' said the voice.

Lucius was using an unremarkable hired Mini Metro. He'd left his Alfa in the garage. It was too distinctive a vehicle. He was already across the river when the open truck drew up on the crown of the bridge. He confirmed that his instructions were being obeyed and continued on down Borough High

Street for half a mile. He passed the church on his left and found a parking space in a side street.

He poked the walkie-talkie aerial out of the window, pressed the transmit button and said: 'Proceed down Borough High Street.'

He imagined the policeman starting up the motor. After one minute he said, 'Halt outside St George's church.'

Firth had the church in view as Ringrose shouted the instructions down to him, and pulled the truck in behind a parked line of three black limousines, each bedecked with white ribbon and silver horseshoes.

Firth looked over his shoulder and gave a what-now? shrug. He cut the engine. A moment later the walkie-talkie crackled and the voice said, 'You have five minutes to clear everyone – repeat *everyone* – from the church.'

Ringrose and Firth raised eyebrows at each other. Ringrose said into his lapel, 'You heard that, Control. For God's sake, don't let anyone walk away with the suitcases while we're inside.'

Around them, he knew, an invisible force of police was moving into position.

The two detectives ran up the steps through the open double doors and into the nave. Tom stopped dead and said, 'Good Lord!'

A plump clergyman, white-cassocked, was in full spate at the zenith of a wedding ceremony. A young bride and her groom stood rapt, staring into his solemn face as he intoned, '. . . hath joined together let no man put asunder . . .'

Ringrose felt a complete swine. 'Stop!' he shouted, running forward. The wedding couple and the congregation swivelled to witness two demented men in orange working clothes, rushing between the pews.

The rector's prayer book inadvertently closed with a snap. The bride burst into tears while her father and the best man took angry swings at the two detectives. Ringrose fended off the blow and fished for his warrant card. 'Police!' he shouted. 'We have reason to believe there's a bomb in the church,' he invented desperately. 'Don't panic – but get outside as fast as you can.'

292

He grabbed the clergyman and pulled him aside as a tide of wedding guests swept out of their pews, jabbering wildly and scattering hymn books and hassocks in their wake.

'Stay with me, sir,' hissed Ringrose. The priest tried to speak but Ringrose would not give him time. 'Just listen. I'm Commander Thomas Ringrose of Scotland Yard and we're engaged on a life-and-death operation. There is no bomb, but your church must be empty of people within the next four minutes.'

He shouted at Firth, 'Check the gallery and the steeple,' and said to the rector, 'Who else is here?'

'Only a couple of ladies and sidesmen in the vestry.'

'Let's get them out,' said Ringrose. 'What about downstairs?'

'No, it's locked.'

'Do you have keys?' The man nodded. 'Then let's open up and take a look.'

They went down to the vestry and winkled out the church helpers. The priest then led Ringrose to the crypt, switching on the lights as they went, his ecclesiastical robes flying bat-like behind him.

Ringrose scanned it. There was a push-bar exit in the east wall and another small door used by the Boy Scout troop in the south wall. 'Are those the only ways out of here?'

'Yes.'

'All the exits from the building come out onto the pavement?'

'That is correct.'

'So anyone entering or leaving the church would be in full view outside?'

'Absolutely. The church is surrounded by roads. They would have to be crossed. Only an invisible man could enter or leave unseen.'

They met Firth in the main entrance. 'All clear up top, guv. I've chased the organist out.'

Ringrose spoke again into his lapel. 'You got that, Control? I want all sides of the church covered.'

He swept Firth and the rector outside. The wedding party was clustered in distressed knots on the opposite pavement.

'Go over and move them away, sir,' Ringrose said to the

clergyman. 'But please keep yourself available.' The bride was weeping.

Ringrose and Firth had returned to the truck.

Lucius had seen enough. Smiling, he strolled back to his car and said into the walkie-talkie, 'Take the ten cases, place them alongside the font and come back out, closing the church doors behind you.' He'd also realized what had been bothering him.

He pressed the transmit button again. 'Commander Ringrose, you and your colleague will then sit patiently in full view in the back of your truck and make no move until you receive further instructions from me. Within forty-five minutes two men wearing red berets will enter the church to make a physical examination of the suitcases and contents. They are to be allowed to enter and leave unimpeded. Any attempt to accost or to follow them will result in the operation being aborted. The first execution will follow automatically. Do you understand and agree?'

'Understood and agreed,' said Ringrose, tersely.

Lucius stowed the walkie-talkie under the car seat, locked the door, and strolled round to mingle with the crowd now congregated outside the entrance to the Borough underground station.

He watched as the two detectives struggled up the church steps with the suitcases. Finally Ringrose came out and Lucius watched him pull shut the tall black doors. He enjoyed the spectacle of the so-called great detective, puce-faced with the exertions of the past quarter of an hour. The two men climbed, obedient to his diktat, into the back of the truck and perched themselves impassively on its sides.

Satisfied, Lucius retreated into the tube station, bought a one-station ticket and descended to the platform. He remained in the white-tiled corridor until he heard a train approach, stop, discharge and take on passengers, and move out of the station.

Lucius walked past the alighting passengers onto the emptying south-bound platform. Within seconds he was the only person visible along its gloomy length. He moved swiftly to the left-hand edge where he was able to stare directly into the black void of the tunnel. From his observation post, a hundred yards inside the blackness, where the disused line diverts from the Northern Line, Dickie Biggs-Salter could see Lucius quite clearly.

Lucius watched until Dickie acknowledged his sighting with two brief needle-flashes of light from a torch. From his overcoat pocket, Lucius took a smaller version of the walkie-talkie he had left in the car. It was almost a toy but its range was sufficient for his present purpose. He whispered, 'The money is inside the church and you have a maximum of forty-five minutes. Check the cases carefully. I suspect the Americans have had a hand in supplying them, which means there's funny business afoot. The lock combination is one seven seven six – the year of the Declaration of Independence. Not very clever.'

That's what had been bothering him. He put away his walkie-talkie and stood, suddenly drained, waiting for the next train to carry him a station down the line to the Elephant and Castle. He had gained them forty-five minutes and events were now beyond his influence.

Ringrose said into his lapel mike, 'Will someone get the rector to take a little stroll over here?' He turned to Firth. 'None of this adds up. Why go to these lengths? They could have had the men in the red berets examine the load at Hyde Park Corner.'

'Don't want us to get too good a look at them,' suggested Firth.

'They're going to get that anyway. We're not exactly going to be sitting here with our eyes closed.' Ringrose said into his lapel, 'Control, I want the biggest possible blow-up photographs of the beret men if they show up.'

He scanned the surrounding rooftops. He could detect no movement but he knew that at least twenty officers in the back-up force must be in range.

A detective dressed as a bus inspector had whispered to the rector, who now bustled anxiously over to the truck. Ringrose, taking a chance on flouting the kidnappers' instructions, jumped down onto the pavement. The walkie-talkie remained dormant.

Ringrose said, 'I must ask you again, sir. Is there no possibility at all of anyone being able to carry those cases out of the building without us seeing them?'

The priest drew himself up, affronted. 'I've been the incumbent for only a year, but I assure you, Commander, I do know the fabric of my own church.'

Ringrose was still uneasy. He said, 'Control, how are the signals from the suitcases?'

'The cases are still stationary inside the church.'

Ringrose sighed. His whole being screamed hoodwink.

Chapter Thirty-nine

Five segments of darkness detached themselves from the black maw of the open air-raid shelter emergency exit. They wore black overalls to protect ordinary day clothes, with black hoods. Bruiser, his Heckler raised, moved silently on rubber boots ahead of the party. He took the crypt steps two at a time and opened the understairs door on the ground floor of St George's. He slid through a glass-panelled door and found himself in the body of the church, the evidence of its rapid evacuation scattered around him. He raised a cautioning hand and the raiding group halted while he made a swift circuit of the nave, checking the pews and the pulpit.

Rolly Ponsford made a similar search of the gallery.

Reassured, Bruiser took up a stance with his submachine gun facing the closed main doors of the church. He could hear traffic and the murmur of voices outside. He looked at his watch. Five of their forty-five minutes had already gone. The two Cockneys stood hypnotized at the sight of the suitcases. Teddy had one gloved hand on the font where he had been received into the Christian church.

Dickie took out the bug detector and switched on. Immediately the instrument emitted a faint, low bleep. Dickie passed the detector over the entire line of cases. 'Shit and derision,' he said. 'These cases have more bugs than a camel's backside.'

'Didn't really anticipate anything else,' said Bruiser. 'Must expect underarm bowling from now on.'

Teddy and Lenny had their own set of mismatched cases ready.

Dickie took hold of the first of the originals and said, 'Let's get them all open.'

The sight that had entranced Lucius through his binoculars

now enslaved them. 'Did you ever see such a wonder?' said Rolly, in a reverential whisper. In the quiet church, the intake of breath was palpable.

'Save it for later,' snapped Bruiser. 'Let's have the test for secret dyes.'

Rolly was carrying a small battery-operated machine like a miniature disc radar. He switched on and carefully bathed each case and its contents in the ultra-violet light which would reveal any attempt to betray them with invisible dyes that could stain their clothes and skin.

'Well, that's one ball they haven't tried to pitch at us,' said Rolly. 'The top layers of the notes are clear.'

They began to transfer the long lines of notes, their hands trembling like those of old gamblers whose nerves have gone.

Bruiser remained with his back to the other four, his eyes and weapon undeviating from the main door. He brought his watch up to eye-level. They'd already been inside the church twenty minutes. Behind him he heard Triggs curse and the sound of banknotes falling to the ground and scattering.

'Easy! Easy!' he heard Dickie say soothingly. 'Work methodically. Don't fumble.'

Four cases were packed and the two Cockneys went to stack them on the tunnel stairs. At intervals, Dickie and Rolly operated their detection instruments over the money bundles.

Presently Rolly called out to Bruiser, 'They've made a damned clever job of doctoring these cases but they've not interfered with the money.'

'Just keep going,' said Bruiser. 'We've already been up here twenty-five minutes.'

Behind him, the banknotes were piling up in ziggurats on the stone floor alongside the discarded FBI suitcases.

Ringrose was torn between an urge for physical action and the need to do nothing that would enrage the kidnappers. The briefing sessions he'd held during the previous night had all ended with one message to his officers: 'We can always recover the money but maybe not the girls' lives. This is a tailing operation. I want them to lead us to the hostages. That is the sole purpose of today's exercise.'

He said to Firth, 'We've been sitting here for half an hour.'

At that moment, Control came through with their regular thirty-second check. 'Still receiving the signals from the cases loud and clear. There's no movement.'

Ringrose watched the clergyman recross the street and scurry towards him, looking concerned. Accompanying him was a frail, white-haired man in a black vestment. Ringrose recognized him as one of the sidesmen he'd ushered unceremoniously out of the church front door.

The rector was breathless. He said, fretfully, 'I fear I may have inadvertently misled you. Mr Simkins here has been in the parish far longer than I. His memory of St George's goes back a long way. I think you'd better listen to him.'

The old man steadied himself against the side of the truck. He was not accustomed to rushing. He said, 'The rector, bless him, couldn't have known about the Deep. He's far too young.'

'The Deep?' asked Ringrose, baffled.

'During the war,' said the old man cryptically. 'Safe as houses it was. Even the V-2 rockets couldn't reach down that far.'

'A shelter? An air-raid shelter?' said Ringrose, light dawning.

'Yes, sir. A disused tube tunnel. It ran right under the High Street.' The sidesman beckoned Ringrose down. 'Come with me a moment, sir. Let me show you.'

Ringrose jumped to the pavement and Simkins led him to the north side of the church. A small graveyard nestled under the windows.

The old man said, 'Look at the wall that divides the graveyard from the pavement. Observe the two places in the wall where the bricks are not the originals. That's where people used to get into the Deep – through the wall and down into the earth. It was all bricked up and earthed over when the war ended.'

Ringrose said, 'I'm still not sure I'm with you.'

'Well,' said the sidesman, 'the rector says he told you there was no hidden way into or out of the church. And maybe he's right. All I can say is, I have a clear recollection of an emergency exit that could take you from the crypt into the Deep.'

The old man gazed sympathetically into Ringrose's face. 'It's just a thought and I don't want to waste your time. But we've all been standing over on the pavement working out what you've carried into the church. And it'd be a pity if those evil men get away from you. Just suppose they know about the tunnel. And you sitting out here . . .' The old man's voice trailed away.

Ringrose muttered an oath that did not quite reach the rector's ears. He said urgently into his mike, 'I want one officer to break cover and fetch two torches.' He turned to Firth. 'Let's get these bloody silly orange suits off. I think we're more likely to end up as lemons.'

They were struggling out of the overalls when a young officer with a green and pink punk haircut ran across and handed his superiors the required items. Ringrose said, 'Lionel, keep your hand near that gun. We're going inside.'

Ringrose went first, gingerly pressing one door with his fingertips. Inside nothing moved. Behind him, Firth drew his revolver and the two men, crouching below the level of the glass panes of the inner doors that now faced them, scuttled forward until they could raise themselves up to get a view of the font.

'Sweet Jesus!' groaned Lionel, stricken. The pillage was total. The FBI suitcases were strewn in a semi-circle around the font, which was as empty as the cases themselves.

The two detectives burst through the doors. Ringrose's foot raised a fluttering at floor level. A member of the gang had dropped a packet of Swiss francs. They'd not bothered to retrieve this valuable detritus.

'Two men in red berets!' exclaimed Firth. 'They never existed.'

But Ringrose was not listening. In staccato style he issued orders into his lapel mike: 'I want the priest, Mr Simkins and ten armed men inside the church on the double. Contact London Transport and get me a fast rundown on the disused tube line that lies beneath Borough High Street – its exits, entrances, everything they can tell us.'

He was dismally aware that obtaining fast answers on a Saturday afternoon was a slender hope.

The police back-up party came charging through the doors, weapons at the ready. Ringrose grabbed the rector and his sidesman. 'Lead the way, Mr Simkins. Show me the emergency exit into the Deep.'

300

The rector struggled with his vestments to get at the church keys in his pocket and the party made a cautious advance into the crypt. The gang had relocked every door behind them. The sidesman pointed to the boiler room and said, 'As far as I remember, the door was in there.'

The rector found a key, opened the boiler-room and stood aside. Firth went first with his drawn revolver. At the rear of the small room the wartime emergency door lay half hidden behind the fuel tank. It was barred from the far side.

Old Simkins complained, 'During the war the bolts were on our side.' Ringrose and Firth put their shoulders against the steel plates. The door would not budge.

Ringrose spoke into his mike. He got only a distant, garbled reply. The walls of the crypt were interfering with the radio signals. He raced upstairs and tried again. 'I want axes and sledgehammers – fast!'

Ringrose was heart-stoppingly aware that the situation was slipping from his grasp.

The gang bumped, dragged and carried the ten strong fibre cases, each weighing forty-five pounds or more, down a hundred steps into the west tunnel. They had brought with them two wooden doors torn from their hinges at the King William Street station and Rolly, displaying the resourcefulness he had learned at Sandhurst military academy, had attached skateboards to the corners of each, thus creating two sturdy, low-slung moving platforms. They were loading five cases onto each door when the first booming sound, like the detonation of a distant cannon, rolled down from surface level.

'They've found the door,' said Bruiser. 'Let's hurry it up.'

They began to push the two loads, each of $12.5 million, in the direction of the Thames, their torch lights bouncing urgent, nervous shadows off the arching walls. The solid wheels of the skateboards rolled easily over the old shelter floor.

Two burly constables swung their hammers at the steel door. Ringrose and Firth stood back, racked with doubt and foreboding.

They heard the bottom bolt break away and the two

constables attacked the upper section of the door with renewed fury. Suddenly it shot open and almost bounced shut again in their faces under the ferocity of the blows.

Ringrose and Firth went through first. Their torches followed the trail of disturbed dust downward. The two men, their armed back-up in their wake, leaped down the staircase.

At tunnel level they crawled through the broken wall to be confronted by the two abandoned tube tunnels. Their torches swept the floor for tell-tale track signs, but the constant ventilation had prevented dust from collecting here.

Ringrose shouted back up the stairs for Mr Simkins. Two officers carried the old man down into a place he had not seen in more than fifty years.

'Which way, Mr Simkins?'

'If you go left you'll end up being electrocuted on the Northern Line,' said the old man. 'The crooks must have turned right.'

Ringrose said, 'Lionel, you take half the men down the right-hand tunnel, I'll take the left one.'

Ringrose pounded down the west tunnel, marvelling at its fine state of preservation. He could see nothing ahead except pitch darkness.

Their breath came in lung-scouring rasps. In their hurry, both Teddy Triggs and Bruiser had tripped over their loads and crashed painfully to the tunnel floor. They notched up the first half-mile of their underground run as they reached the staircase leading up to London Bridge Street. They ignored it, pushing on towards the river wall. A hundred feet beyond the staircase the shelter floor ended.

They hoisted the doors onto their shoulders, and crunched through the slime that ran in a rivulet along the tunnel bottom until they reached the first water gate. The cases would now need to be manhandled for the quarter-mile journey under the Thames to the King William Street exit.

They pushed and dragged them past the iron floodgate that Rolly had shattered with his explosive. He was handing the last of the Hecklers through the hole when he looked over his shoulder. A long way back he could see a dancing spot of light.

'Christ,' he said, 'the hounds have picked up the scent.' He shouted through the hole to Bruiser, 'You push on and I'll go back and hold them off.'

'Balls to that,' said Bruiser. 'It's not part of the plan.'

'They'll be on top of you before you can get the cases out of the tunnel,' said Rolly. 'I'll divert them to give you a breathing space, then beat a retreat by way of the London Bridge Street exit. I'll rendezvous with you at Kew.'

Bruiser made to pass back a Heckler but Rolly said, 'No! Keep it. We can't let it fall into their hands. Only give the game away. And I can't run through the streets with it in broad daylight. Don't worry. I've a handful of surprises for them.' Then the darkness swallowed him.

There were now just four of them to drag ten heavy cases for a quarter of a mile. 'Take two each and drag them along by the handles,' said Bruiser, slinging a Heckler over each broad shoulder.

'What about the other two cases?' said Teddy Triggs.

'Leave 'em,' said Bruiser.

They began the long haul along the stalactite-spiked tunnel under the river.

Rolly raced back, heading towards the moving light, until he reached the staircase leading up to London Bridge Street. He unzipped his black overall and tossed it aside, then wiped his face with the hood and then threw it after the overall.

In the dark, he felt the comforting bulge around his waist and unzipped his windcheater to expose his belt. Clipped to it were a number of green, lemon-sized objects. Rolly took one in his hand and waited patiently while the lights and voices approached along the west tunnel. As if he had aeons of time, he moved into the centre of the floor, primed the clockwork lever and sent the green object skittering towards the lights.

The stun grenade detonated nine feet in front of Ringrose. The effect was devastating. Simultaneously, he was blinded by a brilliant light, lifted off his feet and thrown backwards into the body of men immediately to his rear. He experienced a concussive clap of thunder as if two boards had been smashed together to sandwich his skull. He became vaguely aware of a roar of alarm and outrage as officers from the vanguard of the party leaped over his crumpled body and pressed on. One began to fire a weapon.

'For Chrissake, no!' called Ringrose weakly.

Rolly felt something sear the top of his right thigh and heard the unmistakable crack of small-arms fire. But he was still on his feet. He gritted his teeth. If that was the way they wanted it . . .

He could see and hear the distant mêlée and men's silhouettes. He unclipped a second grenade and sent it scurrying after the first. He watched the bold front-men hurled back. For good measure Rolly pitched a third.

After the thunder and flash, he saw with satisfaction that there wasn't a man left on his feet. Torches shone at crazy angles from the crumpled black groaning heap.

Rolly made his way rapidly up the stairs and into the old lift shaft that led to the oak door on London Bridge Street.

At the top he paused. God knew what he looked like. He zipped up the windcheater, smoothed back his hair with his gloved hands and uttered a silent prayer that he appeared at least half-way presentable. At least he had diverted the chase. They'd come after him now instead of pressing on under the river. He sent one last stun grenade down the shaft to let the police know which direction he had taken, opened the door and stepped out into the approach to London Bridge railway station.

The streets were uncomfortably quiet. On Saturdays, little happens in the area. Blinking in the afternoon light, Rolly turned away from the railway station and made his way towards London Bridge where, on the far side, Bruiser and the rest of the party should soon be emerging above ground with the money.

It occurred to him that he had better not cross the bridge. If anything went wrong, he'd bring the chase too near to them for comfort. He slipped into Tooley Street, wishing there were more people about so that he could merge into the landscape. He slowed his pace – hurrying would draw attention. On his right soared the massive, blackened brick arches on which the railway station was built. At last, a hundred yards ahead, he saw a large group of people forming a queue. They were alighting from two coaches. Rolly saw the perfect camouflage. He nipped neatly into the line. Now where the dickens were they headed? Up front he could see a black-painted doorway with medieval-style lettering above it. Rolly craned his neck. The legend read, 'All Hope Abandon, Ye Who Enter Here.'

Ringrose and his men spilled out onto the pavement of London Bridge Street, dazed and befuddled by the stun grenades. Ringrose shook his head like a wet shaggy dog. He was shocked by the blast and staggered that London should harbour such a vast disused tunnel complex. But right now he had to get a grip on his thinking. He said, 'We must spread out. We're looking for people, most probably male, who look as if they've been hurrying. They may be dirty and wearing old clothes. I should say they'll also turn out to be young or youngish. Down there's no place for old men. If you find anyone of that description, don't approach them. Just keep after them. It's the girls we want.'

He sent three men off into the station to search the platforms, then ran down with the others into Borough High Street and its desultory afternoon traffic. The pedestrian railings at the kerb edge forced him to turn right and he hurried along, scanning faces.

The warm autumn weather had returned and the atmosphere was somnolent. He was still being compelled to take the direction dictated by the pedestrian rails. He glanced up at a sign. Tooley Street. On his right, Joiner Street burrowed through arches, emerging near Guy's Hospital. Three meths drinkers sat on the ground in pools of their own urine.

Ahead a pair of coaches, not unlike the missing one, disgorged the last of a party of Japanese tourists, twittering at the anticipation of pleasure to come. They fell in line for the London Dungeon, a bizarre exhibition of the history of torture and man's bloody past housed in old wine vaults under London Bridge station. Ringrose stopped and stood close to the wall.

An athletic, fair-haired man in his early forties, wearing a khaki windcheater, was shuffling forward in the line. What made him impossible to miss was that he stood a head taller than any of the dark-haired Orientals surrounding him.

Ringrose took a deep, shuddering breath. The medium who, years ago, had admired his aura and psychic sensitivity would have understood the sensation that now oscillated within him. He knew, *he just knew*, that this man had a connection with the kidnappers. Ringrose moved forward to take his place at the back of the line.

Rolly Ponsford loathed the inaction of the queue. His body screamed for movement. He wanted to sprint pell-mell from this dangerous place. He looked around with distaste at the tourists and their damned cameras.

His eye came to an abrupt rest on the Westerner who had joined the end of the queue. The fellow was keeping his head down, studying his shoes. But Rolly would have recognized that silver forelock anywhere. God knows, he'd seen it enough times on the news bulletins. Ringrose.

A great calm washed over him as it always had in times of the greatest peril. He looked straight ahead and drew himself up. As he edged forward towards the pay booth, his right hand slowly tugged down the windcheater zip. He remembered he needed money and fished in his jeans pocket. Thank God he'd kept a tenner on him.

Rolly pushed the banknote under the grille, received a ticket and his change, and pushed through into the gloom.

A guttering candelabrum threw flickering light into a guillotine with a stained blade. He shouldered his way through the tourists and found himself in a long avenue of surprisingly elegant vaults. The smell of must, the scabrous walls and the fine soaring archways reminded him of decaying Venice.

The light was subdued and the damp air was rent by the recorded sounds of the damned and the dying. Screams, moans and cries for mercy echoed off the thick walls. Rolly looked back to see the silver forelock caught in the candlelight. He ran into a side alley and bumped his head painfully on a dangling object that swayed and squealed in protest. He looked up.

Above him rocked a rusting set of gibbet irons containing the rotting corpse of a medieval malefactor. The skull peered down, the bony mouth open in a silent leer. Rolly cursed and ran on, past woodcuts of unspeakable tortures and a tableau of Sir Thomas More's daughter nursing her father's severed head.

Rolly slipped into a cell-like opening and crouched in the shadows, watching for Ringrose. Beside him a leather-jerkined executioner was using a gore-covered blade to disembowel a condemned man.

Rolly shrank into the shadow as Ringrose passed by, then shook off the straw that in 'Merrie' medieval England had soaked up the flowing blood. He doubled back along the avenue, black wispy curtains brushing his sweating face like cobwebs. He ducked under the Tyburn gibbet, ignoring the piteous sight of Simon, Lord Lovat, whose head gazed up from a basket at the stump of his neck still on the axeman's block.

This place was giving him the willies. Rolly looked wildly around for an exit sign. Beyond a tableau of an unfortunate being stretched on the rack, he spotted one and trotted openly towards it. He burst through a door to discover a further walk along an empty corridor. Shit!

He glanced over his shoulder. In the prevailing twilight he imagined he saw a head hastily withdraw behind a wall. Rolly knew he could not afford to hang about. The area would soon be swarming with cops. He felt the top of his leg where the bullet had split his jeans and created a shallow furrow in his flesh. The bloodstain on the blue denim was becoming increasingly noticeable.

At last he reached the push-bar door. He put his weight against it. It opened six inches and was stopped by something soft. From the far side he heard slurred complaints. Pushing angrily, Rolly forced an exit to find three drunks.

'Out of my way, you scum,' said Rolly. In his haste he tripped over the legs of one man and staggered into the road. He was still looking back at the meths drinkers and the exit door, waiting for Ringrose.

Rolly heard but did not see the petrol tanker. He had one of his stun grenades in his right hand, ready for Ringrose, when the nearside fender of the vehicle caught him and tossed him into the air in full view of the startled driver.

His body came down hard against the windscreen and the tanker swerved onto the pavement and into the wall. The impact sheared a feed-pipe clean off its mounting. Rolly slid down, semiconscious, into the growing pool of fuel, his grip on the grenade slackening.

Ringrose, following the sudden gust of outside air, was almost at the iron exit door when an immense explosion rocked the London Dungeon. The doors held but a long tongue of flame licked underneath. Ringrose threw himself down, feeling the hot breath of the holocaust pass overhead.

He picked himself up. The exit doors glowed red hot. Beyond them, seemingly, was the fiery path to Hades.

The heat forced him back. He beat a way through the screaming tourists, retracing his path to the main entrance and racing along the road to Joiner Street, which was already belching black smoke and flame. Nothing could have lived in that brick-lined hell.

Later that day the firemen found the incinerated remains of the tanker driver, three meths drinkers and the man Ringrose had been following. He was identifiable only by an ammunition belt and the remains of the three stun grenades that had detonated and ignited the petrol. He had been destroyed as effectively as if he had spent an hour inside a crematorium oven.

Chapter Forty

From their hired cabin cruiser, gliding gently on the Thames towards Southwark Bridge, Bruiser, Dickie and the Cockneys watched a dense plume of smoke billowing upwards beyond the square tower of Southwark Cathedral. It came from the direction of London Bridge station. 'A bit of a bonfire,' said Bruiser, with satisfaction. 'That should take interest away from our little caper for a while.'

They were not to know of Rolly's part in this catastrophe until the evening's television bulletins. They sailed under Southwark Bridge as a fire engine, siren howling, crossed above them.

The eight suitcases, containing the equivalent in hard currencies of twenty million dollars, were stacked in the cabin as they headed up-stream, in the opposite direction to the course the *Freda* had sailed when they had snatched the queens.

Bruiser glanced at his watch. If all had gone tickety-boo, Lucius would be waiting for them at the riverside flat in Kew. He gazed fondly at the turgid water. The river had been their unfailing accomplice in the grand design and now it carried them serenely along to safety.

Bruiser said to Dickie, 'You'll find a bottle in the transom locker. Let's splice the mainbrace.'

In Chelsea Reach they put the bleep detector, the ultra-violet lamp and a bundle of weighted black clothing overboard. And Teddy Triggs whispered to Lenny Belcher, 'Fair's fair. We've earned at least two of these cases. Just sitting on them's burning my bum.'

By 6 p.m. the souvenirs of the day's work had been gathered and the extent of the shambles fully realized: the ashes of the grenade-thrower, the mute walkie-talkie, the two abandoned suitcases of currency, the makeshift tunnel trolleys, Rolly's cast-off black hood and overalls, the hastily sketched maps of the old underground system provided by a London Transport executive who had been dragged from a rugby game, the accounts from Bill and Flo Beer of the indignities they had endured.

Ringrose returned bleak-faced from a painful interview with Sir Travers Horder. The Commissioner had wavered between concern for the Yard's reputation and an ill-concealed glee at the Ringer's public humiliation. 'You have now, through a personal blunder, brought about the death of one of their number. God knows what revenge they will take on the girls.'

To this tirade, Ringrose had no answer. His one lead was now only a charred, stinking corpse.

The Commissioner dismissed him with the words: 'The Prime Minister has called a meeting of the Emergencies Committee for tomorrow to review the situation. He is interrupting his weekend at Chequers to take the chair. At that meeting I shall recommend you be relieved of continued responsibility for the investigation and that the Assistant Commissioner (Crime) should take over. That will be all, Ringrose. Good evening to you!'

Ringrose climbed wearily onto his thinking chair. Firth, who had brought a mug of tea, said, 'What's Plan B, guv?'

'Plan B,' said Ringrose, 'is to finish developing all the photographs taken by our people around St George's today and get them along to the wedding party we upset. I want every face isolated that the happy couple can't identify as friend or relative. The man on the other end of the walkie-talkie was in sight-contact with us at one stage. And it could be that unwittingly we were in sight-contact with him.'

'What about the meeting at Number Ten?'

'We're back to Scarlett O'Hara. I'll think about it tomorrow.'

Ringrose raised his mug. He would match the wisest of Chinese mandarins with his faith in the restorative powers of the emollient brew.

Under cover of dusk, the eight suitcases were transferred discreetly from the cabin cruiser to the flat leased by the dead Nancy Cornmorris.

'Eight? Where're the other two?' asked Lucius, as the last one was hauled in. Bruiser explained but Lucius exploded, 'You've bloody well thrown away five million dollars as if it were Monopoly money! You should have gone back for it.'

'Go fuck yourself, Lucius,' said Bruiser shortly. 'I was in charge of the show down below and it was my decision. The police were right on our heels. In any case, for once your meticulous plan overlooked what could have been an effective means of delaying them.'

'Oh?' said Lucius, stung. So far, his plans had stood above challenge.

'Yes,' said Bruiser. 'If we'd taken along two padlocks we could have made it impossible for them to follow us under the Thames by relocking the iron grilles protecting the two water gates. *Then* we might have had time to return for the rest of the luggage.'

Lucius was resentful. 'We had no reason to suppose the police would be so close behind you.' Then, viciously: 'That bastard Ringrose has broken every undertaking. They set a trap with the bugged cases – as if we were village idiots. Well, they'll pay. We have to make an example of one of the girls.'

'Stow it,' said Bruiser. 'As the French say, "Revenge is a meal best eaten cold." And you're overheating right now. We have the money so let's turn the girls loose. In any case, none of us will be out of pocket. The money we chucked amounts precisely to the share that was to be set aside for the Source. And, as the lady is no longer with us, the necessity no longer arises.'

Lucius jumped up, screaming in rage, 'You shit, Bruiser. You're not going to renege now. The money was promised. I've never agreed that the Source was Lady Cornmorris. The fifth partner's identity is a secret between her and me and you accepted that condition before we went into this thing using my plan and her inside information.'

They were still quarrelling as they removed all the bankers' wrappers around the wads of notes, burned them in the fireplace and flushed the sooty residue down the lavatory.

Bruiser wondered what was delaying Rolly. He was still wondering when, at 8.50 p.m. a BBC newsflash made the first connection between the tunnel escapade and the Joiner Street firestorm.

Bruiser and Dickie Biggs-Salter looked at each other and sat down, their faces ashen.

Lucius was shocked to see them gripping each other's hands tightly and fighting off tears. The catastrophe halted the squabble and also silenced Teddy Triggs, who had been about to enter his, Lenny's and Jessie's claim for a larger share of the loot. Bruiser took no further part in the night's work.

By 10.30 p.m. they had repacked the cases and carried them into the bedroom, which had recently been repapered in all but one section. Lucius lifted out a raw plasterboard to reveal a space between the wooden studs supporting an internal wall. The cases were stacked one upon the other up to the ceiling and Lucius screwed the plasterboard back over the niche. He took two previously cut lengths of matching vinyl paper and pasted them into position, carefully wiping away the surplus glue. He dragged back into place the bed where, with his gloves on, he had made love to Nancy Cornmorris.

The concealment was complete. Lucius stood back. 'The paper will be dry by morning,' he said. 'Even if we had burglars, they'd find nothing.'

The queens had been almost silent, paralysed by tension since dawn. Today was ransom day. Even Prentiss, nominally an Episcopalian, had felt like joining the Catholics in their makeshift chapel. What was the old soldiers' saying? There are no atheists in the trenches? None in the cellar either, thought Prentiss grimly.

Would the money be handed over? Would the captors keep their word to release them unharmed? Prentiss wrapped her arms around herself, paced and brooded.

Confirmation of the day's importance came with the coffee-and-bread breakfast. Nanny, enigmatic behind her mirrored visor, delivered it alone and stood well back while they reached through the bars and served themselves. She appeared again in mid-afternoon with apples and soup, and maintained her wary distance.

Soon afterwards, Mathilde de Montméja, as composed as ever, came to Prentiss Decker and said, 'I think Nanny is alone in the house, yes? Tonight she may come for me again. This may be our last chance to achieve something for ourselves.'

Prentiss was torn. 'I don't know, Mathilde,' she said. 'You're asking me to play God and tell you to try to kill her. It's a monumental risk. Suppose they really are going to release us, as they say. If your attempt on Nanny backfires, they might leave us to rot.'

Mathilde, with the cold logic for which her fellow countrymen were notorious, said, 'Yes, but suppose they *don't* intend to release us? It will be an additional danger for them. What are they to do? Open the doors and just let us walk out so that we'll be able to tell the police where they've kept us hidden? Blindfold us all again, put us in a truck to drive to some remote spot and risk being stopped by a police patrol on the way? Drop us one by one in different places, multiplying the risk of being detected by exactly forty-nine times?'

Prentiss said desperately, 'They've been ingenious so far. How can we say they don't have a perfect plan to set us free and at the same time foil the police?'

'And how can we say they do?' said Mathilde, flatly. 'We have no reason to believe assassins will keep any promise.'

The French girl dropped her disconcerting, matter-of-fact pose. She gripped Prentiss's arm. 'Your ruse with the Morse Code signals was very clever but it has failed, my dear. I have an instinct that we are now at the moment of greatest crisis. We must not lie back passively like farm animals waiting for the slaughterman.'

Prentiss struggled silently with her doubts, chewing her lip and stalking up and down, frowning at the flagstones. Finally, she said, 'Okay, do it! I can't bear the thought of an epitaph that says: "They Sat On Their Beautiful Asses And Hoped For The Best."'

The Thai girl, Khun, spent the rest of the afternoon dividing Mathilde's hair into two long plaits. Into each she inserted one of her long steel pins and tied the two plaits across the skull, clear of the French girl's ears.

Prentiss rotated Mathilde this way and that. The needles were invisible from every angle.

Jessie had found a music programme among the boring Saturday sports broadcasts. She hummed to herself as she luxuriated in Constanza's marble bath then snooped through her wardrobe. Teddy and Lenny had given her a sketchy idea of the plan to seize the ransom money and she kept an ear open for any radio news flashes, but there were none.

She consulted her watch. They had said she was to have sandwiches cut and hot drinks available; she could expect their return any time during the small hours. She had another whole wonderful evening ahead as sole mistress of Moxmanton House.

Jessie went to fetch Mathilde de Montméja shortly after 6 p.m. This time she took no chances. Not only did she carry with her the manacles and the cut-throat razor but she also made the queens lie face down on the floor before she opened the gate and extracted Mathilde from the grimy mob.

The French girl froze as Nanny placed the mask over her eyes. The elastic came within a hair's breadth of snagging on one of the hidden needles. Upstairs Mathilde hastily removed the mask as soon as Nanny freed her hands.

Nanny had gone to some trouble. She had set out a small table with cold meats and a chocolate cake. But she offered only half a bottle of burgundy – Nanny was running no risk of becoming befuddled through alcohol – and the cutlery was plastic and as harmless as that issued to the girls when they had first been herded into the cellar.

On the bed, Nanny had set out two of Constanza's evening dresses. Mathilde watched as she stripped to her ski mask, slipped a vivid mauve-satin number over her nakedness and stepped into a pair of matching high-heeled shoes. The bodice was starkly slashed and held open even further than the designer had intended by the firmness and weight of Nanny's breasts. She gazed with self-approval into the floor-length mirror.

'I thought we'd make an evening of it,' she said. 'You never know, it might be the last chance we get.'

'What do you mean?' said Mathilde, chilled.

314

'Today's the day we get the money and then you'll all be off.'

'Off?'

'Home, I suppose.'

'Is that the plan? Have the men told you that?' asked Mathilde, intently.

Nanny sniffed. 'They don't tell me anything. But what else would they do with you?'

'They could kill us,' said Mathilde.

Nanny shrugged. 'They're a hard bunch of bastards but I'd have thought it would be more bother than it's worth.' She turned on Mathilde irritably. 'Look, are we going to enjoy ourselves or are we going to play Twenty Questions?'

Mathilde looked at her with the appraisal of an executioner. 'We're here to enjoy ourselves, of course, *chérie*,' she said. Nanny did not observe that Mathilde's eyes were suddenly slate hard.

'You'd better take a dip first,' said Nanny grumpily. But when she tried to turn on the shower over the bathing girl, Mathilde stopped her.

'I must not clean my hair,' she extemporized. 'The last time, one girl became jealous and I was attacked.'

Although the needles were almost weightless, they pressed on her scalp like metal ingots.

Afterwards, she stood compliantly as Nanny draped her in Constanza's cream dress over a pair of black stockings, elasticated at the thigh. She was given no other underwear.

Nanny clamped on the leg irons again and sat Mathilde down to eat, which she did with genuine appetite. Nanny had not risked making coffee: she did not want a boiling cupful dashed into her eyes. Instead, she took out a cigarette machine and rolled two generous joints.

They smoked languidly until Mathilde placed her hand inside Nanny's gaping neckline and began to palpate an eager nipple.

The girl without a name began to murmur and groan. Mathilde laid her sideways on Constanza's chaise longue and arched Nanny over the arm so that her breasts were pushed upwards, tightly constrained by the mauve satin.

Mathilde wormed her hands up the sides of the neckline and eased both breasts out into the light. She lowered her lips and caressed them with genuine appetite. After a while, Nanny stiffened and her mouth fell open, coral lips forming a long 'Ohooooooo.' She came without Mathilde having touched her anywhere below the waistline.

Mathilde's questing hands rustled over Nanny's satin-covered frame. Slowly she gathered the garment up under Nanny's armpits while fingers, palms and tongue invaded and explored. Mathilde poured all her lovemaking skills in the sexual excitation of Nanny's quivering body. Mathilde wanted her relaxed and off-guard.

'Christ, you're sensational,' said Nanny, leaping up from the chaise longue. She pulled off her dress and manacled the French girl's hands behind her back. This was not what Mathilde wanted, but she had no choice.

Nanny picked her up in her arms, carried her to the bed, threw her down and began to rip voraciously at the white dress, shredding it in her burning desire to plunder Mathilde's cool, creamy body.

Nanny ravished her repeatedly while Mathilde gasped, twisted and turned, not only in reciprocated passion but to keep Nanny's hands away from her hair.

Mathilde began to feel desperate. The evening was slipping away and she had had no opportunity to reach unobserved for the needles. Finally, they both lay back on the pillows satiated. Mathilde asked for another joint. Nanny would have to free her hands if she were to smoke it.

They both drew deeply. Nanny said, 'That was better than I've ever had it with a man.'

Mathilde looked at her lazily. 'It is not over yet, *chérie*. I have one more pleasure for you.'

'A surprise?' asked Nanny, with lip-wetting relish.

'Yes, a surprise,' agreed Mathilde.

Mathilde forced herself not to hurry. Leisurely she finished the joint and waited for Nanny. Then she took Nanny's hand and said, 'Come.'

Moving awkwardly with the leg irons joining her ankles, she led the masked, naked girl into Constanza's exercise room and switched on the sunbed. Mathilde guided her onto the litter of dazzling light and, moistening her palms with Constanza's sun oil, began a deep, lingering massage from the neck down the back to the buttocks and thighs.

Nanny murmured appreciatively. Mathilde took care to keep at least one hand in contact with Nanny's body all the time. Her jailer would be alerted if physical contact was broken.

'Now turn over,' she said. Nanny obediently rotated and put on, over her mask, a pair of dark goggles to protect her eyes from the overhead bank of lights.

Mathilde found this comforting. The concealment of the watchful green eyes made Nanny seem less human.

This time Mathilde began at Nanny's feet. She worked slowly up the other girl's body devoting attention to her clitoris until Nanny openly cried out in ecstasy. The moment had to be soon. She dare not delay much longer. The time must already be 10 p.m.

Mathilde's educated hands slid upwards. Nanny's tongue was already lolling wetly between her lips in anticipation of their reaching her breasts once again.

Dear Holy Mother, the moment had to be now. Mathilde could not tell if Nanny's eyes were open or shut behind the smoked glass, but she continued the upward massage with one hand and, casually reaching into her hair, as if to scratch her scalp with the other, withdrew one needle from the plait.

No indication of alarm came from Nanny. Mathilde's left hand soothed its way along the ribcage until two fingers rested above the ribs under Nanny's left breast. The supine girl was making small sounds of satisfaction.

Mathilde sent up another, hurried prayer, poised the five-inch prong between the two fingers and rammed it downwards with all her might.

Nanny gave a terrible, high scream of pain and shock and Mathilde, sobbing, threw herself into the sandwich of light and pressed down heavily on Nanny's jerking body.

Mathilde was astonished at how easily the point had plunged through the wall of Nanny's chest. She pushed home the needle to its furthest extent, until it was stopped by the tiny end button. She clung on in panic. Nanny was in spasm beneath her and making gurgling noises in the back of her throat. Mathilde dared not look at her head – she would be sick.

Her left hand had now found a grip on the far side of the sunbed and Nanny was secured firmly in place beneath her despite her struggles.

Mathilde reached up again and removed the second needle. 'It has to be done! It has to be done!' she repeated to herself, like an incantation. She raised herself a fraction and found another spot between Nanny's ribs, a little under two inches from the first site, and ruthlessly plunged the needle home. Nanny's body gave another compulsive start and her legs came up, striking the overhead fitting and setting it rocking on its safety chains.

Mathilde remained pinning Nanny to the sunbed. She could feel her own exposed skin beginning to tingle from the lights.

Nanny gave a shuddering heave and was then frighteningly still. Was she faking? Mathilde continued to hold on. Finally, she ventured to look at Nanny's thrown-back head. She prised aside the sun goggles and shuddered. Nanny's green eyes were rolled up into her head, leaving the whites to gleam in the glare of the lamps. Her chest was still.

Mathilde collapsed on the floor, weeping and shaking. Some time passed before she could collect herself sufficiently to be reminded of her plight. She hopped around the suite hunting for the keys that Nanny had hidden. She found the one to the leg irons under the plate from which Nanny had eaten her supper.

Mathilde freed herself and slipped on her boiler suit. Nanny's cries had raised no alarm. The house was silent.

She tried the panelled door. It was locked. She pulled back the curtains and, after a struggle, opened a long wooden shutter and raised a sash-cord window. A wonderful, intoxicating rush of country night air greeted her. Mathilde drank it in deeply. She leaned out, wondering whether to shout for help.

She could hear the nearby sound of rustling trees and deduced that the house was probably remotely situated. If she cried out, perhaps only the kidnappers would answer. She turned back into the room. She would free the other girls and they could all make a break together into the night.

She began dementedly pulling out drawers and tipping the contents onto the floor in her search for the door key. After some minutes had elapsed she made a determined attempt to calm herself and think with her customary clarity. The key would be somewhere quite logical.

She stood in the centre of the room and turned slowly, trying to put herself in the mind of the dead girl. She stepped over to the stout door again and, on tiptoe, felt carefully along the architrave. Her fingers swept the key onto the carpet. She gave a tiny cry of triumph and scooped it up.

She pressed the switch by the door and plunged the bedroom into darkness. But a brilliant light still slanted from Constanza's exercise room. The room was as fiercely illuminated as a theatre set. And, stage centre, Nanny lay stretched out like some naked sacrifice to an Aztec sun god.

Mathilde averted her gaze and let herself out into the corridor of a house she had never seen before.

To her left a passage lined with doors ran towards a subdued light. She advanced noiselessly towards it, pausing frequently to listen. There was not even the sound of distant traffic. Truly, they must be in the heart of the countryside. England? She supposed so.

Her heart jumped as a distant clock chimed midnight and, as she emerged onto an upstairs gallery overlooking a large, tiled hall, she could hear it ticking.

An elaborate brass light was suspended in the stair well. Mathilde followed the curve of the stairs downwards. In most houses, entrance to the cellar was gained under the stairs. But no door existed here. She tried the doors of several rooms: a heavily furnished drawing room, a study, a billiards room.

She knew the cellar entrance had to be on the inside. None of them had felt fresh air on their faces since their imprisonment.

She was becoming more agitated until she opened another door and found that the quality of the decoration changed. She deduced correctly that she was in the kitchen. She groped about, not daring to call out, within three yards of the butler's pantry and the access to the cellar.

Terror returned as Mathilde heard a distant sound growing nearer. A vehicle was crunching over gravel and coming to a halt at the kitchen door. Nanny had said they had the evening to themselves . . . but the evening was over. The kidnappers were back.

Mathilde stuffed a fist into her mouth to stop herself crying out hysterically. She ran back into the hall, arms stretched in front of her to hurl aside any obstacle in her path. Mathilde de Montméja raced for the front main doors of Moxmanton House and blessed freedom.

Chapter Forty-one

The celebration of victory, the anticipated wallow in a sea of banknotes, never took place. Rolly Ponsford's horrible death – the television cameras had revealed the full, grim story – cast a blight over the evening. Lenny and Teddy were the first to leave Kew, followed ten minutes later by Bruiser and Dickie Biggs-Salter. Lucius was to lock up the flat with its treasure and follow on in his Alfa.

Teddy and Lenny drew up at the side of Moxmanton House in their van, seeing nothing wrong. Jessie must have gone to bed.

They put on the kitchen lights and found a snack of cut sandwiches prepared and some cans of beer. 'She's a cool 'un,' said Teddy. 'I couldn't go to bed without knowing the score. I suppose she's seen it on the telly.'

The two old Etonians were silent during the journey. Bruiser slumped, tormented by his thoughts, in the passenger seat, while Dickie drove. Bruiser was consumed by doubt. The two policemen, the wretched Marble and now Rolly . . . There was too much blood on the money.

Dickie suddenly said, 'What the devil . . . ?' and braked hard. Bruiser pulled himself upright and said, without real interest, 'What's the matter?'

'Take a look,' said Dickie grimly. He reversed the car on the drive for a few yards. The headlights swept back across the front of Moxmanton House and came to rest on the front doors. They gaped open.

Bruiser frowned. 'Bloody careless. Triggs and Belcher are a pair of brainless idiots.'

At the kitchen door, Dickie said, 'You've left the front door open, you young fools.'

But Teddy said indignantly, 'We ain't been near it, mister.'

Dickie and Bruiser came alive. 'Where's your friend?' said Bruiser.

'Must have gone upstairs to get her head down,' Teddy grumbled. 'We ain't seen her.'

Bruiser took the stairs three at a time. His bellow brought the others in his wake. Teddy screamed hideously and passed out at the sight of Jessie's body cooking pinkly under the artificial sun.

Bruiser swore and took a neck pulse. 'Dead as mutton.'

He spotted the needle ends like studs under her breast and swung round, brushing the stricken Lenny aside as he ran for the door. 'Come on, Dickie! The girls!'

The Hecklers were still in the van and Bruiser and Dickie jumped in, dismantled the false wall and retrieved them.

They charged into the cellar and stopped dead. Everything appeared normal. The girls gazed up curiously at them. Yet something *was* wrong. Bruiser hesitated, then he got it. None of them was in bed. He examined the chain on the gate. It was intact. 'All right,' he shouted, 'I want everyone to line up in front of the grille.'

Prentiss Decker realized instantly what was afoot: a roll-call or a head-count. Something had happened upstairs and they were puzzled. They had to be fobbed off as long as possible.

'No!' yelled Prentiss. 'You can go to hell!' She turned her back on the guns and said, 'Come on, girls, everyone hide in the alcoves!'

In a screaming mob, the queens rushed for the protection of the side cells. Within moments a head count was impossible.

A temporal vein in Bruiser's head began to pulsate dangerously. His control was near disintegration point. He thundered to the foot of the steps, thrust the muzzle of his gun between the bars and discharged the entire magazine the length of the cellar into the far wall.

The noise and the whine of ricochets was deafening. Dust and flying fragments of brick filled the cellar. In the alcoves the girls flung themselves down, crying in terror.

When the din had died away, Bruiser shouted, 'You have

ten seconds to line up in front of the grille. After that I fire directly into the alcoves.'

As he said it, he wondered if he could.

The queens picked themselves up fearfully – even Hanna Hansen acknowledged that resistance was futile – and shuffled out to face their captors.

Dickie made the head-count while Bruiser kept his Heckler trained. Then, to be certain, he made the girls pass one by one in front of the grille.

Finally, he turned to Bruiser. 'Shit! Only forty-eight. One's flown the coop.'

'That bloody whore upstairs has been playing ducks and drakes,' said Bruiser. They ran out, slamming the cellar door behind them.

The colour had drained from Prentiss's face. Mathilde was on the run. But something appalling had happened and the two men would realize it later.

In their haste, the kidnappers had forgotten to don their helmets. For the first time, the girls had seen the true faces of two of their captors.

What price, Prentiss wondered with growing dread, would they have to pay for that mistake?

Lucius sprang out of his car, alarmed at the sight of Bruiser and Dickie bursting, armed, from the front door. They briefed him rapidly. Lucius said, 'Which is the missing girl?'

Bruiser waved his gun impatiently. 'By the time we sort that out, she'll be over the hills and far away.' He handed Lucius his Browning and said, 'Just keep it pointed away from yourself. Now take your car and patrol the main road while we comb the estate. We have to assume she hasn't got far. The bed sheets are still wet from their bloody rutting.'

Lucius drove off, scattering gravel, while Bruiser and Dickie split to circle the estate's inside boundary and work inward. They ran in different directions across the drive and disappeared into the bushes.

Mathilde was drenched in dew, lying in the grass, hearing but not seeing the activity in front of the house. There was no moon and she had no idea of where she would find help. She got up and moved off slowly, trying to test the ground with each bare foot for fear of stepping on a brittle twig.

A short distance away, she could hear a body crashing through the undergrowth. After sixteen days of enforced idleness, the sudden spurt of physical action made her feel dizzy; perhaps she should not discount regimented physical training so readily as she had in the past.

Crouching low, she endeavoured to put as much distance as she could between herself and the milord's house from which she had just escaped. Branches whipped at her, and her feet were ripped and gouged by small stones.

She wanted to cry, cover her face and howl like a child. Then she thought of the silent figure on the sunbed and the pale, dirty faces of the girls in the cellar. There was no going back. She came to a low, dry-stone wall, scrambled over it and found herself in a narrow, rutted lane. Her hopes rose. This must lead to some habitation, some sanctuary. Arbitrarily she plunged left, keeping to the side of the track.

Mathilde was now severely short of breath and her heart felt as if it would burst. She risked raising her head above the level of the wall and thought that, in the distance, across a field that had already been relieved of its summer crop, she could detect a glimmer of light. She jumped over and began to follow a straight furrow that aimed towards the beacon.

The old man sat at the parlour table with his ballpoint pen and a neat stack of black-edged stationery, writing replies to letters of condolence. It was two days since his daughter had said she had to get back to her husband and children. He'd be all right now. It was a month since Mother had died, time enough to let the worst of the grief subside.

The old man felt empty. He did not want to live without his wife of fifty-four years. He hoped he would join her soon. He'd had the best this world could offer.

He was sitting, pen poised, agonizing over the wording of the fourth reply when he thought he heard scratching at the door. Then whimpering, as of an animal in distress. He was a

324

man without fear and he crossed the cosy room to fling the door wide open on its long, hand-beaten hinges.

A girl in filthy working clothes, feet and face scratched and muddy, fell into the room and clutched him around the legs.

In her panic, Mathilde forgot all the English she knew. 'Aidez-moi! Aidez-moi! On me chasse. J'ai besoin de secours!' she gasped.

'My God, girl. Whatever's the matter?' He pulled her into the cottage far enough to close the door and then helped her, shivering, to the blazing open grate.

Mathilde clung to him desperately, a chunky, reassuring old man with cropped silver hair. She fought to force air into her lungs, to control the bedlam of her brain, to speak English to this saviour and send him hurrying to a telephone. Finally, still gripping him tightly, she managed, 'I am one of the kidnapped queens. Please telephone for the police.'

The moment she spoke, the old man recognized her. God knows, the television had carried the girls' photographs enough times over the past two weeks. 'We . . . I am not on the telephone here. We'll have to go down to the village or up to the big house.'

The girl began to wail and clutch him even more desperately. 'No big house! Please! It is our prison – the home of the assassins.'

The old man was confused: what was she saying? He said, 'We'll head for the village, then.'

He gave her his dead wife's slippers and took down a jacket from a hook. He was about to fetch his shotgun and a box of cartridges when the door was kicked open and he was confronted by a pink-faced, breathless man, brandishing a sub-machine gun.

'All right, old chap,' said Dickie Biggs-Salter, eyes narrow. 'Just move back and stand beside the girl.' Mathilde fainted.

The intruder gave a piercing whistle into the night.

The old man moved away from the table, one hand dragging across the cloth and scooping the ballpoint pen into his palm. He folded his thumb over it and raised his arms like a prisoner-of-war on a vanquished field.

'That's more like it,' said Dickie, stepping inside, not moving his eyes from the old man.

Before Dickie could take a look round, the old man said, 'Please, sir, don't frighten my missus over there. She hasn't been too well lately.' He briefly nodded to Dickie's near side.

Dickie turned instinctively in the direction the old man indicated.

With a speed astonishing in a man of his years, the cottager took one sharp step forward and rammed the ballpoint into Dickie's throat, ripping open his windpipe. Dickie's neck arched and began to gush blood. His eyes bulged and his fingers tightened in agony upon the trigger.

The old man attempted to move out of the firing line, but not fast enough. The muzzle of the Heckler spewed a short, lethal burst, blowing away the old man's side. Dickie was already falling and his assailant fell on top of him, about to be reunited with the wife he'd buried three weeks ago.

The deafening sound of the gunfire broke through the grey blanket enveloping Mathilde's mind. Shakily, she sat up. She could feel the heat of the coal fire on her back. Then she screamed hysterically at the gruesome mound of blood and gore still stirring in death throes on the carpet.

Red-tinged bubbles rose from the ruined throat of the man with the gun. He attempted to raise a hand and Mathilde shrank away.

She saw that the cottage door was still wide open, the night air fanning the fire. Gibbering mindlessly, she scrambled across the room on her knees. She could think only of the protection of the dark. Mathilde pulled herself to her feet and ran headlong down the narrow lane.

A slipper fell off but she did not slacken her pace. She burst out into a main road and a sliver of optimism pierced her terror.

She kicked off the other slipper and began to run, her bare soles slapping hard on the smooth macadam.

Suddenly she sobbed in renewed hope. A car's headlights were sweeping round a curve, dancing over tree trunks and roadside hedges. Please, Holy Mother, that the nightmare should be ending.

She ran onto the crown of the road, arms waving wildly. She

was determined that the car should not pass her. She'd throw herself onto the bonnet if she had to.

The headlights filled her eyes but she heard the car squeal to a halt. Thank God! Mathilde touched the hot radiator as if bestowing a benediction on the machine and ran round to the driver's window.

'You murdering little cow,' said Lucius Frankel, and pressed the Browning into her temple.

Something snapped inside Bruiser Moxmanton's head. Brokenly, he said, 'It's Dickie – and Colour Sergeant Wally Barnes. Two of my dearest friends. They've done for each other.'

Lucius looked appalled at the carnage in the cottage. 'You knew the old man?'

Bruiser nodded, punchdrunk from grief. 'Saved my father's life in the war. Taught me how to fend for myself.' He knelt down and cradled the silver head in his lap. 'He was a second father.'

Lucius was trying to hold on to his own equilibrium. A few hours ago they had had the money, had outwitted the country's police forces – but, in the short time since, that French bitch he'd just locked in the boot of the car had come near to wrecking a work of genius. He felt homicidal.

Bruiser gave him an old, weary look. 'It's time to chuck it, Lucius. We gave it the best we had – and almost pulled it off. But I've lost my friends, my name, my honour. Like you, I had a dream of . . . of bigness, I suppose. Like you, I wanted to achieve something grand. I understood your dream, you understood mine. We were afraid we would always remain tiny.'

Lucius dropped to his knees beside Bruiser and put an arm round his shoulder. 'No, no, Bruiser. Do you want the tiny people to drag us back down to their grubby level? Do you want men with moronic faces and vulgar voices to watch you swab floors and empty pisspots for the next twenty-five years? Mean, little men. The rabble that poor Dickie lying there so rightly despised?'

He shook Bruiser hard and whispered fiercely, 'Never, never, never. This is the moment of our greatest test. We have already brought off miracles. It's never been just the money. For you and me, this has been a pursuit of excellence. A demonstration that there are men still capable of snatching away the breath of the world. Do you want that same world now to turn away laughing in contempt?'

Lucius was not sure his weasel words were sinking in.

Bruiser was only half listening. His eyes were unfocused. 'It's no use struggling further. We've left too many droppings on the path.' He waved a vague hand. 'How can you explain away this appalling cock-up?'

Lucius had no convincing answer. He glanced at a clock on the mantelshelf.

'Look, Bruiser, it's gone one in the morning. You're shattered. Why not go back to the house and sleep on it? I'll stay up a while longer and see what I can salvage.'

Bruiser allowed himself to be led towards the door. 'The walk back will help to clear your head,' said Lucius, injecting a note of sympathy into his voice.

Bruiser glanced back once at the two dead men on the carpet and walked out slowly into the dark.

Lucius closed the cottage door and gazed thoughtfully into the dwindling fire. He teetered, he knew, on the brink of the abyss. But not yet . . . not yet, dammit . . .

During the course of the pre-kidnap planning, Bruiser and his friends had provided a number of pieces of military equipment not readily available in surplus stores – Rolly's grenades and plastic explosive among them. These had come through old Army connections or as hold-overs from their service days. Among the items laid by for an emergency was a survival kit provided by Bruiser from which Lucius had extracted a handful of benzedrine tablets. He groped now in the glove compartment of his car for the tin, listening to the French girl kicking against the inside of the boot. He'd trussed her hand and foot.

He swallowed two bennies – after a long, fraught day up in London his body was beginning to flag and they would wake him up.

He returned to Wally Barnes's cottage. He needed to spirit away the bodies. Return the place to an appearance of normality. The disappearance of both dead men could not be concealed in the long run, but there was no reason why the corpses should be linked to the queens.

The carpet was blood-soaked and would have to go with the old man. A 9mm bullet had passed through his body and embedded itself in the wall. Lucius fetched a knife and fork from the kitchen and dug a crude crater in the plaster that could have been made by anything. He prised out the bullet, cleaned away the mess and rehung, over the hole, a framed photograph of the young Wally Barnes, proud in his dress uniform, arm-in-arm with his wartime bride.

A glance at the black-edged stationery told Lucius the remainder of the story so bravely embarked upon all those years ago by the open-faced young couple in the picture. Life had never played fair.

He took a torch and, outside, located the milk-bottle crate. He went back in, took a black-edged sheet of paper from the kitchen table and printed, 'No deliveries until further notice. Gone away to sort myself out. Thanks. Wally.' He placed it in the crate.

By 5 a.m., when the still-black horizon was beginning to be pierced by the lights of rising herdsmen, Lucius had completed his task and was exhausted. The cottage was cleaned and locked, the bodies sealed in black plastic garbage sacks and transported to Moxmanton House. For the moment the trail was camouflaged.

Lucius found that Bruiser had drunk himself into a stupor. Teddy and Lenny had covered Jessie's body, and hovered uncertainly in the corridor outside the death room. He brushed aside their whining questions. 'The best thing for all concerned is that you sleep for a few hours. We'll be able to think more clearly in the morning,' said Lucius.

'Her mum'll never forgive us,' said Teddy.

Lucius shot him a look of disgust.

'Her mum,' repeated Lucius sarcastically, 'is not going to know anything to forgive you for.'

He turned his attention to Mathilde. One thing was certain. She could not be returned to the cellar to tell the other girls all she'd seen.

And then there was Bruiser. The girls downstairs had seen his face . . .

For the most part, the girls were attempting to sleep when the slim kidnapper came to single out Prentiss Decker.

For the first time in the girls' recollection, he was carrying a firearm. He blindfolded Prentiss and led her a few paces beyond the cellar door. She tensed herself for a blow. Had Mathilde talked?

It came as an intense relief when the Welshman growled, 'I want you to memorize these two sentences and speak them into a tape recorder.'

Lucius was not going to be betrayed by a voice print of his own speech pattern. He'd already risked one direct call to Ringrose.

He rehearsed Prentiss and then she made the recording: 'This is our reply to your treachery of yesterday. The rest of the queens cannot be released until all your activities cease.'

Afterwards, Prentiss said, 'What have you done with Mathilde?'

For her pains, she was given a rough push down the cellar steps and told, 'Shut your fucking face.' Lucius unplugged the cellar heater and carried it away.

As the upstairs door closed, the other girls crowded round her.

'Something bad has happened,' Prentiss said, picking her way diplomatically through a choice of alarmist words. 'There's no sound of either Mathilde or Nanny upstairs.' She relayed the message she'd just been compelled to record.

Mirabelle Montcalm said, 'The ransom handover must have aborted. But what can this "reply to yesterday's treachery" mean?'

A number of the girls began to murmur and sob. There was no more sleep in the cellar that night.

Some time in late afternoon they were given their only food of the day. The slim man, still toying with a gun, supervised while the two Cockneys distributed a makeshift meal of cold water, dry bread and yet more windfall apples. If the meal was an accurate reflection, the situation above ground was deteriorating fast.

One of the Cockneys was making sounds inside his helmet. When the kidnappers had again retreated upstairs, Mirabelle said, 'Did anyone catch what he was saying?'

'He wasn't saying anything,' said Hanna Hansen, appalled. 'He was crying his heart out.'

Commander Tom Ringrose walked across Horse Guards to the back door of Number 10, Downing Street, with an anguished heart. The Prime Minister, looking as fresh as Ringrose felt jaded and downcast, opened the proceedings of the Emergencies Committee.

Immediately Ringrose interjected, earning a hostile glare from Sir Travers Horder, 'Perhaps, sir, you would let me impart some distressing news that has only just reached me. The French girl, Mathilde de Montméja, was found dead this morning on the Guildford bypass. The preliminary pathology report suggests that she was killed some time during the early hours of this morning by means of an asphyxiating plastic bag placed over her head.' A ripple of surprise and horror ran round the assembly. He went on evenly, 'The girl was dumped upside down in a refuse bin. In the pocket of a boiler suit, which was her only clothing, was found an audio message, recorded by one of the girls – the American we think.'

Ringrose did not need to consult his notes as he repeated the words burned inside his head as if etched there by acid. 'The message reads: "This is our reply to your treachery of yesterday. The rest of the queens cannot be released until all your activities cease".'

He added, 'The message was addressed to me personally.'

Sir Travers snorted. 'It is typical of the highly personal methods adopted by Commander Ringrose that not even his Commissioner was made aware of this development prior to this meeting.'

Ringrose tried to explain that the news had come through from Surrey as they were all heading for Number 10, but Sir Travers waved him down and pressed on with his threatened proposal to have the Assistant Commissioner (Crime) moved in to take command of the operation.

The Prime Minister said impassively to Ringrose, 'What do

you say to that, Commander? Have you botched the investigation?'

Ringrose briefly showed the palms of his hands in a gesture of distress. 'I can only give a subjective reply to that. We shall only know the truth when we have the criminals' side of the story. Meanwhile, I should say there stands only one major decision I took that is open to challenge. Should I have detained Lady Cornmorris longer and pressed her harder? Perhaps I could have broken her under intense interrogation. But would that have saved the girls? Perhaps we would have got the gang. But if they fled abroad, perhaps not. I'm much more concerned with getting a lead to the victims while we still have a chance of finding them alive. Where I have been frustrated is in not appreciating the utter ruthlessness of Lady Cornmorris's secret lover.'

The Prime Minister raised his eyebrows. 'Secret lover?'

'Yes, the man who had a key to her flat and killed her. The man who has been making love to her for the past eighteen months.'

'That sounds very precise,' said the Prime Minister.

'That is when Lady Cornmorris went to her doctor and asked to be fitted with a diaphragm. Her late husband favoured condoms,' said Ringrose, baldly. 'My instinct says: "Find the lover and we find the girls."'

'Lady Cornmorris was short of money, but she required something more – an enslaving passion, I'd say – to push her over into a crime of this magnitude. The task of investigating all her known associates during the relevant period is enormous. She was a very social lady. But we are pressing on.'

From the long-lens photographs taken around St George's Church yesterday, all but three figures had been eliminated overnight. Tom found himself drawn to one unidentified face in particular, a sallow-skinned man who appeared twice in the photographs, once mingling with the wedding party, although the happy couple had disclaimed knowledge of him, and once in profile, entering the tube station across from the church. He wore a hat, a pencil moustache and thick horn-rimmed spectacles. Could he be Lady Cornmorris's lover and puppet-master?

Even as the Emergencies Committee sat discussing Ringrose's fate over his head, artists at the Yard were sketching their impressions of the man, *sans* glasses, *sans* moustache, *sans* hat. Ringrose had patiently opened up yet another monumental line of inquiry.

The Prime Minister's irritated voice broke into his thoughts. He was saying, 'Well, I don't like it. No one at this table has put a finger on any serious dereliction on the part of Commander Ringrose. The criticism is that he has not produced results. Therefore the real question is, could any of us have handled the matter more skilfully? I'm ready to listen to a *detailed* reply from anyone who can say yes.'

He gazed around the table, finally allowing his eyes to rest coolly on the Commissioner who said weakly, 'Perhaps a fresh, more senior, mind on the subject . . .'

The Prime Minister added, when no one spoke further, 'I propose that Commander Ringrose be allowed to get on with his difficult and painful task. Even on the level of public relations, a switch now that we have the first of the hostages dead on our hands will be seen around the world as a sign of our confusion and impotence.' He sighed. 'You had better leave now. I have a distressing telephone call to make to the President of France.'

Chapter Forty-two

Bruiser, bleary-eyed, unshaven, breath reeking of whisky, said, dully, 'We should release the girls today. No further good can come of holding them.'

At least he was no longer talking surrender.

Lucius was placatory. 'It's not as easy as that, Bruiser. Since yesterday's bad experience we know we cannot rely on the word of the police to lift the roadblocks. While you've been asleep, I've taken the first step to punish them – to bring them into line. When they see we mean what we say, they'll stop trying to trick us and then I'll draw up a plan for the girls' release.'

He told Bruiser what he had done with Mathilde de Montméja.

'You – you – you madman!' said Bruiser. 'What point is served by more killing?'

'Thanks to that little Cockney whore, the French tart learned too much,' said Lucius. 'Blame her, not me. Anyway, she's paid for it.'

He led Bruiser through into the billiards room. The three bodies in their black plastic shrouds were lined up neatly on the floor. 'Tonight we find a little-frequented spot on the estate and dig a burial pit. In time, the fact that a number of people you knew have vanished is bound to bring the police to your door. But if the house is clean and restored and you keep a grip on your nerve, you'll come through *intacto.*'

Lucius continued to lie persuasively. But he knew that Bruiser was lost. Even if the girls had failed to memorize his face in the dim cellar light, the village copper already had the clue that would condemn him.

How could Bruiser produce the non-existent cellar rats and

the non-existent rat-catching firm? It was a lie that one day he would have to answer for.

Lucius Frankel knew that he was now tidying up only on his own behalf. He would sink with the others unless he distanced himself fast.

'There are some curious features,' Professor Franklyn Dart was saying. 'The stomach contents and associated odours show that the girl had ingested a substantial meal, consisting mainly of meat and some alcohol, most probably wine. On her arms and upper back there were changes in pigmentation that I could not associate with after-death lividity. Possibly caused by a sun-lamp. And on the body there were bites and bruise marks that are typical of vigorous lesbian horseplay. No sign at all of penile penetration.'

Ringrose sat back in his chair. Wine? Suntan? Lesbian sex play? He'd never felt bewilderment so acutely.

The telephone call from a quietly satisfied Charles Bollam at the Departmental Records Office came in the early evening. 'Commander Ringrose,' he said, 'the girls here have come up trumps. Have you paper and pen handy?' Ringrose could barely keep his writing hand steady.

Bollam said, 'Photocopies are already on the way to you by courier but here's the gist. Peter Linden was captured by members of the Home Guard within minutes of his parachuting into a field near Detling in Kent in the early hours of the third of September nineteen forty – the first anniversary of the outbreak of war. The Heinkel III of which he'd been a crew member had been shot up by an RAF night-fighter and crashed soon afterwards in a school playground at Bearsted. The body chits show Linden was handed over to the civil police that same morning and taken to the headquarters of the Kent Constabulary in Maidstone. He was held there for the remainder of the day and overnight until the next morning – the fourth of September – when he was collected by the Military Police at seven.'

Ringrose scribbled madly. 'And then?'

'Well, he obviously remained in MP custody until they realized they were dealing with a very interesting fellow and handed him over to the Security Services at the Royal Patriotic Schools on the seventh.'

Ringrose said desperately, 'The vital date for us, Mr Bollam, is the fifth. Where the hell was Peter Linden held by the Military Police on the fifth?'

The silence on the other end of the line was agonizing. Finally, the civil servant said, 'I'll switch the girls to the Military Police archives with particular emphasis on wartime establishments within the Southern Command area. We're narrowing it down, Commander, wouldn't you agree?'

'Yes Mr Bollam,' said Ringrose, dashed. 'Don't be discouraged. Just turn me up a piece of paper that has the fifth of September nineteen forty written on it.'

Special Agent Joseph Bakunin of the Federal Bureau of Investigations would never have made the grade in J. Edgar Hoover's day. Hoover liked his men tall, a latter-day Frederick the Great's bodyguard. Hoover also liked 'em lean, neat and all-American.

Joe was of only middle height, overweight, rumpled and of Russian extraction. He just happened to be a good, wise old cop.

The hunt for Peter Linden had led him a merry dance through the marbled halls of Immigration, Social Security, computer print-outs, bureaucratic boondoggling that evaporated magically when he pointed out – always mildly – that he was working to the direct orders of the President, from Yorkville, Manhattan, a centre for people of German extraction, to several small townships in Montana where everyone could boast German forebears.

His quarry had undergone two changes of name since his arrival in the USA: the first, apparently, to eliminate the last connection with his pre-war political allegiances, the second to escape creditors of a small-town newspaper that he had launched with a conspicuous lack of success. However, he had ended his working life selling a moderately profitable commercial printing outfit in Colorado Springs and retiring to California. His name now, they told Joe, was Peter Lodge.

Joe sat sunning himself on the concrete housing within which could be found electrical, telephone and fresh-water connectors. A similar life-support locker was perched at the lip of every yacht berth along the quay.

Oxnard, California. Not a bad place to end your days, Joe mused, eyeing the empty rectangle of the Pacific Ocean where 'Peter Lodge' kept his thirty-two footer.

'He'll be out for the day, now,' they'd told Joe at the clubhouse.

The local Bureau had been gung-ho. 'Let's call out the coast-guards – run a "make" on everything under canvas,' the chief had suggested.

'It's a nice day,' said Joe. 'There are hundreds of boats out there. He'll be coming home. Let's wait.'

So Joe sat watching the sun roll down towards its nightly dousing in the ocean. At 6 p.m. Peter Linden, as was, came down the main channel on the auxiliary. He was tall, muscular, his head tanned the colour of a saddle. He was almost totally bald, which somehow lent him a powerful aspect. For a man of his years he moved nimbly. He eyed Joe curiously as he made fast and stepped ashore.

Joe laid the ID on him straight away.

'Mr Peter Lodge?'

'Yes, that's me.' Only a careful listener could detect a Teutonic intonation in that voice.

'Also known as Peter Linden?'

The yachtsman's pale blue eyes narrowed. 'What is this about?'

Joe told him. Linden said, 'Leave me out. That all happened many years ago, another life. I'm retired now. I paid the penalty for being a silly kid. I was a civilian but the Brits kept me in a prison camp for six years. That wasn't justice.'

'At least they kept you out of the war and from getting killed,' said Joe.

'And now they can keep me out of this. I want to telephone my lawyer.'

'Be my guest,' said Joe amiably. 'And while you're talking to him you'd better brief him on the illegal-entry charge.'

'Illegal entry?'

'Sure,' said Joe, still affable. 'You're a citizen of the United

States by virtue of the fact that you omitted to give an interesting piece of information on your immigration forms. Still, I can see your point. Even now it's not chic to admit you were once a member of the Nazi Party.'

Peter Linden eyed the FBI man and his undisciplined body with plain contempt. 'You're blackmailing me.'

'You've got it,' said Joe. 'In case you haven't been reading the papers, Herr Linden, there's a whole wagonload of little girls who've been snatched by a bunch of apes over there in London. Somehow, Scotland Yard believes you can help.'

Joe consulted his watch. 'The time in Britain is now two thirty-eight a.m. We're going to take a ride to the local FBI bureau. There's a nice man named Ringrose in London town who wants to talk to you more than anyone in the whole wide world. And I ain't about to let you disappoint him. Get my meaning, meine Liebe?'

A sleepy Tom Ringrose put the call on the voice box so that Firth could hear. Across six thousand miles, Peter Linden sounded grudging and impatient.

'Just start from the police station in Maidstone,' urged Ringrose.

'It's a lifetime ago. My memory isn't so good,' came the German's resentful voice. 'The police took my clothes and gave me a blanket. Oh, and a cup of tea. Later they seemed excited by my civilian suit and accused me of being a parachute spy. They were obsessed by the idea that I had buried a radio transmitter somewhere before I was captured. The police officers who came to speak to me in my cell became more and more senior.'

'What happened next morning?' Ringrose asked. There was a crackling and silence from Linden.

'Was that the day those Military Police thugs came for me? They pushed me around very badly.'

'Yes, that was the day – the fourth of September,' Ringrose encouraged him. 'Where did they take you?'

'I ended up in a mansion at Kensington Palace Gardens that I later learned was called the London Cage. I was driven from there to a school with the children's desks still stacked at one end of the room. This is where I faced my interrogation board and finally convinced the British I was who I said I was.'

Ringrose and Firth exchanged looks of dismay.

Ringrose said carefully into the mouthpiece, 'I want you to take your time, Mr Linden. You've missed something out. Your interrogation took place on the seventh of September. On the night of the fifth of September you were held in some intermediate staging post before being brought to London. You left your name there. Can you remember?'

'Left my name there?' echoed the man.

'Yes. Together with the date. Perhaps you signed a document? Carved your name on a desk? On a wall?'

'Sometimes I have done all those things,' agreed Linden. Ringrose's eyes flashed exasperation. 'September the fifth?' The German was pondering. 'Ah, yes. That is what, for a long time, I called my day of silence.'

Ringrose and Firth stiffened.

Linden went on, 'I remember it because, after the multitude of questions from the civilian police on the previous day, I was asked no further questions at all. I realized later I was being kept on ice for the specialist interrogators who came later. It was boring and frightening alone in the cell. I was afraid they were going to take me straight out and shoot me without trial. I wanted to leave a sign, a mark, that I had passed that way. Yes, I remember now. They gave me some clothes, including sneakers – plimsolls you would call them. I took out the laces and used the metal end-tabs to register my existence on the cell wall and indicate my fate.'

Ringrose and Firth drew deep breaths in unison. Ringrose said, 'Where was that cell, Mr Linden?'

'In a house. A large house. A country house.' Memory was flooding back. 'The wine cellar had been divided into cells.'

'What period of architecture?'

'I was hurried inside straight from a closed truck. The decorations were rather fussy and the tiling sombre. Probably nineteenth century – Victorian in English terms.'

Ringrose and Firth breathed again. Everything was fitting.

'Were you ever told the name of the house or its location, Mr Linden?'

'No. As I say, they kept me deliberately incommunicado.'

'All right,' said Ringrose. 'You were collected from the Maidstone police headquarters by the Military Police and placed in a closed truck. Could you see anything?'

'Nothing. I believe the theory at the time was that German prisoners needed to be protected from civilian lynch parties. The canvas flap was tied down.'

'How long did your journey take to the house of silence?'

'My God, you ask too much. It was a time of many journeys for me.'

'Try,' pleaded Ringrose.

'It must have been short. Maybe twenty minutes to half an hour. We were still in the countryside. It wasn't yet London.'

'What sort of speed?' Ringrose fished on for every particle of memory.

'Not too fast – very correct, I should say. Far more correct than the way they manhandled me. Those Military Police were brutes.'

'So,' said Ringrose, ignoring the rebuke, 'you drove for up to thirty minutes at a reasonable speed – say twenty-five to thirty miles an hour. A maximum of fifteen miles radius from Maidstone?'

Over the link they could almost hear Linden's mind turning. Finally, he said, 'Yes, I'll settle for a fifteen-mile radius.'

For two further hours, Ringrose and Firth kept Peter Linden on the line, drawing him out, testing his memory, approaching his story from every conceivable angle, adding detail.

Afterwards, Ringrose turned to his coloured wall-map of Kent, placed the point of a pair of compasses squarely onto the town of Maidstone and drew a fifteen-mile radial line.

The drawn circle had the appearance of a bullseye in the centre of what the British call the Garden of England.

'We're creeping up on it,' said Ringrose. 'We're creeping up.'

In his grief, Teddy Triggs found an angry, bold voice. 'You can't just dump people in a hole like sacks of horse-shit,' he said. 'We want to leave Jessie where she can be found – and get a proper burial. She can't just disappear off the face of the earth. Not knowing will drive her mum round the bend.'

'Don't be a sentimental fool,' said Lucius, rummaging in the barn for suitable digging tools. 'Do you want to spend the rest of your lives in prison?'

'Me and Lenny ain't the ones what did the killing,' said Teddy, defensively. 'It ain't down to us.'

Lucius Frankel wheeled round, eyes blazing dangerously. 'I know the way your feeble little mind's going. You have a cosy picture of walking into a police station and saying, "Please, sir, it wasn't us. It was those nasty other men. And if you'll forget we've been naughty boys we'll tell you all about it."' Lucius cruelly mocked Teddy's fractured Cockney speech.

'Leave it out,' said Teddy sullenly. 'We're not grasses.'

'Oh, no?' Lucius took a fistful of Teddy's jacket. 'Don't tell me you've not thought about it. You think you can do a deal with the police? Well, let me disabuse you of that idea. There's no going back. There's been too much of a world outcry for any of us to get a deal. Your cunt-struck girlfriend let more than the French girl out of the cellar. And what we're doing now is trying to shut the door.'

Lucius drew Teddy close and, turning to Lenny Belcher, said, 'The pair of you had better listen to me good. If I end up behind bars, I shall swear that I personally witnessed the execution of Mathilde de Montméja and that her killers were you two. I shall say you were taking your revenge for Jessie's death. After that, there'll be no way either of you would be allowed to turn Queen's Evidence. Do I make myself more than clear?' Lucius hissed, so vehemently that spittle fell on Teddy's face.

'You rotten bastard,' said Lenny. 'You killed that girl. And after all the help we've given you. We've gone along with everything. You couldn't have pulled off the job without us.'

'You've gone along and you'll continue to go along,' said Lucius. 'That's if you want your money . . .'

Teddy tugged himself free of Lucius's grasp. 'Don't you come the old acid with us. We've earned that money – and more. You never told us all what you was planning – and we didn't know neither that you was a bunch of fucking lunatics.

'We thought you was gentlemen. It wasn't until the snatch

341

that Lenny and me really cottoned on that you was all deadly serious. By then, poor old Marble had turned up his toes and we was in the shit up to our necks.'

'Triggs,' said Lucius, with menace, 'I don't want to listen to your pathetic bleatings. You knew the score. You were just a pair of grubby little thieves and I promoted you into the first division. You'll never do anything as staggering again in your lives. I expect gratitude from you, not this snivelling. Now, how much do you want?'

Teddy shuffled and said, 'For a start, you can forget all that bollocks about putting our money into bank accounts. We want our cash in our hands – and Jessie's share too. We'll have to bung her old mum.'

'And what do you think Jessie's old mum is going to say, coming into this sudden fortune?' asked Lucius, sarcastically.

'Fortune my arse,' said Teddy. 'You're trying to palm us off with the scrag end. You've got twenty million dollars behind that wallpaper and we want our share. Two suitcases. With that much, Lenny and I can go away some place in the sun.'

'And you think no one will notice these two Englishmen, suddenly and mysteriously wealthy?'

'Well, we know we'll have to box a bit clever. But it's not impossible,' said Teddy. He looked pathetically inadequate.

Silently, Lucius came to a decision. He said, 'All right. Perhaps you have a fair argument. Let's get this pit dug and tomorrow I'll send the pair of you up to London to collect a couple of suitcases.'

Lucius found Bruiser brooding in the sitting room. 'You'll have to lend a hand,' he said. 'It has to be a bloody deep pit.'

Bruiser heaved himself out of the armchair and wordlessly accompanied the burial party to a corner of the kitchen garden that had not been cultivated since Constanza had moved to the South of France. They did not risk lighting a lamp until they had got down four feet and the sides began to crumble. Lucius went to find boards and pit props.

Bruiser shifted more earth than any of the others. The strenuous work demonstrated that he was, by far, the fittest of the quartet, which worried Lucius.

The sky was beginning to lighten before the three bodies

342

were laid in the bottom of the pit. Water was already beginning to ooze through the clay and both Teddy and Lenny started to snivel.

Bruiser suddenly said, 'As from this morning Dickie is absent without leave from his regiment. It's a damned miserable ending.'

They refilled the pit and thinly scattered the excess soil over a field. Despite his tiredness, Lucius fussed over the grave, brushing the soil level and insisting that the tools be cleaned and dried in the house before being returned to the barn.

They all climbed the stairs to their beds at 5.45 a.m. The queens were securely battened down. There seemed no point in keeping a sentry in the butler's pantry.

Lucius took another bennie to stay awake. He waited thirty minutes, then edged along the corridor past Bruiser's bedroom door to Rolly's room, from which they had yet to clear the dead man's things.

Lucius found his knapsack in the foot of the wardrobe. He breathed a lot easier after he had fished out Rolly's remaining stock of the dirty grey plastic explosive and a detonator set. He had observed the preparations closely when Rolly had blown a hole in the Thames floodgate.

He now moved silently downstairs and let himself out of the side of the house where Teddy's van was parked.

The headlines said: 'BAMBOOZLED' and 'BRING ON THE GIRLS' and 'DEADLY SILENCE FROM KIDNAPPERS'. To avoid being hampered by hordes of reporters trampling the ground, Scotland Yard had deliberately limited the release of information concerning progress in the case. By so doing, they had risked international ire in the media. And this they were now suffering.

The story of the ransom handover and the significance of the petrol-tanker holocaust at London Bridge had been publicly fathomed. Criticism of the police and grave concern for the girls were now being given strident voice. In addition, the *Daily Mail* had been telephoned by a Yard contact and given the first intimations that a move had been made to replace the Ringer.

All in all, the Tuesday-morning newspapers did not make happy reading for Ringrose as the concentrated search moved quietly into the heart of Kent.

Ringrose had inserted another 'Lord Grey' message in the *Times* personal column that morning. It said simply: 'Everything at a standstill until you deliver.' He did not expect to be believed. But, then, if he *had* brought the investigation to a standstill, the kidnappers would not have believed that either. It was what his CIA friend Jake Bishop would call a 'no-win situation'.

Ringrose normally took his work calmly but now his stomach lurched in anxiety. *Could* they kill all the girls?

He closed his eyes but all he saw was the canvas screen being lifted in front of him by a respectful uniformed constable, Mathilde de Montméja's legs sticking up in the air and, down below, her blue face squashed obscenely against the wire mesh of the refuse bin.

The quartet slept until mid-afternoon when Lucius remembered the queens in the cellar. For all his ingenuity, he had failed to devise a foolproof method of releasing them – even assuming that that had ever been his intention. He was not certain himself. Was there something missing in his emotional circuitry? The thought was interesting.

He supervised while Teddy and Lenny took down soup and bread. He wrinkled his nose. The cellar stank of fear and chemical lavatories. The girls shuffled woefully up to the bars.

The American girl had guts, he had to say that. She had pushed her smudged face to the bars and said, 'Don't you think it's about time you told us when we're to be set free? You must have the money by now. Some of the girls are in a bad way and I don't know how much longer we can hold up without some news – some hope.'

She shut her mouth abruptly. A note of pleading had entered her voice and she wasn't going to give the bastard the satisfaction of hearing it.

Lucius lied, 'It's being arranged – even though you were foolish to conspire with the French girl.'

So Mathilde had failed. Prentiss said, 'Why don't you bring

344

her back here to her friends?' She waited, dreading the reply.

'You wouldn't like that one bit,' said Lucius, viciously, behind his visor. 'She stinks even more than you do.'

'How do you mean?' asked Prentiss uncertainly.

'She's been a corpse for the past two days,' said Lucius. And he closed the door on them for the last time.

Bruiser listened curiously as Lucius briefed the Cockney pair. What the hell was he playing at? Despite his devastated spirits, Bruiser was intrigued.

Lucius gave Teddy a key to the Kew flat and said, 'All right, you set out at six p.m. in the van and return by ten with two of the cases. The money will be counted here and the pair of you will be signed off. You'll take no further part in the operation and you will both go abroad immediately. Is that understood?'

Teddy and Lenny both nodded eagerly. 'That's fair enough, guv. You won't cause any trouble for us and we won't cause any for you. We'll have enough to keep our noses clean for the rest of our lives,' said Teddy.

They scampered away to gather their meagre kit.

Bruiser said, 'You can't be serious. You'll never see hide nor hair of those two again.'

Lucius said, in an oddly airy manner, 'I think you do them an injustice, Bruiser. As hired help goes, they've been highly satisfactory, provided they weren't called upon to use their grey matter. We don't want two disgruntled former employees going around purveying unflattering tittle-tattle about their employer, do we?'

Lucius gave him a sly, sidelong glance in which there danced considerable inexplicable amusement.

Teddy Triggs and Lenny Belcher were ready to go promptly at six, hardly daring to believe their luck.

Bruiser had disappeared but Lucius walked them to the van. He said, almost avuncularly, 'Now, drive carefully. You don't want to draw attention to yourselves. And make sure you lock the flat securely before you leave.'

They both nodded again, anxious schoolboys indulging Teacher's homilies at the start of the hols.

The evening was already drawing in as Teddy let in the clutch, then drove round the side of Moxmanton House and down the main driveway. The genial mask dropped from Lucius's dark face as he watched their tail-lights recede.

He wheeled round at an unexpected sound. Bruiser was coming up behind him in his own car. Lucius went to the driver's window. 'Where are you going?'

Bruiser put an elbow on the sill. 'Sorry, but I don't buy any of that funny business with Triggs and Belcher. I don't know what's going on between you and them but there's too much of my friends' blood on that money for me to be indifferent to it. I'm going to keep an eye on those little jokers.'

Lucius said, alarmed, 'Don't go, Bruiser. Take my word – letting them go is all for the best.'

'Then you must be a bloody fool, Lucius,' grunted Bruiser. 'What's to stop them cleaning out the flat of every last penny? And I don't remember you consulting me about paying them off with such a handsome bonus. I'll see you later.'

Lucius opened his mouth to speak but Bruiser's car shot from under his hand and roared down the drive. 'The stupid, meddling fool,' cursed Lucius. He went back to the house to begin dismantling his video studio and to pack his belongings. Everything was coming to a headlong finale.

Bruiser got as far as the village green. He braked opposite the war memorial, its plinth a wartime machine-gun post. As if someone had thrown a pail of arctic water at his head, Bruiser had suddenly seen the significance of Lucius Frankel's sly demeanour. 'Rolly's bangs bag!' breathed Bruiser. 'The maniac has been at Rolly's bangs bag!'

He threw the car into a U-turn, almost knocking the vicar off his bicycle. He was back at the house in six minutes. He fumbled for his key and charged through the front door, bellowing, 'LUCIUS!'

The club owner came warily to the top of the stairs and peered down. Bruiser, fuming, appeared enormous. He shouted up, 'You damned madman. You've rigged a bomb in the van, haven't you?'

Lucius's uneasiness was confirmation enough. 'Calm down, Bruiser. It's the best way. They'd never be able to keep their mouths shut. They won't know a thing – and it'll blow away one of our biggest headaches.'

Bruiser shook his fist. 'You cold bastard. Those poor little sods deserve better than that. How long have they got?'

Lucius shook his head obstinately. Bruiser said evenly, 'If you don't tell me right away, I'm coming up there to throw you over the landing.' He walked to the foot of the stairs.

'Dammit!' exploded Lucius. 'I'm doing it as much for you as for me.'

'No, you're not,' said Bruiser. 'Sooner or later I'd be the next name on your hit list. You have an unpleasant appetite for death, Lucius. I only wish I'd appreciated that a lot earlier. I've killed out of duty but I've never killed for pleasure or as an act of treachery towards a comrade.'

Bruiser put a heavy foot on the bottom tread. 'Now, are you going to tell me how you've set the timer?'

Reluctantly, Lucius consulted his watch. 'They have about another twenty-five minutes. I timed it so that they'd be well clear of the village before it happened,' he said, sullenly.

Bruiser ran for the car and hurtled down the drive, gravel showering the bushes.

He ate up ten of those twenty-five minutes zig-zagging his way through home-bound traffic to reach the M20. If Triggs and Belcher had opted for a less direct route into London there was nothing he could do. Bruiser moved sharply into the fast lane and jammed his right foot to the floor.

Teddy and Lenny were cruising along at a steady forty. Teddy was saying, 'It's fishy – I mean, just giving us the key and trusting us like that. They ain't never left us alone before with the money or the guns. You don't think we're being fitted up, do you?'

'Can't see how,' mused Lenny. 'If we're nicked, we'd know who put us in the frame. And they know we'd shop them.'

'Well,' said Teddy shortly, 'what's to stop us taking all eight cases?'

Lenny turned on him sharply. 'Forget it, Teddy. Christ! Ain't two enough? So we lift the lot. What happens then? We'd be lying on a beach in Brazil and one day we'd look up and they'd be standing over us and about to pull the trigger.

Remember the two coppers? They didn't fuck about with them. We got to go along with them.' He placed a hand on his friend's shoulder. 'You can't take it out on them because of Jessie. I may be out of order here, but she brought it on herself. She must have been out of her fucking mind to do what she done with that French girl. I didn't even know she were like *that*, did you?'

Teddy, gazing ahead at the unreeling road, pressed his lips into a thin, morose line and shook his head slowly.

Three miles behind, Bruiser, flashing his headlights to clear a path, was coming on at ninety.

He did not see the van until he was parallel with it. It was shielded by a car transporter in the centre lane. Bruiser swore and fell back, switched to the middle lane and came alongside Teddy and Lenny, jabbing at the horn.

Teddy glanced across the narrowing gap and screamed, 'It's them! The bastards are after us!' He accelerated and the high-sided van rocked on its suspension.

Bruiser cursed again as the van shot away. He put down his right foot and once again came up alongside. He could see Belcher's face, drained of colour, staring at him. Triggs was concentrating on the road and pushing the van's speed to its limit.

Bruiser took his left hand off the wheel and made a waving-down motion. 'No, no, you fools!' he shouted. 'Stop! Stop!' But his words were lost in the scream of the two engines.

'Oh, Christ!' Teddy wailed, wrestling with the wheel. 'I *knew* the bastards were up to something. They've got us away from the house to kill us!' He crouched lower over the wheel.

Lenny said: 'I can only see the big bloke, I can't see no shooter.'

Bruiser moved closer to the van. He edged forward until he was half a length ahead and then crossed into Teddy's path in an attempt to slow and halt him.

Teddy screamed, 'He's trying to drive us off the road!' He jabbed suddenly at the footbrake and the tyres shrieked in protest. The van lurched dangerously as the pursuit dropped to below thirty m.p.h.

Bruiser braked with relief. At last the idiots were seeing sense.

348

He eased back until, looking over his left shoulder, he had the two men in his sights in the van's cab.

What happened next could have taken only milliseconds, yet Bruiser saw it all elegiacally. The two Cockneys were mouthing at each other when the cabin was illuminated by a searing light, endowing them with the innocence of choirboys. Then the fireball rose up from the secret compartment at their backs and consumed them and the cab, which disintegrated before Bruiser's eyes. A front wheel detached itself from the van and Bruiser raised an arm instinctively to protect his face as his own vehicle ran on through a shower of blazing fragments.

The loose wheel hurtled into his path. He felt it smack into his radiator and jam on his underside. His car flung itself into a road-churning skid beyond his control, and headed inexorably for a high parapet.

Bruiser, who had spared no time to put on his seat belt, hit the door handle, threw himself out and went into a falling roll, kicking clear of his car. His body spun away from the hurtling metal and his head cracked sharply against concrete.

Chapter Forty-three

Prentiss Decker had her head pressed against the bars, thinking. By the calendar scratched on the wall, the queens were in their twentieth day of imprisonment and her stomach told her that they had not been fed for some time. But it was not so much hunger as fear that made Prentiss feel hollow and helpless.

The spite in the Welshman's voice had convinced her: Mathilde had been executed and, somehow, the ransom demand had gone horribly wrong. Was the lack of food just a short-lived punishment or . . . ?

Prentiss pressed her head harder against the iron as if to expunge the foreboding.

How long could they hold on without food or water? A week? Two weeks? And then what? Would some estate agent one day bring people to view a desirable country residence, open the wine cellar and be met by the vile, choking smell of the charnel-house?

Prentiss drooped but, feeling Hanna Hansen's comforting arm on her shoulder, straightened up again.

Prentiss said, 'Do you think the English have given up on us?'

Hanna said, 'No, but there's a saying of those mad Scottish soldiers that we Krauts always admired. The Scots say, "If the English give up, it'll be a long war." I'd say that the whole country is still being ripped apart in the search for us. They can't be long . . . And if the English give up, others won't.'

The English had not given up. Ringrose, flanked by maps on easels, addressed a roomful of officers from the rank of sergeant upwards, at the Maidstone police headquarters.

He said, 'I know a fifteen-mile radius doesn't sound much

but we're talking of an area comprising seven hundred square miles. All the evidence we have suggests that the girls are somewhere within this perimeter.' Gravely he added, 'The kidnappers are not responding to my latest efforts to contact them and, as far as we know, they have made no attempt to live up to their side of the deal. But that was a major risk from the start. Our chief concern has been to recover the girls and *then* go after the perpetrators. However, the very act of releasing the girls must mean that the criminals expose themselves to chance discovery. So far, they have not taken that chance.'

A uniformed chief inspector risked breaking into his superior officer's briefing with a question. 'Surely, sir, keeping the lid on the girls is an even greater liability?'

'Not if they can be left to die in some godforsaken hole,' said Ringrose bleakly.

A murmur of anxiety ran round the room. 'Ladies and gentlemen,' said Ringrose, 'we're dealing with people who have shown both extraordinary flair for crime and extraordinary cruelty. Our psychiatric experts tell me they are capable of any psychopathic deed necessary in their self-interest.'

A woman inspector asked, 'Sir, if, in fact, time is running out for the girls, isn't it the right moment to call in the Army for assistance – impose some kind of martial law within the search area and bring everything to a standstill while a massive comb-out by combined police–military forces is undertaken?'

Ringrose shook his head. 'It's a course I've considered – and from the start a company of the Special Air Service has been on stand-by. But my own feeling is that if I ever need them I will have failed. They're a crude instrument – rather like a house-holder chasing a burglar and smashing up his own furniture in the process. It's the girls alive we want – only then may we unleash the SAS. As for martial law, surely it must only alarm the kidnappers to such an extent that they will be forced to entomb all forty-eight surviving girls and make a getaway?'

The word 'entomb' sent another uneasy murmur around the room.

'No,' said Ringrose. 'Despite all pressure from outside – and there has been plenty – we shall continue this hunt as a police operation.'

He turned to one of the maps. 'Notionally, the ground within the target area has already been gone over once and all likely buildings inspected. Well, we're now going to assume we're dealing with virgin territory and begin all over again. This time, we're armed with some clues that may narrow the search. Take the type of building in which we suspect the girls are being held . . .'

In the cellar, the second day passed without anyone coming to feed the queens. They were all accustomed to strict dieting but thirst and lightheadedness were exacting a toll. No one now exercised to maintain fitness: movement was exhausting. The girls slumped on their mattresses in apathetic groups, mostly too weary for either hysteria or to continue the circular conversation about their plight and chances of rescue.

Prentiss Decker knew that they would also now start to lose their accurate measure of the passing hours.

Some time during what she assumed to be daylight, Mirabelle Montcalm said, 'The chemical toilets have started to overflow. It's disgusting down there.'

Prentiss said, 'That'll be the least of our worries. There can't be much left inside any of us to add to the mess.'

For the first time there was a note of hopelessness in her voice. Mirabelle shuffled away, disturbed.

The inexplicable explosion that had destroyed a van and its two occupants on the M20 and caused three other casualties became an immediate matter for investigation by Scotland Yard's Bomb Squad.

The identities of the dead men were speedily established by means of fingerprint fragments taken from their scorched and blackened hands. Their files were retrieved from the Criminal Records Office and the deduction made that here were two petty criminals who had gone in for a spot of safe-breaking with insufficient skills and had blown themselves up. The calamitous results in no way indicated any connection with the kidnapping of the Queens of the Earth.

Detective Inspector Walter Fisk of the Stone's End Street police station, as guv'nor of the manor on which the deceased twosome lived, was peripherally involved in furnishing the Bomb Squad with his personal observations on Teddy Triggs, Lenny Belcher and their known associates.

A date for the double inquest was set, although this hearing was expected to be adjourned by the coroner, pending the availability of witnesses, including Sir Brewster Moxmanton, Bt, of Lowndes Square, Belgravia, at present unconscious in hospital.

The whole mucky episode seemed just a sad little tale of two small-time dreamers overreaching themselves and injuring innocent citizens in the process.

At least, it did until Friday, 21 October, when, for the second time in nine months, Mrs Martha Triggs presented herself at the Stone's End Street station, demanding to see Walter Fisk. With her, she had dragged her reluctant husband.

They had both recovered from the initial, overwhelming grief at having lost their son. Now Mrs Triggs was ready to tell Fisk of suspicions that she had been nursing – suspicions that she had withheld from the officers of the Bomb Squad who had called earlier.

For a few minutes Fisk listened attentively then placed a guard over the interview room and headed for his telephone.

Thirty minutes later, Commander Tom Ringrose and Detective Inspector Lionel Firth were speeding along the M20 towards London.

They slowed for a brief inspection of the spot where Teddy Triggs and Lenny Belcher had been blotted out. Passing traffic had not yet erased the black heat marks in the road.

Walter Fisk and the Stone's End uniformed superintendent waited on the station steps to receive their high-ranking visitors. The four men made straight for the interview room where the grim, bereaved mother said, 'My son and young Lenny Belcher were murdered. I want you to get the bastards what done it.' She prodded her uneasy husband with a rod-like finger. 'Harry, tell them what you know.'

Mr Triggs squirmed. Volunteering information to the police outraged his moral code. Tom Ringrose waited patiently.

'I suppose the missus is right,' he began miserably. 'We both think Teddy and Lenny was caught up with a dodgy crowd.'

'Any names?' asked Ringrose.

'No, nothing like that. I don't think they was local or I'd have heard a whisper. Whatever happened started about the time Martha came round here to see Mr Fisk. She was worried because Teddy had done a vanishing act with Jessie Moss.'

Ringrose glanced at Fisk. 'Jessie Moss?'

'Teddy's girl-friend, sir. There's been no sign of her since Teddy's death was reported, which is unusual.'

Mrs Triggs began to sob at the word 'death'. Her husband squeezed her hand and went on, 'Some odd things started to happen. Teddy and Lenny kept disappearing for days on end and they changed their appearance. We was worried about Teddy losing so much weight. He let his hair grow long.' Mr Triggs looked disgusted. 'And he were tinting his hair and eyebrows blond. My boy's always been straight but suddenly he was acting like a bleedin' nancy-boy.'

'Did you ask him what he was doing?' Ringrose asked.

'Too bloody right I did!' said Harry Triggs. 'But he cocked a deaf 'un. All he said was, ''There's a nice little drink on the way, Dad. So ask no questions and you won't hear no porkies!'''

Mr Triggs let go of his wife's hand and wiped his brow, looking confused. 'It's only when the news broke in the papers about the death of old Marble – Frank Simpson – that I got a whiff of what Teddy was into. But how the heck could it happen? He's never been big-time. The silly little sod, God bless him, ain't never done nothing but Mickey Mouse tea-leaving.'

Ringrose said, 'What was so special about the news of Marble, Mr Triggs?'

Mr Triggs could not look Ringrose in the eye. He studied the backs of his hands and said, 'Well, it was me what put Teddy on to Marble, wasn't it? About six months ago he said, ''Dad, I need a bloke can operate a big crane.'' I'd worked with Marble on the docks so I told Teddy to get him.' Mr Triggs stirred unhappily. 'Now I know I done wrong in not coming to you right away. But Teddy was my son – and you don't drop your own in the shit, do you? I daren't tell his mother. She'd have had a fit. After Marble's body were identified I went round Teddy's place but there weren't no sign of him or Jessie. I went round her parents and Lenny Belcher's. Same story. None of us ain't seen any of them in the past three weeks. Until I went up the mortuary on Tuesday.'

Walter Fisk stepped in with a question. He was holding his diary. He said to Mrs Triggs, 'Martha, I have my notes here on your previous visit to Stone's End Street when you thought Teddy had gone missing. My note says he had told you before-hand he was going for a ride in the country. But those weren't his exact words, were they?'

Mrs Triggs lifted her plump, wet face to look at him questioningly. 'I can't remember . . .'

Fisk said, 'Come on, Martha. You've got to think about it.'

The woman pondered. Finally she said, 'Do you mean what I said about 'oppin'?'

'That's it!' said Fisk, instantly. 'Teddy told you he was going down to where the hops are picked.'

Ringrose and Firth stiffened. The processing of hops with sulphur had come into the investigation before – when the 'sulphur' signal from Prentiss Decker was being pursued – and discounted.

Ringrose said, 'Mrs Triggs, did Teddy know that part of Kent well?'

'Oh, yes. He loved it. He had the first 'olidays of his life there. We used to take 'im 'oppin' with us when he was a kid – East Peckham, Paddock Wood, Medsham.' Her face darkened. 'Then they took it away from us, like everything else, and picked the hops with machines.'

Firth had his map of Kent spread upon the table. He looked up. 'East Peckham, Paddock Wood and Medsham are all within the target area, sir.'

Ringrose took Firth's pencil and circled each of the tiny communities, three wheels within the big wheel. 'Let's make them three areas for priority effort, Lionel. I don't believe in coincidence.'

Ringrose took Fisk aside. 'I want you to go and comb out the parents of Belcher and Moss while DI Firth and I get back to Maidstone. And get hold of the E-Fit pictures of the two men who drove the coaches on the day of the kidnapping. I'm willing to bet a month's wages the families will identify them as reasonable likenesses of Triggs and Belcher. We'll also need photographs of the girl, Moss, to circulate.'

On the way back in the car, he said, 'I'm willing to bet a second month's wages that we'll never find Jessie Moss alive. Marble ... Triggs ... Belcher ... Nancy Cornmorris ... They're killing off the hired help.'

'And the girls?'

Ringrose shook his head. He said slowly, 'The way things are developing, it seems presumptuous to dare to hope.'

Chapter Forty-four

For two days Bruiser Moxmanton had been rising through layers of consciousness, until light and awareness revealed the reality of the white-walled room.

His eyelids fluttered and he was aware that someone was with him.

He had not seen his wife, Celia, in two years, but somehow it seemed perfectly natural that she should be seated quietly at his bedside.

'That you, Cee?' he asked hoarsely.

She was out of the chair and bending over him. 'Yes, it's me, darling. Are you At Home to callers?'

He knew it was a joke but felt too tired to smile. 'Just about,' he said weakly.

'By God, you've had a lucky escape, Bruiser,' said Cee. 'You've cracked a couple of ribs and you've been severely concussed. I suppose it's the least you can expect if you get in the way of a couple of incompetent safe-breakers. At one stage, the quacks wrote you off.'

What was she saying? Bruiser began to fit together the recent past. At some time, Cee disappeared and he fell into a dreamless sleep. Later he woke again and she had returned. So had mocking memory.

He tried to reach for her with a hand covered in dried scabs. 'Listen carefully, Cee. What day is it?'

'Saturday.'

He could not comprehend this. Then Cee added, 'October the twenty-second. You've been out cold for almost five days.'

'Christ!' whispered Bruiser. He made another futile attempt to grab for her. He said desperately, 'Please, Cee, go away and find me all the newspapers since Monday.'

'Don't be silly, darling. You're in no condition for reading.'

Bruiser said, 'Please, Cee. Take my word. It's a matter of life and death.'

She looked at him curiously, shrugged and went. Bruiser slept again until she returned.

Cee placed pillows behind his head and helped him to sit up. His white-turbaned skull throbbed.

Bruiser's battered hand tore through the printed pages. He read the published accounts of the M20 'accident' in which his photograph was prominently displayed. In every account he featured as an innocent passer-by. In some cases the story was in coincidental juxtaposition to the latest bulletin on the missing queens. There were no reports of them being released.

Five days! thought Bruiser. Lucius Frankel had had sole charge of the forty-eight girls for five days.

He said to Cee, 'Don't argue, Cee, just get me a telephone.'

Cee did not object, but the nursing staff did. 'You either bring a phone or I discharge myself and crawl out of here to the nearest public box,' he said.

Bruiser let the Moxmanton House number ring for a long time. Then the number for the Kew flat. He tried Lucius Frankel's private quarters above his club. Nothing.

He reached Maurice, Lucius's manager, on another line. The man was surprised and gratified. 'Sir Brewster! How nice to hear your voice, sir. We were all extremely sorry to read of your accident. Mr Frankel was most upset. He'd given you up for dead. He said as much after he had telephoned the hospital.'

'Did he, by Jove?' said Bruiser, grimly.

'Yes,' said Maurice. 'He'll be overjoyed at your recovery.'

'I daresay,' said Bruiser. 'I'll break the news to him myself if you don't mind. Is he there?'

'I'm afraid not, Sir Brewster. He returned briefly to his flat on Wednesday, made arrangements with the bank for me to sign the staff cheques, packed a bag and was off with his trailer.'

'Trailer?'

'Yes, sir. Mr Frankel had hitched a trailer to the back of his car. He said he was taking a touring holiday. I don't expect him back for some weeks.'

Bruiser knew why Lucius had hitched a trailer to his car. He put down the phone. Blood thudded in his head. He said to Cee, 'Don't ask me any questions. Just go away and come back with a suit of clothes, some money and a car with a full tank.'

Celia was silent for a moment. Then she said, 'You're in hot water, aren't you, Bruiser? Do you want to tell me about it?'

Bruiser looked at her and felt an ache that was no part of his injuries. He'd wrecked his chances. Wrecked everything.

He said, gruffly, 'Best you don't know, my dear. There's a bit of a shambles I have to put right.'

When Cee returned with his clothes Bruiser rocked on his feet, dizzy with exertion. A young doctor was calling him every kind of bloody fool. Bruiser waved him aside. 'Discharging myself. Every man's right,' he said unsteadily. 'I'll do my recovering at home.'

Cee helped him downstairs to the car park. He endured sharp, stabbing pains from his strapped ribs and his head, still bandaged, beat out a throbbing rhythm.

He climbed painfully into Cee's car. 'Where to?' she said. Bruiser gave her the address of the Kew flat and fell back in the passenger seat. She parked outside the block and Bruiser climbed slowly onto the pavement. He said, 'Wait here.' She gazed anxiously after his shambling figure.

He hauled himself up the stairs by the banisters to Nancy Cornmorris's hideaway. There was no sound from within and no answer to the bell. Bruiser tested the door with his body-weight. The timbers creaked but did not budge. He moved back and, gritting his teeth against the inevitable pain to follow, kicked out. His ribs seemed to explode and Bruiser staggered, but then the red hot mist behind his eyes cleared and he saw that he had jumped the tongue out of the lock's striking plate. He pushed the door and lurched in.

Nancy Cornmorris's bed was on its side, the vinyl wallpaper lay in coils upon the carpet and a floor-to-ceiling hole gaped emptily where twenty million dollars' worth of hard currency had been secreted.

Bruiser went back down the stairs. A woman poked her head out of a doorway. 'Sorry about the noise,' he grunted. 'Damn lock got jammed.' She withdrew hurriedly at the sight of his stature and battered appearance.

Back in the car, he debated whether or not to ask Cee to drive him to Moxmanton. No, he had to keep her clear of the firing line.

She took him to Lowndes Square. 'I want you to come in for a minute,' said Bruiser.

In the drawing room she gazed around, remembering. Since she had walked out Bruiser had not changed so much as the position of a single chair.

He was acting like a man obsessed. He poured them both a stiff whisky and she watched while he gripped a pen with difficulty and wrote a long letter, sealed and addressed the envelope, then placed it within a second. The writing paper displayed the Moxmanton armorial bearings.

Cee raised an eyebrow when Bruiser found a candle and a stick of red sealing wax. The hot blobs fell like gore onto the flap and Bruiser pressed his signet ring into the thick ooze.

He said to her, 'I want you to go now and take this letter with you. If you haven't heard from me by noon on Tuesday, break the seal and deliver the contents to the person named on the envelope.'

Cee tried to speak but Bruiser placed a hand tenderly over her lips. 'Please, old girl, don't say anything. I've been such a fool.' He groped for the right words of explanation and apology. 'It's all been so tiresome. I've always thought the world should be a grander place but knowing that it isn't hasn't been very good for my character. Do you think you can understand that?'

Cee was worried. She said, 'Bruiser, why don't you go to bed and I'll stay the night within shouting distance? I don't think you should be alone. You're not well.'

But he was steering her towards the door. He pecked her on the brow and said, 'Thanks for coming to the hospital and doing picket duty. Now go home and get on with your life.'

Stepping out into the square, Celia found that she was crying.

Bruiser had left his Browning at Moxmanton House. He found his father's old captured Luger and a magazine, and consulted his watch. It was almost 10 p.m. He set the alarm for 3 a.m., stretched fully clothed on his bed and fell into a sound sleep.

At 3.20 he was sitting in his car obliquely across from

Lucius's club. The five-hour rest had transformed him. The throbbing in his head was reduced to a moderate pulsation. His timing had been good. He watched the last of the customers straggle off noisily into the Mayfair night and the more sober departure of the staff. He waited patiently until Maurice himself appeared, in his topcoat and trilby, perched at an unbecoming angle upon his brilliantined head. As he was locking the front door Bruiser materialized silently at his side. The manager's face registered first surprise and then alarm.

'Sir Brewster! What a sur—'

'Shut up, Maurice,' said Bruiser. 'We're going back inside.'

'But, sir, as you can see, I'm just closing—'

'No buts, Maurice. Get the door open again.' Bruiser brought the Luger up to eye level.

Stunned, the manager obeyed. 'Now disconnect the burglar alarm,' said Bruiser, and prodded him with the gun.

At last, Maurice found his voice. 'Sir Brewster. This is terrible! You're breaking the law.'

'Don't worry, Maurice. I'm not here to steal anything or to harm you – unless you misbehave. I only want to know where Frankel is.'

'But I've told you already, sir. He took off in his car without leaving me any further information. He's getting out of the club business and has invited me to form a consortium of the staff and make him an offer for the business.'

'Right,' said Bruiser. 'Let's open up his private office and flat.'

Maurice wriggled unhappily. 'Mr Frankel will be furious, sir. I'm not permitted to enter his quarters when he's absent.'

Bruiser waved the Luger. 'This is all the permission you need. Get going.'

They climbed the panelled staircase and Maurice opened the door to the top storey. Bruiser waved him into a seat while he ransacked Lucius's office. Then he pushed the man ahead of him into the private quarters. In the process of tearing down everything from the walls, Bruiser discovered the safe, concealed behind a mosaic plaque depicting the Aztec serpent god, Quetzalcoatl. It seemed apt.

'Combination!' demanded Bruiser.

'I'm not allowed to touch that safe. It's meant only for Mr Frankel's private papers,' said Maurice, looking haunted. 'I only have the numbers in case of an emergency.'

Bruiser took first pressure on the Luger and Maurice snatched shakily for his keyring and sorted through the bunch until he found a small brass tab etched with some numbers. 'You start at eight, and it's three left, four right and three left again,' he said.

Bruiser scattered the safe's contents across Lucius's bed – cash, a bunch of IOUs and postdated cheques, documents relating to the South Audley Street lease, a magistrate's liquor licence . . .

Bruiser riffled through, finding nothing of interest. He was left with a photograph album. He turned the pages. At the beginning there were pictures of a gaunt, upright woman, whom Bruiser assumed was Lucius's mother. Then came several of Lucius in white tie and tails, apparently performing some theatrical act. The bulk of the collection was of Lucius with celebrities who frequented his establishment. Bruiser found himself, Rolly and Dickie. He felt a pang of sorrow. They all looked so carefree. Could it have been only a year ago?

He stopped at another page, identifying Nancy Cornmorris in a group photograph. Lucius was there, but at the edge of the crowd. She was smiling radiantly, like a woman in love.

In one of the clear plastic pouches towards the back of the album, Lucius had tucked a handful of Polaroid shots. Bruiser could see why they had not been mounted with the others. The colours in the first few had darkened but there was no mistaking the activity frozen frame by frame. Lucius was on a bed, romping with a slender, naked woman. In one he was clearly penetrating her and her head was thrown back in ecstasy.

Bruiser flipped on, intrigued. He came to one in which Lucius's bed partner figured alone. Lucius was apparently on top of her pointing the camera downwards to capture by flash the woman's *moment suprême*. Her mouth gaped and her teeth were bared, caught in an orgasmic scream. Her wide-open eyes threw back into the lens two brilliant diamonds of light.

Bruiser stood up, dropped the photographs and knocked over a chair. He gave a terrible, anguished moan, followed by an enraged bellow.

Bruiser Moxmanton at last understood the total nature of his humiliation – understood how, in the bold, buccaneering enterprise, he had been no less a miserable pawn than Triggs, Belcher and Marble. He had been manipulated from the start like the dolt he was.

Bruiser sat down heavily, fighting an urge to be sick. He stirred only when he saw Maurice make a move for the door.

'It's all right,' said Bruiser, tiredly. 'You can clear up this mess and go home. I've got what I came for.'

He made his way leadenly down the stairs. By the time he reached the pavement his resolve had returned. At least he now knew where to look for Lucius Frankel.

He drove slowly back to Lowndes Square to pick up his passport and the car travel documents.

Chapter Forty-five

Another Sunday and again the Prime Minister had interrupted his Chequers weekend. Officials led Ringrose through the narrow corridors of Number 10. The Prime Minister had the morning newspapers strewn in front of him. 'GRAVE CONCERN FOR GIRLS,' said the *Sunday Times*. The *Mail on Sunday* put it more bluntly: 'QUEENS FEARED SLAIN.'

'The foreign press is even worse,' said the Prime Minister. 'The whole question of the government's competence is being debated from Greenland to Tierra del Fuego. The work of the Foreign Office and our overseas missions is almost at a standstill while our people seek to placate the governments of the countries involved. Heads of state are chasing me with telephone calls all the hours God sends.'

The Prime Minister handed Ringrose a cup of coffee. 'Here,' he said, 'you look as if you need this.'

Ringrose had not seen himself in a mirror for at least a day. He guessed he must look shattered. The sweep of central Kent had gone on throughout the night. He said: 'I'm certain we're on top of the hiding place. In our target area we're visiting every structure larger than a dog kennel.'

'It's been three and a half weeks,' said the Prime Minister. 'Most people would find it inconceivable that you could keep forty-eight people hidden against their will so long in this densely populated little island.'

Ringrose sighed. 'The gang, whoever they are, planned for a long time to make the inconceivable possible.'

'And what condition will the poor things be in if we do find them?'

'That's my one real fear, sir. I don't believe the gang even thought beyond collecting the ransom. The irony is that it's probably more difficult to release them than it was to snatch them.'

The Prime Minister put down his cup. 'Now, Commander, I must say something unpleasant to you.' Ringrose waited for the axe to fall. He went on, 'As you know, I've been under considerable pressure to replace you but I don't believe in change for its own sake and, hitherto, I've sent your critics packing. You've confronted an intractable problem with great energy and ingenuity. I now have to tell you that you will be replaced on Tuesday afternoon when I plan to make a statement to the House of Commons. I'm afraid the public temper has turned against us and I have to throw you to the wolves. Do you understand my point of view?'

Ringrose nodded and stood up. 'Yes, sir.' He felt choked. 'But God help the girls.'

'You have until I get on my feet in the House at three p.m. on Tuesday.'

He escorted Ringrose to his office door and offered him an automatic press-the-flesh handshake, already withdrawing into the politicians' carapace, protectively distancing himself from a potential disaster.

'So sorry,' he said, and closed his door softly, leaving a lackey to usher Ringrose to the garden exit.

Bruiser took Le Shuttle to Calais. The holiday season was almost over but he made poor time heading south. His residual concussion tired him easily and from time to time he had to pull off the *autoroute* to catnap.

His Luger was in the back of his belt under a loose leather jacket. He had removed his head bandages and wore a cap to prevent his wounds attracting curiosity from Immigration and Customs officials.

He reached Cap d'Ail in the pre-dawn of Monday. He could smell bread baking as he parked off the *corniche inférieure* by the church, and proceeded on foot downhill through the lanes until he came out to the rocky path that follows the shoreline where Winston Churchill used to walk. He padded on eastward, a black silhouette against the lightening sky, until he rounded a promontory, bringing the lights of Monaco into distant view. This was the place.

Bruiser looked for the foot and handholds of boyhood memory, found them and, exerting himself against the restrictions of his injured ribs, scaled the rock face to the foot of the concrete wall that marked the edge of the garden of the Villa Apollo.

He threw his jacket over the strands of barbed wire strung along the top, reached upwards, took a grip and hauled himself over. He landed on his knees on the grass, checked that the Luger was still in his belt, retrieved his jacket and moved cautiously up the slope to the main building.

His blood sang almost happily as he spotted the trailer. Lucius had parked it on a side terrace in the lee of the house. The curtains were drawn but the door was unlocked. Bruiser peered inside. Two wall panels leaned against a mini-refrigerator. Lucius had removed the stacks of banknotes concealed in the wall cavities but had not yet restored the trailer's interior.

Bruiser kicked a wheel. Clever, clever, Lucius. He had even thought to over-inflate the tyres to compensate for the secret extra weight.

The villa was silent. Bruiser circled the building, testing for entry, but all the ground-floor shutters were locked. Finally, he returned to the trailer, climbed onto its roof, reached for a balustrade and drew himself up and onto a balcony.

The high french windows were ajar and Bruiser eased himself inside. He was in the principal guest bedroom. The bed was made up and the coverlet turned down. But no one had slept in it. Bruiser recognized some of Lucius's clothes on the nightstand. Beyond it was the door that connected with the main suite. It was ajar.

They slept together, naked on an ice-blue satin sheet, she with her arm across his chest and golden hair fanned across the pillow, and he on his back, legs apart, a man sated. A conqueror.

Bruiser had a momentary impulse to place a bullet straight between Lucius's eyes. But that would be too merciful.

The man's penis hung soft and wrinkled on the cushion of

366

his scrotum. Bruiser took out the Luger and icily flicked the limp thing with the muzzle. Lucius gave a murmur of approval. Bruiser flicked it again, harder.

Any tendency it might have acquired towards engorgement evaporated as Lucius's dark eyes snapped open and he found himself examining the Luger's foresight.

'Oh, my Christ!' he whispered. He cowered from the gun as far as he could, sliding up against the bedhead. Constanza, Bruiser's stepmother, opened one eye sleepily, then screamed.

'I ought to put the pair of you down here and now,' said Bruiser.

She squealed and huddled her golden body against her lover.

'For God's sake, Bruiser,' gasped Lucius, holding a palm up in front of him as if that could ward off a bullet. 'You're not seeing things clearly.'

'I'm seeing clearly all right,' said Bruiser, evenly. He swung the barrel towards Constanza. 'It wasn't Nancy Cornmorris who was the secret partner, it was you. The silly woman was disposable once her usefulness came to an end. And I daresay that's how the pair of you saw me. A disposable yokel with more brawn than brain.' Bruiser experienced a flash of anger. 'My God, you had me trained like a bloody gundog. You knew I'd come down here to plead with you to help bust the trust. And I thought you were being generous when you agreed to the wine sale! But you had to have the use of Moxmanton, the cleared cellar and me, if Lucius's scheme was to work. You set me up so that I had nowhere else to turn for money.'

Constanza sat up, her breasts quivering. Desperately, she said, 'Bruiser, you've got to listen to me. We didn't want to deceive you, but we didn't think you'd go along if you knew that Lucius and your dead father's wife were lovers. Lucius's plan was brilliant and we couldn't risk family quarrels getting in the way. Believe me, we would have told you eventually.'

'Yes,' said Lucius, eagerly. 'Once we were in the clear, there would be no reason to hide anything from you.'

'No reason at all – but how much more convenient if I were pushing up the daisies with the rest of 'em,' said Bruiser. 'I've lost my best friends because of you. Even Wally Barnes, who had no part in it.'

'Bruiser,' pleaded Lucius, 'you can't blame us for any of that. You knew the risks.'

'Did those poor little Cockneys know the extra special risk of working with you?' asked Bruiser. He levelled his gun. 'No, it's quite apparent to me that you planned all along to dispose of us.'

Bruiser had a further thought. He said to Constanza, 'I shouldn't be a whit surprised if you weren't intended to follow me. I can't see our wily Lucius leaving anyone breathing who would have a lifetime's hold over him.'

'Bruiser,' said Lucius hoarsely, 'you must stop this. I've brought the money out of the country at enormous personal risk. It's all here and locked in the attic. A third of it is yours. What else could I do once you were taken into hospital? How the hell could I predict that you'd go racing after those two little monkeys? You must have known in your heart they had to die. They could never have kept their mouths shut.'

Bruiser stared down at them, their fright subsiding, their oiled tongues rewriting events to suit the calamity that had overtaken them.

'Get out of bed,' Bruiser said flatly to Lucius. He gestured with the Luger.

'What are you going to do?'

'It's what you're going to do that matters.'

Constanza fell on her knees on the mattress, clutching a pillow to her sleek stomach. 'Please, please, Bruiser! Don't do anything to Lucius! I love him! Just take your share of the money and go. You're spoiling everything for all of us. This is madness.'

'Shut up, Constanza,' said Bruiser. He was gripped by disgust and betrayal. She'd not blubbed that much even at his father's funeral. He waved the Luger again at Lucius. 'Come on, get dressed.'

Lucius slid onto the cool white marble in his bare feet, his body still arched in a cringe.

Bruiser said, 'You're going to reload the money into the back of the Rolls and then we shall all drive home to England.'

'England!' shrieked Lucius. 'What the fuck are we going back there for?'

'I should say for a thirty-year stay in one of Her Majesty's maximum-security establishments, wouldn't you?'

Bruiser was quite calm now. He had been ill and he had behaved badly. Inexcusably badly. He knew what had to be done. He looked at the couple almost sorrowfully.

'And what about you?' Lucius was screaming. 'What do you think they'll do to you? You'll be in the next cell, you damned fool!'

Bruiser said calmly, 'I shall hand the pair of you over to Ringrose and then I shall do what has to be done.'

Constanza bounced on the bed. 'He's talking of blowing his brains out!' she cried.

'Christ!' said Lucius, disbelieving. His voice rose to a roar: 'This isn't some bloody *Boy's Own Paper* escapade where everyone ends up doing the decent thing. We've pulled off one of the biggest crimes in history.'

'My mind's made up,' said Bruiser, implacably. 'Nothing has happened the way I expected. For a while, I admit, I had my vision of achieving great things but everything has turned out as downright butchery. It's all over. Get your kit.'

'It's in the other room,' said Lucius quietly. He walked across the floor, shoulders sagging. Bruiser followed. Lucius, he knew, would make his play soon.

At the door, Lucius turned slowly, looked at Bruiser with dark hatred and said over the bigger man's shoulder in a conversational tone, 'Constanza, kill him!'

Too late, Bruiser remembered that he had handed his Browning to Lucius on the night the French girl had escaped. He started to turn. He saw Constanza kneeling upright, holding an object concealed and muffled by the pillow.

Before he could bring his Luger round, the shiny satin surface erupted in a spout of goose down and Bruiser felt something smash into his right side, throwing him against Lucius.

Propelled by a savage animal instinct, Bruiser's mighty left hand found Lucius's throat and began to squeeze. The other man was flattened against the bedroom wall, gurgling and struggling. Bruiser attempted to raise his right arm to draw a bead on Constanza. But his wound was already causing a spreading paralysis. He crushed Lucius's throat harder against the silk-hung wall, watching his beautiful step-mother uncoil and come off the bed like an avenging goddess.

The pillow spouted again and another great hammer blow shook Bruiser's huge frame. Constanza's face was distorted by a murderous rage. Bruiser made one more effort to raise his firing arm but he could no longer feel his fingers. He heard a clatter and knew that the Luger had dropped to the floor.

As the world began to recede, Bruiser turned a dignified face towards Constanza. She stood, tall and magnificent. Diana the huntress, a spewer of death.

She stepped lithely to one side, so that her lover should not be in the firing line, then venomously pumped two more shots into Bruiser's shattered flank. His grip loosened on Lucius's throat and he toppled to the floor. Lucius slid down after him, his face congested with blood, a livid weal encircling his neck.

Constanza threw down the pillow and the Browning and leaped to his aid over Bruiser's expiring body, sobbing with relief. She ran to the night table to fetch a tumbler of water. 'The bastard! The bastard!' she wept. 'Oh, my darling, he could have killed you.'

Lucius gazed up weakly at her. 'You got him, Connie. You got the crazy bastard.' Gratitude and adoration overwhelmed him.

Half an hour later, Lucius was once again all icy intelligence. Before the servants were up, Constanza had helped him to wrap Bruiser's body in a sheet and drop it over the balcony. Then they tiptoed down to the terrace and stowed it in the trailer.

'I'll take a drive into the Alpes Maritimes and put him over a cliff,' said Lucius. 'They won't find him for months.'

Back inside, they swabbed the blood from the marble floor and swept up the scattered feathers. Lucius returned to his own room. By the time Rawlings served breakfast, all traces of Bruiser's arrival had been expunged.

Lucius said, 'He must have come by car. There are no night flights from London. I'll scout around for it later.'

They spent the remainder of Monday monitoring the BBC World Service. The girls were still being hunted. The Prime

Minister intended to make a statement in the House of Commons the next afternoon.

That evening they dined by candlelight with Bruiser's body lying a dozen metres away. Lucius raised a glass of chilled Blanc de Blancs. 'To the victors the spoils,' he said.

Prentiss Decker felt as if her lips were splitting. Her body temperature was dropping and every movement brought on a bout of dizziness but, slowly, more than forty of the girls shuffled or crawled into the centre of the cellar. Muslim, Hindu, Buddhist, Christian, they huddled together while Fran Pilkington intoned a prayer, improvised from a dimly recollected psalm: 'O Lord our God, in Thee have we put our trust, save us from all them that persecute us and deliver us: lest they devour our souls, like a lion, and tear them to pieces, while there is none to help . . .'

The lovers lay side-by-side, naked once more. Constanza asked tremulously, 'Is there no safe way to let the girls go?'

'None,' said Lucius. 'Ringrose will be waiting for that. Waiting for a mistake.'

'What do we do now?'

'Beyond dumping Bruiser and distributing the money to a widespread number of new bank accounts, we sit still. If Rolly Ponsford's remains are not identified and linked by close friendship to Bruiser, it may even be possible for you to resume your role as lady of the manor.'

'God forbid!' said Constanza. 'I could never go back to live in that house. And what about the girls?'

Lucius looked up at the ceiling striped by the slanting light pattern of the window shutters. His eyes were so black they seemed like vacant sockets. 'You can put the girls from your thoughts. Before I left I filled in the cellar doorway with a nine-inch brick wall. It should have hardened nicely by now. We can leave the whole place sealed for five or ten years, if you like. Then, perhaps, one day if you wanted to sell the house, we could send the servants away while I break in and clear out whatever's left . . .'

Constanza rolled over so that her body pressed against his.

She placed a hand over his mouth. 'Don't say any more. For pity's sake, do something to me, Lucius. Take my mind off everything outside this room.'

Lucius Frankel, smiling indulgently, obliged his goddess.

On the telephone, Charles Bollam sounded exhausted and vexed. 'The house must have been requisitioned by one of the service corps, with Intelligence or the Military Police given the run of one section. There's absolutely no trace of any such I corps, or MP unit having sole possession of a property that fits your information. I'm in the process of redirecting the whole team to the records of service corps wartime requisitions. It could take days . . .'

Ringrose put down his telephone. He glanced at his watch. Nine a.m. In six hours the Prime Minister would stand up in the House and he'd be put out to grass amid many polite expressions of regret and tributes to his, regrettably, unavailing efforts.

Ringrose wondered at what stage he should break the news to his haggard aide. However, he said, 'Get your hat, Lionel. Let's do the rounds of the search centres.'

Chapter Forty-six

The two detectives spent the morning visiting the outposts, questioning operations officers, studying maps. A list of properties had already been re-examined and eliminated from the investigations. But the hunt continued. Photographs of the two dead policemen from Hotel Five were prominently displayed in every control room. This had been Ringrose's idea.

It was already past noon when Ringrose and Firth, being driven along a narrow, russet-and-gold lane, first had a moment to note the glory of the day. Wearily Ringrose wound down his window. He thought of the girls as, in the past, he had thought of dead friends. Never again to see a bright shining morning . . .

Simultaneously he and Firth registered the smell. 'What the hell is that?' said Firth. He wound down his own window and they both began to sniff at the air like frenzied hounds.

'Sulphur!' shouted Ringrose. 'It's sulphur!' He tapped their driver on the shoulder. 'Stop the car!'

They both climbed out. The smell was acrid, unpleasant in the lungs and seemed to be hanging in the trees.

The two men ran back and forth along the lane, trying to locate the source. 'Go further along the road,' Ringrose instructed his driver, and grabbed the hand-mike. He ordered up India Nine Nine, the Bell Textron 222 helicopter manned by the Air Support Unit. India Nine Nine was overhead and in radio contact within fifteen minutes.

Ringrose said, 'Down here we're sitting in a cloud of polluted air. Can you lead us to its source?'

After a few moments, the observer's voice came in clearly: 'From three hundred feet we see it as a scattered mist. Stay where you are, sir, while we track back along the line of drift.'

The helicopter was back in two minutes. The radio crackled: 'The source is an oast-house, sir, about three-quarters of a mile to your east. Just follow us.'

The young man sitting on the plump khaki pokes was drinking a can of beer. He was wreathed in choking vapour, swirling from the swinging white cowl of the oast, but did not seem to mind. He wiped a hop-stained hand across his rubicund face and laughed. 'It's my dad,' he said. 'Likes to keep up appearances. He could have given up using the sulphur with the rest of the hop-growers years ago but he's determined to have the best-looking hops until he gets planted beneath 'em. The sulphur keeps them a lovely green, you know. He sells a lot of them for exhibition.' He tilted his can again and looked up at the helicopter. 'It ain't no crime as far as I know. The Hop Marketing Board haven't told him he mustn't do it.'

Ringrose asked, 'Was the oast-house putting out a sulphur cloud like this on the evening of the twenty-ninth of September?'

'Last week in September?' asked the young man rhetorically. 'We'd have been in bloody big trouble if it weren't. The harvest was late this year but not that late.'

Ringrose turned urgently to Firth. 'What was the wind direction that evening?'

Firth fumbled in his documents case. Presently, he said, 'South south west. Light to moderate breeze.' He fished out his compass. 'As a matter of fact, conditions are similar now.'

'Right,' said Ringrose swiftly. 'I'm going up in the chopper. Follow in the car.'

In response to a call, the pilot brought India Nine Nine down in the wagon yard attached to the oast. A member of the crew strapped Ringrose in among the surveillance equipment and the helicopter rose vertically to two hundred feet.

The sulphur fumes drifted away from the oast, spreading in a wedge shape. Ringrose took the navigator's map and began to shade in the area covered by the white plume. 'Follow the smoke line slowly,' he said. They moved down it for three-quarters of a mile.

The pilot said, 'The smoke peters out at the edge of Medsham village, sir.'

Below was the redbrick and tile straggle of a typical Kentish town. Ringrose could see that his shaded area covered at least a dozen large buildings set in the countryside. He had the helicopter put down on Medsham Pilgrims' Green next to the scuffed, yellowing cricket pitch. Firth was already coming up fast in the car.

Ringrose, clutching the map, ducked out under the whirling blades and ran to meet him. 'Let's find the village bobby,' panted Ringrose.

Firth looked around. 'Over there, sir.' Ringrose followed his finger. The blue sign could be seen plainly opposite the lychgate of the church. The police car screeched to a stop and Ringrose and Firth galloped up the path.

PC Bob Malley jumped to attention the moment he opened his door. He needed to see no warrant card to recognize Commander Thomas Ringrose.

Ringrose brushed past him into the tiny neat office and spread his map on a desk. 'Constable, point out to me every building within this shaded area that could possibly be Victorian or could house a minimum of fifty people.'

Malley jumped to comply. 'There's Medsham Manor, Medsham Place, Moxmanton House, Medway Abbey, which is really a residence, and The Firs.'

'Has each of these been visited and searched?'

'Every one, sir. I've called on each house-owner.'

'And?'

'Nothing, sir. Everything was as normal.'

Firth broke in. 'Were any of these used by the military during the war?'

The bobby shrugged. 'I wasn't even born then, sir. I've never heard mention of anything.'

'Who would know?'

Malley thought. 'I suppose old Miss Collinson's the best bet. She was headmistress of the village school before they closed it down. She once wrote a historical pamphlet on the area. She's at Georgian Cottage.'

'Let's go,' said Ringrose.

Miss Collinson was frail but her mind was still as sharp as her darting yellow eyes.

Ringrose spread out his map. 'Miss Collinson,' he said, 'were any of these fine houses occupied by military personnel during the Second World War?'

The old lady muttered to herself and pored over the map. Ringrose and Firth waited. She raised her elegant ebony walking stick and brought it down with a firm smack on the paper.

'That one,' said Miss Collinson. 'Moxmanton House. The scene of some mysterious goings-on. They even had a sentry-box at the main gates and blocked the public footpath across the property.'

Ringrose asked, 'What sort of goings on?'

Miss Collinson said, 'They pinned one of those wretched acronyms onto Moxmanton House. ALI-something-or-other. Sounded Arabic.'

'ALIPROC. Alien Process Centre,' yelled Firth, loud enough to cause Miss Collinson to shoot him a severe glance.

The two detectives turned to Constable Bob Malley. Ringrose said quietly, 'Officer, did you examine Moxmanton House?'

Malley shuffled. 'I did, sir. The owner, Sir Brewster Moxmanton, conducted me round in person.'

'Hold on,' said Firth. 'That name's been in the frame recently.'

'Yes, sir,' said Malley. 'Sir Brewster's in hospital, the victim of a nasty accident on the M20. It was in the papers. A van exploded—'

Ringrose interrupted, with frightening intensity, 'Constable, tell me about your search of the house. If you value your career, leave nothing out.'

Malley licked his dry lips. 'I walked through all three floors, sir. All the doors were open. I could see into every room. There was nowhere to hide forty-nine girls.'

'All the doors were open?' said Ringrose. 'Like a conjuror showing you his empty top hat? Didn't that strike you as suspicious?'

'Not at the time, sir,' said the policeman, unhappily.

'And what about the cellar? I take it that there is a cellar?'

PC Malley sat down heavily at Miss Collinson's dining table.

He buried his head in his hands and said, 'May God forgive me. I never saw the cellar, sir. Sir Brewster told me he had rat bait down . . . I took his word for it.'

Ringrose and Firth raced for the car radio. Ringrose shouted over his shoulder, 'Come with me, constable. You can do your crying later.'

Within ten minutes a force of 250 men was on the road from Maidstone and a squad setting out for the baronet's hospital bed that they would find empty.

Ringrose, Firth and Constable Malley broke through the boundary hedge and scuttled across open parkland to where they had an uninterrupted view of the frontage of Moxmanton House on its knoll. Malley was babbling all he knew of recent happenings at the house. Through binoculars, Ringrose scanned the premises.

Two gardeners were burning leaves on the edge of a clump of sycamores but otherwise there was no sign of life. The shuttered windows gazed enigmatically out over the grounds.

'The two gardeners are from the village,' said Malley, eager to ingratiate himself.

'I want them out of the way,' said Ringrose. 'Get some help, come up through the trees and take them into custody. Make sure you're not seen from the house.'

Ringrose said to Firth, 'When the men arrive, deploy them out of sight. We dare not risk a frontal assault in daylight. If it's girls rather than rats that Moxmanton has in his cellar, we don't want a gun-to-the-head hostage drama or wholesale slaughter. Meanwhile, I'm going to scout the place alone.'

'There's a bloody great open space to cross, guv'nor,' said Firth. 'Are you going to disguise yourself as a tree?'

'No,' said Ringrose. 'Both end walls are windowless. I'm going to have the helicopter approach on the flank and lower me to the roof and fly away fast. They'll hear the noise inside the house but, with luck, won't catch on.'

'Guv'nor,' said Firth firmly, 'you can have me up on a disciplinary board later but I'll knock your block off rather than let you go in there unarmed.' He removed his jacket and unclipped his shoulder holster. 'Here, take this and give yourself a chance.'

'All right, Lionel,' said Ringrose. 'I'd hate to miss the finale.'

The helicopter swooped a bare twenty feet above the slate roof of Moxmanton House. Ringrose landed on the sloping attic roof with a heavier thud than he desired, dislodging several grey slates. He unclipped himself from the cable, raised an arm as a signal and the chopper raced away over the treetops.

Ringrose was on his own. He crab-walked down into the gutter and peered through a window into the unoccupied servants' quarters.

He traversed the frontage, checking each window and finally, unknowingly, came to the broken attic window through which Teddy Triggs and Lenny Belcher had made their first entry into Moxmanton House. He reached in and lifted the latch.

Lying on his belly in a rhododendron bush, Firth sweated. He consulted his watch. The guv'nor had now been inside almost twenty minutes. The house continued to present an impassive face to the world.

'Nobody is to move until I give the word,' murmured Firth into his radio, for the third time in five minutes. 'No one, repeat, no one.'

Another eight minutes crawled by. Suddenly Firth tensed. One of the front doors was opening slowly. 'Hold it! Hold it! Hold it!' rapped Firth into his mouthpiece.

Ringrose was on the doorstep, signalling. Firth jumped up and raced across the grass and gravel.

Ringrose wasted no words. 'The house from the ground floor up is unoccupied.'

They stepped into the hall. Firth gazed round at the decorations and tiling. 'It fits Peter Linden's description. But where's the cellar?'

'I'm still looking,' said Ringrose. 'It's been well concealed.' The two men separated and each took a wing. It was Ringrose who found the plastic bucket under a sink in the kitchen. A few grains of powdered cement still clung to the bottom. He put his head outside the kitchen door. On the ground were traces of sand and cement where mixing had taken place recently. A dark dread began to form in his mind.

He studied the kitchen floor. The red quarry tiles had been wiped over, but only in places. He followed the dried water marks and found himself facing the butler's pantry. He pulled open the door. The small room had been jammed to the ceiling with old items of furniture.

'Lionel!' Ringrose bellowed and began tearing at the stack. Behind a cupboard door in the rear of the room they discovered the raw brick wall.

'The air!' Firth shouted. 'The bastards have sealed off the air.'

They both scratched futilely at the new brickwork, which was well set. 'Get those two gardeners here – fast!' Firth shouted into his radio. 'We need pickaxes and shovels.'

Chapter Forty-seven

If she were not so tired, she could probably work out the formula. First take the cubic volume of the cellar, subtract the space occupied by forty-eight females, average weight now about a hundred pounds, multiply the volume of carbon dioxide being produced by forty-eight pairs of lungs, calculate the volume of renewed oxygen supply from the vents, a supply seriously reduced since the door had been sealed Lord knows how many days ago . . .

Prentiss Decker's brain gave up the task. The answer, common sense told her, could add up only to one thing: oxygen was losing the battle against carbon dioxide. If they did not die of thirst, they would suffocate.

Through stiff, split lips she croaked to Hanna Hansen, 'We must get everyone to take turns breathing near the vents.'

Distantly, she could hear a heavy pounding. Prentiss assumed it was the blood booming in her head. She closed her eyes to rest a while.

Ringrose and Firth attacked the wall like madmen. Firth got a purchase between two lines of bricks and began to lever frantically.

Working with difficulty in the cramped space, the two men started to make headway with a hole at waist level. A brick in the second layer split and they could at last see the timbers of the cellar door beyond.

'No time to clear the whole frame,' gasped Ringrose. 'Let's go straight through the wall and door into the cellar.'

They swung furiously, scattering dust and brick splinters, rubbing their palms red raw. They scarcely noticed.

Suddenly Ringrose's pick made a different noise as he achieved the first head-on strike at the door's panelling. They pulled away brick fragments with their bare hands, widening the gap until the whole centre panel was exposed. 'Sledge-hammer!' he shouted.

They both caught the putrid odour as the wood splintered under the onslaught. Choking, Ringrose thrust his head into the cavity. He felt Firth lifting his legs, pushing him through. He was heedless of the splinters tearing at his clothes. His hands found the cold stone landing at the top of the cellar steps and he hauled himself right through.

So far, he had been conscious only of his own heavy breathing and the encouragement from the kitchen side of the door. But now he could hear other sounds: a low moaning and a strange guttural noise.

Whoever had constructed this tomb had forgotten to switch off the lights. And then Tom Ringrose looked down the stairs at a scene that might have come from a wartime concentration camp.

Reedy, bedraggled figures were pressed against the bars, gaunt faces staring up at him with hollow, luminous eyes. Several were attempting to speak but producing only the sounds of shifting corn husks in the backs of their throats. Finally, one managed a sentence, 'Water and food, you bastard.'

Ringrose's swelling heart threatened to make him as inarticulate as the girls. He had to turn away from the pitiable sight for an essential duty. He shouted through the hole, 'Major emergency, Lionel! We want every ambulance in creation, doctors, nurses, and forty-eight hospital beds. And someone fill that bucket with water and hand it through.'

He jumped down the stairs, shouting at the dazed creatures shuffling up to the bars: 'It's the police! The *policia*! *Polizei*. The cops!'

Some girls were still sufficiently composed to grasp what he was saying, and began to scream hoarsely and thrust their hands through the bars to clutch at their deliverer.

Prentiss Decker looked dazedly at this tall, dishevelled man with silvering hair. The cops! He'd said THE COPS!

She dragged herself upright, swaying with the effort. She tried to raise a cheer but nothing would come so she began to weep instead.

Firth crawled through the hole with the bucket. At the sight of water, the girls at the front turned frantic. The two men took out their handkerchiefs and started to squeeze droplets onto blackening tongues thrust beseechingly between the bars.

Ringrose rattled the chained gate impatiently. He shouted up the stairs, 'Get that sledgehammer down here.'

For the next hour pandemonium existed in the cellar as Lucius Frankel's wall was smashed down and medical teams moved in.

Finally Ringrose and Firth fell against the cellar wall, exhausted and exhilarated. The dust and dirt caking their faces was criss-crossed by rivulets of what looked suspiciously like tears. All the girls were still alive and in the weeping mass, Ringrose found Prentiss Decker. They clutched each other's hands in mutual gratitude.

'You did it, you know,' said Ringrose. 'You and the smell of sulphur.' She fainted clean away and he placed her gently on the next stretcher.

He remembered something and looked at his watch. It was two thirty. He said to Firth, 'I'd better get a call through to the PM before he stands up in the Commons and makes a damned fool of himself.'

Afterwards, when the tumult had faded, when the two grimy detectives had faced a chaotic, mammoth press conference, when the sealed letter from Bruiser Moxmanton explaining everything had been placed in his hands by Cee, Ringrose said to Firth, 'I don't know what we shall do for the rest of our lives. This is the best day we'll ever have.'

But there was to be one other.

Chapter Forty-eight

Overnight, the licence number of Lucius Frankel's car and a description of his trailer were circulated internationally via Interpol. The French were hungry for revenge. Their outrage at the murder of Mathilde de Montméja was acute.

So it happened that, at midnight on Tuesday, a dispatch rider of the *gendarmerie* was going about his routine duties when he fell in behind a car towing a trailer on the Col de Braus, travelling towards l'Escarene.

Lucius was returning to the Villa Apollo after disposing of Bruiser's remains.

He had smiled in the dark as the naked body tumbled and bounced down the rock face. What price now all that careless ease, that lofty arrogance, that insolence of birth and office? I'm more of a man than you ever were, Lucius thought.

The dispatch rider had the presence of mind to keep his motorcycle in the trailer's blind spot, switching off his own lights and riding down to the coast in Lucius's wake. In this fashion, sometimes free-wheeling, he stuck to Lucius Frankel all the way to Cap Fleurie before making his report.

Early-morning television was monopolized by dramatic pictures of the girls being wheeled off to hospital, of Commander Ringrose's press conference and of fulsome praise from the British Prime Minister.

The hunted baronet, Sir Brewster Moxmanton, was clearly the chief villain; there was no reference to anyone else.

Constanza said, 'All the same, I'm bound to get a police visit as joint beneficiary of Moxmanton House. You'd best make yourself scarce for a few weeks until the fuss blows over.'

They were still having breakfast when Rawlings answered the front door and was brusquely brushed aside by an aloof, wavy-haired man, who was followed into the house by a number of heavily armed gendarmes.

The man threw open the breakfast-room doors and said to the thunderstruck couple still seated at the table, 'I am Commissaire Victor Massillon. You, sir, are under arrest for murder, kidnapping and extortion. You will be held in custody pending extradition to the United Kingdom. You, Madame, will accompany us, pending inquiries into your complicity in this affair.'

Lucius came to his feet, sending the table and breakfast things flying. 'No, not me! You can't mean me!' he screamed. He ran onto the veranda, recoiling only when he saw the line of uniforms advancing across the lawn.

Lucius's face collapsed. He fell at Constanza's feet, clutching her round the knees and gibbering, 'Tell them it wasn't me! Tell them! For pity's sake, tell them!'

Commissaire Massillon watched with disdain. He raised a hand, clicked his fingers and said, '*Menottes!*'

A junior officer ran forward, unclipping a shiny object from his belt.

Commissaire Massillon turned to the lean, tired man standing behind him, gave a small, courtly bow and proffered the handcuffs.

'Commander Ringrose,' said the Frenchman, 'I believe the honour is yours.'

THE END

384